Ten Tales

of Improbable Escape

Stolen

by Marshall Evans

from the Thief Giovanni Boccaccio

Printed in the United States of America
First Printing, 2015

ISBN 978-0-9970127-1-2

Land's Ford Publishing
Spartanburg, SC, USA

Cover design by Fayssoux Evans

This book is a work of fiction. Any resemblance to actual events or
persons is accidental and completely unintentional.

To Ann

Contents

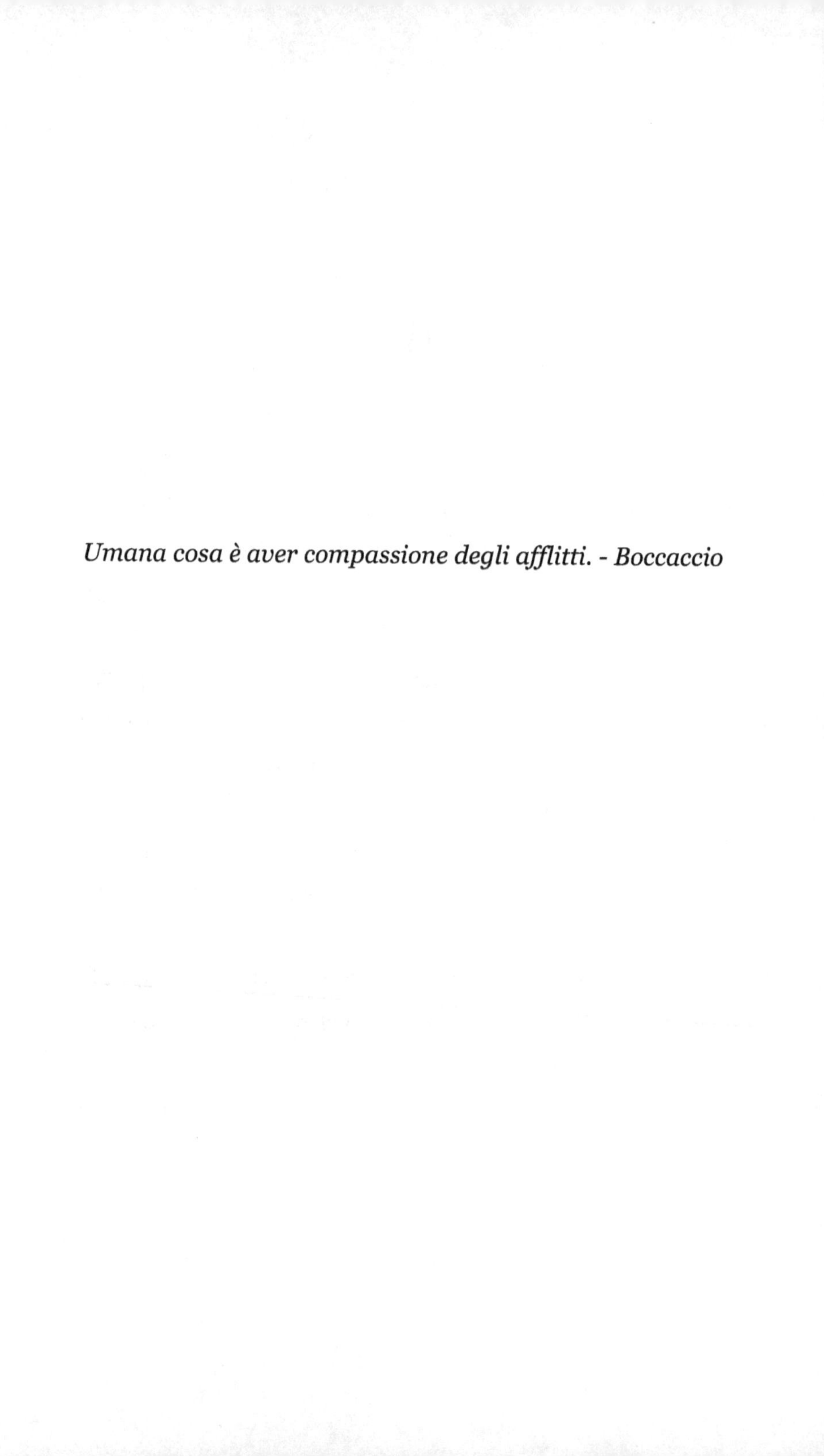

Umana cosa è aver compassione degli afflitti. - Boccaccio

Prologue

In the middle of the way of our life, I found myself in a very dark place, indeed. The Great Recession had broken me. Or I had broken myself. At any rate, I was middle-aged and broke and out of work, and I found myself with the time to dig into that back closet of the unused bedroom, to throw aside the hand-me-downs our adult daughters had left behind, and to pull out the boxes stuffed with the detritus of my youthful writing career.

The dust was thick. The manuscripts unread, lo, this quarter century. With them were bulging folders of rejection letters- often surprisingly chatty, many quite encouraging- from the leading New York editors and agents of another era. I had come so close but had landed so very, very far away. Nothing! Out of all the books and stories and essays and poems and screenplays, nothing had ever been published, nothing ever bought, no screenplay ever produced. What incurable vanity had induced me to schlep these cardboard boxes full of useless manuscripts from house to house, apartment to apartment, country to country over the decades since? But I had, and it was all still there. Being broke and middle-aged and completely out of something to do, I sat down and started to read some of it.

One of the books caught my attention. I gloated secretly to myself. It was good. It was funny. I found myself laughing out loud. It drew me in.

I began reading it so avidly my youngest daughter said, "Dad, you're reading that stack of paper like it was your job."

Oh, well.

Eventually I found a paying job, but one that gave me time to write. The youngest grew up and moved out. I pounded away until I finished a new novel. I e-mailed the new novel off to publishers- the old agent- the old editor, now retired, who had seen such promise so many years ago. Once again- nothing.

But times change. The past becomes the past, the new becomes the old, and the old... I'm not sure I like where this is going.

I decided to self-publish the new novel on the Internet.

While I was working on that, the thought came one day, why not also publish that book of stories I stole from Boccaccio so long ago?

Why stolen, you ask? (Or perhaps I overestimate your involvement in this narrative so far.) I stole them because I realized I couldn't invent good plots on my own. The stories I made up myself were just too flat to suit me.

I started copying Boccaccio's plots- at first as a sort of exercise. I began at the front of his book and produced some stories that weren't really any better than I'd written before, but by the time I worked my way around to the second day of the *Decameron* the plot-copying began to bear some fruit. I decided to write a book based on the ten tales in that second day.

I knew Boccaccio had stolen his plots from somewhere else. But as I rewrote these stories- over, and over, and over- things started to come clear that I had never seen before. Even then I didn't always get it.

Once a fiction editor at *Esquire* wrote an encouraging rejection letter, noting the tale I had sent him was obviously the story of Joseph and Potiphar's wife from the Old Testament. Such had never had occurred to me.

Long story short, then, here is that book, dragged out of bedroom-closet purgatory, scanned and digitized and spell-checked. Polished a bit. Regretted in spots.

It's hard for an old man to read the young man's book he once wrote. The person who wrote that book is almost like a character in the stories themselves. Who was that guy? Whatever happened to him?

I guess I ought to know, now. Still, I find myself wondering.

The First Tale
Earnest witnesses a miracle.

It was typical Willy, didn't call or write or anything. I was sitting at the computer, staring out the window on a pretty spring day. The dogwood petals were blowing off the trees in the front yard. Mary Ruth was still at work. The little street of white frame houses was quiet. Soon the neighborhood kids would come walking and riding their bikes down from the school. Mrs. Wilson's dachshund wandered across the street, sniffed around in my yard near the sidewalk, and took a crap.

All of a sudden there was this roar of a sports car winding through the gears from the main street. Boy, that always tees me off, some guy rednecking it through the neighborhood like that. Here came this bright white and black Porsche tearing down the street, and then right in front of my house it brakes so hard the tires screech, and it turns into my driveway. The driver opens his door, runs his fingers through his curly blond hair and checks himself in the mirror, takes off his Vuarnet sunglasses, steps out of the car, and it's Willy Stahl. When the other guy got out he accidentally kicked a couple of beer cans into my driveway.

I had a lot of work to do. I was desperately trying to finish up a novel. The baby was four months old, and Mary Ruth had already laid down the law three or four times since she found out she was pregnant. Either I had to start making some money or I was going to have to get a job. I had a lot of work to do. And I sure didn't need to be spending time with Willy Stahl.

I've got to admit I had a little animosity built up towards Willy anyway. He had gotten a good role on that soap opera, *What the Heart Knows.* So he had made it as an actor, or, no, I should say he was making a lot of money as an actor, and I wasn't making jack.

There I was in Columbia, South Carolina, unknown and unpublished, and here he came in his Porsche Turbo Carrera. The other guy with him was an actor friend of his from New York, Dennis Warner.

Mary Ruth came home about five. She was happy to see Willy, because really we had wondered if he would keep in touch now that he had hit the big time. We decided to cook out that night, so Willy and I went to the supermarket together to get some beer and burger stuff. We rode in the Porsche. The main thing I remember was that Blaupunkt radio on a flexible wand, so the driver could tune it without taking his eyes off the road. I liked roaring around Columbia in that car. I hadn't felt that way since right after college.

So we're in the supermarket getting the burger stuff, and the first one to recognize Willy was a blue-haired, fat woman in her fifties or sixties. She was wearing a navy-blue, print dress and slippers that were crushed over to the side. She came up and asked like a schoolgirl if he was Louie Stoddard (Willy's name on the soap). He said, yes, he played that part. He signed an autograph for her. Before we got out of there the word spread, and he must have signed twenty or thirty. They had him autographing the back of checks, even a cereal box, anything they could find for him to write on. When we got to the cash registers, women were crowded all around him, asking questions about where he lived and what he did, and what the other characters on the soap were like. He was really good at it. He handled them all very professionally and graciously. You could tell he just loved it, too.

So anyway later that night, after we cooked out, and after the baby was down for the night, Mary Ruth went to bed, because she had to go to work in the morning. I stayed up with Willy and Dennis. We got down the bottle of Glenfiddich Mary Ruth's father gave me for Christmas and were taking hits of that and chasing it with beer. We watched T.V. and chatted about our romantic lives as artists.

At eleven o'clock *The Witness for Truth Club* came on the channel we were watching. Dennis and Willy and I stopped talking and watched the beginning of *Witness for Truth*, which I had never really watched before. Dennis said he couldn't believe poor fools were still sending money in for this kind of stuff. The host of *Witness* came out in a navy pinstriped suit cut like something a game show host would wear and started singing with a grin that was so calculatedly ingenuous I couldn't stand it.

Dennis and Willy just howled. I thought they were going to wake up the baby.

I told them the show was taped right outside of town, at the Truth Ministries Village, which they hadn't known.

So anyway, I don't know how this came to me. I didn't think about it at all. It just popped into my head, and I had had enough to drink that it ran straight to my mouth without being considered, and I said, "Hell, we could ride out there tomorrow and see them tape the show, if you want to."

Willy Stahl, once he latches on to an idea, just won't let it go. He's always been like that. For some reason my idea lit a fire in him. So when they started flashing the toll free prayer and pledge number on the T.V. screen, Willy called it and said he had come all the way down from New York, and could he come watch a taping of *The Witness for Truth Club*? It turned out they taped the thing every afternoon at two o'clock and would be taping the next day. The woman had him hold while she checked. She came back on the line and said she was sorry, all the tickets had been sold two months in advance. But would he like to make a contribution anyway?

Willy said no thanks, but after he hung up he sat there in my recliner thinking, even after Dennis and I had changed the channel and were talking about something else.

I knew perfectly well what was going through his mind.

The next morning Mary Ruth was in an ill mood. She had to get up and go to work, and the den had empty beer cans all over it.

I was trying to keep her quiet so we wouldn't wake Willy and Dennis up. I told her, yes, I was going to get some work done that day, but we would probably take a drive out to the Truth Village before Dennis and Willy left, and that sort of thing was important to a writer, too, damnit. You have to have those experiences to write about. I said I couldn't get it all sitting in a little white frame house taking care of a baby. I was keyed up about this lately. It could have been a bad argument if we hadn't had guests. Mary Ruth said, well, I would have to do what I thought was right, and she stormed out of the house.

So I took the baby over to my aunt's for the day. Willy and Dennis and I took off for Truth Village in the Porsche with the roof off. We had a cooler of beer with us. We did Tequila shots before we left, and we were smoking dope on the way down. I rode in the back, with my head sticking out of the roof, because I was the smallest.

We were pretty stoned when we pulled up to the main gate. Willy asked where we should go to see *The Witness for Truth Club.* The guard said they had already sold out all the studio tickets in advance, and you had to write two or three months ahead of when you wanted to come. He was hostile. That Porsche just pissed people off, I think, but when Willy asked how to go about ordering tickets he warmed up a little. Willy finally got from him that it would be o.k. to drive down to the studio anyway. We might get a glimpse of the stars while we were down there.

I guess I ought to add that one reason my wife put up with Willy Stahl as much as she did is because he was such a charmer. In fact I guess that's about the only way he got away with a lot of the stuff he did, because he seemed like a cute boy with curly blond hair and blue eyes who had done something bad, and it was hard for people to hold a grudge against him.

We drove down to the television studio thinking we would be able to talk our way in, since we had talked our way into plenty of things in the past. But when we got down there, the crowd was backed up from the entrances to the studio three or four hundred feet.

This is where things started to go bad. We roared through the parking lot to turn around. We passed a bus parked near the woods, where it would be in the shade of the oak trees during the show. It was one of those big ex-Greyhounds with the name of such-and-such Gospel Church from such-and-such Tennessee on the side. There wasn't anybody on the bus, but the luggage compartment underneath was still open, and there were three folded up wheelchairs sitting in there. Willy stopped the car and looked around the parking lot. The bus hid us from the crowd that was waiting to get into the studios. Willy jumped out of the Porsche, went over to the bus, untangled one of the wheelchairs from the other two, and pulled it out. He grabbed a blanket that was in the luggage compartment, sat down in the wheelchair, and tucked the blanket over his lap and legs.

"You guys can wheel me in like this," he said, and he laughed that snickering laugh of his.

And I said, "Bullshit, Willy."

"Willy," Dennis said, "You can't do that. People are going to recognize you. "

Willy laughed. He wheeled himself around the Porsche a couple of times in the chair. He tried to pop a wheelie, and he almost tipped himself out.

"Famous," he said. "Too damn famous."

Then he started laughing again. He winked at me, and he began twitching all over and lolling his head around. He twisted his face up and stuck his tongue out and grunted so that you couldn't even recognize him. He drew his cheeks back until his teeth showed in a distorted grin. He sucked his chin in until it almost disappeared. He stiffened his fingers and cocked his hands over at an unnatural angle and waved his arms around. It must have been the actor's training, but it was terribly convincing.

Listen, of course you aren't supposed to laugh at that stuff, but I was drunk, and I had been smoking, which Mary Ruth hadn't let me do in a long time. Anyway, he got me laughing, and then Dennis couldn't help but laugh, and this just egged Willy on even more.

I've got to square with you, I hadn't smoked dope in a long time, and I just wasn't thinking right. I don't know how I let myself get caught up in this. I never do really know how I let myself get caught up in these things until it's too late. I've got to say, Willy didn't look at all like himself. He looked exactly like the kind of person he was imitating, and somehow the spirit just took hold of us, and Dennis and I wheeled Willy across the parking lot in the wheelchair towards the studio. I had to bite my tongue hard to keep from breaking up and laughing. I couldn't help grinning, which maybe just came across to the crowd as the grin of a pious man who was about to see *The Witness for Truth Club* live.

Dennis led the way and politely asked the little old ladies and the men in their polyester jackets if they could move aside and let us get Willy out of the sun. They all backed up, murmuring and smiling.

When we reached the door, the man taking tickets asked everybody else to step aside. He let us on in without asking any questions. He grabbed me lightly by the arm once I got in. He beckoned across the lobby to a security guard who was standing at one of the double door entrances to the studio. He asked the guard to lead us around to the handicapped entrance. The guard took us through a side door and down a hallway to the studio. He seated us on the front row- on the studio floor, really, right behind the television cameras, and there we were all of a sudden in front of a studio half-full of people and filling up fast.

Willy couldn't let off his act then. He spasmed and grunted.

Dennis and I were sitting in folding chairs to one side of Willy. On the other side of him were two other people in wheelchairs. One of them was a young girl who had cerebral palsy. Her mother was sitting beside her, and every now and then the mother would reach over and wipe her daughter's mouth with a handkerchief. There was an old, old woman in the other wheelchair, who was fairly alert and just looked like she might be too old and sick to walk.

Let me tell you, I have felt like slime before. Lots of times I wouldn't really want to remember. But right then I felt more like slime than I have ever felt in my life. But there was no apparent way out except to keep up the act.

Within a very short time the studio filled up. The audience lights went down, and the orchestra started up, and they started taping the show. Which was a relief to Willy, because he was able to let off his act. He sat slumped over in the wheelchair with a blank expression on his face and jerked and grunted every now and then for effect.

Then the host came out, dressed today in a baby-blue, polyester suit. Live, you could see the outrageous makeup caked on him and the hair impossibly stiff with hair spray. He had four or five huge gold rings and a gold chain bracelet. Oh, he was something else. He sang with that same outrageous smile, and the crowd just loved him.

They all applauded and cheered and shouted to him. You can't get the feeling of an audience over television. Sitting in the studio it was a lot more electric, and I began to feel very bad for doing what we were doing, and also a little bit scared.

Then that goddamn Willy Stahl. Damn his eyes. When the crowd started cheering, he started shouting and grunting and twisting his face and trying to clap his hands. Every time he swung his hands together he missed. I couldn't help it, I burst out a laugh, and Dennis stomped down on my toe so hard it brought tears to my eyes.

The co-host came out and joined the host on the living room set. They began the show with pitter patter. Then the co-host read some viewer mail to the host, and they congratulated themselves and praised the Lord for all the good they did.

The host told a church joke, and Willy laughed, "Ahunga, hunga, hunga, hunga!" louder than anybody else in the audience.

"Oh bless him," a blue-haired woman said behind us.

Then the host introduced the first guest. She was a tall, blond woman, middle-aged, slightly overweight, with enormous breasts. She looked familiar, but I couldn't place her, and the name didn't ring a bell at all. She was wearing a conservative, gray suit. Her hair was cut short.

When she spoke, she had an unusual, throaty voice that was familiar to me.

I forget her real name. I'll say it was Rose Crenshaw. Anyway, she had founded a home for runaway children in Los Angeles. She described the work of the home and told stories of runaway children, and told how she had run away from home herself. She had gone to Hollywood to become an actress, but Hollywood had been tougher than she imagined, and she had ended up making porn films.

The host looked very sad. "Your screen name was something else, wasn't it, Rose?"

And Rose said, yes, her screen name had been Melinda Bender.

Melinda Bender! Talk about fleeting youth. Or maybe she still looked good with all her clothes off, doing those things she used to do in front of a camera.

Willy slapped me on the thigh with his twisted hand, and he winked at me with a spasmed grin.

"Now most of us can't understand, Rose," the host said, "how a beautiful young girl can end up doing something like that. How can one of God's creatures degrade herself in those- and I'm going to use this word very loosely- films?"

The question didn't endear Rose, but she told her story. Rose had a quiet, sincere way of speaking, and she looked right at the first row of the audience as she spoke, so I felt like she was looking at me and Willy.

"You know," she said, "I could never have been drawn into making porn films if people didn't watch them. If ordinary people didn't rent them and take them home to watch on the VCR, there wouldn't be any money to entice people to make them. What people don't realize is that those are real people on the screen, real people with spirit and hope. People who want to be loved.

"My story, it's not easy to tell." She paused and gathered her breath. "When I was twelve, my uncle began having sex with me." She started to cry. The tears rolled down her face first, and then it affected her breathing.

The host had this grin on his face. He was twisting it to make it look sympathetic.

"It happened over and over...," Rose tried to get out. But she couldn't finish that sentence.

There was a silence here. Rose cried quietly.

"It never really stopped," she said.

"Eventually I ran away. But by then people could tell. There are people who find children who are victims of abuse- who prey on them. They can tell. It's like they can smell it."

She put her face in her hands for moment and choked. Then she made herself keep speaking.

"So many people I worked with were abused as children. Most of the people I worked with in porn. If you ever got to know them, you heard it sooner or later. That was how they found us, I suppose. They could tell. They knew we would do what they wanted. What everybody wanted."

Rose gathered herself a bit here.

"You know I stopped caring for people," she continued. "They were just there. I mean they were just there like the street signs or something. It was like I couldn't see they were people, because I couldn't see myself as a person." She was really crying now, but with a magnificent sort of dignity.

Willy reached over and tapped me on the knee. He had stopped his act. He nodded toward the exit door. And I don't know why I did it- I suppose to make the exit a little less humiliating- but I cradled him under his arm as he stood up out of the wheelchair.

That seemed to inspire the actor in Willy. He rose shakily to his feet, slowly standing to his full height.

People behind us started talking quietly to each other.

Then all of a sudden the blue-haired woman behind me screamed out, at the top of her lungs, "It's a miracle! Praise the Lord!"

The host and the porn star stopped hugging and turned to look into the audience.

The woman behind me jumped up and started dancing and shouting, "Praise Jesus, praise the Lord, oh blessed Jesus." She was pointing at the stage, I thought. I tried to see what she was pointing at. I looked up into the audience, but everybody was looking at me. No, they were looking at Willy, and pointing and shouting and praising the Lord and throwing their hands up in the air. The camera crew turned the cameras around and put the lights on us. The lights were so bright Willy held his hands over his face. And Willy appeared on the T.V. monitors overhead, standing beside his wheelchair.

The host came toward us carrying his microphone. There were tears still running down his face. His makeup was running. He was smiling and holding his hands in the air.

"Oh, my goodness," he said. "It's been so long since we've had this. Praise the Lord."

Well, it all happened so fast. They came and took Willy by the arms and led him up on the set with the host. Willy was still holding his hands over his eyes to try to block the lights.

The host wanted Willy standing right beside him while he talked to him. He was trying to guide Willy onto the camera marks on the floor, to get him standing on the right pieces of colored tape.

Willy must have gotten used to the light, or the host pulled him off balance, because he dropped his hands from his face and was standing there full-faced and upright in front of the cameras and the audience.

It took a little while. A few seconds at least. The host was asking for his name when a woman far back in the audience stood up and shouted, "That ain't no cripple! That's Louie Stoddard!"

Well, Willy panicked. He tried to get away, but the host was holding him tight on the marks, and trying to get him to look the right direction. Willy shoved him to try to break loose. He just shoved a little too hard, is all, or maybe he was panicked enough that he didn't care how hard he shoved, but he knocked the host back across the coffee table and onto the porn queen. The sofa rolled over backwards and spilled the host and the porn queen on the floor behind it. All I could see were her legs and slip and panty hose as she tried to get him off her.

Willy bolted off the set, trying to get away from the cameras and lights, but a big young man who looked like a football player dived out of the front row and tackled him before he reached the door. Willy got up swinging. He caught this guy a great, left roundhouse to the ear that knocked the big guy down. At that the seats in the audience emptied. Two older men in leisure suits got between Willy and the door before he could get out. Willy tried to burst between them, but they grabbed him and held him long enough for the others to get there, and then the whole mob, men and women, starting beating holy hell out of Willy. It was an ugly scene.

At first I could see Willy fighting back. Then I lost sight of him in the mob, and I could just hear him screaming and begging for mercy.

Of course, Dennis and I were in deep danger ourselves, so I tried to get lost in the fracas and tried to get as far away from Dennis as I could. The security guards, four of them, came running through the entrance Willy and Dennis and I had come in, and after a struggle, they got the mob off Willy. His jacket was ripped all down the back, and the collar of his shirt was hanging off. Willy was cursing and shouting at the mob. One of the security guards, a man with silver hair who looked like somebody's grandfather, pulled a blackjack off his belt and started beating Willy savagely while a younger security guard held him.

Well, I scatted out of the studio through one of the main entrances and took off down one of the side halls. There was an office door open. Nobody was in the office, and there was a desk with a telephone on it, so I went in and closed the door and locked it and dialed the operator and had her get the sheriff's office. I told the dispatcher there was a terrible emergency at the Truth Ministries Village, in the television studio, and to send some patrol cars immediately. She asked for my name, but I said I didn't have time, it was a matter of life or death, and hung up.

I was still in that office staring at the inspirational paintings of Jesus and the host and a print of the *Last Supper* by Da Vinci, trying to decide whether to go out and try to get away or to stay in there until the sheriff's deputies came. I was convinced if that mob caught me they would beat hell out of me, too. But it couldn't have been more than a few minutes before I heard the siren coming. The police car came flying into the parking lot, and I heard it stop in front of the studio.

I left the office and went carefully back down the hall. Just as I was going into the lobby, the two sheriff's deputies came out of the studio doors dragging Willy between them. One of his eyes was swollen shut. His nose was bleeding, and there was a huge bruise coming up on the side of his face around the shut eye. The mob from the studio was right behind them, shouting. Another sheriff's patrol car pulled up in front, and two black sheriff's deputies got out of it and came in. The host was in the mob. He was pointing and shouting at the sheriff's deputies. His hairsprayed hair was sticking up, still mussed from the scuffle. He was shouting something I couldn't understand, and so were some of the others in the mob. Then I understood, they were saying, "Search him, search him."

I could tell the sheriff's deputies wanted to get out of there. But two deputies put Willy up against the wall and spread his hands and legs and searched him. When the deputy got to the side pocket of Willy's jacket, he said something to the other, who whipped his pistol out of its holster and dropped to a crouch, aiming it at Willy with both hands. The deputy who was searching Willy reached into Willy's jacket pocket and pulled out a snub nosed .38, or that's what it looked like from a distance.

The crowd was howling. The host looked up to heaven, and I thought he was going to faint. I couldn't figure out what was going on. Willy couldn't figure it out either. He was so confused he couldn't do anything while they handcuffed him. But then the host held his hands up to the mob and got them quieted down enough that he could shout over them, and he said, something to this effect, "Brothers and sisters, this is not the first time, and this will not be the last. We have had those before who would destroy this ministry, who would destroy me, so that I won't be able to spread the gospel of our Lord Jesus Christ."

Well, it was something to that effect. I can't remember exactly how he put it. Nobody could talk like that guy. He said he was willing to die for the Lord. This was as close as he had come, ever, he said.

When Willy finally understood what this guy was saying, he just went berserk. He broke away from the sheriff's deputies and rushed toward the host, screaming, "You son of a bitch. You fucking fraud."

The deputies caught him and held him off the host, but I've got to admit, if you hadn't known what was the truth, it looked awfully bad. Willy fought like a madman after the deputies caught him. They delivered several blows to his head with their billy clubs, and finally all four of them picked him up off the ground and carried him horizontally out to one of the cars. They shoved him in the back seat, shut the door behind him, got in themselves, and both patrol cars pulled away with the sirens wailing.

It all happened so fast. It hadn't been forty-five minutes since Willy and Dennis and I drove into the studio parking lot. I caught a glimpse of Dennis across the lobby. He jerked his head in the direction of the car, and that was all I needed. We slipped out the front doors and met at the Porsche.

We caught up to the sheriff's patrol cars on the highway and followed them into town to the county courthouse. By the time we got downtown there was a caravan of cars from the Truth Ministries Village behind us. They all followed the deputies' cars into the parking lot. I got Dennis to drive down a few blocks and park the Porsche where they wouldn't find it.

We sat out in the car and talked about what to do. Dennis didn't want to go in the courthouse at all. But I said, wait a minute, this was the county courthouse. We couldn't get beat up in there. And this assassination plot thing was so outrageous there was just no possibility.

By the time we got inside the courthouse, the *Witness for Truth* crowd had already coagulated at the magistrate's office. We just followed the noise. The office door was open, and the outer office was full of people. The secretaries were leaning back against the wall behind their desks with their arms crossed, watching. Willy and the host were in one of the inner offices. I couldn't see much, just caught a glimpse of Willy between the two black deputies, and the host in there with them. They were talking to the magistrate, who was seated at a metal desk.

All of a sudden I saw Willy start struggling, and I heard him cursing. I saw one of the white deputies pull out his billy club and start to move toward him, and then somebody closed the door from inside. I could hear Willy shouting as they beat him.

Then somebody grabbed Dennis by the arm, and a couple of the Truth Ministry people started questioning him hostilely. He had drifted fifteen feet or so away from me in the mob. When I saw that, I ducked into the hallway and dashed down the nearest stairwell into the basement.

So there I was, walking around in the basement of the county courthouse, trying to find some way out, and wondering whether I should run away or stay. I went down one hallway and then another, looking for an exit. I passed the main stairwell, and I thought I heard people running down it.

I was outside the county assessor's office, where they keep the plats and the aerial photographs. I ducked into the office. I went into the back, where the drawers containing all the aerial photographs were, and where the plat books were out on the tables.

I went to the drawers, started looking at the labels like I knew what I was looking for, opened one of the drawers, and pulled several sheets of photographs out. Then I sat down at one of the tables with my back to the door and pretended to be studying them.

I was breathing pretty heavily at this point and was concentrating hard to calm down. I had no idea what to do. I could get out of the courthouse after a while, I was sure, but I couldn't leave Willy and Dennis up there.

And then Fred R. Helms walked in.

Fred R. was my father's college roommate, now chairman of Darness Mills, and he was a man of enormous wealth. He was dressed in a leather jacket and slacks. He went to a file drawer and pulled out a couple of aerial photographs. He was carrying them to a table when he saw me and came over to talk. He was careful to roll the photographs up so I couldn't see what property he was looking at.

Well, there I was. It's not like Fred R. had never heard of me being in trouble before. And it's not like I hadn't ever heard of him being in trouble himself, to tell the truth. Well anyway, when he asked me what I was doing at the courthouse, I told him. The whole story.

He made me repeat the story until it was clear to him. Then he laughed and thanked me for telling him. I couldn't imagine why he thanked me. He told me to sit tight. He would make a phone call.

Fred R. left the office, and I sat back down and studied the photographs I had gotten out. They showed the Sandhills patchwork of abandoned farm fields and pine plantations and hardwood forest down along the creek beds- and every once in a while an Interstate highway cutting right through the middle of it all. From the air you can see how an Interstate cuts the old roads and the old farms and the property lines at random, like someone dropped it down on them from the sky.

I don't know how long I sat there. After a while a sheriff's deputy in uniform walked in. I tried not to look at him, but he walked right over to me, laid his hand on my shoulder, and asked me to come with him. The Realtors and law clerks sitting in there looked at me like I was an escapee from the jail.

The deputy took me upstairs. When we entered the main hallway I could see the mob down by the magistrate's office. There were newspaper reporters, and the television people were there, too.

Someone pointed me out to them, and a bunch of people came running, but all I could see were those television cameras aimed at me. The deputy pulled me across the hallway into an office and closed the door behind us, and I was safe.

In the office was a conference table. Seated around it were Fred R., a state senator I assumed was acting as his attorney, Willy,

Dennis, the magistrate, and the host of *Witness for Truth*, along with his lawyer.

They were going at it. Fred R. and the state senator were talking about a tax audit for Truth Village, and all the stories about it that might appear in the press, and then what kind of stories would break out when the registration was traced on the revolver that had been found in Willy's pocket. The host got red in the face and got up and started pacing and spouting all this stuff about how his ministry had been assailed and persecuted since the beginning. Fred R. just slid back in his chair and listened, smiling.

The host's lawyer got the host down to the point where he was talking about forgiveness, and how he could take Willy out in front of the reporters and publicly forgive him for the assault. Fred R. let him huff and puff and posture, and when the host was finished, he made his proposal. The host's lawyer took his client into an adjoining room. When they came back in a couple of minutes, the lawyer said the arrangement was acceptable to them.

The host and his lawyer left the office by the front door.

Willy, Fred R., the state senator, Dennis, and I went through a couple of connecting doors into another suite of offices, out into another hallway, and out the side door of the courthouse, so nobody saw us leave.

Mary Ruth was irate when I called her and told where I was. But that evening, when we were all sitting at home, the whole thing started looking funnier and funnier, and she ended up laughing about it more than we did. Poor Willy was beaten black and blue. He couldn't open one eye, and his lips were purple and swollen. He had a couple of cuts on his forehead and scalp, not big enough for stitches, though we debated that. Mary Ruth had to wash the dried blood out of his hair with a warm washcloth.

Willy kept looking in the mirror and saying he couldn't possibly act like that. He was awfully worried about it. In the end, as a matter of fact, they did have to write Louie Stoddard out of *What the Heart Knows* for six weeks.

But what really had Willy worked up that night was the possible publicity. He had moaned and moaned about that in Fred R.'s Mercedes as Fred R. was driving us to pick up the Porsche. Fred R. had just laughed at him and said, "There won't be any problem with that, son."

That's all he had said. And frankly, none of us had believed him. I was sure the incident would make the news. We got home too late to watch the six o'clock news that evening. But we watched the late news at eleven, flipping from one local station to another, waiting with dread to see the report come on. There was no mention of Truth Ministries at all.

The next morning I got up before Mary Ruth and ran out to get the paper. Willy and I searched the thing from front to back, but there was nothing about the incident. I was astonished, and honestly, a little bit scared that Fred R. could pull off something like that.

That afternoon Willy and Dennis took off for Florida in the Porsche. They started drinking hard before lunchtime, and they were well on their way when they left. Willy caught a wheel as he pulled out of our street onto the main street. I heard the Porsche roaring and the tires spinning and shook my head. Then I went back inside to get the baby up. She was starting to cry in her crib.

A couple of days later I was sitting in front of the computer, staring out the windows, and watching Mrs. Wilson's dachshund wander into my yard, when something started eating at me. Why had Fred R. Helms been so quick to help us, and why had he taken such a personal interest in the affair, when he was such a busy man? Sure, he was an old, old friend of my dad's, but he could just as easily have sent a lawyer down to get everybody bailed out and then let things straighten themselves out. I certainly had never expected him to get involved personally.

That ate at me for a couple of days as I sat at the computer and stared out the window. Finally I put it down to a simple dislike for the Truth Village people and for the host in particular. You know how those people are. That's the way I got it figured out at least, and I put the whole story to rest in my mind.

Several months later, Mary Ruth and I were riding down to the beach with my parents for the weekend. We passed the Truth Village exit on the Interstate, and I didn't even want to look at it, the memory was still so fresh. I certainly had never mentioned the incident to my parents. And Mary Ruth had gotten a little sorer about the affair after Willy and Dennis left.

But as we drove under the overpass, I saw a huge new construction project going up beside the highway. Grading pans and bulldozers were clearing a hundred acres or more. Where there used to be a billboard proclaiming the incipient construction of the Tower of Truth, there was an even larger billboard announcing a new office space and shopping mall complex, with an artist's rendering of the completed project, its parking lots full of cars.

My dad pointed it out, and he told us that was Fred R.'s new project. I put my hand on my forehead and leaned against the window behind my dad and smiled at Mary Ruth.

Mary Ruth looked at me like she would kill me if I opened my mouth.

The Second Tale
Roy Derwelt goes to the big house.

Roy Derwelt had been in prison, sent there for stealing a car, which you wouldn't think would have gotten him a prison sentence on a first offense. But he had led the police on a high speed chase from South Carolina up through the North Carolina mountains and into Tennessee. Drunk. The interstate flight landed him in the federal penitentiary down in Atlanta for three years.

Roy was not a hard man, and prison life was tough on him. To cope, Roy got religion and soon became a sort of inmate missionary.

After Roy got out of prison and went back home to the dark corner of Greenville County (that corner right up under the first range of the Blue Ridge), he considered the missionary work his true calling. He lived with his mama and let her support him, and wouldn't get any kind of paying work at all. He lasted a few months like that until his mother finally started raising Cain for him to get out and get a job. His sisters, who lived nearby, had been bending her ear about it for a long time. They figured Roy was living off their inheritance, which, judging from the Derwelts' one-acre estate and tumble-down frame house with a house trailer attached, couldn't have been much. But small estates often rouse firier passions than grand ones.

That was back in the early part of the eighties, when work was scarce, and a man, even a trained welder, could claim to be looking for work for quite some time without finding a job. So Roy made it on into December before his mama finally just told him he would have to hit the road. It was one of those terrible rows that take place in tumble-down frame houses way out in the country. At least all that suffering and noise can get lost in the empty countryside.

Roy had heard welders were being hired at New York wages on a nuclear power plant on Long Island. He didn't want to go that far, but he didn't have much choice. There really was nothing happening close to home, so on a cold day in December Roy told his mama good-bye, threw a couple of paper sacks full of clothes in the back seat of his car, and pulled away from the red mud parking area in front of the Derwelt house and attached trailer.

Not long after Roy began his trip it started to rain. When he got up around Salisbury, North Carolina on I-85, the rain turned to ice. Sleet was popping on the hood and the windshield, and the road was getting slick. The trees beside the road were starting to bend under the weight of the ice on their limbs, but Roy didn't have enough money with him to stay in a motel, and it was too cold to sleep in the car, so he decided he would just have to keep on going.

The more Roy thought about his money situation, though, the more he began to get kind of worried. He was driving a sixty-eight Ford Galaxy, two-tone, midnight blue and white, jacked up with wide, white-lettered tires in the back, and roaring with Glass-Pack mufflers installed by Roy himself. But the car was out of tune and seemed to be burning a lot of gas. Gas had gotten to be a good bit higher than it was before Roy went to prison. Roy was trying to calculate if he had enough money to buy gas all the way to New York. It looked pretty grim, and Roy even thought of that as an excuse to turn around and go home. But about that time Roy spotted two boys standing under an overpass thumbing. The visibility was so bad he didn't see them until it was too late. He had to pull over and back up in the emergency lane to pick them up.

The boys were wet, and they smelled pretty bad. They were young boys, maybe in their late teens, early twenties, with long stringy blond hair, both of them. One was short and fat, in a wet, blue denim jacket. He had a double chin and gaps in his teeth, and scars from acne. He got in the back seat. The skinnier one, with a sharp nose, deep blue eyes, and a few days' growth of beard, was wearing an old Army fatigue jacket. He got up front.

They were both smiling when they got in the car, which was certainly understandable, because it was an awfully nasty day to be out hitchhiking.

The boys thanked Roy for picking them up, and he said it was no problem at all really, and he asked where they were going. They said they were just going up the road a ways. Roy asked where, exactly, and they said they weren't really sure. They looked at each other and laughed.

"Just outn the rain, is good enough," said the skinny one. Roy drove on in silence for a while, with the sleet popping on the windshield.

"I ain't never seen no plastic Jesus like that," the skinny hitchhiker said, talking about the one riding on the dashboard of Roy's car. This was a plastic statuette of Jesus with wavy, light brown hair and a goatee. He was wearing a blue outer robe over a white inner one.

"Well," Roy said.

They rode on in silence, and Roy had just about gotten up the nerve to ask them if they could pitch in for the gas, when the fat hitchhiker in the back seat said, "What, you some kind of preacher?"

"Well, really I'm a missionary."

That was an honest enough answer, because Roy at this point in his life thought of himself more as a missionary than a welder. He was only going to work to get some money to live, because he couldn't see any other way at all. That didn't mean he had to stop spreading the good news, and, as a matter of fact, these two boys right here might be someone he could witness to.

First things first, though. The needle on the gas gauge was below empty and was delving into that zone Roy knew so well, right before the car would start to skip and then die. Roy knew exactly how far down that needle would go. Roy started to ask the boys for some gas money, but the hitchhiker in the front seat all of a sudden asked him where he was going, and Roy told him, and the one in the back seat said, "What? You goan preach up there in New York?"

So Roy told them both the whole story, except the part about his being in prison. He was going to ask if they could pitch in for some gas since he had such a long way to go, but the boy in the front seat said, "I don't know, that religion just never did nothing for me. I mean all that stuff my mama was always talking about, it seemed kind of silly to me. "

This irritated Roy, because it just wasn't said in a friendly way at all. Roy took a deep breath and calmed himself down, and said, "Well, and maybe you ain't never been in prison, neither."

But the two hitchhikers just burst out laughing when he said that.

Roy didn't like this, and he was thinking maybe he could pull off at one of the exits ahead and leave these boys at a gas station or something. But the hitchhiker next to him said, "You think Jesus is goan take you all the way up to New York safe and sound today?"

"Well, as a matter of fact, I'll be honest with you," Roy said. "I ain't got a whole lot of money, and I'm running short on gas, and it might show you something or it might not, but I said a little prayer for some help just before I saw you boys hitchhiking back there."

This was greeted by silence.

"What, you mean we goan pay for the gas?"

It was about all Roy could do to keep his cool, and he decided he would pull off at this next exit, and just pull into a gas station if there was one and tell them to get out.

But Roy couldn't help throwing in a little preaching. "Boys," he said, "When I said I prayed a little prayer, I mean I prayed that the Lord would just see fit to take care of me today, and I put it all in his hands. That's all I did. It ain't like you thinking, or everybody else is always thinking or talking about. The Lord just don't work that way."

"No, no," the one in the front seat said. "It might just be the Lord answered your prayers after all. We'll pay for some gas. I got nothing against that. Why don't you take this exit up here?" The boy in the back seat laughed.

Roy looked up at the next exit, and he couldn't see a gas station. He hadn't seen any signs, so he said, "They ain't no gas up here, I'll go on to the next one."

And the boy beside him said, "No, I think they's a station here. I seen a sign back there. It's a Texaco."

"I'll tell you," Roy said, "they ain't no gas up there. Look, you can see, they ain't one of them tall signs, and we don't need to be making no side trips. This girl's low."

"I think you ought to take this one," the boy in the back seat said. Roy shook his head, and he was just about to let them both have a piece of his mind, when he heard a click and felt cold metal press against his neck. The boy in the back seat stuck the barrel of a revolver behind Roy's ear and said, "Take the exit."

Roy was right, there was no gas station at this exit. There were no stores, no houses, nothing but a two-lane country highway bordered on both sides by thick pine woods. Roy leaned his head away from the pistol as best he could, and the hitchhiker in the back seat told him where to go.

They turned to the right on the two-lane, which was beginning to ice up. They passed a couple of frame houses and then drove another mile or so through country that was either pine plantation or recent clear-cut. The hitchhiker told Roy to turn left down a tar and gravel road marked only by a county maintenance number.

Roy drove another two or three miles down that road and didn't see any houses or trailers at all. Then the hitchhiker told him to take a right onto a gravel road. The pine trees were coated thick with ice and hung all down in the road and scraped on the windshield and the roof of the car. The rear tires slipped and spun.

Way, way down in the woods, where the pine trees were thick and bending double under the ice, the hitchhikers told Roy to stop the car. The hitchhiker with the gun got out and pointed the gun at Roy while he got out. The other hitchhiker reached down in his duffel bag and found a wad of manila rope and a roll of duct tape. The two of them walked with Roy into the pine woods.

Roy was thinking the whole time about making a break for it, but the fat boy was walking right behind him and would have two or three point-blank shots at Roy's back before Roy could duck behind a tree.

Roy was wearing a quilted, Sears work jacket and no hat. The sleet and rain quickly soaked his head and his shoulders. The boys led him a hundred yards back into the woods. The pines here were short, twenty or thirty feet tall, just prime for pulp wood. Roy was remembering how his daddy had taken him out to cut pulp wood when he was a boy. It was one of the countless things Roy's father had done to pretend that he was providing a living. Roy was remembering this and more, when the fat boy hauled off and hit him in the back of the head with the butt of the revolver. Roy landed face down on the icy pine needles. Roy rolled over and faced the two boys. The fat one was grinning and breathing hard. His breath was steaming.

"Where was you in prison?" the skinny boy asked him.

"Atlanta," Roy spat out. But Roy wasn't tough. He had had to take care of himself, but he wasn't tough.

"Why don't you go on and start taking them clothes off," the fat boy said, and he waved the revolver at Roy.

"Uh uh," the skinny one said, and he shook his head. "No, we ain't goan do it. All we want is the car."

"All you want is the car," the fat one said.

"That's all we goan take," the skinny one told him, and even though he wasn't holding the gun, the fat one seemed to be scared of him. "All we goan take is your car, man," the skinny one said. "We goan have to tie you up, is all, so you won't come after us.

"That's all we goan do."

"Bullshit," the fat one said."Uh uh, not me."

"You shut the fuck up," the skinny boy said to him, through his teeth and with his eyes hot. The fat boy shut up.

The skinny boy made Roy crawl to the upright trunk of a tree and had him sit up against it. He tied Roy's wrists tight together behind the tree. He lashed Roy's torso to the tree so tight Roy could breathe only in shallow breaths. Then he took the duct tape and started to tape around Roy's mouth, but he laughed and stopped himself.

"What'd you say you got sent up for? Stealing a car?"

Roy didn't answer him.

The skinny hitchhiker laughed and taped over Roy's mouth and around the pine tree. "Well this is maybe Jesus paying you back for what you done. 'The Lord works in mysterious ways,' my momma always said."

The hitchhiker was tickled by that. He was grinning as he taped Roy's eyes shut and wrapped the tape tight around the tree again.

Then Roy heard the revolver being cocked close to his head.

The skinny one said in a tone that was terribly menacing, more menacing than anything Roy had heard in prison, even, "Don't you do it. Leave the boy alone."

"Shit," the fat one said, "he goan freeze to death anyway."

"Leave him alone," the skinny one said.

Roy smelled one of them leaning down close to him, and whoever it was kissed Roy on the cheek. The skinny thief said right beside his ear, "You better pray real hard to Jesus, friend." He laughed.

Roy heard the hitchhikers crunching away over the icy pine needles. He heard his Galaxy crank and crank and finally start up. The rear wheels spun in the mud, and he could hear the two boys shouting at each other. The Galaxy finally caught traction. Roy heard its Glass Pack mufflers throbbing off through the woods.

The sleet was falling harder. Roy was shivering. Cold water was running down his neck. The woods were silent except for the sleet rattling and limbs cracking and falling occasionally.

Water was running into Roy's ears where the duct tape held them flat. Roy could feel water pooling and running under his clothes. Sleet pelted the top of his head. He was shivering. He struggled to get his hands free. His shoulders and biceps ached. The struggle warmed him a little, but it was terribly frustrating, and he wanted the whole time just to give up. Somehow he kept struggling.

Roy struggled for two hours, or it may have been more, until the ropes began to get a little looser, and he was able to get one loop off his wrists.

From that point it didn't seem nearly as long, maybe a half hour or so, until he was able to get his hands free. He reached up and pulled the duct tape off his mouth and down over his chin.

His fingers were numb, and he could barely feel the tape. He managed to tear it in two.

He worked the tape off his eyes and over the top of his head. Once he could see, he found the knots that held his torso against the tree. They were frozen, but eventually he got them undone and pulled the rope from around him and stood up.

Roy was soaked to the skin and was aching. He walked out to the dirt road. He looked in both directions. There was nothing. He was shivering. His teeth were chattering. He was very, very tired, and he wanted to lie down and go to sleep, but he knew if he did he would die. Roy thought how far it was back to the nearest house. He figured it had to be close to four miles, and he knew he couldn't walk that far in this weather. It was getting to be dusk. The gray woods were even grayer than before, and the sleet kept on just as hard.

Then Roy remembered something he had learned as a boy scout, that when you are lost you should go downhill. The road definitely went downhill in the direction opposite from which he had come, so he decided to try it.

Within three or four hundred yards Roy came to the shore of a lake. In the twilight across the cove he could see the lights of a couple of houses, and this gave him new energy. The houses weren't more than a few hundred yards away across the water, but the way around the cove on foot would be long. It was getting darker and darker. The pine branches hung down to the ground, coated with ice. Sometimes the branches were so thick Roy had to bull his way through. His teeth were chattering loudly.

At one point the shore of the lake was an eroded red clay bank about eight feet high. As Roy was thrashing his way through the branches above, the ground underneath him gave way, and he slid into the lake below.

The lake water almost felt warm, but that sensation quickly went away. Roy stood up thigh deep, and the water made his legs ache. God, they ached. He tried to climb the bank, but it was too steep, and the clay was too slick. He slid back in with his hands full of mud.

Roy had to wade down the bank forty or fifty yards. With each step his legs were hurting so and he was shivering so he was sure he couldn't make it. He was crying, and when he finally found a place where he could pull himself out, he sat on the bank for a while and fought with himself, because he wanted to lie down and go to sleep and die.

Roy kept on along the shore. He was out of the pine woods now, into scrub oak and underbrush. The brush got thicker and thicker. He got into a blackberry bramble. The briers tore his jacket and his shirt and scratched him, and he struggled and fought. Roy didn't think he could go any farther at all, when suddenly he burst out of the briers.

Roy was disoriented. He was on grass, and the grass was cut short. He looked up, and he was on the lawn of a big house.

It was a very big house, a two-story modern design with cedar tongue-and-groove siding and cedar shingles on the roof and two wings that stretched out along the top of the hill. There were lights on inside. Roy hurried up the long lawn. Roy was soaking wet and covered in mud and scratched all over. His clothes were torn. He could smell an oak fire burning in the fireplace. He went around to the front of the house where a two-door, silver Mercedes coupe was parked. The front porch lights were lit as if visitors were expected. Roy climbed the redwood steps onto the front deck. He slipped on the ice and almost fell down.

The door was huge, beautifully varnished and intricately carved. Roy rang the doorbell. He was shivering, and his teeth were chattering. He could hear someone coming, and then the door opened, and the warm air came out. It was an old, black woman. She screamed and tried to slam the door.

"Please, for God's sake, no," Roy said, "Please help me." He tried to stop her from closing the door, but this scared her worse.

Someone else came running through the house shouting, "What is it? What is it?"

Roy let go of the door, and the black woman got it shut. Then he could hear the other woman talking to her, and Roy said, "Please, in the name of God help me, I done fell in the lake and I'm goan freeze to death. I just cain't go no further. "

He heard the two women talking again, and the black woman said loudly and emphatically, "Uh uh, uh uh."

All of a sudden the door opened wide. The most beautiful, amber-haired white woman opened it. She was dressed in a black dinner dress. "What do you want?" she said, "What are you doing here?"

Roy told her he had been robbed and tied up in the woods and left for dead, but that he had escaped, and he just couldn't go any farther at all, and could they please help him, even let him come in and warm up by the fire for a few minutes, and let him call the police? Roy really didn't want to call the police. He'd never had anything but trouble and beatings from them in his life. He just said that because it sounded like the right thing to say.

As cold as Roy was, and as wet and miserable, he couldn't help noticing that this was a very good-looking woman he was talking to. Not the maid, but the white woman. She was in her forties, at least, but she had quite a body, with large, firm breasts that filled out the sheer dinner dress. Her amber hair hung around her neck and was pulled back behind her ears, and she was wearing a long string of pearls.

"Sophie," she said, "would you get some towels, and a blanket?" Then she asked Roy to come into the flagstone entry hall, and she had him stand there dripping until the maid came. The maid brought several towels and a red blanket. The white woman took the blanket, hesitated, then gave it back to her and said, "Why don't you get that Army blanket in the hall closet?"

Right when the maid came back, the phone rang, and the woman in the dinner dress went into another room to answer it. Roy dried himself off as best he could without taking his clothes off. He wrapped the blanket around him and stood there dripping. The maid watched him like she was standing guard. She didn't say anything.

Roy heard the white woman's voice started off plaintive. Then it got louder until he heard the telephone receiver slam down. "Son of a bitch!" the white woman shouted, and she came storming out, worrying her string of pearls. "Sophie," she said, "There is no need to start the *a la greque*." She paused. Sophie didn't understand.

"Our plans have changed," the white woman said, obviously not comfortable speaking in front of Roy.

The wind roared outside through the trees, and there was a loud splitting noise and a crash as a big limb fell.

The woman told Roy if he took his shoes and socks off, he could come in and stand by the fire.

On his way into the living room, Roy noticed the dinner table was set with candlesticks and wine glasses and fancy silver and china. He went to the fireplace and stood on the slate hearth in front of it. There was a nice oak fire going, with a big, red bed of coals and blue flames coming up between the logs. Roy stood in front of it and turned himself to warm front and back. The woman in the dinner dressed asked him if he wanted to call the highway patrol or the sheriff's department. He didn't want to call either, but he figured he'd be better off taking his chances with the local sheriff, since he had particularly unpleasant memories of the North Carolina Highway Patrol.

She went to the telephone right there in the living room, picked up the receiver, and listened. She clicked the button a couple of times, and listened again. She tried to dial, and listened, then she slammed the phone down and said, "Fuck."

"Sophie," she said, "the goddamn phone is dead. Oh, why in the hell does this always happen to me?"

Then she went in the kitchen where the maid was, and they talked a while, and the white woman walked back through the living room a couple of times while Roy was standing by the fire. It was like she didn't even notice he was there. Roy was feeling a lot warmer. He was no longer shivering, but his head was swimming a little. The woman went to the bar in the corner of the living room, poured herself a glass of whiskey over ice cubes, drank about half of it down, and filled the glass up again. Roy watched her do this. She turned and saw him and gave him a look that told him to mind his own business.

"We're going to have to drive you to the police station," she said, "I suppose. Would you like a drink?" Then as an afterthought,

"How about some brandy? That's probably the best thing for you. Sophie, bring me a brandy snifter please."

The maid brought the snifter, and the woman in the dinner dress poured Roy a drink and brought it to him. Roy thanked her. He was bashful about taking a drink of liquor in front of these two women like this, but he turned it up anyway and took it all down in a couple of gulps, even though he hadn't had anything to drink since he got out of prison. It went down like unproofed corn liquor, only not as smooth. Roy gasped and said, "Jeezus," before he could catch himself. He had been trying not to use the Lord's name in vain.

Well, Roy was already light headed, and the liquor was burning in his stomach. He felt himself getting dizzy as he stood on the hearth and listened to the woman talking to her maid about taking him to the police station. The woman wanted Sophie to drive him, but Sophie said she didn't have any gas. Sophie had a disapproving scowl on her face, especially when she looked at Roy. The wind whined on the eaves of the house, and ice rained down from trees onto the roof, and Roy felt himself going. He started to ask if he could sit down, but he never got it out. His head was spinning.

His legs went weak, and he lost consciousness.

He woke up in a warm bath. The bathroom was like nothing he had ever seen before. The walls were all mirrored, and the mirrors were steamed up. The plumbing fixtures were gold-plated. There was marble tile on the floor, the counter tops, and around the tub. The toilet was built low like something out of a rocket. The bathtub was a couple of feet deep, and warm water was whirling out of little gold jets set into the sides. The toilet lid was down, and Roy's wet, nasty clothes were in a pile on top of it.

And there, at the other end of the room, sat the maid on a foot stool. Roy covered himself with his hands.

The maid stood up. "They's clean clothes right here," she said, pointing to a stack of clothes on the vanity top. "And Miz Wickerson done poured you some more liquor." Sophie looked thoroughly disgusted. "You ain't goan drown now, is you?"

Roy said no, he was o.k., and Sophie left the bathroom and closed the door behind her.

Roy leaned back in the bathtub and enjoyed the hot water. His feet were warm and tingly, and his hands were no longer numb. He was tired, but he felt much better than he had earlier.

Roy got out of the tub and toweled himself off. He walked onto the thick carpet in the adjoining bedroom. Apparently nobody slept in this bedroom. There were two twin beds, and flowered wallpaper and ruffled bedspreads. At one end of the room were two armchairs with a side table between them.

Steam was rolling out of the bathroom. Roy went back in. On the vanity was a stack of clean clothes and another snifter of brandy. Roy took a drink, but he couldn't get it all down like the first time. He put on the clothes--madras cotton pants and a pink, starched, oxford-cloth shirt. The clothes fit very well.

Even the bright penny loafers fit. Roy looked at himself in the mirror. He slicked his hair back with a silver brush that was on the vanity, and he took another drink of the brandy. He drained the tub (which took a little figuring), and then he found his way out and down the hall to the living room.

The lady was at the bar fixing another drink. She raised her eyebrows when she saw Roy. "My goodness," she said.

"Would you like something to eat?" she said. "I'm sorry, I didn't ask your name."

"Roy Derwelt," Roy said, and there was something about that smile, that was so real, and so happy. Roy could feel it as he smiled.

She shook his hand, and said, "I'm Eva Marie Wilkerson, Roy." She led him to the dining room table and told him to have a seat. She went into the kitchen and told Sophie to serve him the dinner. There was no sense letting it go to waste, Eva Marie said.

Sophie brought out a bowl of watery soup, and Roy's heart sank. He slurped through that in no time. Eva Marie sat at the table across from him and drank her drink and watched him eat, and then she told Sophie to bring the rest of it out all at once. She asked Roy if he would like some wine, and he said, well, maybe he oughtn't, but she said, "Oh, come on, you've been through a terrible ordeal." Roy gave in, and she had Sophie bring out a bottle of wine, too.

Sophie was scowling when she served Roy. She set the plates down hard in front of him. But what a meal. There was roast leg of lamb and several different vegetables and a casserole and a salad and bread and butter, and some kind of fabulous cake covered in whipped cream and liquor, and then some cheeses Roy didn't care for, and more brandy after all that. Roy ate like he had never eaten before. Eva Marie had Sophie bring her a plate, too, and she had some wine with Roy, and then a glass of brandy herself.

Roy told how he had gotten robbed, and where he was from, and where he had been going. After dinner they moved in and sat in front of the fireplace and drank some more brandy and talked about a lot of things. You know how these things go, or maybe you don't. Anyway, the wind was getting stronger outside, and the sleet was beating up against the sliding glass doors, and there was plenty to drink and a warm fire. Roy told Eva Marie about his missionary work, and his job search, and his mother and his sisters, and about cutting pulpwood with his daddy when his daddy was alive, and even later in the evening, Roy told Eva Marie how he used to help his daddy make liquor, and how they would run it down to Atlanta and sell it to the nigger bootleggers. And then, after a few more drinks, Eva Marie told Roy about her children and her ex-husbands, and then Roy told her about the theft of the car and the high speed chase through the mountains and even about going to prison, and Eva Marie told him about Fred R. Helms, the man who had stood her up that evening.

They both laughed long and hard as the night went on.

Later that evening the power went out, and they had Sophie bring some candles and light them. Roy and Eva Marie kept on talking and drinking, and really just lost all track of the time, until Sophie came out of the kitchen in her raincoat.

"Miz Wickerson," she said, "I got to feed my family tonight. "

"Oh Sophie, I'm sorry, I just wasn't paying attention to the time. Take some of the leftovers, help yourself."

Sophie was already carrying a stack of leftovers wrapped in tin foil. She stared at Roy until he looked away. "You want me to send Joseph to take him to the police?" she asked.

"Oh thank you, no. No. I can take Roy to the police station myself. Is that o.k., Roy? I don't think the storm is as bad now." The wind whipped the sleet against the house.

"You go ahead," Eva Marie said. "We'll leave right now. Would you let me change my shoes, Roy? You'll need a coat, I think. There's a coat for you in the hall closet, I'm sure."

Eva Marie went into her bedroom and came back in a fur coat and rubber boots. She found a golf jacket for Roy in the hall closet. She told Sophie good night and told her they would go out the front door to the Mercedes. Sophie left with the scowl she had been wearing all evening. She walked hunched over her armload of leftovers.

Eva Marie led Roy to the front door. Roy heard Sophie's car crank and crank and sputter to a start and then roar as Sophie floored the accelerator. He saw the old Chevrolet Impala pull out of the driveway.

Eva Marie stopped right at the front door, and turned towards Roy and looked into his eyes. She put her arms around his neck and kissed him.

Roy could see Sophie's car through the window, and just for a second he saw her looking in at them, and then the car rolled slowly on off.

Now if you had told Roy Derwelt that morning when he left Greenville County what was going to happen to him that day, he would have said you were absolutely crazy.

Roy spent a long time up in Eva Marie Wilkerson's king-sized bed, until the candles they put on the bedside tables burned all the way down and went out, and Eva Marie pulled the covers up over them both, and they went to sleep.

When Roy Derwelt woke up the next morning, the first thing he saw was the sunlight coming through the glass doors that led onto the deck. And God, it was bright, reflected off the ice trees swaying in the wind. Roy turned away, and lying there beside him in the king-size bed was Eva Marie Wilkerson, with her face all puffed up and her red hair tangled. She was snoring.

The light was so bright Roy's head throbbed. He put his hand on it to try to keep from throwing up. His mouth felt like a cat had slept in it. He had heartburn up to his throat.

On the table behind Eva Marie were pictures of the children she told him about the night before. He looked down at the foot of the bed, and there was a white, long-haired cat lying at his feet. Roy tried to swallow. He reached up and pulled cat hairs out of his mouth. He spat and spat. Cat hairs were all over the blanket near his chin. Eva Marie moaned. She rolled toward him and put her arm over him and breathed into his face. Her breath was eight-hour-old leg of lamb and liquor.

Roy lifted her arm off and got out of the bed and ran to the open door that he thought was the bathroom. It wasn't. It was Eva Marie's closet, with rack after rack of clothes and shelf after shelf of shoes. Roy's head was pounding, and his jaws were tightening. He almost tripped over a pair of high heeled shoes, and then he stepped in the cat droppings, right in the middle of the carpet, in his bare feet. When the smell hit him, Roy lost it, in a corner of the closet under the evening gowns.

It was a big, wine-colored stain with bits of food, but Roy couldn't look. He rubbed his foot on the carpet. The smell was terrible. He went back into the bedroom, expecting Eva Marie to be awake, but she was sprawled all the way across the bed now and was snoring again. The wind was howling outside. The sky was bright blue, and the icy tree limbs whipped in the sunlight.

Roy tried not to wake Eva Marie. He went into the bathroom and closed the door and cleaned his foot off with a wash rag. Then he got a towel and meant to go clean up the closet, but just the thought of it made him nauseous again. He gave that up.

Roy looked at himself in the mirror. His eyes were red, and he was pasty white, with scratches on his face from the brier patch. He wet a brush and slicked his hair back and got his cowlick to stay down. He went back in the bedroom. Eva Marie was snoring still.

She rolled over and said, "Fred, Fred, will you see who that is?" Roy started to answer, but he saw she was just talking in her sleep. Roy found the madras pants and the pink Oxford cloth shirt he had been wearing, and the penny loafers, and he pulled them on. Then he found the golf jacket. It wasn't much, but it was something at least. Roy could feel drafts coming in around the sliding glass doors.

Roy quietly opened the door to the bedroom. The big cat jumped off the bed and ran out the door past him. Eva Marie snorted. Roy waited and watched for a second, but she didn't wake up. He left the bedroom and went downstairs quietly. The wind was roaring around the house. Limbs were falling and ice was raining out of the trees. Roy went to the front door and opened it. The cold wind blew into the house. He closed the door and searched through the coat closet and found a stocking cap and some man's driving gloves.

Roy went out on the deck, walking very carefully in those loafers so he wouldn't slip. The sun was so bright he had to shut his eyes for a moment. Roy went down the steps and walked past the silver Mercedes. He looked it over and whistled. Then Roy turned down the driveway and started to walk away.

He went about twenty feet and stopped.

Roy turned around and went back to the Mercedes. He tried to look in the driver's side window, but the whole car was covered in a sheet of ice. He took off one of the penny loafers, stood on his other foot, and scraped some of the ice away with the sole of the shoe.

A gust of wind blew, and a tree limb fell in the driveway. Roy opened a clear spot so he could see in, and there were the keys hanging from the ignition.

"Roy! Roy!" Eva Marie was standing in the front doorway in her housecoat. "Roy," she shouted over the wind. "Wait a minute and I'll take you. Come on in."

Roy went in, and Eva Marie said, "God, did you smell in the bedroom? The damn cat went on the carpet again."

Roy shrugged. Eva Marie ran upstairs and put on pants and a sweater and a kerchief, and a good bit of make-up, and came back down. Roy scraped the windows of the Mercedes for her, and they drove off towards town to take Roy to the police station.

They hadn't gone too far, maybe three or four miles, when the road began to look familiar to Roy- the narrow two-lane, the dark pine woods, the two frame houses he remembered. And then there was a car parked up ahead on the side of the road, within sight of the Interstate. As they got closer, Roy saw it was the Galaxy.

"I be damned," he said.

They stopped, and Roy got in the car. There was no sign of the hitchhikers. The keys were gone, but that didn't matter, because the switch was broken, and you had to hot-wire it anyway. Roy bent under the dashboard and touched two wires together. The motor turned over fine. But it wouldn't start. So Roy held the wires together and twisted his head around to where he could see the gas gauge. Sure enough, it was down to that spot Roy knew so well.

Eva Marie took Roy three or four miles on the two-lane to a gas station. Before she pulled into the station she put on her big dark glasses and pulled her kerchief around her face.

Roy had to borrow a few dollars from her to pay for the gas and to leave a deposit for the can. Eva Marie drove him back to the Galaxy. He gassed it up and cranked it and cranked it. It finally kicked over. Roy left the car running and went back to the Mercedes. He stuck his head in to say good-bye, and he couldn't decide whether to try to kiss Eva Marie or not. She quickly pointed toward the Galaxy.

"What is that huge thing on your dashboard, Roy?"

"Oh, that's my plastic Jesus," Roy said. Eva Marie started to giggle, but she stopped herself.

"God bless you, Roy," she said. They said good-bye again, and they kissed.

Roy directed Eva Marie as she turned the Mercedes around in the highway. She waved to him in the rear view and took off down the road. Exhaust steamed out of the dual tailpipes of the silver Mercedes coupe. The whole countryside was so lit up with ice Roy couldn't look after her for long.

So Roy Derwelt got back in the Galaxy, and he had just enough gas to get back to Greenville County that morning without picking up any hitchhikers. When he got home to his mama's house he took a long nap to get over his ordeal. In fact he slept almost till supper time, when the smell of fried pork chops and black-eyed peas woke him up.

His mama carried on like she was irritated to have him back already, but when she said grace over the pork chops and black-eyed peas and rice and gravy and biscuits and turnip greens and Roy's glass of buttermilk and her little tumbler of well water that evening she thanked the Lord for bringing her boy back to her safe and sound.

The Third Tale

Earnest is surprised by a young man from the East.

I picked up my canvas bag and walked out of the station onto the street, and there I was in Rome, sixteen years old and on my own. It was hot, mid-morning in August. The flashy billboards around the square sported Italian jingles. The crowd was loud and lively. The roofs of the buildings were red tile, and the walls were a yellow stucco. It's still alive in my memory after all these years-hundreds of little cars whining around the square, weaving amongst each other with their horns blaring. In the early seventies Rome was the Old World, and a fabulous place for a sixteen-year-old boy to find himself.

I wandered across the square and down one of the main streets to an inexpensive cafe. I found a table outside, ordered a cup of coffee, and waited, tired from the overnight train trip, for the morning to get a little older before I searched for a place to stay.

Three young people came walking down the street from the direction of the train station- two girls who looked to be in their early twenties, and a boy who looked even younger than I. The girls were carrying backpacks. The boy was dark-skinned and was carrying a heavy, leather suitcase. They stopped on the sidewalk and read the menu. Then they propped their backpacks and suitcase against a table and sat down to order.

The waiter took his time coming to them. The girls asked him in loud, Yankee accents if he spoke English, and he shook his head no.

"Two cappuccinos", one of the girls said. She asked the young boy with them, "You want cappuccino? Three cappuccinos." She held up three fingers (the American way, not the European way.) "And rolls. Bread." She hefted an imaginary loaf of bread in front of her.

The waiter acted as if he didn't understand.

"You know," the girl said, irritated. "Bread. Rolls. Eat." She put her hand to her mouth and bit her teeth together.

The waiter mumbled and walked away.

I sat there at my table reading my book and pretending not to notice the other Americans in the cafe.

The waiter came back with the cappuccinos and three menus. "Great, they're in Italian " one of the girls said. She looked Jewish- long dark hair and a pretty, white complexion. Connecticut accent.

The dark-haired Jewish girl tried to point out something to eat on the menu, and the waiter pretended he couldn't understand anything she was trying to get across to him. The waiter played this scene for several minutes. He finally disappeared with the menus, grinning.

The other girl had short, straight blond hair, and round, wire-rimmed glasses. She was tall and slender. Unusual looking, but attractive.

The guy I couldn't figure. He was dusky-skinned and had curly, black hair with a girlish face. He could have been two or three years younger than I was. Very slight. Very quiet. It was easy to be quiet with that couple of girls.

The blond was the first to talk to me. She said something about the book I was reading. We spoke across the tables for a while, then they invited me to come sit with them. The waiter brought out a basket of rolls, along with plates of bacon and eggs. They had been brought the tourist breakfast, and they were going to get stuck with a stiff bill.

"Oh damn it, " said the Jewish girl.

"We might as well go on and eat it," said the other girl. "I'm starving."

The Jewish girl picked up a soggy piece of bacon and chomped on it. The other girl buttered up a roll and ate it. The Arab boy asked what the bacon was. They told him it was bacon. He didn't know what that was. I told him it came from a pig, and he didn't eat it.

He had slight, feminine features and big, brown eyes. His polyester print shirt was too big for him, as were his double knit pants. Remember, this was the early seventies. He probably was wearing a wide white belt with two rows of holes all the way around it. Or maybe I was. I can't remember.

"Ooh, pork, pork," said the Jewish girl, chomping on the bacon and waving her hands in front of her in mockery. "What would my muthah say?"

We found out where we were all from. The Jewish girl was from Rhode Island. The blond was from somewhere out west. I want to say Arizona or New Mexico, but I've really forgotten now. She told a story about riding motorcycles in the desert. I remember that.

The Arab boy was from Kuwait. They had met at a youth hostel in Milan, and they had taken the train down together to Rome.

The two American girls were in Europe for their Grand Tour, having finished college the previous spring. I had met plenty like them that summer. I had never met anyone like the Arab boy. Jamil was his name. He was so young. Usually people were amazed to learn I was traveling on my own. But he looked two or three years younger than I. He was quiet and very soft spoken when he talked. He had a soft, high-pitched voice. His eyes avoided mine. He felt more comfortable speaking to the girls.

We decided to look for a place to stay together. I didn't want to stay in a youth hostel. My guide book had given the names of a few *pensiones* off the main avenue we were on, and I suggested we check them out.

So we took off, me carrying my little shoulder bag, the two girls carrying their overstuffed backpacks, and Jamil dragging a full-sized leather suitcase.

Jamil was huffing and sweating when we got to the first *pensione*. The owner of the *pensione* took one look at us and sent us on our way. The Jewish girl, whose name was Miranda, was indignant. We listened to her tirade as we trudged to the next few *pensiones*, where we received similar treatment.

Being sixteen, and being even more blunt than I am today, I told them the people were being rude to us because of the backpacks, and perhaps we would have better luck if Jamil and I went to the door of the next *pensione* alone.

"I don't know," Miranda said. "I'm ready to go on to the fucking youth hostel and get a decent shower."

I persisted. Jamil and I went to the door of the next *pensione* alone. The owner said yes, he had a room, and then I asked if he had a room for our friends. The girls appeared, and he reluctantly said yes, he could take them, too.

This *pensione* was on the third floor of an apartment building with a grand, winding staircase. I remember the mahogany stair rail, the marble treads and risers, the cast iron balusters, and a cage elevator coming up through the center of the stairwell. It's been a long time ago, and these memories are getting to be like dreams.

Was there a reception counter, or was there just a desk in the living room of the *pensione*? I can't remember. A hallway led off to the right from the reception area. The toilet was at the end of the hallway. We asked to see the rooms before we took them. The rooms we were shown overlooked the roofs of the buildings next door. There were clothes lines out on the roofs with clothes hanging stiff in the morning sun.

The rooms came with only one double bed in each. But they were reasonably clean, and we said yes, we would take them. Jamil was not comfortable with the idea. And frankly, neither was I particularly. But I suppose I saw it as the thing to do.

The owner made us pay in advance. As soon as he left the room, I opened my canvas bag and pulled out some clothes to change. Jamil excused himself and left the room. After I had changed, I went down the hallway to the toilet to wash up. The door was locked. I waited outside until Jamil emerged with an embarrassed look.

When I came out of the toilet and returned to our room, the door was locked there.

I went to the reception area and had a seat to wait for the others. I picked up a copy of *Paris Match* and tried to read it. I couldn't read much French back then, but this was sure to impress the girls when they walked out.

We decided to get lunch together and then go sightseeing. I was very tired from the train trip, and it would have suited me to sleep in that afternoon, but the girls were not leisurely tourists.

We had a conference there in the reception area about where to go. We compared guidebooks. Jamil had a little green book written in Arabic with fold-out maps. He wanted to go see the Forum, and nobody else objected, so we went downstairs, bought some items for a picnic, and caught the appropriate bus.

The layout of Rome is still pretty clear in my mind. Probably not to scale, but I can remember where the Vatican and the Forum and the Palatine Hill and the Coliseum and the Spanish Steps were. I can remember walking in the Forum amid the ruins and climbing the Palatine Hill and looking over to the Circus Maximus.

On the Palatine Hill, we had a picnic of bread and cheese and sausage and wine. I remember the bright Roman sun. Bright like the courtyard of an Italian Renaissance painting. Bright like *Ben Hur*.

I wish I knew what kind of tree we were sitting under on the Palatine Hill. I remember the sparse, grassy forest with the ruins of palaces scattered in it.

Jamil drank no wine, explaining that it was against his religion. That led to a discussion on religion. You know how you can get into those discussions with strangers when you're far from home.

Forgiveness was the most important topic to me back then. I asked Miranda if Jews believed in forgiveness. She said, yes, of course. Well, I said, but what about sin? Did Jews believe God forgave you for your sins? Why yes, Miranda said.

"I don't think there's really anything like sin," the blond said. (I've forgotten her real name, so I will call her Beatrice.)

This created an awkward silence.

"How can there be no sin?" I said. "You mean there's nothing right or wrong? We should just do whatever feels good?"

"Well, that actually sounds reasonable to me," Beatrice said.

"Oooh, honey," Miranda said, "Watch what you're saying." Jamil said nothing. His eyes were wide.

"Well, it's silly to me," Beatrice said, "this idea of sin, of certain things being bad. Who says they're bad?"

"God does," Miranda said.

"What, did He tell you?" Beatrice asked. "Did He say, 'Miranda, I don't want you smoking any more pot. That's a sin.'"

Miranda didn't answer, but I did. "Don't you think you have an innate sense of what is right or wrong?" I asked. I was raised as a Presbyterian.

"No, I'm not sure that's so," Beatrice said. She thought about it a minute. "No, I don't think so."

"Oh come on!" I said.

"What do you mean by right or wrong?" Miranda asked.

"I mean what is morally right and morally wrong. I mean what you feel in your stomach is right. I'm not talking about what you learn in Sunday school, or wherever you learn it, but what you know in your gut is hurting other people and you shouldn't do it."

"So," Beatrice said, "you're saying like cannibals in New Guinea, when they kill somebody and boil them and eat them, they know in their guts that what they're doing is wrong, without even going to Sunday school to learn that it's wrong?"

"I'm not a cannibal from New Guinea," I said, "and I've never known one. But I suspect there is some feeling of pain and regret in those cannibals. That's just my gut feeling. I've seen on like National Geographic specials where they show some primitive tribe somewhere, there's always some ceremony where they atone for the sin of killing the animals they eat. They have to atone the animals' spirits or the forest's spirits or something. I mean I think there's some real feeling of loss, or what?"

The conversation stopped for a while, and the subject probably would have changed, but Jamil spoke up.

"Do you think it is wrong for men and women to sit together like this?" he asked.

"What do you mean?" Miranda asked.

Jamil was very shy, and it was hard for him to make himself talk. His voice was soft and high. "Do you think men and women should be together like this?" he asked.

"Of course. Why not?" Beatrice said.

"And is o.k. for women to dress like this when they are with men?" Jamil said. He said it in an honestly inquisitive way, not a judgmental way. Miranda and Beatrice were wearing shorts, hiking boots, and T shirts. Neither was wearing a bra, and Miranda's large breasts waggled deliciously inside her shirt.

"Why on Earth not?" Beatrice said. She was offended.

"You know in my country is not allowed. In other countries is even more sin."

"That makes me so furious," Beatrice said. "It's so medieval. What, do you think men and women can't be around each other without being overwhelmed by lust?

"Do you think that there are no feelings to make you, what?" Jamil searched for a word.

"Sin," I said. "To make you want to sin."

"Yes," Jamil said. "Do you think there are not feelings to make you sin when men and women are so close together?"

"Well, I don't know about you two, but I've got perfect control over my hormones," Beatrice said. "And if I did want to do it with somebody, I can assure you I would."

Jamil got red in the face. Not angry red. Embarrassed red. "Without being married to him?" he said, astonished.

"What the hell is marriage but a piece of paper?" Beatrice said. "My parents were married for twenty-one years. Now they're both divorced and sleeping with people my age.

"Sex to me," Beatrice continued, "is something you do because it feels good, and because it makes you feel good to be with the person you're doing it with. Modern science has made it just that, and it's time for the world to catch up with reality."

"You can't say that," Miranda said. "What if the girl gets pregnant?"

"Having sex and having children are two entirely different things," Beatrice said. "There is no need in the modern world to confuse those two things."

"Well, you can catch diseases," Miranda said.

"No need for that, either," Beatrice said. "They can be prevented or they can be treated. I'm telling you, all of these medieval attitudes about sex have been rendered completely obsolete by the realities of the modern age."

"Well, what about love?" Miranda asked.

"Well," Beatrice said, "to tell the truth, love doesn't necessarily have anything to do with it now, does it? I mean you and I may wish it did, and maybe we can make a personal choice that it does, but it doesn't necessarily have to play a part. Screwing is screwing and love is love, and I don't know about you, but it's been perfectly obvious to me a time or two that the two don't necessarily go together."

This conversation was tearing me up. Women talking about sex. Imagine. I had never even come close to having sex, although I wasn't going to admit that in conversation.

"I think it is impossible to be with someone without being married," Jamil said, and this stopped the conversation dead.

After a long silence, Beatrice said, "Well, maybe in your culture- but we are from a different culture and a different age. That is what I am talking about.

"Speaking of a different age," I said, "think what went on in these palaces two thousand years ago. Orgies. Nubian love slaves."

I don't think Miranda followed me.

"They were pagans, infidels," Jamil said. "They had no religion. They had no enlightenment from God."

Again, this created an awkward silence. Beatrice spoke to Jamil as if she were speaking to one of those cannibals in New Guinea.

"Jamil," she said, "we just look at things differently in America. Things change with time. The world changes, and humanity changes. I respect your religious beliefs, but I really feel I should be honest with you. You travel to learn, and here you're getting a chance to learn how other people look at the world. Look at what Miranda and I are doing. Do Kuwaiti women ever do this sort of thing?"

"No," said Jamil. "Is impossible."

"Well," Beatrice said, "there may be a great deal of good in that, but I can tell you there is a great deal of good in the way we are living, also. Good that women have never had a chance to experience- because of these old attitudes about sex and what is proper and what is sinful."

Jamil didn't argue. I wanted to argue, but I didn't. It was just too beautiful a Roman sun to waste on this discussion. And Miranda wanted to stretch back on the grass and take a nap, with her nipples erect against the flimsy knit of her t-shirt.

That night we ate at a Spanish restaurant within walking distance of the *pensione*. The restaurant was a dark place on the basement level, with a sunken entrance beneath a neon sign that advertised Sangria. The ceiling was low. It seemed as if it were only two or three feet above the bar top. The men's room was a concrete trough in the rear alleyway. I drank Sangria that night with fruit in it and thought it was too sweet, while Miranda and Beatrice loved it.

Jamil asked me if he could taste my sangria. There was a look of determination on his face. Like he was climbing over a wall. I felt kind of bad handing the glass to him. I was really too young to be drinking myself, and he was younger than I, and it was clearly against his religion.

Jamil sipped the sangria with a serious, contemplative look.

He didn't say anything about it, and we didn't say anything. When we ordered dinner, he ordered a glass of sangria for himself. I remember his eating the fruit off the rim of the glass first, before he began drinking.

I ate paella, the first time I ever had it, and I can still taste it, the salty seafood and the spicy rice. Who knows what the others had? It's strange how you can remember certain vivid bits of your life, and the rest is lost in a haze. I can remember Jamil's face as he began to get drunk. The laughter in it, which I had not seen before. I remember the blush and the shiny brown eyes. He didn't have much to drink, probably two or three glasses of sangria, but as small as he was, and having never drunk before, it had quite an effect on him.

That night we talked about what we wanted to be when we grew up. Miranda and Beatrice feared only that the jobs they found wouldn't be exactly what they wanted to do. Miranda's mother wanted her to be a lawyer, but Miranda wasn't sure this was her true calling. Jamil was fascinated by this possibility.

"Is so different with you," he said.

We all got tipsy. Miranda told us about some of the men she had had sex with. The boys, I should say. She had a one-night stand in her past that she was quite ashamed of. She couldn't remember the guy's name. He had picked her up in a college bar and took her back to his apartment. Miranda must have been quite drunk to tell us about this, but we were in Rome, in that dark cellar of a Spanish restaurant, and she had never known any of us before and would never see any of us again.

We left that restaurant and walked to the Piazza Navona, where we ate ice cream and drank more wine and listened to a bad Italian rock band play. The night was warm, and the Piazza was lit in a soft, incandescent light. I can feel the texture and the click of the stones on the soles of my shoes.

Somehow Jamil and I ended up walking back to the *pensione* without the girls. He was laughing and weaving, walking very effeminately, really, and he was walking too close to me. I felt uncomfortable because of it. He told me he had a big secret he might tell me. He stopped on the sidewalk and held his finger to his lips and shushed me to be quiet. Then he stood and thought to himself and grinned. He shook his head and said nothing and started walking toward the *pensione*.

We got to the front door of the building and used our guest key to open it. I remember the huge mahogany and marble staircase more clearly now, with the black elevator cage rising through the middle of it. I remember Jamil's big brown eyes looking at me and smiling as we rode in the elevator. His eyes were laughing.

I got my toothbrush from our room and went to the bathroom immediately. I locked the door and sat on the toilet for a long while, even though I didn't need to go.

When I got back to the room the light was off, and Jamil was in bed with the covers pulled up to his chin. I stripped down to my shorts. The night was humid and warm, and there was no breeze coming through the open window, only traffic sounds and the sounds of Italians speaking loudly in other buildings. I climbed in bed beside Jamil, rolled toward the window, and closed my eyes. There was a buzzing in my head from the wine.

"Earness", Jamil said softly. That was the way he said my name.

"Earness."

I tried to pretend I was asleep.

Jamil's voice was very soft now. It was soft and laughing. "Earness, I tell you my secret."

Jamil put his hand on my back, and I tensed up. His hand was soft and warm.

"Earness, you will not believe it."

I turned away from him. He tried to take my hand in his. His hand was so small. I didn't know what to do. Maybe such behavior was acceptable in his society.

"My name is not Jamil, Earness." Jamil giggled. I was most uncomfortable.

"Earness, I have done a bad thing. I have left my family." He was drunk.

"They make me marry, is a terrible man. Oh, he's so old- he is ugly and terrible. He has already two wives, and they are very unhappy. He, he...," Jamil searched for a word. "He hit them. Is always hit them.

"Ooooh," Jamil moaned. "He is so terrible." Jamil let go of my hand and sat up in the darkness. "I hate him, Earness. He touch me and I hate him. I cannot live with that."

I lay in silence. I didn't know what to think. The curtains blew lightly in the night breeze.

"I have taken my brother's passport, Earness, and I have cut my hair, and so I have come here to escape. And now my life is over."

And Jamil began to cry. "I can never see my family again. I cannot see my sister, my dear sister. Jamil covered his face and broke into sobs, and I knew the whole story, then.

She sat with her face in her hands and sobbed so long, like my wife has done, and I'm surprised at that age that I had the strength and the understanding to reach out and hold her. She put her head against my neck, right under my chin, and sobbed. I could feel the tears against my chest.

She must have been filled with fear, because it took her several minutes to get it all out. She let me hold her as she cried, and I stroked her hair.

When she finished crying, we sat up against the pillows in the dark and she told me the whole story. Her name was Marium, and she was fifteen years old. She had been married a very short time. I remember the husband's name clearly- Khalid Mustafa.

Khalid Mustafa. How that man has loomed in my imagination.

Now I can remember the smells of that night. The slightly oily smell of Marium and her strong perfume. The mildewy smell of *pensione* room and the sweet, pungent night smell of Rome. I remember the texture of the lumpy mattress, the coarse weave of the bedspread.

I was a very shy boy. I had only kissed two girls before I met Marium. I never kissed a girl before I was fifteen. I had never run my hand under a girl's blouse.

Marium's breasts were little mounds, with boyish nipples and large, soft aureolas. Her pubic hair was smooth- not very thick. She didn't shave her legs or under her arms.

I remember the entire event now as a matter of fact, but at the time I was astonished.

Young Marium was passionate. God had miscast her as an Arab girl. She would have done better, I think, as an American high school girl.

The love-making didn't last long, but Marium didn't seem to mind. She held me and rested her chin on my shoulder.

Marium told me stories of her family and her home and the evil Khalid Mustafa. She told me about her brothers and sister, and how she had cut her hair and stolen her brother's clothes and passport and planned and executed her escape.

She lay in the dark with the covers pulled up to her chin, her English falling to pieces. She told me a story about camel races. I can't exactly remember how camel races fit in, but I remember the camel races now like they were a dream. I've always imagined them as something like a steeplechase back home, but with the men in their Kuwaiti headdresses and the women in their veils, and the flat desert stretching endlessly to the horizon in all directions.

We talked a long time, without turning the light on. She told me how her parents had arranged for her to marry a man who was nearly sixty years old. He was wealthy and very powerful, so it was a good marriage for her family, and now she had ruined her life and her family. There was no way she could leave Italy, she said, because the customs men would look at her passport. The authorities would have been alerted by now to look for her brother's passport number.

By the faint light from outside her features were very soft.

"Your parents will not choose your wife?" she asked me, and I laughed and said, no, that was unthinkable in my country.

I tried to kiss her again, this time on the lips, and she let me. I tried a little tongue, and her lips opened up, and I was on fire. She pushed me lightly away.

"Then we could be married, here in Rome," she said. "We could be married tomorrow, and we will be as husband and wife tonight." There was desperation in her voice.

I stopped trying to kiss her.

I didn't know what to say. I sat up in the bed and raised my knees so the bed covers wouldn't reveal how aroused I was. "I," I said, "I wish. I wish that were possible. "

"Why it is not possible?" Marium said. "We can be married in a Christian church. It is all the same. I cannot return to my family or my home. I will become a new woman."

I sat in silence. And being sixteen, and being in Rome on a warm summer night, in bed with a naked girl after much wine, I gave a lot of serious thought to what Marium was proposing.

"You have seen, I can be a good wife," Marium said. "There is nothing wrong..." And she burst into tears when she said this.

The import of what we had done began to come through to me then. The import to me. I didn't for years begin to realize what had happened to her.

Marium got out of the bed, turned on the bedside lamp, found her clothes, and began to get dressed. She was in fact the first live naked girl I had ever seen. She wobbled as she pulled her pants on.

My mind was spinning through possibilities. What if I did marry her? It would save her. Well, maybe it would, but then again how would we deal with her traveling on a stolen passport? I didn't know what to think.

Marium put her clothes on and sat in the small wooden chair in the corner, staring out into the room with a lost look.

"Earness," she said, "you are a very good man. I think I am a very bad woman. You must not be with me."

"Marium," I said. It was the first time I had said her real name. "You are not a bad woman. I have not known you long, but you are not a bad woman at all. You are a very brave and a very good woman. I don't think you were wrong to leave."

Marium clasped her hands and squeezed them between her knees. I felt bad. I hated myself for doing what I had done. I remember the emotion clearly. I was embarrassed and ashamed. No, that wasn't so much the feeling. I hated that I had hurt her. I put my face in the pillow.

Marium came to the bed and sat down beside me and held me. "Is all right," she said, stroking my hair. "Is o.k."

I cried. I cried for a lot of things. For being sixteen years old and being on my own in Rome and for being bad. Marium hugged me and said with her lips close to my ear, "Is o.k. my baby. Cry. Cry."

I fell asleep like that, with Marium sitting on the side of the bed, holding me.

And when I woke she was gone. The sun was up, and the morning air was already getting hot. The curtains billowed ever so slightly in the breeze. I looked at my watch. It was seven-thirty or so. I thought she had gone to the bathroom, so I rolled over and closed my eyes. When she didn't come back after fifteen minutes, I looked for her suitcase. It was gone. I got up and looked around the room. I checked immediately for my money belt. My French franc travelers' checks, my passport, and my airplane ticket were all there.

I pulled on my blue jeans and a shirt and shoes and went out into the reception area. No one was there. I walked into the breakfast room. A number of guests were eating their rolls and coffee, but Marium was not to be seen. The people eating breakfast stared at me. My long hair was mussed from sleeping.

The owner of the *pensione* came in from the kitchen, carrying a basket of rolls and coffee cups. He gestured to me to sit down, but I shook my head no thanks.

I went back to my room, got washed up and dressed and packed, and for several minutes I sat in the little wooden chair Marium had sat in the night before, wondering.

When I went downstairs again for breakfast, Miranda and Beatrice were already seated and eating. Neither looked as attractive as I had remembered them the day and evening before. They asked where Jamil was, and I shrugged my shoulders and said he was gone.

"Where did he go?" Miranda said.

"I don't know," I said. "I just woke up and he was gone. No sign."

"Did you check your money belt?" Beatrice asked.

"Yeh," I said. "It's all there."

"Humph," said Miranda.

"I always knew there was something fishy about that kid," Beatrice said.

We were silent.

"You don't think we could have made him mad yesterday talking about religion?" Miranda asked. She was paying more attention putting sugar in her coffee than to Jamil's disappearance.

I didn't respond. I just sat down. The owner caught sight of me and started making another cup of coffee.

Miranda buttered and spread jam on a roll and took a big bite. "Boy," she said, "you can't ever tell about people, can you?"

The Fourth Tale
Chester Thoms goes to sea.

Chester Thoms was from one of those fabulously wealthy families who summer in Newport, Rhode Island still and spend the winter in Palm Beach or Palm Springs and never have to work, although some of them take on ambassador or publishing or patron-of-the-arts jobs.

Although there is a slim chance that you may be one of these people yourself, the chances are damn slim. So you probably don't understand those circumstances of life any better than I do.

Chester Thoms was the only heir to a fortune that was made in shipping and minerals in the early part of the 20th century. Chester's father, Raoul Thoms, the son of the original fortune maker, never worked a day in his life except at politics. He was a U.S. Congressman and a passionate champion of the rights of the working man. Chester was a disappointment to his father. Chester, from the time he was at Yale, disdained politics. He had some ferocious confrontations with his father during his college years and after he left Yale. Raoul had groomed Chester for a career in politics. Raoul Thoms considered it his family's duty to use their wealth and leisure to benefit those less fortunate. Chester had endured the lectures and the political meetings and the tacky, classless political operatives who came to visit his father when Chester was a teenager, but as he reached his early twenties, he finally got up the courage to tell his father he wasn't interested in that kind of thing at all.

Raoul was furious. After two or three years of fierce arguments between father and son, Chester and Raoul stopped speaking to each other altogether. In those stormy years before and right after Chester left Yale, Raoul had some terrible things to say about his son, and as is usually the case, Chester began to believe what his father said. So Chester, who already loved parties and women and yachts and the races and the beach club, became more or less a party bum. His father cut him off entirely shortly after they stopped speaking, but his mother had enough of her own money at her disposal to allow Chester to lead a jet-setting life.

Chester's mother doted on her only son, and when Raoul died suddenly a few years later, she was able finally to give Chester all the money he wanted. Chester was in his mid-twenties at the time, and his mother lived another fourteen years. She and her advisers took complete care of the family investments. Chester had no job and no need for one. She gave him as much money as he asked for, and he had no qualms about asking, so Chester Thoms led one of the most profligate lives imaginable until he was nearly forty years old.

Chester spent a lot of time in Europe and in the Caribbean and a lot of time in Newport and Palm Beach. He was a regular at every America's Cup, back when that was a regular event in Newport. He went salmon fishing in Norway and grouse shooting in Scotland, and went on camera safaris in Africa and trips to see Inca ruins in the Peruvian Andes. He crewed on a friend's yacht on a sail to Tahiti, and he jetted to the Seychelles or Mallorca in season. He was a regular on the largest yachts of the world, and an invited guest of pretending royalty. To be a world class socialite on this scale, and to maintain a subtle enough profile to allow others to carry most of the bill for it, was a full time job, and Chester was as adept at that job as a Hollywood agent is adept at his or hers.

The spiritual price anyone would have to pay for this life may be obvious to you, or maybe it isn't. No one can do that sort of thing for very long and think very much of themselves. Plus you have to remember, Chester had been attending cocktail parties eight hours or more a day, six or seven days a week, for many years. And towards the end of it, when cocaine became the in thing, he got into that, too.

Chester's mother was diagnosed as having liver cancer when Chester was thirty-nine. She lasted only nine months after the diagnosis. Chester stayed by her side at Sloan-Kettering the entire time, and later, when she was sent home, at the Palm Beach house. That June, when she was still able to travel, she asked to go to the Newport cottage for the summer, and Chester took her there, sparing no expense and arranging the minutest details to make the plane trip as easy as possible. When his mother died in Newport a couple of months later, Chester was inconsolable.

Perhaps you can see just how hard this could have hit Chester Thoms. He had no family left, he had never done anything worthwhile in his life, he had just turned forty years old, and now his mother, the only person he had ever loved, or the only person who had ever returned his love, was gone.

It's easy to see how upset Chester could have been, but it is impossible for us truly to feel the depth of another person's anguish. That would be too hard, and we can barely handle our own depths when they come.

That was a bad year for Chester. Within a couple of days of the funeral, his mother's financial advisers and lawyers began trying to get Chester to sit down with them to go over the estate. He avoided them and sat at home in the Newport cottage alone and drank. A few friends came to visit him and tried to console him. This went on for nearly a month, until his mother's lawyers and accountants and stockbroker finally came to the house and confronted him. They caught him early in the morning and made him sit down with them in the breakfast room overlooking the entrance to Narragansett Bay. They read Chester his mother's will and went over his new financial statements.

Chester was shocked. He had always thought there was simply no end to the money. His mother had never mentioned her financial affairs to him in the fifteen years since his father's death. Whenever he had asked for money, it had been immediately forthcoming, and in fact a little more than he asked for always came. Chester now discovered that he, and to a much lesser extent, his mother, had been digging deeply into principal for more than a decade.

"The bottom line is," one of the lawyers said, a brash young New Yorker whom Chester didn't like at all, if you continue to live as you have, you'll be bankrupt by the time you are fifty."

Probably only Chester Thoms's style of life could consume all that money in ten years. The fortune was still quite huge by most people's standards. But for the first time ever, Chester was confronted with the need either to make money or to spend less of it, and the confrontation was quite a jolt.

Over the next couple of months Chester stayed at home in Newport and thought about what he could do. The America's cup trials were being held, and he went out with Cynthia Cheatham on her father's boat to watch them most days. He talked to anyone who would listen about his dilemma, although most people didn't care to listen. Cynthia did. Chester had been a dear friend when she was leaving her first husband. Finally she recommended Chester go to see a psychiatrist in New York who had done a world of good for her. After a couple of visits the psychiatrist, who was quite expensive, suggested Chester look into pursuing a career.

It was a week or two later, at a benefit for the Guggenheim in Manhattan, that Chester ran into an old, old friend from Yale, Ned Waterman. Chester hadn't seen Ned in close to twenty years. Ned was going through a mid-life crisis of his own. He had just left his wife and his three children and was living in an apartment by himself. He and Chester got together for a few drinks after the benefit, and they ended up commiserating. Chester told Ned about his talks with the psychiatrist, and how he was thinking about what kind of work he should get into. He was really excited about the idea of making money. He thought it was sort of a masculine need, something he had been denying himself for too long, but he was having a hard time deciding what he should do. He had thought about a lot of things, but nothing he had come up with really excited him.

"Well," Ned said, "Have you applied for any jobs, sent any resumes out?"

No, actually, but Chester just wondered whether he could fit into the corporate organization, after so many years of being on his own." It would be one thing if I were twenty-five," he said, "but I don't know."

Ned had made a fortune in the minerals trading business, something his father had set him up in years ago, and he was very skeptical about the psychiatrist's advice to Chester. "One thing I can tell you," he said, "is it's not going to make you happy. It might fulfill some masculine need, like you say, but I'm even beginning to have my doubts about that."

Chester stayed in New York that week, since he had another appointment with the psychiatrist the following Monday. He and Ned hit the singles bar scene together every night and spent a lot of time talking about what was eating them. Chester couldn't really put his finger on the exact night it first came up, but Ned and Chester started to agree that maybe the best thing for Chester to do would be to invest some money in Ned's mineral trading business, become a financial partner more or less, and let Ned provide the work and expertise while Chester learned the ropes and made some money. "It's a damn risky, business, Chester, " Ned told him, "and I wouldn't let anybody else into it, to tell the truth. But I've got a vague idea of the kind of money you're talking about, and I think you've got the wherewithal to withstand some shocks and maybe reap the rewards, which," he gave Chester a look like those businessmen in Fortune magazine ads, "can be quite substantial."

Chester was ecstatic after that. It was so, what? Daring. Masculine. Substantial. He even rented a flat in New York and moved in and started going to Ned's office nearly every day. He was serious and eager, at least before lunchtime, and loved learning what he learned and answering the phone as Ned's partner when Ned was out of the office, although Ned diplomatically put a stop to that after a few days. Chester felt better than he had in his whole life. He noticed he carried himself differently at cocktail parties and spoke to the men more. He stood up straight and spoke confidently instead of gossiping like a woman.

Chester and Ned worked together for some six months before the Mexican deal. They lost a little money at first, but when they made half a million dollars on a shipment of copper ore from Chile, Chester just went wild with pride. Ned cautioned him that you had to take the good with the bad, and the big hits only came every now and then. It took discipline, he said. And control. But you also had to be willing and ready to strike when an opportunity arose.

The opportunity came on Mexican talc. Ceramic grade talc from the Sierra Madre. The kind of thing that is used to make bathroom sinks and toilet bowls. Ned heard about the mine through his countless connections, and somehow he dug up a couple of ceramics manufacturers who had low inventories and tremendous production runs coming up. He went to Mexico to inspect the mining facility and see what grade of talc they were digging. He had to fly by chartered plane from Mexico City and then had to ride some hundred miles or more on dirt tracks in a Jeep. Chester loved hearing Ned talk about the deal and hearing him describe the characters he would have to negotiate with. Chester told Cynthia Cheatham about the whole affair after Ned left for Mexico, and she looked at Chester like she was seeing a man she had never known.

Chester didn't hear from Ned for nearly a week after he went to Mexico. Then one day, as Chester was getting ready to leave the office for the squash club, he got an overseas call from Ned, a radio patch from the Sierra Madre.

After some confused talk in Spanish between the operators, Ned came on, shouting to get across the bad connections. This might be the opportunity, he told Chester. This had the makings. He couldn't go into the details over the radio, he said, but what it was going to take was money, a lot of it, and fast. The window of opportunity was very small. They needed seven million dollars for thirty days, at any price, it didn't matter, they could afford to pay twice prime for it if they had to, but it had to be in their Swiss account within forty-eight hours. This was a hell of a thing to be putting on Chester, but Ned couldn't possibly make it back to New

York fast enough to put together the financing himself. Ned told Chester what banks to call, and which vice presidents to deal with. If Chester didn't feel that he could do it, fine, he shouldn't take it on unless he felt comfortable, but the opportunity was just too damn good not to present it to him.

Chester had been in business with Ned long enough to understand the subtext of what Ned was saying. Something not entirely above board was going on, but Ned knew his way around in these matters. If he said he needed seven million dollars, it was worth getting into. Some Mexican bureaucrat might get very rich, but Chester and Ned would probably get richer.

This was right up Chester's alley. He hadn't done anything at all, no real business dealing, just putting up money and learning up to this point. Now was his chance. He told Ned he would be back in touch the next afternoon, and Chester set immediately to work.

He was able to raise three million of his own money from his liquid investments. His financial advisers howled when they found out what he was doing, and his mother's lawyer visited Chester at Chester's apartment that evening to tell him he couldn't advise Chester strongly enough not to do this. This was extremely dangerous and imprudent, and the man couldn't in good conscience continue as Chester's adviser if Chester didn't spread the risk among other investors. The lawyer was willing to find some investors if Chester wanted, for a reasonable finder's fee, of course. Chester told the man to go to hell, right there in his apartment, and fired him. Chester felt fabulous when he told the man to find his own way out.

The next morning Chester had breakfast with a group of vice presidents from one of the largest banking houses in New York. The negotiations stretched throughout the morning, but by lunchtime Chester was able to raise the other four million dollars. Chester had to sign away everything he had, except the Palm Beach house, as collateral. It was a huge gamble, but the talc was always going to be worth something, and even if they lost money on the deal, even if they lost a lot of money, he would be able to repay the bank loan from the sale of the talc.

By four o'clock that afternoon, Chester was able to raise Ned through a telephone-radio patch and advise him that seven million dollars had been deposited in their Swiss account and could be released by Ned's number at his discretion. "Fabulous, Chester," Ned said. "You're a hell of a man."

That was the last thing Chester ever heard from Ned Waterman.

Chester waited for three days before he called Mexico again. *Senor* Waterman had left the mine in the Sierra Madre three days earlier. The seven million dollars had been withdrawn from the Swiss account. Ned's estranged wife had heard nothing from him. Their divorce hearing was coming up the next week, she told Chester, and Ned had to be in New York for that. Ned's wife started digging Chester to find out how long he had been associated with Ned, and what kind of business dealings they had had, and when Chester realized she was collecting information for the alimony suit, he hung up on her.

Chester contacted the Mexican police, and, after a few days, the FBI and Interpol, but by that time Ned Waterman had disappeared from the face of the earth, with all of Chester Thoms' inheritance in tow.

There was a terrific investigation. Chester enlisted the help of his father's former political associates to keep the matter out of the press. The FBI, and later the IRS, were professional and determined, if bureaucratic, but they were unable to trace Ned beyond the jungle airstrip where his chartered plane had landed in Honduras. Chester retained new counsel to represent his interest in the investigation and to protect him from Ned's creditors. The new lawyers took him for twenty thousand dollars in legal fees the first month. Chester had practically no money left to live on. In fact he had to take a mortgage on the Palm Beach property.

The owner of the talc mine in Mexico was arrested for a short time but was released when there was no evidence to bring him to trial. Ned's wife was left penniless, and the divorce proceedings were in limbo.

That was a really bad time for Chester. Some of Ned's other creditors named Chester in lawsuits, claiming that as Ned's partner he was responsible for what Ned had been up to before he disappeared. The whole affair was much too complicated to go into here. Chester spent some three months in New York, frantically trying to stay afloat, and then he decided to flee to Palm Beach.

Now how Chester first got involved with drug smuggling, I don't know. You have to take into account that he was drinking heavily, and doing a lot of cocaine, and he was undeniably in deep financial trouble. I suppose when the idea first came up, Chester couldn't see himself doing something like that at all, but as time passed, and his situation became more desperate, well.

It helped that he was in Palm Beach, where he had always been a little wilder. His recreational suppliers there had very close connections to some big people in the trade, and when Chester dropped the hint he might be interested, they arranged a meeting between Chester and a middle-aged Cuban man in a high-rise office building in Fort Lauderdale. The man was dressed immaculately in a very expensive, olive suit with a Latin cut. His curly dark hair was graying and dignified. The two never discussed drug shipments at all. The conversation was more like Chester's conversation with the bankers in New York, the main topics being net worth, collateral, and credit history. At the time, Chester had already begun lying to some creditors about when he could pay them. And he lied to this man, a convincing and elaborate lie that placed his net worth at something close to the pre-Ned Waterman figures.

The other thing you have to keep in mind is the depression that set in. This business of making money seems to be very important to a certain part of the middle-aged male ego. Chester had made his bold move, the first bold move he had ever made in his life, and it had been a disaster. his self-confidence was destroyed, and he was having trouble with outbursts of anger, especially towards the end of a long night, when the cocaine was working overtime.

I won't take you through everything Chester Thoms did in Palm Beach. The fact is, he developed the necessary connections and made the necessary arrangements. This was in the late seventies, when the drug business in South Florida was still a sort of romantic endeavor. Independent smugglers brought cocaine and marijuana in from all over the Caribbean and Latin America. The big boys had not yet consolidated their power and begun eliminating all free-lancers. The coast of Florida, with its inlets and islands and rivers, and its tremendous pleasure boat traffic, was virtually unpoliceable. Smuggling dope back then was something college dropouts did on a lark. After a few years at it they became more professional, and some ended up very rich and others very dead. But it was not beyond reason for Chester Thoms to think he could pull off his own drug run from the Bahamas.

Chester was a real stickler on this point. He demanded to make the run himself. He wasn't going to hand over a substantial sum of money this time unless he could put his hands on what he was buying. There was a lot of resistance to the idea at first, but after a few days the resistance suddenly melted away, and a rendezvous point was picked and the price set.

So Chester went to a local bank, lied on his financial statement, and used his family's good name to mortgage the rest of his Palm Beach property. He had his man Antonio drive him to Miami, where Chester shopped for half an afternoon and then wrote a personal check for a drug boat.

That was a black-hulled, forty-two foot luxury offshore cruiser that was supposed to do fifty knots stock, but whose engines had been built to do a lot more than that. When the salesman opened the engine compartment hatches, and Chester saw the chrome flame arresters and the chrome valve covers and the bright yellow paint on the exhaust headers, the boat was sold already. After a wild test ride on Biscayne Bay, Chester wrote the check. He had Antonio drive the car back to Palm Beach while Chester took the boat himself, driving up the coast so fast at one point the bouncing threw him out of the driver's position and onto the deck.

When Chester pulled his throbbing black, plastic boat up to the dock behind his mother's house that afternoon, poor Antonio was mortified. Mrs. Thoms had moored her stately yawl there in the past, with its oiled teak decks and varnished mahogany wheel house. Now this plastic monstrosity was there, belching water out of the exhaust outlets, with low, chrome handrails and red vinyl seat cushions. The portholes were covered with darkened Plexiglass.

Antonio had been with Chester for twenty years and had suffered patiently through his myriad indiscretions, but he wouldn't speak for two days afterwards.

Chester loved his new boat. He was the talk of Palm Beach for the rest of the week. He took girls in bikinis out on it and opened the throttles up and bounced and skipped wildly over the swells until they screamed and begged him to stop. He roared up and down the waterway and sprayed Mrs. Helms's dock, scandalizing a lawn party she was having.

Chester had done a lot of sailing when he was a boy, but he had gone out on other people's boats for the last twenty years or so, always with a professional crew to run them, and besides, Chester never had been too good at navigation. When he told Antonio one evening he was going to make the run over to Bimini in his new boat, Antonio asked if Mr. Thoms thought that wise, considering that he had been so badly lost that time when he was home from boarding school and took his friends out in the haze off Newport.

But Chester assured Antonio there was nothing to the navigation here in South Florida, and besides, he had a brand new Loran that could tell him his position instantaneously anywhere over the area he would be cruising. After Antonio had served him dinner and a few drinks, Chester led Antonio across the lawn to the dock and took him aboard his new boat, Chester got out his plastic chart tube, spread the Cape Canaveral to Key West NOAA chart out on the small chart table, turned on the Loran, and showed how it gave their position exactly. For added effect, he gave the coordinates for Bimini, and the course and time that he would run to get there. Antonio, though he wasn't reassured, was at least silenced.

The next morning, shortly before lunch time, Chester left the dock and motored out through Lake Worth Inlet, passing the Coast Guard station to port and the north end of Palm Beach to starboard. He set his course, not for Bimini, but for the middle of Northwest Providence Channel. He opened the throttles. The engines roared, and the boat splashed and then pounded and then skipped high and wild over the swells as Chester headed out into the Gulf Stream.

It was a beautiful day. The sea was sapphire blue and raised in three- and four-foot swells. The spray flashed clear in the sunlight, and the breeze almost blew Chester's baseball cap off his bald head. Flying fished skimmed the wave crests. The boat jumped and roared and plunged and bounced, and Chester felt like a king.

This was the most magnificent, most daring, most inspiring thing he had ever done. There's something about modern American life that kills a man. It crushes all that is the man in him. But out there in the Gulf Stream, driving at close to sixty knots towards a rendezvous to break the law, Chester felt better than ever. And perversely, even though Chester had spent most of the last three months hating Ned Waterman, out here he began to feel a little bit of what Ned must have felt. He laughed when he realized that.

Chester ran at close to full throttle until higher seas in the middle of the Gulf Stream slowed him down. After a couple of hours he slowed his boat to idle and went below to check his position.

The motion was entirely different now, as the boat rose and rolled and dropped and wallowed in the swells. The cabin was hot and smelled of motor oil and bilge water. The boat rolled and threw Chester against the chart table as he got the chart tube down.

Chester pulled out his chart, spread it, read the numbers from his Loran, and plotted his position. That put him somewhere west of Miami, so he read the numbers again carefully and took his dividers and read the interpolation scale in the corner of the chart, and plotted his position again with his parallel rules .

Chester was getting nauseous. Working below decks in a boat on the open sea is the quickest way to get sea sick. The boat rolled erratically. The engine exhaust bellowed as the pipes rose and fell in the water. Chester was satisfied with this position. His jaw muscles were tightening as he drew another course line and memorized the heading. He dashed up the companionway.

Chester opened the throttles again, and the breeze and the clear horizon and steadier pounding made him feel much better.

He ran another four or five hours in building seas as the breeze freshened and clocked to the east. Late in the afternoon Chester made his landfall. He got out his yachtsman's guide to the Bahamas and carried it to the helmsman's position and studied the drawings of the islands and read the text. After about a half an hour of searching, he found the passage he was looking for and followed the directions given in the guide. The sun was setting in front of him, so he couldn't see into the water, but he recognized the ranges that marked the channel.

Chester followed the directions in the guidebook exactly. He kept the hill on the south end of the island in line with the rock off the near point until the white beach on the neighboring island was abeam to port. Then he turned and steered for the middle of the line of palm trees until the cove opened up to starboard and revealed a hut and a small dock and the most beautiful pink beach backed by casuarina trees. Chester motored to the dock and moored his boat, with a bow line and a stern line and one spring line aft to hold it up against the dock for loading. He stepped ashore, glanced at his watch, and looked impatiently for the people who were supposed to meet him.

When no one appeared Chester went back aboard and read his guidebook carefully. He had to be at the right place. He checked his watch. He was half an hour late. Chester went below and took a beer from the refrigerator. When he climbed back into the cockpit a red-headed man was walking lazily out the dock toward him. The man was young and fat. His red beard looked at the most a week old, and he was wearing ragged shorts and a dirty T-shirt and blue-tinted sunglasses. His redneck accent was so thick Chester almost laughed. "This is a private island, man. You can't just come in here and tie up."

Chester felt all the more bold, seeing these smuggler types were nothing to be feared, and he said in his snootiest Thoms accent, hardly looking at the man, "I was sent by Rafael. I believe there's something here for us."

The red-haired man chuckled. "Where you from?" he said.

"I've come today from Palm Beach," Chester said.

The redhead chuckled again and signaled up the hill to someone Chester couldn't see. In a few minutes a rusty Land Rover came over the hilltop and down towards the dock.

"Let's see the money," the redhead said.

"Let's see the merchandise," Chester said.

So they waited until the Rover pulled up. Two other drug smugglers were in the Land Rover. Both looked young enough to be in their teens. They had long hair and immature beards and dark tans. The driver was lanky and tall, with dark, curly hair. The other, who was carrying an Uzi machine gun, was quite good-looking and well-proportioned, with sandy, shoulder-length hair. Both were dressed only in dirty shorts.

The driver opened the tailgate of the Rover and showed Chester the bales of marijuana wrapped in green, plastic garbage bags. He opened one of the garbage bags, and Chester saw the marijuana baled tightly in clear polyethylene inside. Chester went back aboard his boat, went down below and took a nylon carry-on bag full of cash from the hanging locker. The redhead counted through the money on the dock, rather carelessly, Chester thought, and then the three of them began loading the bales onto Chester's drug boat.

They formed a chain, with the redhead and the boy with the Uzi on shore, and the other boy in the cockpit of the boat. Chester packed the bales down below, starting in the forepeak, and stacking them tight up to the headliner. Then he filled the hanging locker and the head and started filling the main cabin. They stopped every now and then for the two boys to go for another Rover load.

It took some two hours. Chester was huffing and sweating as he crammed the last bales into the galley. His boat was completely filled with plastic bales, so there was only a couple of feet of space left below the headliner in the aft half of the main salon. Chester was shaking. He was so nervous, but he felt fabulous. He felt the most alive he had ever felt in his life.

"Hey," the redhead said as Chester packed the last bale in.

"Come out here, man. Get the fuck out here."

When Chester came out into the cockpit, the redhead was kneeling over the nylon carry-on bag, counting money.

"Where the fuck do you get off, man?" he said. "Get the fuck over here."

Chester was sure all the money was there. He had counted it twice the night before, and once again this morning. He stepped onto the dock.

Chester saw one of the boys moving around behind him.

"Come here," the redhead said, and Chester knew he was being cut off from his boat, but there was no way to watch all three of them at once. He kept an eye on the boy with the Uzi, and he was judging the distance to the water, thinking he could dive in and swim underwater to keep out of the gunfire. He lost sight of the boy behind him. Almost immediately Chester was knocked face down on the dock by a heavy blow. The redhead jumped on Chester and pinned him to the dock, while the boy with the Uzi came running. The driver of the Rover cut Chester's spring line and bound Chester's feet together and bound his hands behind his back.

They turned Chester over, and the redhead was standing over him with the Uzi. He knelt and stuck the barrel of the Uzi up Chester's nostril. The gun oil on the barrel stung.

"You dumbfuck," the redhead said. "You lousy rich dumbfuck. You think you can come down here and waltz into this? You think fucking money buys everything? How'd you like me to pull the trigger? Blrrraaapppp." He imitated the noise of the Uzi, and Chester jerked his head away. The redhead laughed and shoved the gun barrel back into Chester's nose.

"Pig brains. Everywhere. All over the dock," he said. He got down close to Chester's face "I'd love to do it. I'd love to kill one of you rich bastards and watch you jerk around like a dead pig. That I would really love. But the man ain't goan have it that way. He says I got to deliver you in good shape. And he wants me to tell you, so you can start thinking, it's goan cost you to stay alive. A hundred grand a week. Where we're taking you they's a telephone, that's all you got, and you got to start raising a hundred grand a week. We take you to Nassau to the bank every now and then, is how it works. The man has all the details worked out. He just wants you to be thinking. And if the money runs out before the man is happy, maybe I get to kill you."

The redhead pushed Chester's head back with the gun muzzle until Chester was staring at the casuarina tops behind him.

"Load him on the fucking boat," the redhead said.

The two boys carried Chester aboard his boat and threw him down below on top of the dope bales. The sun was setting. The sky was orange behind the hill to the west. The boys closed the companionway hatch, and the cabin was dark except for the fading light from the darkened Plexiglass ports.

The drug smugglers cranked the engines. Chester heard the gearboxes being engaged and heard the water rushing through the jet intakes. The boat turned and headed smoothly away from the dock. As the boat moved into the passage between the two islands, Chester felt it start to rock in the surge. When the throttles opened up, and Chester's drug boat started pounding into the swells, it was already dark night outside. The sun sets quickly in the Bahamas, and there is very little twilight.

The boat moved sluggishly with all that weight on board. The motion was especially uncomfortable when the boat turned to the south and began running with the swells on its beam. The boat rolled and pitched irregularly, rose high on the crests and then wallowed and slid sideways into the troughs. It didn't take long for the engines to heat up the cabin, and the smell of oil and pot was strong. Chester couldn't see anything at all. The noise was terrific, and the swells seemed to be much higher and were torturously irregular, and Chester felt horrible. He felt the beginnings of nausea, and his head ached. His jaw muscles started to tighten. He tried his best to hold it back. He swallowed hard and fought it, but he didn't even feel it coming when he vomited like a cannon into the darkness.

That made the plastic bags slick. Chester started sliding back and forth over them as the boat rolled. He banged his head and his knees and couldn't do anything to stop it, couldn't even get oriented. The smell of vomit was strong in the hot cabin. Chester vomited again and again until he was retching and nothing would come up, and he was soaked.

The boat ran on for maybe fifteen or twenty minutes. Then the hatch opened. One of the boys looked in and shouted, "Oh my God, he's puked all over the dope."

They stopped the boat. The two boys pulled Chester out of the cabin, dragged him to the gunwale, and untied his wrists so he could hang on. The redhead opened the throttles back up, and they were off again.

Now that the fresh air blew on his face and the cool spray hit him every now and then, Chester felt better. But that let him start thinking about what was going to happen to him. There was no money left to give these hoods. There would be no money even to service the mortgage on the Palm Beach property now. Everything had been riding on this deal. Whoever these thugs worked for might be an intelligent being. The man in Fort Lauderdale had been professional and reasonable. They might kill Chester when they found out he had lied to them, but maybe he could reason with them. He was useful alive. He was useful, damn it. If they would just let this deal go through, he could get back on his feet financially. Surely they could use a man with some financial clout. With his background.

It was all the desperate rambling of a useless man, Chester knew. These dealers handled more money in a week than Chester had to offer. They didn't take him seriously. They never had. Ned Waterman hadn't taken him seriously. Ned had known from the beginning what he could do to Chester. Chester was someone to be used, and now that he was all used up, they would dispose of him. They all hated him. Deep down inside they all hated him for what he was. No matter what he ever did, Chester realized, they would always hate him for being born what he was.

He thought about jumping overboard, right out in the middle of the ocean. His chances would be practically nil, he knew. But at least he would have some hope of surviving until daylight and being picked up by a passing boat. He kept telling himself he could do it, but it was no use. In the darkness the swells looked tremendous.

Chester ran through a hundred scenarios of what he could do and what the consequences would be, but as is usually the case, none of those scenarios even came close to what was really going to happen. It was a dark night, with no moon, and the drug boat was running at close to thirty knots with no lights, plowing and roaring through the waves. The sailboat had to be running without lights also and was probably surfing on a broad reach. Over the rush of the water and the wind the crew of the sailboat never heard Chester's drug boat until it was too late.

Chester never saw anything at all. He just heard something like tin being shredded, then he was thrown out of the cockpit and into the darkness. He landed on the water with such force he skipped, and his swimming trunks, which were all he was wearing, were torn off. When he fought his way to the surface, the only sound was the combing of the wave crests and a man screaming in the distance. The screaming died away very quickly. Chester dolphined with his bound feet to stay up, until he brushed against something plastic that was floating, and he grabbed it and held on. It was a dope bale.

This all happened that quickly, two or three minutes maybe, although it's ridiculous to talk in terms of minutes here. It just happened that quickly. One moment Chester was a prisoner on his roaring, speeding drug boat in a rough night sea, and then there was nothing. Chester was floating naked in the warm water, holding a dope bale. The contrast was so sudden and so great that it was hard to comprehend. If you think back on it is hard to comprehend. Chester was living it, so it didn't matter if he comprehended it or not. Chester could see the stars overhead in an unbelievably clear, moonless sky, and he rode up and down in the warm swells, hugging his dope bale for flotation.

He tried to untie the bonds that held his ankles together, but the knots had swollen with water. He worked for a long time, but he couldn't see what he was doing, and he couldn't keep his head underwater for very long. It was too much of a struggle. He could swim with them bound together anyway. He rode pretty well, except when the occasional comber broke on him. From the crests of the waves Chester looked all around him on the horizon and saw only the darkness where the stars ended. Occasionally during the night other flotsam from the wreck washed close by, but there was no sign or sound of other survivors. Twice Chester saw the red or green lights of a passing boat far in the distance, but there was no way to signal for help.

Chester hung on his bale, exhausted and scared, nodding occasionally but never falling asleep. Often fish bumped against his feet or legs, and Chester would force himself to stay still. And time passed, time that seemed as if it would never end.

When daylight came the next morning, Chester was still hanging on his dope bale, and there was still nothing but water and wreckage to be seen in any direction. A somewhat gentler breeze blew the swells from the east. Before the sun came up, when the clouds in the eastern sky were red, and the swells were still dark, Chester tried again to untie his ankles, but the knots were swollen hard. He worked with them until he nearly drowned himself. It was no use.

The water was warm, and as the sun climbed in the sky the water turned a beautiful cobalt blue, infinitely deep. The sky was filled with high white clouds in shapes no man could imagine, and they blew to the west with the wind. The swells were steep but were no longer breaking, and when a crest of one of them rose against the sky, the sky shone through it crystal clear for a flash.

There was flotsam from the wreck around Chester- pieces of wood, Styrofoam plates and cups, little oil slicks. Chester hung on his bale and rode the waves and looked out for boats for several hours, checking the time on his Rolex, until sometime mid-morning, around ten o'clock, he looked up and there was another bale of dope floating near him. Chester dolphined over to it. He held the bale he already had between his legs and held the new bale in his arms and floated a little higher and easier. And then he started thinking. These bales were worth what at street value?

Forty-, fifty-thousand each. If the right person picked him up. Hell, anybody on a boat in the Bahamas might be the right person. He could split it with them, one bale for himself, one for them. That was enough to go to South America. Make another start.

He could even get into the drug trade down there. What the hell, he'd had an education. An expensive one, but he was still alive. As far as he could see he was the only one still alive. That would count for something.

Chester worked through lots of scenarios. About noon he drifted near a big yellow horseshoe buoy, the kind of lifebuoy that hangs on the taffrail of a sailboat, but that didn't interest him much. Floating right behind it was another bail of dope. Chester kicked over and grabbed the bale. It was getting a little harder to hold on, with one bale under each arm and one between his legs, but Chester was just ecstatic. A hundred twenty, a hundred fifty thousand, he was talking real money now. Chester began to plan how he would handle the negotiations with his rescuers. The main thing would be not to get killed. He had to offer them something that would make him useful. He would say he knew where to sell the stuff. Would play the part of the seasoned smuggler. Offer them risk-free cash if they would help him.

Chester held on and rode well until later in the afternoon. His bald head was painfully sunburned. He was dreadfully thirsty and sick to his stomach from swallowing salt water, but still he held on. The tuna tower of a sport fisherman had passed on the southern horizon around one o'clock. Of course there was no way they could spot Chester from that distance, but Chester believed he might be close to the over-the-banks route between Bimini and Nassau, and if a boat would pass a little closer before nightfall ...

The sky to the west started to darken. Chester heard thunder boom, and he watched a black, huge, anvil-shaped cloud grew and come towards him. From the wave crests he could see the rain underneath it and lightning cracking. That's a beautiful thing to watch, a thunder squall growing and coming towards you over the Bahamian sea. The sky and the sea are turquoise around it and deep black where the squall is.

The easterly wind died, and after a pause, the breeze began to freshen from the direction of the storm. This breeze running against the direction of the swells confused the sea, and the swells became steeper and choppier, with more white water. The storm filled more and more of the sky, until the water began to darken around Chester. The breeze was whipping, and the sun was blocked out. The waves grew steeper and darker until the sky was black. The wind blew in bursts. The waves began to break, and the water turned whiter and whiter. Chester had to fight hard to hold onto the bales and keep his head above water.

When the squall hit the wind was ferocious. The sea was foaming. Breaking waves rolled Chester over and over, and still he fought, until he lost his grip on one bale. Lightening cracked and thunder boomed all around him. Chester was rolled over again, and when he came back to the surface, he was holding one bale of dope and one torn, empty, plastic garbage bag. The flotation wasn't enough to keep him up, but he held tight to the one remaining bale and did the best he could to swim with his free hand and his bound feet. He could barely stay up, but he didn't let go of the bale.

When the rain came, it fell in tremendous drops. The wind died, and the rain came in sheets, so that Chester couldn't see more than fifteen or twenty feet. These squalls are quick. They are ferocious, but they are usually over in thirty minutes or so. The rain was as hard as Chester had ever seen. It beat the waves calm, and in fifteen or twenty minutes, when it stopped, Chester was floating with one bale on an oily, sluggish sea. The sea around him was filled with flotsam from the wreck. But there were no more green plastic bags, only the horseshoe buoy floating about twenty feet away. Chester rolled onto his back and hugged the one bale he had left and began to piece together some more modest plans for his future. Maybe he would just go to Mexico, hang out on the beach, and see if he could run into something. Chester squeezed the bale tight. It gave a little, like it was getting softer. Then something brushed against the front of his legs.

Chester panicked and kicked. The bale gave way, and Chester saw a cloud of marijuana leaves dispersing in the clear water around him. The plastic garbage bag he held in his hands had torn open and was almost empty.

"Oh fuck it," Chester screamed, but he had to struggle to keep his mouth out of the water to curse. "Fuck it all. Fuck every goddamn bit of it." Chester slung the plastic bag away from him and went underwater when he threw it. He might have wept, but he had to swim the twenty or so feet to the lifebuoy. He just had enough strength to tuck the buoy under his arms, so that he was wedged tightly into it, and his head was out of the water. Chester was surprised at how low the buoy floated. He wondered if it too, was leaking, but he was too tired and too desperate to worry about it. He didn't care if the damn thing sank and he sank with it. He just gave up and floated in the sea on his lifebuoy. The wind was dead calm, and the swells were long and flat and gentle. Chester waited for the sun to go down and for the sharks to find him.

I think the nicest thing about the Bahamas is that they are so much of a mystery, in a world that is no longer supposed to be mysterious. The Defense Hydrographic Mapping Agency charts of the Bahamas have large expanses that are labeled as coming from nineteenth century surveys, or are labeled simply as inaccurate.

There are notes about currents that fluctuate in direction and velocity, depths that are reported but not confirmed, islands and banks that shift and are uncharted. The lights are unreliable, the positions of some islands on the chart are unreliable.

I'm just trying to justify in my mind, here, as I look at the chart showing New Providence Island and the Tongue of the Ocean and the Great Bahama Banks, what current carried Chester Thoms ashore on Andros. But I don't know. Do you know that the Tongue of the Ocean off of Andros is over a mile deep? And the ocean floor drops vertically from the thirty fathom curve to beyond the thousand fathom curve?

That's neither here nor there. The next morning at sunup, Licia Kettering was walking alone on the beach in Andros, about half a mile up from the Lost Cove Bay Club. Licia was thinking about taking her bathing suit top off just for the hell of it, but she was afraid some locals might be working nearby. Her black hair was peppered with gray, and her thighs wiggled as she walked in the coarse coral sand, and she was thinking just how wonderful all this was, how great it was to be back at Lost Cove Bay, where the bungalows had only rusty screens for windows, and where everything was loose and slow. Her ex-husband would never have appreciated it. There was so much she had been able to do without the bastard. Still, Licia was very lonely this morning, walking on the beach so far from the club, with no one waiting for her back at the bungalow.

Licia looked out over the calm shallows to the reef. She noticed something floating out there, but she didn't pay much attention. She was thinking about the third chapter of her dissertation and when she was going to get back to work on it. She kicked in the sand and walked on down the beach, and then she looked up again. The thing that was floating was curious. It was low and round, bright yellow with a sort of red bulb on top. Things seen across the water in the Bahamas can be so curious. The mind can make them anything. This was a jellyfish, then some sort of garbage, probably thrown from a cruise ship. Licia walked up the beach to get a different angle. It almost looked like a lifebuoy except for the red bulb. She couldn't figure it out until she looked away and let her mind form another image with the information it was getting. Then she saw it was a man.

Licia got kind of limp and a little bit queasy, the way you get when something horrible you thought would never happen is actually going to happen. Licia was going to discover a corpse.

She could make out the nose now on the sunburned face- the ears, and a ring of hair around the back of the head.

The body was motionless, hanging in the lifebuoy. And oh my God, Licia thought, who knows what the fish had done to the part that was underwater. Licia wanted to run back to the club and get help. No part of her wanted to see this. But then again, hell no, what if the man were alive? Licia was surprised by her own behavior. She ran splashing into the water, waded out as far as she could, and then swam out to the man, a distance of two- to three-hundred yards. She approached cautiously, doing the breast stroke. He was alive. He was unconscious, but she could hear him breathing. She took him by the hand and started swimming toward shore, careful to keep away from him in case he came to and panicked.

Licia had a hard time once the water was too shallow to swim. She had to take the man by the shoulders and drag him the last hundred yards or so to shore. The water inside the reef at Andros is very shallow. The man was naked, and she saw that his ankles were bound together. She couldn't help but notice the size of the man's genitals, which were quite large. As were all the male genitals she had ever seen, they were unique in their shape and proportions.

The lifebuoy fell out from under the man's arms, and Licia worked the man around to where she could kick the buoy ashore. The man's head and shoulders were horribly sunburned, blistered and bright red. Licia was a gentle as she could be, but the man was fat and very heavy. She dragged him most of the way out of the water and turned him face up.

Licia knelt and put her ear to his mouth to listen for his breathing. He was breathing, faintly, but Licia was facing the man's feet, and she saw a surer sign of life, an involuntary reaction, which was very embarrassing.

She didn't have anything to cover it up. She laughed. It was really huge, and she didn't want to look.

The man was too heavy to drag farther ashore. At least he was out of the water. There was nothing nearby to cover him up with. Licia hated to leave him there, but she couldn't do anything more by herself. His bound feet. She tried to untie them. The knots were swollen tight, but with her fingernails she was able to work them loose. She took the rope off and rubbed the man's feet to get the circulation going again. He moaned and moved his legs.

Licia looked around in the scrub palmetto beside the beach, trying to find something to cover Chester while she went to get help. Chester lay naked on the beach with a hard-on. Licia shook her head and took off running for the Lost Cove Bay Club, her feet sinking deep in the coral sand.

When she came back with the men from the club, Chester was starting to get pink on the part of his body that had been underwater. They wrapped him in a blanket and carried him back to the club, and Licia volunteered her bungalow to put him in.

To get Chester to a hospital, they would have to radio from the Lost Cove Bay Club to Nassau and get a Bahamas Air Sea Rescue Association helicopter to fly over from New Providence Island. But the radio at Lost Cove Bay had been broken all week. The staff kept telling Licia they were going to fix it any day, but she was beginning to wonder if the thing hadn't in fact been broken a long time, and they just told everybody who came that it broke just before they arrived and would be fixed soon. The only communication with the outside world was by Jeep from Andros Town, and that took a couple of hours at least to drive. It was getting late in the afternoon and most of the staff were getting ready to walk home.

They didn't particularly want to be bothered with this new arrival.

Licia raised hell and cursed, but that only made the staff angry at her. She liked them. She knew most of them, and even though they had that Bahamian aloofness, they had always been friendly to her. Besides, when they got the man into her bed and gave him a sponge bath and rubbed him down with Aloe lotion, he seemed to be doing better. Licia gave him sips of orange juice and water. While she practically had to pour the first sips into his mouth, he roused a little and was able to drink the rest of what she gave him.

"The police will be here in the morning," Nigel, the bartender, told Licia. "They can take him if they want. The mon is all right. He don't want to go to the hospital. You know what he is."

Well, yes, she knew perfectly well what he was. And yes, she supposed he might not want to go to the hospital, and he was regaining consciousness.

When Chester opened his eyes he was alone in the bungalow with Licia Kettering sitting beside the bed, smiling at him. "You're a strange thing to find on the beach," she said.

Chester asked her where he was.

"At the Lost Cove Bay Club," she said. "On Andros. It's a very out of the way place, somewhere I discovered with one of the biggest assholes on earth, once, really. "

Chester didn't like her at all when he first heard her talk. He lifted his head off the pillow, and saw the bottom half of her body, and he wanted to groan.

Licia Kettering was in her bathing suit still, with a beach towel wrapped around her hips. She gave Chester a sip of orange juice and asked him if he preferred that or water. Water, he said, so she gave him that. He had the strength to hold the glass and drink the water himself.

"I really should rub you down with Aloe again," Licia said. "If you'll just think of me as your nurse." Chester didn't object. She carefully rubbed the lotion on his head and shoulders, and then she pulled the sheet back and began on the rest of his body.

Licia squeezed the aloe on Chester's plump chest and rubbed it in. She worked down his belly and rubbed over the round part and carefully covered the love handles on his flanks. Then she squeezed lotion down each of his legs. She worked that in with both hands, and when she turned and saw Chester watching her, she put down the bottle and moved to the head of the bed and kissed him.

I don't know. I want to say it was the brush with danger. It was certainly the remote location and the hot climate and the salt breeze. I don't know. It was a naked man and a woman in a bathing suit in a bungalow by the beach on Andros. And that was enough.

There was nothing more than a bad sunburn and a bathing suit holding them back. When Licia kissed Chester, he didn't resist at all. This was before AIDS, almost before herpes even. I think Licia and Chester would have been shocked if you proposed to them that it would happen like this, this suddenly, and this feverishly.

Licia didn't show up for dinner that evening in the dining room. She wandered in right before the kitchen was closed, got the cook to give her some conch fritters to go, and a couple of Heinekens, and took the plate and the beers back to her bungalow.

The kitchen and the dining room staff were laughing out loud about the noises coming from Licia Kettering's bungalow that evening.

When Chester woke up in the morning and saw Licia lying naked on the bed beside him, with the sheets kicked down around her ankles, well, he was a little repulsed at first. There was all that cellulite, and the thighs sagged as she lay on her side. But something in him was irrepressible, more than since he was a very young man. His head was splitting, a terrible headache, but he woke her up and was making love to her before she was even fully conscious.

That took a long time that morning. People were walking back to their bungalows from breakfast before Licia and Chester finished. When Chester and Licia lay back in the bed, they could hear the other guests talking just outside through the screens.

When the people had walked on to another bungalow, Licia asked Chester what he was going to do about the police.

"The what?"

"The police are coming up from Andros Town this morning," she said. "Of course I'm sure they would have nothing on you. I mean, you don't have anything in your possession."

Chester didn't respond. He was thinking. He got out of bed.

His legs were weak. He had to sit down on the edge of the bed. "What day is this?" he asked.

"It's Thursday, I think."

Thursday. He had been gone, what, two days? Surely Antonio would have notified the Coast Guard by now. He couldn't pass as someone else. The police would be looking for him.

"I really hope they aren't nasty," Licia said. "Everybody knows exactly what you were up to. The bales have been washing up on the beach since early yesterday."

Chester started to feel things tightening around him.

"I'd love to take you with me," Licia said. "I've been wasting my time with the most boring slug of a man. Professor of Developmental Psychology. Jesus, how do I get hooked up with these guys? But I'm afraid you're in a hell of a fix, and I don't know how to get you out. Surely you people have some way of dealing with the local authorities."

Chester heard the whine of a Jeep driving into the club compound. He jumped to his feet.

"You've got... No, listen, you don't understand, I can't face the police," he said. "I've got to get out of here. My God, I need some clothes. "

Licia got out of bed. Chester heard the doors of the Jeep slam. Licia was frowning now. Then she got a wicked grin on her face. "You can wear my shorts. Here." She picked a pair of khaki shorts off the back of a chair. "If they fit you I'll hate you. "

They fit Chester a little tightly. He sucked his stomach in and fastened them. His love handles rolled over the waistband.

Chester went to the door and watched the police go into the dining building.

"Here," Licia said, "You'd better take this. Don't want to leave any evidence." She picked up the lifebuoy Chester had been floating in and brought it to him. Chester didn't want that worth a damn. But he took it from her. She stood naked and watched him to see what he would do.

The police were out of sight now. Licia gave Chester a deep kiss, and as he started to leave she grabbed him playfully by the crotch. He opened the screen door and hurried around the corner of the bungalow and across the club compound, carrying the yellow horseshoe buoy. His stomach was jiggling, and his feet were tender.

Seventy-five yards and he was on the beach. He hustled around the brush pile at the edge of the club compound so he was out of sight of the club buildings. Then he ran, as hard as he could in the loose sand. The sun was hot on his sunburned head. He ran as far as he could, and then he walked on as fast as he could for an hour or two, out of breath, sticking close to the edge of the forest to stay out of sight. Slowly he let himself accept that no one was following. He paused to look down the beach behind him.

Chester was in the middle of the most beautiful nowhere. The multicolored shallows lay calm out to the reef. Clear wavelets washed on the beach. The pine forest was dark and humming with insects. A long way down to the south a lone, black fisherman was skulling his boat over the reef. The sun was just high enough the colors of the coral and seaweed were showing up in the water.

The whole thing was so bizarre to Chester, because for once, here he was with absolutely nowhere to go and nothing to do, and no way out, but it really wasn't so bad at all.

This is the way the climate in the Bahamas can affect a man.

Chester sat down on the beach and began to daydream. Not daydream with any purpose, really, he just laughed at himself and wondered how in the hell he would ever get out of what he was in. He looked at the lifebuoy he was carrying. The cover was coming unsewn, which was probably why it was leaking and floating so low. Chester picked at the cover while he was daydreaming and pulled the stitching out until he had one side completely open, and the stuffing fell out. Out dropped three plastic bags, one filled with kapok stuffing, and two filled with a white powder. He tore the corner off one of the bags of powder, stuck his finger in, and tasted some. His tongue numbed. Chester tore the rest of the cover apart, and out fell four more bags of powder and three more of kapok stuffing.

Chester squeezed the bags of powder like he was kneading dough.

He was laughing, and he stood up and did a little dance in the sand, holding the bags of cocaine over his head. "Hah, hah," he shouted. "Hah!"

The Fifth Tale
Earnest robs a grave.

The first, the only check I ever got as a writer was for one hundred dollars from a major southeastern newspaper. They bought a little travelogue I wrote about going to the Outer Banks. The trip itself, a camping vacation with my wife, cost us around three hundred dollars.

I can't tell you how much that check boosted my spirits. After three years of calling myself a writer, finally I was a professional writer. Not only that, the editor took up an idea I had thrown out in my cover letter and asked me to do a piece on migrant workers in the Southeast.

That came from my having been a peach farmer, which I was for five years before I started trying to write. I never made any money at it , but I borrowed a lot and lived well and repaid it all by the skin of my teeth. I still have an outstanding commercial credit history for someone with no job and an average annual income for the past three years of thirty-three dollars and thirty-three cents.

Well, I'm straying, because really what I want to get into is migrant workers. I worked with migrant workers for five years, Mexican, Jamaican, Haitian, American blacks, even a crew of white American drunks. I don't even know where to begin telling about them, except to say that I knew very little about them before I became a farmer. As much as I had read or as much as I had seen on T.V. about migrant workers, I knew very little. I have never seen a report by a journalist that didn't look at migrant workers as a shame, or a problem to be solved.

Well, that's saying a lot more about it in a direct way than I really want to say. The editor offered to pay me four hundred dollars if they published my article, and in the rush of excitement over getting my first check in the mail, I showed Mary Ruth the letter. She was wonderful about it and said if I sold a couple more like this, got some credits, and then started getting some more income- any income at all, maybe I wouldn't have to get a job.

There was an idea, though, that had been floating around in the back of my mind for a long time, ever since I was a peach farmer, really. I had always daydreamed about working as a migrant worker for a few weeks, to see the situation from the other side. I already had a perspective that very, very few people ever get, that of employing migrant workers, of actually doing the exploiting that allows well-to-do Americans to eat fresh fruit and vegetables year round and despise those who make poor migrant workers live in such terrible conditions.

Oh, hell, there I go again. I don't want to get into that. Anyway, I realized long ago that I had an opportunity that most people never have to see both sides of this fence, and as a writer I ought to take advantage of it.

I hit Mary Ruth with this proposition. I could get in touch with Javier, who used to be my foreman on the farm, and who still lived near home and still had a lot of relatives and friends who were migrant workers. I would ask him if I could join up with his brothers for a couple of weeks, let's say a month, in Florida. It was orange picking time in Florida. Mary Ruth was only six months pregnant, so I would be back in plenty of time for the baby. Well, let's say three weeks.

Mary Ruth was not keen on the idea at all. But I put it to her this way. I was going to have to get on the road for a week or two to research the article anyway, and all those expenses would come right out of our pockets. This way I could earn my travel expenses, and if I got into some good picking, I might even bring money home. Plus it would give me an unusual angle on the story, both sides of the fence, so to speak, and an unusual story was more likely to be bought.

I had known and worked with a lot of migrant workers and had done much the same work they did from time to time when I was a farmer. On slow days, when the crew was small and things in other parts of the operation were running smoothly, I would strap on a pick sack and help pick, trying to dump equally in everybody's bin, so it didn't look like I was playing favorites. And I had spent a fair amount of time down at the labor camp, drinking beer, playing pool, eating dinner every now and then. I really enjoyed that. Frankly, it was what I enjoyed most about farming. Mary Ruth knew all this, and that helped win her over.

What really won her over, though, was later that night when I said I felt it was something I ought to do, something I owed to these people, that they couldn't speak for themselves to the kinds of people I could speak to. Mary Ruth doesn't usually go in for that kind of thing, but, and maybe it was the way I said it, I think that's what finally convinced her to let me go.

So I called Javier and asked if I could drive up from Columbia to see him that afternoon. He still lived up near the farm. When I got to his trailer late in the afternoon, there were twenty or thirty chickens running around the yard, and a goat tethered to a stake in the spare grass sticking out of the red clay. There were two cars parked out front, a seventies model pickup truck and an early seventies model Buick Electra. And a satellite dish. Inside the kids were watching a movie on the VCR. I think Javier has done better for himself since I quit farming.

When I told Javier what I wanted to do, I could tell he thought the idea was ridiculous. But Javier is a nice guy. He wouldn't tell me to my face it was ridiculous. And I think his wife kind of appreciated it. She said it would be good for me to get out and do some hard work. She said it wasn't good to stay home all day by myself. She had done that herself with five babies.

Javier told me he would call his brother, who was down near Orlando picking oranges, but it would be a couple of days before he could get back to me.

I went home and spent three restless days. A couple of rejections came in the mail. They had been a long time coming, and I had convinced myself that both of them were taking so long because they were being passed up the ladder. But they came back with the stock, printed rejection slip. That hit hard.

Anyway, when Javier called me up and said there was a lot of work down in Florida, and his brother and cousin were expecting me, I was just ecstatic. Here was not just an adventure. I've been on lots of adventures, but this might be something substantial.

I went through the closets, trying to find something to pack my clothes in, but all the bags looked too new. So I finally got a couple of plastic garbage bags and stuffed one inside the other. I got out the rattiest old work clothes I could find, preferably something about ten years out of style. The best stuff was left over from high school, and it just did fit me.

Mary Ruth was in the bed watching me pack, and she started to have second thoughts about the whole thing. You know what hormones do to a pregnant woman. I looked over, and she was crying, and she wouldn't tell me what it was about. So I sat on the bed beside her and held her. I would be fine, I told her. She knew Javier's brother and cousin. They had worked for us one summer on the farm, and they were nice boys, just country boys from southern Mexico, not hard boys. Plus I could speak Spanish plenty well enough to get along.

She drove me to the bus station the next morning. When I kissed her good-bye she started crying again, but she said she was really proud of me. She said what I was doing was a good thing, and she was glad to see me working now on what I knew in my heart was right "That's what you've got to work on, Earnest," she said. "You've been selling yourself short. If you're going to do it, you have to write about what really matters to you."

It was hard to leave her, but I got on the bus and I felt pretty good about myself. I felt good about myself all the way to Orlando, a fifteen hour trip. Javier's brother met me at the bus station there, along with one of the boys from camp who had a car. They took me to a concrete block labor camp on a hill in the middle of an orange grove. The place was dirty, and there was trash all out in front of it. But I'll tell you the truth, I knew good and well it was like that because the people who were living there had made it like that. Well, anyway, Mary Ruth wouldn't have liked it, but it didn't bother me being that dirty.

I'm really not going to go into the time I spent in Florida, because it's not the best part of the story. The people in the camp were very kind to me for the most part. The picking was heavy, and we worked our asses off every day. I couldn't keep up with them. We were getting paid by the bushel, and I made some good money, but not like those guys were making. This was the gravy train for them. The gravy train only comes every now and then, and they were riding it as far as they could. The physical labor did me a lot of good. I was exhausted at the end of every day, and it was all I could do to wolf down a few tacos, wash the dishes, and crawl in the bed. I had to wash the dishes since I couldn't cook Mexican food. I was sharing a kitchen with Javier's brother and his cousin and a couple of boys from their home town in Mexico. They taught me a lot of

Spanish slang and curses I didn't know before. We watched baseball on an old T.V. they had bought at a pawn shop in Orlando. Told dirty jokes. Talked about women all the time.

The hardest part for me was having some Florida cracker lording it over me all day in the field. This guy was the farmer's nephew, weighed about two-twenty, red neck. Literally his neck was red, and he was dumb as mud. But after a few days he figured out I wasn't a social worker or a union organizer, which he had thought at first. I told him the truth. Well, not about the newspaper article. I told him I was an ex-farmer myself, and was now a writer, and I was down doing some research for a book. A novel.

"A novel? What kind? Fiction or non-fiction?"

I get that question all the time. When he found out that I had been in his shoes once myself, he was pretty decent to me. We spent a lot of time talking during the hottest part of the day, and I probably would have earned more money if I hadn't been so willing to stop picking and talk to that guy.

Anyway, I'll be honest with you, or I'll try to be. You may think I'm crazy, but those were two of the best weeks of my life. They really were, and I'm not going to try to justify that statement.

There was one ugly incident on a Saturday night when some of the guys in the camp got drunk. But I won't go into that.

Anyway, it was just about the end of orange picking season in Florida. As the work started to slow down, some of the crews were moving up to Georgia to thin peaches. And since I had had such a nice couple of weeks with this bunch, I decided I might ought to check out another crew, particularly a crew of black migrant workers, since I knew the situation would be entirely different with them than it was with the Mexican crews. Oh, there, that gets your hackles all up, but it's the plain truth, and I don't think you would find anyone who has spent any time in contact with these people who would tell you any differently. I don't know why it is. I suspect it's partly because American born migrant workers come from the most down and out part of our society, while Mexican migrant workers have to travel thousands of miles to work illegally in a foreign country, and that takes a lot of initiative and determination. To hell with that. I don't know the reason, and I'm not going to try to explain it.

I went to the crew leader of one of the black crews working on the farm with us. This guy's name was Leonard Robinson, and I could just tell when I met him he was a shifty son of a bitch. He was one of the shiftiest crew leaders I have ever met, which means he was shifty as hell. He looked like Idi Amin in a pair of blue-lensed, sun-sensing glasses. He owned a tremendous red Cadillac Sedan de Ville, and a ratty green Ford panel van for the crew to ride in. When I met him I should have known what I was in for. Well, I partially did. That's why I wanted to go with him to Georgia.

He was suspicious when I first approached him and explained what I wanted to do. Again, I didn't mention the newspaper assignment. He knew I had some kind of ulterior motive, but in the end I talked him into it. He said, just rough as hell, "O.k., I'll take you along, but I ain't putting up with no shit. You work just like the other niggers, and I ain't goan have no stirring shit up. You crazy."

And ooh, I was filled with righteous indignation, because I always had hated these guys, on the one hand because they had always, always done their best to rip me off when I was a farmer. It was their every waking thought, how to rip somebody off. And on the other hand, it made me feel good to tell myself that I, the rich white guy, was trying to do what was fair and right, and it was these black pimps that were ripping the poor drunks off, and they were the real villains of the situation.

So I said good-bye to Javier's cousin and his brother and all the guys at the Mexican camp and went over to Leonard's camp that afternoon. I walked down one hill and crossed the highway and cut up through another orange grove. Weeds and grass were growing up in the orchards where the fruit had already been harvested, and some of the limbs were broken from the picking.

Leonard was supposed to be packing up to go to Georgia, but when I walked into the camp he was just raising hell, throwing stuff in the trunk of the Cadillac and cursing his girlfriend and the one other black guy who was there. I asked him what was going on. He told me there was just no way he could take me, that the whole thing was called off and he didn't know where he was going, and that he might just quit being a fucking crew leader and working with these goddamn drunks. It turned out that his whole crew had walked out on him at lunchtime and left him with just his girlfriend and her brother. I watched and waited for him to blow off steam. I'd watched it all before a dozen times. Different crew leader, same tirade.

He calmed down after a while, then he said, well, he guessed he'd go on up there anyway, and go through Atlanta and pick up a new crew. And I got him to take me with him. I had to do some fancy talking to keep him from charging me car fare to Georgia. In fact he may have been planning to deduct it from my pay when we got to Georgia.

I rode with his girlfriend's brother in the van to Atlanta that night. We spent a few hours in a rest area in Central Georgia, trying to catch a few z's on the bench seats. I didn't see Leonard and his girlfriend at the rest area. I figure he spent the night in a motel.

We met them the next morning out in front of a mission in downtown Atlanta. Leonard parked his Cadillac right in front of the mission, and we parked on the opposite side of the street and down the block a ways. Leonard picked up five or six men there, old drunks, all black. All of them had done this plenty of times before. Then we went to a couple of liquor stores, and Leonard got seven or eight more men there, including a couple of fairly young boys who were out of work and were naive enough to believe him when he told them how much they could make picking peaches. Sure, they might make that on a good day. Well, they might make it. Migrant workers in the East are paid by the bushel mostly, and I doubt those boys would ever work hard enough to make that kind of money.

The best couldn't hope to make that much but every now and then. You have to figure on all those weeks when they make almost nothing, because there's nothing much to pick.

We were going to thin peaches in Central Georgia. That's when you knock the little green peaches off the tree in the spring, ideally spacing the peaches so there is one every six inches along the limb and they will be able to grow to full size. I say ideally. The workers get paid by the tree, and you have to stay right behind them all the time to get them to do a decent job.

Anyway, we drove that afternoon to a farm in Central Georgia, not terribly far from Macon, and moved into a labor camp there.

This was pretty swanky as far as labor camps go. It was a converted peach-packing shed, a big, open building that had been enclosed and divided into hallways and rooms. It had two stories, with a kitchen and a large combination rec room and dining room downstairs. Also downstairs were a shower room and the crew leader's room. Upstairs were the bedrooms for the crew.

I say it was swanky. It was swanky for a labor camp. A bunch of the windows were broken out, and there was graffiti and red mud all over the walls. The place was on a hill in the middle of a peach orchard, surrounded by high grass and weeds. It had the funky smell of fried foods and spilled beer and dirty people about it. The furniture was broken. The beds were very old. But the building was spacious and was built to withstand some heavy duty partying, which may be why it had been assigned to Leonard Robinson's crew.

We got there on a Sunday afternoon, and there was no work to be done until the next day, so as soon as we got there Leonard opened up the bar. This was in the rec room/dining room. Leonard had three items for sale, wine, malt liquor, and generic cigarettes.

Well, four items. He had pot for sale, but he was demanding cash for that, instead of marking it down in his notebook to be deducted from the next paycheck. Nobody had enough cash to buy any. Except me. I had a lot of money with me, which was making me kind of nervous. Mary Ruth had insisted before I left that I take a couple of hundred dollars in cash with me, just in case of emergency, since we had cut up all the credit cards earlier that year. Then when I was working in Florida, I had cleared another couple of hundred dollars over living expenses, so I had a good-sized roll of money stuffed in my sock.

Leonard left his girlfriend to tend bar while he took the Cadillac to get groceries for dinner. All the guys lined up and opened their charge accounts. Leonard had his girlfriend stuff the old jukebox with quarters to get the party atmosphere flowing. And there was a pool table with threadbare felt.

I bought a sixteen-ounce can of malt liquor from Leonard's girlfriend. I would have paid cash, but everybody else was charging it, and I didn't want to stick out, so I told her my name and had her start a tab. I watched as she jotted down the entry. I was astonished at the price. Well, I decided what the hell, I'd better buy a pack of cigarettes, too, as this promised to be a stressful situation.

After a while Leonard came wheeling back from the store with the groceries. He had a large roll of bologna, several loaves of sliced white bread, and a bag of beans. That was dinner, and I think he ended up charging us a couple of dollars apiece for it. But that part is hazy. What is not hazy is the four women he brought with him.

They were all black, and there was no question how they earned their keep. Two were skinny girls, flat-chested and dark skinned, maybe sixteen or seventeen years old. One of them was missing her front teeth, when she smiled. There was a woman who might have been fifty years old. Her hair was graying. She was no more than five feet tall, and she had a kind of a square shape, but she apparently knew Leonard and his girlfriend's brother very well, and she was the most forward in approaching the other men. The fourth woman, though, was the one who attracted the most attention. She was somewhat lighter-skinned than the others, and while I wouldn't exactly call her pretty, she was built like a brick house. Really too plump to be considered attractive in high society these days, but well enough endowed that she looked like she might explode out of her skirt and blouse. My guess is she was in her twenties. She had straightened hair with a wave on one side of her head. She seemed very shy at first, but whenever someone said something that interested her, she would get an almost wicked grin on her face. She had a little boy with her, too, I would say about eight years old.

Elmira. That was her name. I'm not real sure how I learned it . She was wearing a black knit skirt, one of those tube things, and my goodness, did she fill that thing out. Her blouse was of a gold satiny material, a little old, and with little polyester balls coming up on it.

At first I thought they were all whores who had come to turn tricks. But they weren't easy pick ups. I mean the men had to buy them drinks and give them cigarettes, and maybe they were just there for a good time. I don't know.

I said before it was all a little hazy, and the reason is this.

I don't know if you've had a sixteen-ounce can of malt liquor recently. I probably hadn't had one since college. But those things pack a wallop. Now I've always known I couldn't handle my liquor very well. But I did think I could control it. I'll just have to be honest with you, though. By the time I finished my first malt liquor I was feeling good enough to be playing pool. And I thought, well, just one more. And after one more malt liquor I was playing pool maybe the best I had ever played it in my life.

Not saying much. Just playing, and taking my time and concentrating on the shots, but I was loose. And hot. I couldn't miss. I was starting to win a little money, too, which Leonard's girlfriend was keeping track of in the notebook, too, so we could settle up when we got paid. I think that's how it worked. I'm not real clear on that.

Late in the afternoon, close to supper time, a horn blew outside, and it was the man from the state employment agency-- a middle-aged white man in a Massey Ferguson hat who didn't want to come into the camp. I watched from the window, so he wouldn't see me in there. He had a couple of black guys in the front of the pickup with him, and Leonard hired them on. When they got out, I couldn't believe what I was seeing. At first I thought it was just that I was a little drunk. But one of these guys was Gravey Pickens, from back home, who used to work for me on occasion on the farm

I hadn't seen him in three or four years. He had his hair palmated or whatever into those little greasy curls like Michael Jackson, so he looked different, and I thought I might be mistaken at first. But when he came into the camp building I knew it was him. If I had been a little drunker I might have run up and hugged him.

Let me tell you why. I was already starting to realize I might have made a serious mistake signing on with this bunch. With the Mexicans I had gotten along fine, except for that one incident, but here I was the only white guy in the camp, and things weren't going well. I was pissing some people off winning all that money at pool. Plus, to tell you the truth, I may have been pissing some people off the way I was eying Elmira. I've always had a fantasy about that. But growing up the way I did in the Deep South, it was only a fantasy, and one I never would have lived out, or at least I thought that at the time.

But when Gravey showed up, all of a sudden I felt, I don't know, I felt like I had an in. I'll explain.

After I quit farming, when I had just started writing, Mary Ruth and I were still living in our little blue house out in the middle of the peach orchard. I was trying to support the two of us by substitute teaching, which didn't pay much and wasn't very regular. So that winter, when the fellow who was leasing the farm started pruning, I asked if I could do some pruning for him, working with Gravey and the other guys. We got paid by the tree, so it was ideal work for me. I could work whenever I wanted and be free to write or take substitute teaching jobs whenever they came up. Plus it gave me something to do outdoors.

I told the fellow who was leasing the farm what it should cost per tree to do the pruning, and warned him how Gravey and the others would work slow the first couple of days so they could demand a price increase. I had been paying to have the trees pruned for four years, and I knew what the price should be.

It was late in the fall, on a cloudy, cool day, when we started pruning. Gravey and the others were already cutting a few trees when the other farmer and I walked up. The negotiations over the price were friendly, and I kind of mediated. At some point though, I can't remember where exactly or what brought it on, Gravey told the fellow I had leased the farm to, "Man, Earnest just like a brother."

Well, that really meant a lot to me. It's stuck with me a long time.

So when Gravey came in to the labor camp, I was delighted to see him. He didn't recognize me at first, I was so out of place. But when I called his name, you should have seen the grin on his face. Before he could ask what I was doing there, I pulled him over and bought him a malt liquor and took him aside where we could talk. He had run up on hard times at home and hadn't been able to find any work for a while, so he had decided to come down to Georgia and work thinning peaches. The crop up at home was just about wiped out by frost that year, he said. I told him briefly what I was up to, and said I would appreciate it if he didn't call me "bossman" or tell the others what I was doing, because I didn't feel real comfortable with it. Oh, Gravey's a great guy, I tell you. I could have hugged him.

We had dinner about that time, and I had another malt liquor and bought Gravey another one. And, well, we were talking about all the guys back home, and I was playing pool and still just tearing everybody else up. I was getting pretty cocky about it, too, and would raise the cue tip up and tap the felt at the other end of the table when it was someone else's turn to rack. I've just got to be honest with you. I started out to have one or two malt liquors, but I have no recollection at all how many I ended up having. And that Elmira, she was sitting off to one side of the room up on one of the tables, and she kept stretching that tight skirt down over those big brown legs. I couldn't keep my eyes off her. Even made a little eye contact, and she smiled back.

She was sitting right next to Leonard Robinson, and the more I drank, the more I despised that guy. He was such a pimp. Later in the evening, it must have been pretty late, I went over to the bar to buy Gravey and me another malt liquor, and there was this poor drunk trying to buy a bottle of wine. His shoulders were stooped, and he was skinny and gray haired, and he had that sort of milky look in his eyes. And Leonard's girlfriend wouldn't sell him any more wine. She said he had already run up too high a bill, and Leonard said not to let them charge more than they could pay back in one day of working. It really got under my skin. So I said, here, I'd pay for the goddamn thing myself.

"You cain't have no more neither. You done run up twenty dollar already," she said. That made me even madder.

"Here, goddamn it," I said, and I reached down in my sock and pulled the roll of money out. I peeled off a ten and threw it on the counter. "I'll pay you cash for it. And I'll buy his goddamn bottle of wine, too."

Well, that was my big mistake, though I didn't have my wits about me enough to realize it at the time. She took my money, and the drunk got his bottle of wine. He put his arm around me and breathed in my face and said, "Thank you, brother."

I took Gravey his malt liquor and got back to playing pool. I had lost a few games by that time. I still was ahead for the night, though and was determined to get back on the winning streak. But I was a little tight to be playing well, plus, and this was much more disturbing, Elmira started making eyes at me.

I'll tell you, she was looking better and better. I might say fuller and fuller. If she had inhaled deeply her blouse would have burst open. And we were making unmistakable eye contact. Long contact, with an inviting smile. I was thinking hard about my wife, and about the baby coming. I tried not to look over there, as much as my eyes wanted to. But it was hard. Anyway, I think Gravey thought she was making eyes at him, because he went over and started talking shit to her in that real cocky way a black guy will. And I was grateful he had removed the temptation from me.

She got up and went outdoors after a while, and Gravey followed. I figured he was going to hit the jackpot with her, but he didn't stay out there long before he came back in looking deflated. She didn't come back with him. I guess she was going to the outhouse.

Oh, yeh, the outhouses. This camp didn't have toilets. It had running water and showers, and it even had toilet stalls, but the holes in the floor where the toilets had been were plugged with concrete. And outdoors was a men's and a women's privy. I had seen this before. I had some good friends back home who had a similar arrangement. They said they originally had a nice bathroom setup in their camps, but they would have to go down two or three times a week during the season and unclog the toilets from everything the drunks threw in them. One day my friends went down to a camp and the whole bathroom was flooded. The toilets had clogged up, and the drunks had kept on using them and flushing them, even standing on the seats to use them. So my friends brought in a backhoe that same day, dug privy pits, slapped up a shed over each of them, and filled the toilets up with a sack of concrete mix. The OSHA codes allow privies in a labor camp. At least they used to.

Well, I'm not going to argue this either way. Watching Leonard Robinson's bunch in action, it was easy to understand how exasperated my friends could have gotten. I don't know if that was the motivation behind that particular farmer in Georgia's plumbing arrangement. We had had toilets in Florida. And God, were those outhouses raunchy. Leonard and his girlfriend drove up the road to McDonald's to use the toilet.

When Elmira came back in, she didn't pay any attention to Gravey. She was just making eyes at me. I was fighting it. I fought it hard. I tried to ignore her completely. I had a couple more malt liquors to calm myself down, and by this time I was buying drinks for whoever was around me at the bar. And my pool game just went to hell.

I could feel Elmira watching me for a long time, until she finally strolled across the room with her little boy and went upstairs. My goodness, you should have seen her stroll. Every man in the room stopped to watch her leave.

I finally got my opponent's attention back to our pool game. The cues were all warped, and we were missing the twelve ball, so we played a strange game of eight ball. The first man to sink a striped ball was at a considerable advantage. I was concentrating hard. But it was no use. I was having trouble keeping my balance by that time, and my ears were buzzing. You know how you feel when you get really blasted and are still trying to pretend you are sober. Well, maybe you don't, but that's how I felt. I don't know how much time had passed before the little boy came back downstairs. He was tugging on my pants leg before I saw him. He got me to lean over so he could whisper a message in my ear.

Well, like I say, I've always had this secret fantasy. And it was late at night, and I was in the middle of nowhere in Central Georgia, and I was, to put it accurately, shitfaced. All the invitation needed was a little self-justification, and by this time I was a self-justification machine. So I followed the little boy upstairs, grinning like a fool, I imagine. I lit a generic cigarette to steady myself.

I knocked on the door the little boy pointed out to me, and it opened, and there was Elmira standing in a red satin bathrobe that just did fit around her.

She invited me in, a little bashful, really, and asked me to have a seat. It was a small room, maybe ten by ten, with two metal bunk beds pulled together to make a double bed and one purple bedspread across them. There were two old kitchen chairs and a card table, and a closet without a door. I offered her a cigarette. She took it and let me light it, but I could tell she didn't usually smoke. She was nervous, and really, here I felt pretty bad. She was sexy as hell still. The robe was short, and her smooth brown legs were hanging all out of it as she sat on the other side of the card table from me. But she just didn't seem as sure of herself up here. She was a human being, to put it awkwardly. I mean she was a real person up here in this little bedroom in the labor camp, and that has always given me pause.

"Your name Earnest, ain't it?" she said.

And I said, well, yes, it was, how did she know that?

"That friend of yourn, he told me. I got him to tell."

I didn't particularly like that. I thought Gravey had looked pretty guilty after he had gone outside with her.

"You think I'm pretty?" she said. She had that insolent pout to a question that black girls can have.

Well, I didn't know how to answer that. I don't know if she had been drinking or not, but the opening of the robe showed the inside of her thigh about halfway up, and whenever she moved I could catch a glimpse of tremendous cleavage.

"You think I'm some kind of whore?" she said. "I mean what you think coming up here? You think I'm some kind of whore?"

"I... No, I didn't." I was drunk enough to lie before I would tell the truth.

"I ain't no angel," she said. "But I ain't no whore. I don't want you thinking bad about me."

Well, I wouldn't think bad about her. I would respect her in the morning even, I was telling myself.

"You growed up in Spartanburg, what that boy told me," she said, and this took me aback. I didn't want this much information out about me. But I said, yes, I had.

"Your last name so and so," she said, and I said, yes, it was.

Did I know her?

"I growed up in Spartanburg, too," she said, and I asked her if maybe I had gone to high school with her. But she said no, and she kept looking in my eyes like she was looking for something. "My name Elmira" something or other, I don't remember the last name she gave. It didn't mean anything to me.

"You don't know," she said. "You never knowed anything about it."

It was a strange conversation. I didn't know what to make of her. She asked me if, and she gave my father's name, if that was my father, and I said yes, and she started telling me a story. I wasn't even listening to the first part of her story. Just hoping she would hurry up, but then she started to say some things that grabbed my attention.

She knew all about me, who my father was, and where he had worked and how we had moved out to the country and started farming, and what my mother and brother's names were. Everything she told me was correct. I was wondering how Gravey had known all of that stuff about my family. And it was unnerving to hear her tell it. Sort of like hearing a fortune teller tell you what is really on your mind. She told me her mother had lived in Spartanburg and she grew up there herself , and as for her father, well, that was a terribly difficult thing to tell. She paused here, and this is when she really got my attention. I mean she got my attention in a big way.

She acted like she didn't want to tell the rest of the story. She put her face down in her hands and started to cry.

She said she had never told anyone in her life who her father was. Her mother had never let her tell anyone who her real father was, even though her father had come and visited her often when she was a little girl and had helped support her and her mother. They were never allowed to go to see him, and she was never to call him up or go by his house, and she could never, never tell anyone who he was.

My skin started to crawl. "You see, Earnest," she said, "you and me is brother and sister."

Well, you may think you can imagine my shock, but I'll tell you, you can't. Plus, I was awfully drunk and more than a little disoriented.

"I had to tell you, Earnest," she said, "Because your friend, he said you was just like a brother, and he told me what you was doing here, and I knowed. I knowed they was something special about you when I seen you. Your daddy one of the nicest men in Spartanburg. I can tell you his boy. They ain't many would do what you is doing."

Then she came over and hugged me as I sat on the edge of her bed. She wasn't particularly tall, and when she hugged me my head was right between her breasts. She held me tight. "I'm sorry," she said, and she was crying again. "But I ain't never had no real brother. I ain't never got to do this before. I didn't think I ever would do this."

God, those tits were huge. She smelled like a black girl, too, only I never had smelled one this close before. She held me tight, like a sister would hold a brother, and I'll have to tell you I was really unable to take it all in. It was just too much. I mean it was, I suppose, believable. I told myself it was believable. She had a white facial structure, and I thought I could see some of my brother in her, maybe. I don't know.

"This all too crazy," she said. "You don't want to believe me. " She let me go and walked to the other end of her bed and sat down on it and faced away from me and played with the sash on her robe.

"I don't know what the shit I were thinking," she said. "You go on then. Go on and get."

I didn't know what to say or do. I could see her legs sticking way out of the robe.

"Go on and get outta here. Just forget what I said. It were all a lie."

I just sat there. I didn't know what to do.

"What would" and she gave my father's name again, "want with a daughter were a whore? I were crazy. I didn't think of that."

"Listen, Elmira," I said. "If that's your real name..."

But Elmira just shouted at me. "It were all a goddamn lie. I were just trying to get your goddamn money without having to fuck you . Go on. Go on outta here."

She sat on the bed and sobbed. She looked back over her shoulder at me.

"Get out," she shouted. "Go on and get out, or I'll start screaming."

I didn't know what to do. I didn't want her to start screaming.

"Elmira, " I said, "I don't know what to say. This is ..."

"Goddamn your white ass," she shouted. "Go on, get out of here
" She jumped up and came towards me swinging her fists. Her face
was wet with tears. I would have jumped up and run like a rabbit
any other time in my life, I guess. I don't know why I didn't, but I
caught her and held her. She hit me on the back and cursed me, and
I just hugged her. She hit hard, too. And cried. She was crying
pretty hard when she stopped hitting me.

I hugged her while she cried. We were standing in the middle
of the room, and I think honestly that was the first black person I've
ever hugged. Even counting the maids who helped raise me when I
was young. She smelled like those maids. She was warm, and her
tears were soaking my shirt.

She cried a long time, and then we sat down at the table and
had a cigarette each, and she said she didn't want to talk about it
any more. I said I wanted to hear more of her story, but she said she
didn't want to tell it, and she didn't care what I thought.

You know how a woman can get. We'd talk about it in the
morning, she said. I asked her what her mother's name was, and
she looked me straight in the eye like she was surprised, and told
me, but it didn't mean anything to me.

And then later, after a couple more cigarettes, I guess, she told
me I had made a bad mistake. She said Leonard Robinson was as
mean a crew leader as there was, that he had killed plenty of men,
and that she was ashamed to be running around with him. She
didn't know why she had ever gotten in with people like him. Her

mother had tried to keep her from going off with him in the first place.

It wasn't right, she said, what they were going to do to me.

That was a tremendous shock, because I had thought things had been going better since Gravey showed up. The talk was, Elmira said, something was going to happen to me. All the men were plenty damn mad to have me in the camp, she said, but Leonard was keeping me around to get money off me. When I had pulled that roll of money out everybody in the camp had seen it, and if I slept in one of the other rooms someone would probably cut my throat to get it .

"You goan have to get outta here," she said. "They goan cut your ass or shoot you. They ain't goan have no white man in this camp less they got a reason for it."

"You gots to sleep in here tonight," she said, "And I'll lock the door. They know better'n come in here. Leonard won't let em."

God, then she started to look sexy again. But the situation was now very complicated, complicated enough that I got a little common sense back. So I agreed, and we pulled the two bunk beds apart to make two twins. She took some satin sheets from the closet and made up the bed for me and was even going to give me the purple bedspread, but I asked her not to. I didn't want to sleep on her clean sheets in my dirty clothes. I was kind of embarrassed to strip down to my shorts, though.

"Don't look," she said, and she went to the closet and took out a nightgown. So I turned away, and when she said, "O.k.," I turned back around, and she was in the flimsiest red nightgown I had ever seen. It was made of smooth, thin fabric that left nothing to the imagination, and it only came to the top of her thighs.

I was drunk enough then, and I figured the only thing to do was to strip to my shorts, which I did. I was wondering if I could ever tell this story to my wife. Or how I could possibly tell it to my wife, or if I would ever tell anyone.

"You better go on out to the bathroom," she said. "Then I'll lock us in here, and cain't nobody bother us tonight."

Well, I did need to go. I had needed to go for hours, but I had been fighting a battle to contain myself. I don't know if it was the baloney and beans, or the malt liquor, or the delayed effects of two weeks' worth of Mexican food. I said, "O.k.," and looked at my pants hanging on the foot of the bed, where the roll of money was in the pocket.

"You can go on in your undershorts," Elmira said. " Everybody do."

I picked up my pants and started to put them on anyway.

"Earnest," she said, "I don't want you going out there by yourself with that money. You don't know how bad they is."

She looked genuinely concerned and afraid. So I thanked her, left my clothes there on the bed, and went out into the hallway and down the hall to the second floor exit. There were two ways up to the second floor, one inside the building, the way I had come up, and the other up a rickety wooden stairway outside the building, which is the way I went out. The only other way into the labor camp was by the door in the rec/dining room on the first floor.

It was warm and humid. I hurried down the steps in my bare feet, trying to be careful of splinters, but the situation was pressing. There's something about that stroll towards the bathroom that gets the body in the mood. I hurried out through the tall weeds towards the outhouse.

My God, was that outhouse awful. I could smell it twenty yards away. The door was hanging from one hinge, and there were flies buzzing around even in the dark. The light bulb didn't work. I pulled on the string, and nothing happened. It was pitch dark inside, and I had to stand there in the doorway for a while in that awful smell trying to let my eyes adjust. I thought of running out into the weeds, but then I saw the white toilet seat in the darkness, and it looked relatively clean. And there was a roll of toilet paper beside it. I stepped in, and the floorboards creaked and sagged underneath me.

Damn, I thought, this was outrageous. This thing was probably going to collapse some day with some fool in it. I sprang gently with one foot, and the board underneath it was rotten. And I don't know why I did this. It must have been the malt liquor, and I wasn't thinking clearly, but I bounced with all my weight on the boards to see how they would support me. They were flimsy as hell.

"Look at this shit," I said out loud, and I was going to put this in the newspaper article for sure. In fact, I was thinking some pretty righteous thoughts at the time. I had never let our labor camp get in this shape. But I couldn't assume that other farmers were as conscientious as I had been. I was thinking it was maybe a good thing after all that I had come on this trip. I was learning a lot, a lot about my fellow man and myself. And I was so drunk and so righteous I wasn't thinking practically. I jumped up, I mean clear off the floor and was really going to test those boards. And crunch. The boards gave way completely, and I fell about six feet into the mess below.

I don't know how long the outhouse had been there, but I sank in over my knees in the most God awful mess. It still makes me shiver to write about it. It was so slick and cold and deep. I could just reach the floorboards over my head. I grabbed hold of them and tried to pull myself out. I've always been a bad curser. And I've always had a terrible temper. But I'm not going to write the things I was shouting in that pit. I just have to draw the line somewhere. I tried to pull myself out, but that stuff was like quicksand. And the smell, I don't know how I breathed at all. I pulled with all my strength to climb out, and the floorboards gave way again. I tumbled back into the darkness and landed flat on my back.

I don't know what would live down in that pit. A possum. A rat. But some kind of animal ran across my chest in the darkness. Let me tell you. There are reserves of strength in a man that amaze him when he finds them. I don't know what I did. I may have climbed. I may have jumped. I may have flown, but I got the hell out of that pit.

I was covered in, oh, that stuff, I can't describe it. It was slick and smooth and sticky, and it smelled horrible. It was even in my hair. There were streamers of toilet paper hanging off me, and I was shouting and cursing like I have never cursed in my life, which frankly must have been a terrible thing to hear, because I'll curse like a sailor over the smallest thing.

I was going to run right in to the showers and wash off. I went to the ground floor entrance to the camp and tried to get the door open, but it was locked from inside. I jerked on the door and banged on it, but the lights were off in the rec room, and nobody came.

So I ran around to the wooden stairs that led up to the second story entrance. That stuff was starting to dry on me. God, my skin still crawls to think about it. I dashed up the stairs to go in the door I had just come out of. The passage lock was broken on the thing. I remembered it had been held shut just by the friction of the swollen door in the jam. So I knew it was open. But when I jerked on it, it wouldn't come. I jerked again, hard. The damn thing was padlocked from inside.

I called for Elmira, softly, since she was only a couple of rooms down the hall. For that matter she must have heard me shouting when I got out of the pit. I called and waited. Nothing happened.

Then it began to dawn on me what had happened. I banged on the door and shouted for Elmira. "Elmira," I shouted. "Somebody has locked the door. Come let me in." That was loud enough to wake anybody in the camp. Still there was nothing.

I banged on the door, mad now, and shouted for Elmira and said I wanted in. I kicked the door and cursed.

I went back down the stairs, walked around to the side of the camp, picked up a piece of gravel from the parking area, and threw it against Elmira's window.

"Elmira, goddamnit, unlock that door."

I thought I heard laughter inside the camp. I picked up a handful of gravel and slung it up against the tin siding. "Goddamn your ass, Elmira, open that door."

It was unmistakable that time, howls of laughter coming from all inside the camp. And "Ooowheee!"

Well, I've always had a bad temper, but I was drunk and was covered head to toe in shit, and I just lost control completely. I picked up handful after handful of gravel and started slinging it up against the side of the camp, and cursing the whole bunch of them.

"You goddamn thieving nigger bitch. Goddamn all you fucking niggers. Fucking bunch of no-count drunks." I was screaming it, about to burst a blood vessel.

Well, a window opened on the first floor, and Leonard Robinson stuck his fat, black face out, sans glasses, and said, "What the fuck?"

And I was mad enough that I told him what I thought of him. I said he was a whore-running thieving pimp, and whatever else I could string together in the way of racial slurs and things about his mother. I saw him stick the pistol out of the window. I shut up when I saw the pistol. It was one of those big-bore, long-barrelled things. When he shot it the sound was like thunder, and flame shot out of the barrel about a foot and a half. I heard the bullet crack as it went past me, and that was the last I ever saw of Leonard Robinson and that labor camp.

I ran like I have never run in my life. Out through the weeds and across a ditch and down through the peach orchards, ducking under the tree limbs. The pistol fired twice after me, and I swear one of the bullets knocked a limb off a tree right in front of me. I stumbled and rolled and scrambled up and kept running down through the peach orchard. At the bottom of the hill I jumped a six-foot clay road bank and landed on the tar and gravel roadbed below, and I kept running, as hard as I could, down the road.

I may have run the better part of a mile before I stopped, doubled over and gasping. The night was moonless and dark except for the starlight. The road was bordered by pine woods on both sides. I listened and looked. Nobody was coming after me. Still, here I was, somewhere in Central Georgia in my shorts, drunk, covered in shit, with all my money stolen. The first thing I had to do was get washed off. So after I caught my breath enough, I kept walking down the tar and gravel road in the direction I had been running, looking for a creek or a pond to wash off in.

The tree frogs were crying. The stuff covering me was drying and cracking. The gravel of the road was sharp under my bare feet. I walked and walked, stopping to look over the edge of the roadbed at every low spot. But there were only dry ditches, no water to be found. I came out of the pine woods, and the road curved through some overgrown pasture land. I must have walked a mile or two.

Then I saw a light in the road up ahead. At first I thought it was a car with one headlight, but it came very slowly, and I saw it was two men walking with a lantern. I didn't want to face anyone in the shape I was in, so ducked off the road and into an old tumble-down barn about a hundred feet into a pasture. As the men came closer I heard them talking. They were black. When they got up even with the barn, they stopped and held the lantern up, and one said, "Here it is. I couldn't see it in the dark."

They started toward the barn, so I scrambled to the back and crawled behind a stack of half-bushel peach baskets. The men came on into the barn, and their lantern lit the place up.

I peeked between the peach baskets and watched them as they took a sledge hammer and a couple of rusty crowbars off the wall. Then one of them picked up an old truck axle that had been sharpened to a point at one end. One of them was an old man, skinny and slightly stooped. The young man with him was huge, maybe six feet five and well over two hundred pounds. He had a fat, simple-looking face.

"Goddamn," the old man said, "something done crawl up in here and died."

"What," the younger man said. "That ain't me."

"Shit no, they something dead in here, " the old man said, and he took the lantern and traced the smell back towards where I was hiding. "Gimme that axle," he said.

The young man gave him the sharpened axle, and he started to jab it into the stack of baskets. The first jab went right past my knee. I jumped up and said, "No, wait."

You would have thought I was a ghost, the way they shouted and started. "Goddamn your ass," the old man shouted. "What the hell you mean jumping out like that?"

I calmed them down and apologized for scaring them. I said it was obvious what shape I was in and I didn't want anyone to see me. They just stood there, waiting for an explanation, so I gave them one. I said I had been in Leonard Robinson's camp, and I told how I had fallen, and how I had been robbed and shot at.

"Shit, you lucky that all you got," the older man said. "That Leonard Robinson the meanest nigger in this state. What the hell you doing in with his bunch?"

His companion agreed. "You go back there they liable to cut your throat and bury you in a peach orchard," he said. "How you get mixed up with him?"

Well, I didn't want to tell them the truth. It was just too ridiculous. Plus I was drunk, and honestly, I was drunk thinking, insisting on consistencies that were unnecessary, so I told him I had been down and out, had let the booze get me down again, and had needed some money in the worst way, and I had thought the work outdoors would do me some good. Right now, I said, what I needed was some way to get cleaned up and get some clothes and maybe get into town to the bus station.

"How you goan take the bus? You ain't got no money," the older man said. I knew exactly how. I was going to call home collect, but I didn't want to tell him and drop my disguise.

The older man pulled the younger one aside for a minute, and they discussed something in hushed tones. The older one held the lantern up and looked me over. He shook his head.

"Listen, brother," he said. "We might let you in on something, what could get you a little traveling money, if you can keep your mouth shut."

I said I could, and the younger man asked, "You ain't ascared of haints, is you?"

I almost laughed, but I said I wasn't.

"You ever touch a dead man?" the older one asked, and that threw me back a little. No, I said, I hadn't.

"I mean you ascared of them or what?"

Well, I didn't know if I was or not, but I certainly didn't want to be involved in any killing.

"We ain't goan kill nobody," the old man said. "You ever heard of Willis Johnston?"

Frankly, the name did ring a bell, but I couldn't think why, and I shrugged my shoulders.

"White dude, own all these orchard round here. You was goan work for him."

Well, that was how I knew the name. When I was a farmer, I had been active in several farm organizations, among them the Southeastern Peach Growers Conference. At one time I had known most of the major peach growers in the Southeast. I couldn't place a face with the name, but it did sound familiar.

"Well," the older man said, "Old man Willis done passed last Friday, and they buried him this morning, up to the Methodist church. My boy here work down to the funeral home, and he say they laid him in wearing a gold Rolex watch and a big old diamond ring. My boy helped lay the casket in hisself. They had the casket open at the church, and he sealed it up and seen the watch and the ring when they did it ."

He looked to his companion, and the companion nodded. "The thing is," the older man continued, "they ain't buried him. They laid him up in a big vault, up offen the ground. The boy here put the lid on it hisself, and all we got to do is prise it open enough for one man to crawl in. We get that watch and that ring, I know a man will pay us five hundred dollars for it. It ain't much, but I like to help a man out when he down, so we'll split it with you, three ways."

Well, it was a most unusual scheme. And to tell the truth, I was flattered to be invited to join in on it. My pride was still hurting from the affair at Leonard Robinson's camp. Plus, what the hell, stealing from a dead man, that doesn't strike me as much of a crime. And I was drunk, which explains a lot of things. It didn't strike me as a high risk crime anyway, robbing a vault in a country graveyard in the middle of the night.

They carried the sledge hammer and the crowbars and the axle, and I followed them around the barn and down across the pasture. They stayed well ahead of me. At the far end of the pasture we crawled through a barbed wire fence, crossed a short section of woods, and came into another pasture, this one covered with deep, lush grass. We climbed a long, low hill. The faster I walked, the faster the other two walked to stay out in front of me.

The stars were bright overhead, but without a moon it was hard to see anything. I stepped in a couple of fresh cow patties in my bare feet, but that was nothing compared to what I was covered in. All of a sudden the two grave robbers stopped in front of me. "Goddamn!" the older one said in a harsh whisper. "You got to wash that funk off."

I caught a whiff of chlorine on the breeze. My companions led me up the hill to a swimming pool surrounded by a high chain link fence. Just up the hill past it, set back in the shade trees, were two enormous white houses. No lights were on anywhere. The other two boosted me up the fence. I scrambled over and dropped to the concrete deck on the other side. I padded across the deck in my bare feet and lowered myself into the water. It was still early May, and the water was bracing, but it felt fabulous. I waded out into the middle of the pool, took a breath, and ducked under. I wriggled in the cool water and scrubbed the stuff out of my hair.

I'll tell you, the clean surroundings, the smell of chlorine, the feel of the concrete bottom on my feet, it was the first time in weeks I had felt comfortable. It was like arriving in the United States after a trip to a third world country.

I ducked under a few more times, then swam a couple of laps, oblivious of my companions outside the fence. I hung on the edge of the pool underneath the diving board, hyperventilated, held my breath, and swam a lap and a half underwater, holding my breath until my diaphragm was convulsing.

When I burst to the surface, there was the most awful racket.

Two enormous dogs were barking and growling and lunging at the chain link fence. I looked for the two grave robbers, but they were gone. One of the dogs was sort of a cross between a German shepherd and a Lab. The other was a white Malamute. Even in the darkness I could see their teeth snapping.

It is so frustrating hoping a barking dog will shut up, but these dogs, when they saw me come to the surface, went wild. They were jumping their full height up against the fence and yapping and growling and whining.

A light came on up at the house, and then another. I swam to the edge of the pool and tried to keep still, but this made the dogs even madder.

After what may have been a few minutes, the outdoor spotlights came on up at the house, and I heard a screen door slam. I climbed out of the pool and started to climb over the fence, but the dogs came growling around to me and snapped at my hands where I grabbed the fence. Then the underwater lights came on in the pool, and I panicked. The only place to hide was a low pump house, about four feet high, at the far end of the pool deck. I ran to the pump house, opened the door and crawled in beside the sand filter. I closed the door tight behind me. The pump was whirring.

I heard voices coming down from the house, and I heard the gate being unlocked. The dogs came rushing in. I heard them growling and barking right outside the pump house. The voices came into the pool compound. It sounded like a man talking to his son.

"I'll betcha it's a coon, Will," the man said. "See, look where he's muddied up the water."

I heard a shotgun being pumped, and the two voices came towards the pump house.

"Tie the dogs to the fence, Will," the man said. "I don't want them fighting that coon. When you open that door, jump back to the side, behind the building, so it doesn't come after you."

God, I was miserable. I was dripping wet, drunk, in my underwear, in this man's pool house, wondering what in the hell I was going to do. I'll be honest with you, I've been in a lot of terribly embarrassing situations drunk. You run from it, no, let's be more precise, I run from it and run from it until I'm cornered in a situation where there's just no dignified way out. I figured finally the only way out of this was to come clean, just to step out of the pump house and explain to the man what I was doing there and to apologize for trespassing.

"O.k.," the man said, and the door sprang open. I heard the boy scrambling out of the way. And there fifteen feet in front of me stood Willis Johnston, Jr., past president of the Southeastern Peach Producers Association.

I hadn't remembered the name clearly, but the face was unmistakable, even after five years. This was the man who had presented me with the Young Farmer of the Year Award and had taken me and Mary Ruth out to dinner with his wife at the annual convention on Sea Island. He had been on the awards committee that had come up and toured our farm. He had told me I taught him a thing or two about managing peach orchards himself, even though his family had been growing peaches for three generations.

I guess he couldn't see me back in the darkness. I hope he couldn't see me. But all I could think of, no, that makes it sound like there was some reason to my thinking. Actually I was just drunk and embarrassed and scared, and I wanted more than anything in the world not to have this man recognize me. So I burst out of the pump house, screaming and waving my hands in front of my face like a madman. I vaulted over the corner of the pool and dashed out the gate and ran down the hill through the pasture. The dogs were howling and barking, still tied to the fence.

I think I ran faster from that situation than I did from Leonard Robinson's gun. I had seen what may have been a brief look of recognition and surprise on Willis, Jr.'s face, but surely he would never associate what he saw with the promising young man he had met four or five years before.

I put about half a mile between me and that swimming pool before I stopped to catch my breath. I was gasping, trying to hold my hands over my head like I had learned on the cross country team in high school. I had run down through the lush pasture behind the Johnstons' houses, crossed a paved road, run across the earthen dam of an irrigation pond, and up through some hardwoods to the edge of a peach orchard. God knows where I was. I caught my breath some and started walking to my left around the edge of the peach orchard. I guess I had gone two or three hundred yards, when I came to a point of the woods where two orchards met. As I was walking past a big oak tree right at the point, two shadows stepped out from behind the tree.

"No!" I shouted. It scared me so badly I shouted out loud. But they just laughed. It was my two grave robbing companions.

"Did you see them dogs?" the big, young one said.

"You're goddamn right I saw those dogs," I said. "Where the hell do you get off leaving me out here in the middle of God knows where..."

"Shut the hell up," the old man said. "You want to wake up the whole damn country?"

They were carrying their tools, still. They said to keep quiet and come with them, the graveyard was only a little ways off.

By that time a quarter moon had just risen, and in that clear, humid night it lit the fields nicely. Tree frogs were ringing around the pond. The church was only a quarter mile or so away down a dirt road. It was a white, frame, country church with a steeple over the entrance. The dirt road led out of the peach orchards and beside the graveyard. The church was on the main highway, but there was no traffic this time of the night. And the cemetery was screened from the highway by a hedge of red tip shrubs.

Willis Johnston, Sr. 's vault dominated the small cemetery. The vault was of peach colored granite and was set on a pediment a foot and a half above the ground. The vault was huge, much larger than the two coffins it was built to contain, about five feet tall and better than eight or ten feet square. The sides were decorated with a bas relief of all the fruits Mr. Johnston must have cultivated in his lifetime. Willis, Sr.'s name was carved on one end, with his birth and death dates carved underneath it. His wife's name was carved beside his, with no dates yet.

We took the pointed truck axle and stuck it under the lip of the six-inch granite slab covering the vault. The slab was laid with a rubbery sealant that gave us a place to start the point of the axle. We wrapped the axle with rags so it wouldn't make so much noise, then they made me hold the axle while the young man drove it in with the sledge hammer.

He was really swinging that hammer, and it was all I could do not to let go. I was scared he was going to miss. We drove the axle in about six inches, then all three of us put our weight on it and lifted the slab. The old man stuck one of the crowbars in the crack that provided, and we moved around to the side to get a new purchase.

It took us fifteen or twenty minutes of hard work and prising to get the slab lifted about sixteen inches at one end. Just enough for a man to slide in. The slab was propped up with two crowbars, an arrangement that was too precipitous for my taste, but I didn't say anything about it.

When we got that done, I stepped back and wiped the sweat off my brow, and the old man said to me, "You ready?"

They were both looking at me.

"I ain't going in there," I said.

"I be damned," the old man said. "We was nice enough to bring you along on this. Now it time you did some work. "

It wasn't the thought of the dead man inside that bothered me, it was those two crowbars holding the slab up. I said I was sorry, I wasn't going in there.

The young man grabbed me and threw me up against the side of the vault. The old man held the sledge hammer up to my chin and threatened to lay my head open, so I agreed to crawl in. They boosted me over the lip, and I slid into the darkness inside.

The young man handed me a key to unbolt the coffin lid. That was awkward work in the dark. I had to feel for each bolt by hand.

I got the lid unbolted and swung it open. This took a lot of pushing myself, but I reached in to touch the corpse. My fingers hit cold flesh and a day's growth of beard. I couldn't see anything inside the vault, just the two silhouettes of my companions in the moonlight outside. It took a little getting used to. I stuck my hand back in and touched the face several times, until I convinced myself it was dead and inert, and there was nothing to fear from it.

The two guys outside were telling me to hurry the fuck up. I found the mouth and the chin and felt down the neck to the shoulder, then ran my hand down the sleeve of the suit jacket until I felt the flesh of the left hand. There, underneath the French cuff of the starched shirt, was the Rolex. I lifted the hand and managed to get the watchband unsnapped. I pulled the watch off.

"Here," I said, and I held the watch up to the opening. The old man snatched it out of my hand.

"Now get the fucking ring. Hurry up. We ain't got all night."

I didn't like it. I had already been ripped off once that night, and now I smelled rip-off big time. The way he grabbed that watch out of my hand told it all to me.

I reached into the coffin and felt around until I found the right hand. There was the ring, sure enough, and it felt huge. I tried to pull it off, but it was stuck. I worked the arm around to where I could use both of my hands, and I pulled as hard as I could, but it wouldn't come. So I had to get my leg over in the coffin and hold the elbow down with my knee and pull on the ring with both hands.

I pulled and twisted and pulled. Pop! The whole finger came off with the ring on it.

"Goddamn!" I shouted. The shout just died in the granite around me.

"What wrong?" the old man asked.

"Nothing," I said. "I just touched something funky." I pulled the ring off the torn end of the finger and stuck the ring in the waistband of my shorts. I tossed the finger back in the coffin.

Then I patted around loudly on the body. I wasn't going to trust these guys.

"There's no ring here."

"The hell you say."

I patted around loudly again. "Listen," I said, "there's a wedding band here, but there's no big ring. I'm counting down every finger of both hands."

"You bullshitting. Don't pull this bullshit on me," the older one said.

"You want to climb in here yourself and look?"

"Goddamn boy," he said. "You said they were a diamond ring."

 "It gotta be," the young man said. "I mean I saw it. I were there with him, the whole time, except right at the end when them boys shut the coffin up."

"What the hell you been telling me?" the old man said. And he started raising hell. Apparently the young man had not actually bolted the coffin shut as he had said earlier. Two other employees of the funeral home had done that, but he swore the preacher was there with them the whole time, and there was no way they could have taken the ring off.

The two of them argued about this for five minutes or better, and I thought the old man was going to have an apoplectic seizure. The hole in the young man's story was really a stroke of luck for me, or at least I thought so at the time. I been planning to give them the ring, anyway, once I was out of the vault. I just wanted to make sure they didn't run away and leave me stranded here.

After considerable argument, the old man told me to get the wedding band off, that would be worth something. Fortunately it slid off easily. I even took off the cuff links and handed them out to make the old man a little happier.

"That everything?" the old man asked.

" Yeh," I said.

"You sure they ain't nothing more, like a necklace or something?"

"Listen, you want to crawl in here and see?" Neither one said anything. "Do you want me to bolt the lid back down?" I asked. I was ready to get out of there.

"Yeh, you better do that," the old man said.

So I crawled back to the head of the coffin to search for the key, and all I heard was the scrape of the two crowbars on the granite, and then a deep whoooomp! as the lid of the vault fell back into place. I scrambled back to the other end and could just hear the two of them shouting at each other outside.

"Man, you cain't leave him there like that," the young grave robber was saying.

"Why the fuck not?" the old man said. "He just a drunk. A migrant worker. Ain't nobody goan miss him. "

It took a few seconds for me to realize what was going on. I expected to hear the hammering on the vault as they started working to get me out. I heard them pick the tools up, then I didn't hear anything else.

I shouted. That shout was the most stifled, deadest sound, closed in that small place by the granite. I shouted and pounded my fists on the granite. I screamed, as loud as I could, but sound just died in there. It was absolutely dark. I put my hands up and found the lid of the vault and got up in a crouch and tried to lift the granite. I pushed and shoved with all my strength, but I couldn't budge it.

I shouted again, shouted and screamed and begged and pounded with my fists on the sides of the vault, but there was no response.

I went crazy then and pushed and strained and struggled. You know you hear those stories of women lifting cars when the adrenaline gets flowing. I think the adrenaline was flowing that hard in me. I pushed and screamed, with a strength I had never known I had, but the lid didn't budge. Nothing at all. I kept pushing and straining and screaming. I prayed and said the Hail Mary over and over. I cried and banged my head on the slab.

Finally I started quaking, and my legs went weak. I don't know if it was the lack of oxygen or the exertion, but I must have passed out.

I don't know what time of night I went into that vault. So I have no idea how long I lay there. I have no recollection of dreaming, so it wasn't like I was asleep. I was just gone. It's all a blank, until the very end, when I heard something like a bell tolling regularly and far away- ring, ring, ring, ring. I was imagining Frere Jacques tolling the matins. The ringing was coming closer, or I was coming closer to the abbey, and I could see the tower where Frere Jacques was pulling the bell rope. Then as the ringing became quite loud, I came back to consciousness. I opened my eyes, but I couldn't see anything. I felt around, and after some time I realized I had fallen down beside the open coffin.

The ringing kept getting louder, until I began to feel a draft of fresh air, and I heard men's voices, redneck voices. I saw some faint light, like moonlight, above me. The rednecks were telling each other to hurry the fuck up, that they should have come earlier, and it was going to turn daylight if they didn't hurry up. I didn't say anything. I just lay there. I was still weak, and I felt it all might be a dream.

Soon I could see the bar coming into the vault as they worked. The opening grew wider. I could see the men's hands and see their silhouettes outside on occasion. They were saying some terrible things about Willis Johnston, Sr.- what a ring-tailed son of a bitch he had been, and how he had stolen all his damn money anyway. Soon I could smell liquor. They were cursing each other as much as they were cursing Mr. Johnston. All the Johnstons, really. I just lay there as the slab slowly rose. They propped it up with four-by-fours at two corners. When the opening was big enough for a man, they started arguing about who was going to go in.

"I be goddamned if I am," one of them said.

"What? You think they's a haint in there?"

"You should a gotten it off before you laid him in."

"Shit. I couldn't. The goddamn preacher stood there with us till we screwed the top on. And the goddamn nigger was there before that. You know a nigger. He was eying that diamond ring like it was a plate of chitlins."

I smelled liquor again, and I could see them passing the bottle around. They started arguing again about who was going in. None of them wanted to, but finally the one who sounded drunkest said, "Fuck it. That sonbitch cain't do nothing to you dead."

I heard him scrambling on the side of the vault, and then his head stuck in the opening. I reached up and grabbed him by the hair and started pulling him into the vault with me.

I've never heard a man scream or felt a man fight like that in my life. I dragged him about halfway in before the others grabbed his legs and started pulling against me. He was flailing and screaming and writhing and calling on Jesus to help him. I was pulling hard, but the two men pulling outside got the better, and they yanked him back out and left me with two hands full of hair.

They didn't ask what had happened or anything. The man took off running as soon as he hit the ground, and the others took off after him so fast they were already rounding the church building by the time I stuck my head out to look.

The sky was just starting to turn bright to the east. I was still in my underwear and nothing else. I guess after all I'd been through that night it wasn't hard for me to do what I had to do then. I took Willis, Sr.'s ring out from under my waistband and put it on my finger and crawled back to the open coffin. I had to wrestle the body around a good bit, but I managed to get the suit and the tie and the shirt off and the socks and shoes. Though the clothes smelled a little of embalming fluid, they weren't too bad.

I stuffed the body back down in the coffin, face down, but I didn't figure that would ever matter. It took me a while to find the key, and I was beginning to worry about time, but I did find it, and I bolted the aluminum coffin lid down, so the family wouldn't be upset whenever Mrs. Johnston was buried. I tossed the clothes out of the vault and climbed out after them.

Willis, Sr. had been just about my size. Everything fit better than I hoped it would. By the time I snugged the tie up tight, I probably looked pretty damn respectable. The pants were a little too long, but I hitched them up as high as I could, tightened the belt, and buttoned the jacket. It was a nice suit. Felt like a hundred percent worsted. The wingtip shoes were too loose, but not so bad I couldn't walk in them.

By this time the sky to the east was turning red. I stretched myself out and kicked one prop at the same instant I jerked the other one out with my hands. The stone fell so perfectly into place I couldn't tell it had been raised.

I picked up all the tools and props, carried them to the back side of the cemetery, and tossed them into the honeysuckle. Then I went out to the highway and started walking. In a half hour or so I came to an intersection, and I followed the signs towards Macon.

Not long after the sun came up, I caught a ride with a couple of Mexicans in a faded, red van.

There was curtain fringe hanging around the windshield,and pictures of the Virgin and Jesus on the ceiling over the front seats. I acted like I couldn't speak Spanish. The whole way into Macon they talked and laughed about me, a rich, drunk gringo wandering down the highway in the middle of nowhere.

I got them to drop me off downtown in Macon. I found a pawn shop and hung around the entrance until it opened. There was no inscription on the ring. The pawnshop owner looked at me like he could care less what the story was behind it. I made up a name and a local address. The diamond in that thing was a least a carat.

The ring was worth thousands, I'm sure, but he offered me two hundred, and I took it without a word.

I walked up the street to J. C. Penney's and bought a polo shirt and some slacks and cheap tennis shoes. Then I went to the bus station, bought a ticket to Columbia, and changed clothes in the men's room. I stuffed Mr. Johnston's suit in the trash receptacle and covered it up with paper towels.

When I called Mary Ruth from the bus station in Columbia, she was surprised and delighted at first. She showed up at the station with her mother, who had come down to spend the weekend with her.

Her mother even seemed a little happy to see me. I covered my ass with stories about the camp in Florida. They weren't particularly interested anyway. Mary Ruth asked if I had written any of the article yet, and I said I would get on it that week. Her mother just sat there with the corners of her mouth turned down. She didn't say anything at all.

So I waited until that night, when we were in bed, to tell Mary Ruth what had happened. I told her the whole story, the honest truth. She got pretty mad when I was telling about the drinking and going up to Elmira's room, but by the end of the story she was laughing. She wouldn't believe me at first. She said I had to have made it up, but I swore up and down

"Now why can't you ever write anything like that?" she said. "People would buy a book like that." She said it like the idea of somebody buying one of my books was a fantasy of the wildest sort. But she kissed me and said she was glad to have me home.

The Sixth Tale
An unexpected relationship is discovered.

Mr. Rodriguez was a prosperous and well-respected lawyer in a good-sized coastal town in Cuba, not far from Havana. He was a plump but handsome man, in his early forties, with curly dark hair and a dark complexion, and a hairy chest that showed through the open collar of his *guayabera*.

Mr. Rodriguez had a lovely wife who came from a wealthy family. She was some years younger than he. He had married her when he was a young lawyer practicing in Havana, before he returned to his hometown. They had two young sons, small and pretty boys, the older of whom, Juan Jose, was quite a handful for his mother. The baby, Andres, was an angel .

The Rodriguez family had a maid, Mrs. Serna, who was a widow and was childless. She lived in the Rodriguez's house. Her husband had worked for Mr. Rodriguez's uncle at the funeral home before he died. She had been with the family for six or seven years when Castro came to power.

Let me describe the Rodriguez's house. It was on a low hill overlooking the sea. It was on the west side of the town, which surrounded a cove that was home port for scores of small fishing boats, boats that could be pulled up on the beach every day after the fishermen had been out all night. Most of the wealthy inhabitants of the town lived on the hill to the west, along a road that curved up from the beach and followed the coast around the hill. Occasionally North American tourists would mistakenly take that road, thinking it was a highway that led up the coast, but the road dead-ended after a couple of miles at the *finca* of a Havana doctor.

The Rodriguezes lived on the inland side of the road, but from Mr. and Mrs. Rodriguez's bedroom you could see the cobalt blue sea. The sea was always a deep and lovely blue seen from that window, because you could not see the shallows for the trees and the hill slope in front of you, and the sun was always behind you. Even Mrs. Serna would sometimes stop and stare out at the sea when she was cleaning the Rodriguez's bedroom. The trade winds blew in through this open window, and even on the hottest of days, watching out over the palm trees blowing and seeing the tossing sea, bright, clear blue, and no sun reflecting off of it, Mrs. Serna would feel cool.

In the evenings the family often sat on the second floor porch, which stretched across the front of the house. They would enjoy the breeze as Mr. Rodriguez smoked a cigar. Mr. and Mrs. Rodriguez sat in rocking chairs. Mrs. Rodriguez rarely relaxed during these times, because she was scared the two little boys were straying too close to the edge of the porch.

The house was a two-story stucco house with porches all the way across the front of both stories and large windows with heavy hurricane shutters. In the back was a large garden planted in all sorts of tropical plants and trees. It was almost like a jungle, except that it was meticulously maintained, and brick paths led through it to several shaded patios that surprised you when you found them. The garden was walled, and the boys would often play in it when Mrs. Serna was watching them. One of the most unusual features of the garden were the *tinajones*, enormous terra cotta urns that lay on their sides, which had been used in earlier times to catch and store rainwater. Now Juan Jose would hide from his brother and Mrs. Serna in them, but she scolded him for getting in them and getting his shoes wet.

That is as vague and as sharp as the Rodriguez's and Mrs. Serna's memories of their home after many, many years of exile.

Mr. Rodriguez was a compassionate and honest man who had quietly opposed the Batista regime and its corruption for some time. Shortly after the Revolution, he became active in politics and played a conspicuous role in trying to restructure the local government. For several months he was a happy man, working long hours in his law practice and then spending evenings in political meetings and private discussions, working with the new people to see that things went smoothly and well.

But revolutions being as they are, Mr. Rodriguez quickly found himself in a dangerous situation. After the first few months of elation, there was a sobering period, and then there was the mounting fear, quiet fear that they didn't dare confide to anyone, as more and more of their friends left the country. Mr. Rodriguez spoke privately to Mrs. Rodriguez about his fears that he might lose his law practice and his share in the family business, the funeral home and the plantations. They spoke at length for several weeks of how they would manage the family finances in those circumstances. But things go bad faster than we usually imagine they will, and soon Mr. Rodriguez had to arrange for his family to escape from Cuba in the middle of the night. He told no one but his wife of his plans, and he contracted with the captain of a fishing boat to pick him and his family up on a beach near their house one night and take them to Miami.

In the early morning hours of the night they were to leave, Mr. and Mrs. Rodriguez woke Mrs. Serna in her little room off the kitchen. When she saw Mr. and Mrs. Rodriguez standing in her unlit room, Mrs. Serna thought one of the boys had died.

But they told her instead they were leaving Cuba. Mr. Rodriguez had already paid her way on the boat, just in case she wanted to go with them, but of course he would understand if she didn't. He hoped she could tell the authorities she knew nothing about their leaving when she was questioned the next day. Mrs. Serna was not a sophisticated woman, and he was afraid the police might trick her into incriminating herself.

Mrs. Serna had no close family other than her sister, with whom she did not get along. Her sister was a drunkard and was married to a corrupt policeman under the Batista regime who was a brute.

Now he was in prison, and her sister continually came to the Rodriguez house drunk and badgered Mrs. Serna for money. Mrs. Serna adored Andres and Juan Jose, the Rodriguez's two little boys. She had never had children of her own, though her husband and she had prayed fervently for them before he had been killed in a fishing accident. So Mrs. Serna had nothing to lose by going and much to lose by staying. There in her little bedroom, as she sat in the dim light in her nightgown with the bedclothes pulled over her for modesty, she decided she would go.

Mrs. Serna had only a couple of minutes to pack some clothes, no more than she could carry in a handbag, while Mr. and Mrs. Rodriguez awakened the boys. Then they left the house without turning any lights on and made their way down the road in the darkness. They turned onto a path that led to the beach behind their neighbors' house. This house was empty, as the neighbors had left Cuba six months earlier.

The Rodriguezes and Mrs. Serna went down the steep sand path to the beach. The cabin cruiser Mr. Rodriguez had hired was waiting in the swells off the beach. A dinghy came to shore for the family. The surf was too rough for the dinghy to land, so Mr. Rodriguez had to wade out beyond the breakers with each of the boys on his shoulder, one at a time, and hand them to the man in the dinghy. Then Mrs. Rodriguez and Mrs. Serna waded out, and Mr. Rodriguez helped them scramble into the dinghy, which was very tricky, since the boat was small and the swells were good sized, and the women nearly turned the boat over. The dinghy was overloaded with that many people aboard, so they had to make a trip out to the cabin cruiser and load everyone aboard it as the seas heaved them in the dark. Then the mate ran back in to pick up Mr. Rodriguez. By the time everyone was aboard the boat, they had been struggling too long and too hard to do anything but hold on to each other. The captain put the cruiser into gear, opened the throttles, and headed north toward Florida.

They hadn't been running five minutes, and the Rodriguezes were just starting to think the worst par of their ordeal was behind them, when the motor sputtered and cut off. The captain tried and tried to crank it, but the diesel engine wouldn't fire. The captain opened the engine hatches and tried to work with it in the dark. He was scared a flashlight might be seen from shore.

As he worked, the breeze and current were carrying them back toward town and the shore. The captain and the mate worked as hard as they could, but they couldn't get the engine to run, and finally, as the boat was about to wash up on the rocks in the surf, the captain told Mr. Rodriguez that they would all have to jump overboard and swim to shore themselves. Mr. Rodriguez took Juan Jose, since he was the heavier of the two boys, and his wife took Andres, and they all jumped overboard and swam for the rocks.

Mrs. Serna cut her knee badly on the coral coming ashore, and Andres swallowed water and couldn't catch his breath. He was coughing and crying. As they were scrambling up onto the rocks, they heard the motor of the cabin cruiser start up. The captain gunned his engines and took his boat away from the rocks. But the sky was already beginning to turn red, and the surf here was much too rough to try swimming out to the dinghy again. The Rodriguez family walked back to their house. The boat returned to Havana with the other fishing beats that morning.

That afternoon the captain came to the house to beg Mr. Rodriguez's forgiveness, and the two of them made arrangements to try again that night.

So late that night, or early the next morning really, the Rodriguezes and Mrs. Serna all got up and got their clothes together and left the house again. As they were walking down the road, Mrs. Serna was limping badly from the cut on her knee. When they turned onto the path leading to the beach, Mr. Rodriguez grabbed his wife and pulled her into the shadows of the bushes and motioned to all of them to keep quiet. They heard voices down the road, coming up from town, and then they saw a group of men coming toward them.

There, on the instant, because he wanted so badly to do the right thing, Mr. Rodriguez made the hardest and most important decision of his life. He didn't have time to agonize over it, and he would ask himself many times over the rest of his life if it had been the right decision, or if he should have run on down that path with his wife and children and their maid. But that wasn't something he was likely to do, run away like a dog. He told his wife to take the children and Mrs. Serna and run as fast as they could down the path to the sea and get on the boat and go. He would have to join them in Florida later. Actually, I don't even know if this much was said. The men were walking fast, and their voices were quite close, so there was no time for Mrs. Rodriguez to argue. She and Mrs. Serna picked up the two boys and ran down the path to the beach.

Mr. Rodriguez stepped onto the road and walked boldly toward the group of men. When they stopped him and questioned him, he told them he couldn't sleep and was taking a midnight stroll. They went with him to his house and asked him where his family was. He said they were visiting his in-laws. He was taken into town to the police station and held overnight for questioning. The next morning, when the truth was discovered, he was charged with counter-revolutionary activities and thrown in prison without trial.

When the two women and the boys got down to the beach, Mrs. Rodriguez picked up Juan Jose, and Mrs. Serna carried Andres out to the dinghy. Andres was eighteen months old. She had to keep her hand tight over his mouth to keep him from crying. She was scared she was going to smother him. Once in the swell he wriggled out of her arms and was gone, and in a panic she grabbed for him and found him in the water. He was coughing and screaming when she got him out of the water, but fortunately they were beyond the surf, so the noise of crashing waves drowned out his cries, and the policemen up the hill didn't hear. Juan Jose was quite a brave little boy. He didn't cry.

When they were aboard the fishing boat and Mrs. Rodriguez told the captain what had happened, he put the engine in gear and headed north toward Florida, shaking his head and muttering to himself.

Mrs. Serna took the boys down into the cabin and kept them there. Mrs. Rodriguez sat on the deck in the cockpit and watched the lights of Cuba fall slowly behind them. She sobbed, well, you can imagine how she sobbed.

That was a horrible boat ride. The trade winds were strong, and the sea was very rough The boys soon were seasick and were crying, and Mrs. Serna and Mrs. Rodriguez had to hold them out in the cockpit where they could vomit over the rail. They had to hold on tight so the boys wouldn't be thrown overboard by a big swell.

They had been running only a couple of hours, and the last lights of Cuba were just out of sight, when the motor cut off for the first time. The captain and mate opened the engine compartment hatches again and discovered after much work that trash was being stirred up in the fuel tanks by the high seas, and the fuel filters were clogging. The captain was able to get the engine started again after a half hour, and they ran another hour or so before the motor started sputtering and died again. When the mate and the captain went into the engine compartment this time they found the motion of the boat in the swells was causing its seams to open up. The boat was taking on water. After they got the engine started again, the mate had to man the bilge pump for fifteen minutes.

This went on all night. The next morning at sunup, the motor had cut off again, but at least they were far enough to the north to be out of the trade winds, and they were out of danger from Cuban patrol boats. The sea was calmer. They went on the rest of the morning and into the afternoon, fighting the engine. Every time the mate and the captain would open one of the fuel lines to unclog it, the smell of the diesel fuel would make Mrs. Serna seasick. The boys were crying and thirsty, and there was not much fresh water left.

The engine cut off for the last time late in the afternoon. The batteries died as the captain was cranking it. The sea was calm ,and the sun was very hot, and the boat drifted northeastward with the current.

They drifted on through the night, and the wind clocked around and started to freshen from the southwest. When the sun came up the next morning they could see some small coral cays off to the east, about two miles distant. The boat had been leaking more and more since they left Cuba. As the day and night wore on, the seams had opened wider, and now the captain and the mate had to take shifts on the pump and man it almost continually. They were out of drinking water and beer. The two men were exhausted and beginning to get dehydrated. They had an angry discussion when they saw the coral cays off to the east. The sea was still not running high. The breeze was blowing only moderately from the west, and they had the dingy, which was small but could make it that far if they didn't overload it. The mate didn't want to go, but the captain had little faith in his cruiser, so he decided they would go ashore in two shifts. The mate would take Mrs. Serna and the two children ashore on the first trip and then would return to the boat and take the captain and Mrs. Rodriguez.

The trip ashore was longer than it looked and was very rough in that small dinghy. Mrs. Serna and Juan Jose were terrified. Twice small waves broke over the transom of the dingy, and Mrs. Serna had to bail with a tin can to keep them afloat. The breeze was freshening, and when they made it to the beach Mrs. Serna knelt on the sand and held the boys and wept and thanked God and the Virgin for delivering them. The cruiser had been swept a good bit to the north already by the current, so the mate pushed the dinghy back out through the surf and motored into the wind and the waves to pick up the others.

Mrs. Serna and the boys watched as the dinghy fought into the waves. The mate stopped every now and then to bail furiously, and still the cabin cruiser and the dinghy were being swept to the north in the current, and the wind was freshening, and the seas were growing, so the dinghy was sometimes lost to sight in the troughs. The ride was getting wild for the mate, and the cruiser was getting farther and farther away, and the boys could just see their mother waving to them from the cockpit. Both the boys were crying and calling for her. Then the mate turned the dinghy around and started heading back for the cay.

Mrs. Serna was irate when she saw this. She stood up and shouted into the wind and cursed the mate and called him a filthy coward. He couldn't have heard her, as he was a good half-mile or more away, and it was all he could do to keep the dinghy from broaching in the following seas.

The mate steered wildly to keep the dinghy under control.

Several times combers broke over the transom, and he had to bail like mad, until one big wave finally caught the swamped little boat and flipped it over and tossed the man out.

That was the last Mrs. Serna and the boys saw of the mate. He either drowned or was eaten by sharks. They saw the dinghy washed up on a sandbar to the north of the barren cay late that afternoon. As for the cruiser with Mrs. Rodriguez and the captain still aboard, it drifted out of sight to the north within a couple of hours. The cay they were stranded on was one of the many poorly charted little sand cays to the south of Bimini and Cat Cay. There was no vegetation of any kind on it and no fresh water and no way to get out of the sun. They wouldn't have survived very long at all if they had stayed there. By noon little Andres had stopped crying and had stopped sweating. His skin was hot and dry, and his breathing was very slow. Mrs. Serna was sitting on the sand in the shallow salt water on the north end of the cay. She held Andres in her arms, and Juan Jose was curled against her hip, whimpering.

Suddenly, on the horizon, Mrs. Serna saw a magnificent white fishing boat. Well, not really on the horizon. She just looked up and it was there, very close, not more than a mile or two away. It was a sport fisherman trolling down the edge of the banks. The boat would pass very close to the cay on its course. Mrs. Serna sprang up and carried the two boys to the highest part of the island. She jumped up and down and waved her arms and shouted for help. Finally she could see the man on the tuna tower of the boat clearly. He waved to her, and the boat turned toward the cay. Mrs. Serna carried Andres and led Juan Jose to the water's edge.

Mrs. Serna was not an educated woman. She had never been outside of Cuba, and she spoke no language but Spanish. She had never read a newspaper. As far as she knew, she and the boys were fugitives from justice.

The white sport fisherman, a recently painted 57' Robalo, turned toward the sand cay and worked carefully through the reef until it was close enough to put a motorized runabout in. Two middle-aged men brought the runabout to the beach. They took Andres from Mrs. Serna and examined him carefully. They could speak no Spanish, so there was practically no communication, except that they pointed to Mrs. Serna and said, "Cooba?"

She nodded and said, "*Si.*"

I need to go back a few minutes here and tell what Mrs. Serna told Juan Jose as the sport fisherman was working its way in through the coral heads. She shook him by the shoulders and said almost between her teeth- so it really scared him- that he was to speak to no one, no one at all. He was not to tell anyone his name or any of their names, and he was not to tell anyone where they came from, or else they might be thrown in prison. Juan Jose started crying and Mrs. Serna slapped him in the face and cursed him with a curse that only a fisherman's wife would use. So by the time the doctors from Miami picked them up, Juan Jose would only stare silently and fiercely at them like a mute.

The doctors (there were five of them on the sport fisherman) were staunch anti-communists. When they learned that these were refugees from Cuba, they had a long conversation among themselves. This conversation was in the rocking and jumping cabin of the sport fisherman, where the two youngest doctors were working with ice from the bait cooler to treat Andres for heat prostration. The doctors spoke in low, measured doctor tones. What they were talking about, although there was no way Mrs. Serna would have known this, was that if they took her and the two boys to the British authorities at Bimini, there might be great difficulty arranging political asylum for them in the U.S. The most humanitarian thing to do, they all agreed, would be to take them directly back to Miami.

In the end, and Mrs. Serna never really understood what was happening to her until some time later, they decided to take Mrs. Serna and the boys back to Miami with them and concoct a story about how they were found.

They went first to a long dock behind a big, pink stucco house on Key Biscayne. One of the doctors went up to the house and got a maid to come down and explain to Mrs. Serna what her story was to be. There was an old wooden dinghy, with most of its paint blistered off by the sun, lying on the beach beside the end of the doctor's seawall. Two of the doctors walked down the lawn beside the seawall and found the dinghy, dragged it into the water, and waded with it back to the sport fisherman.

The doctor who owned the sport fisherman told Mrs. Serna (through the maid as interpreter) that she was to say she and the boys had been aboard a larger boat, that the Cuban crew had set them adrift in the dinghy when they came within sight of the Florida coast line, and the doctors had found the dinghy in the Gulf Stream several hours later.

Mrs. Serna fudged the story when she first told it to the immigration officials in Miami. She said she had been aboard a shrimp boat crowded with refugees, and that the people had been so cruel they made her and the boys get in the dingy and then had cast them adrift. When Mrs. Serna's story didn't match that of the doctors, the immigration authorities were a little suspicious, but you have to remember the political climate of the time. And you've also got to realize that Mrs. Serna spoke like a fisherman's wife, so the educated translators and case workers treated what she told them as you would treat the story a small child tells you.

Mrs. Serna told the case workers that her name was Riera, and that the two boys were her sons. She was almost too old for this to be believable, but not quite, so she and Andres and Juan Jose were granted political asylum. Within a few weeks they had moved to Philadelphia, because Mrs. Serna (or Riera) didn't want to be recognized by any other Cubans living in South Florida. She feared for her and the boys' safety if their real identity were discovered, plus, to tell the truth, after a couple of weeks of taking care of Juan Jose and the baby, she liked the idea of having the children she had always prayed God would give her.

As for Mrs. Rodriguez and the captain (going back to that day when she was separated from her sons)- the powerless cabin cruiser drifted north in the current, past Bimini and Cat Cay in the late afternoon, close enough that they could see the islands, and they passed within a mile or two of a couple of sport fishermen trolling close to the banks. But they had no flares aboard and no radio, so they were unable to signal for help. That evening the wind shifted back around to the South (an unusual change for that area) and blew at thirty to forty knots. The sea was still relatively flat, because the current was running strong in the same direction as the wind. The boat drifted north across the entrance to Northwest Providence

Channel and, in the dark, early morning of the next day, washed ashore on the reefs of Grand Bahama Island south of West End.

The captain was killed in the surf and darkness when the boat broke up. Mrs. Rodriguez made her way to shore by the grace of God. She was dehydrated and exhausted. She pulled herself up the beach, out of the water, and went to sleep.

The next morning, two Bahamian boys who were out on the beach searching for conch found her. She was barely alive. She had to be flown by helicopter to the hospital in Nassau, and it was several days before she was coherent enough to tell her story.

She told the authorities about her boys and Mrs. Serna, but the story was confused for the first day or two that she could speak.

Mrs. Rodriguez had practically no knowledge of geography or navigation, so there was no way to tell where the sand cay she was talking about could be. Her description fit any one of the dozens or hundreds of poorly charted little sand cays that lay along their probable route from Cuba. The Royal Navy and the U.S. Coast Guard flew several reconnaissance flights over that route, but no sign of Mrs. Serna or the boys was seen. The strong wind that had blown the cabin cruiser ashore on Grand Bahama was the early effect of a tropical storm that had sprung up northwest of Cuba and moved through the area while Mrs. Rodriguez was in the hospital. There were no reports either out of the Bahamas or Florida of two Rodriguez boys and their maid being picked up on a sand cay in the Bahamas. The British authorities finally concluded that the three had been stranded on a particularly low-lying cay, and that high seas from the storm had washed them off of it.

Mrs. Rodriguez was emotionally destroyed. In the course of a few days she had lost everybody she had ever loved. Her husband was probably in prison. Her sons were gone. She was exiled in a strange country where few people spoke her language, and as far as she knew, she may never be able to see any of her relatives and friends in Cuba again.

It was roughly three months before Mrs. Rodriguez was granted political asylum in the U.S., mainly through the efforts of her husband's friend in Miami, an American named Loehr, who had owned a hotel in the Rodriguez's hometown before Castro nationalized all the tourist hotels. He flew to Nassau and took her back to Miami with him.

What happened to Mrs. Rodriguez was sort of strange, strange only in that you and I probably wouldn't have dreamed it up, which is generally the way all of life works out. Mrs. Rodriguez, as I said, was emotionally destroyed by her exile and the loss of her family. A lot of her just wanted to die, and frankly I'm surprised she didn't die, because a person can pine away just as surely as they can die of cancer or AIDS. She wasn't at all the same woman the Loehrs had known in Cuba- a young, pretty, reserved but vivacious upper-class woman. She had aged ten or fifteen years in three months. Her complexion was gray, and her face sagged. Her hair was a duller brown with streaks of gray. She stayed by herself in the guest bedroom for several days after Mr. Loehr brought her to Miami, and when she finally came out of her room, she didn't speak much to the Loehrs at all, giving nothing more than detached and emotionless responses to their attempts at conversation.

Eventually she began leaving the house to take slow and unadventurous walks around the neighborhood, and that gave the Loehrs a lot of hope. But their hope was ill-founded. If anything, Mrs. Rodriguez became more detached once she started walking. She spoke to herself as she walked and looked into the blank air in front of her and chastised it as if there were someone standing there. The neighborhood children, even the neighborhood adults, began to joke and laugh about her.

This went on for months, long past the point where the Loehrs gave up hope of her recovering. Mr. Loehr even discussed with his wife the possibility of sending her to a psychiatrist, but in those days only the insane and the very forward-looking went to psychiatrists. And Mrs. Rodriguez didn't really act crazy. She just acted strange.

She didn't like to come out and sit and talk when visitors came. She would stay in her room with the television on, or she would go in the kitchen and putter. The Loehrs avoided having guests over for several months, but eventually they had to go on with their lives. They certainly didn't want to turn their old friend out, and there was no question of her finding an apartment on her own or supporting herself. So they started having guests over for cocktails or dinner, and they let Mrs. Rodriguez do as little as she wanted. She spent so much time in the kitchen when other people were in the house that it was just a matter of time before someone mistook her for a maid. The Loehrs were terribly embarrassed at the mistake and quickly corrected their guest, but after many more times, they found it more convenient simply to go along than to try to tell the whole story.

Mrs. Loehr started feeling so bad about all the work Mrs. Rodriguez was doing around her house that she hired a maid. Mrs. Rodriguez would go behind the maid, recleaning what the woman had just cleaned and changing her recipes and embellishing the dishes she had already cooked. The first maid quit after a couple of weeks, and after the second maid quit, Mrs. Loehr didn't hire another one. So it ended up that Mrs. Rodriguez lived and worked in the Loehrs' house like a very dear and very close servant, only she didn't get any less strange. She never learned to speak English well. In fact, she rarely spoke at all.

The Loehr's little girls were very young when Mrs. Rodriguez came to live with them. She stayed there for over twenty years, so she raised the four girls. They were dear to her. Well, no, maybe I shouldn't really say that. She was as close to them as a maid of twenty years' service would be to the children of the house. People exaggerate the depth of the attachment in those circumstances, but there is love involved.

The Loehr girls, like so many children of the well-to-do, turned out not to be worth much as they grew up, even though they were charming and pretty and well-behaved when they were children. The third from the oldest, Ree, was especially troubled. At twenty-three she married the son of a well-to-do family from Boca Raton, but he worked for his father, and he didn't work very much. He did a lot of drugs, and so did Ree. The marriage was bad. After several separations and an abortion, they finally split up for good, having been married only fifteen months. Ree had never really had a job of her own, so at age twenty-five, she moved home to live with her parents.

I know I'm moving you along pretty fast here, but things just move along fast sometimes.

Ree moved back home and didn't get along well at all with her father. She could talk to her mother some, but not very pleasantly. She could talk to Mrs. Rodriguez in broken Spanish, and Mrs. Rodriguez could talk to her in broken English. They didn't share much, but at least Mrs. Rodriguez didn't speak to her judgmentally. They didn't talk about all the things Ree had done and continued to do to screw up her life. Life just didn't seem too important to Mrs. Rodriguez, so screwing it up wasn't such a crime for her.

I suppose Ree had been living back home with her parents for four or five months, and had found and lost one job with a bank, when she started spending a lot of time at the swim and racket club. Ree was really much too old to be spending time at the swim and racket club. Most of the young people there were teenagers.

She played tennis and squash with a good many middle-aged men, and she raised quite a few eyebrows for doing it. The middle-aged men didn't speak well at all about Ree in the locker room after they played her.

Ree had been a charming but flat-chested young woman, very pretty when she was a teenager and in her very early twenties. But the strain of a divorce and drugs was already beginning to tell on her, and she looked more and more like a tramp. She hung out at the racket club because she didn't want to stay at her parents' house during the day, and her father had cut her off from shopping, and she didn't seriously want to get a job. Getting a suntan and smoking joints in the lifeguards' station was something for her to do. And the well-healed college crowd that hung out at the club was always ready for a party, though they didn't really enjoy having Ree around that much.

There was a young Cuban lifeguard at the pool, a boy about nineteen years old, who had a fairly light complexion and a roman nose. He was short, no more than five feet seven, but he was very good looking, and he had broad shoulders and well-defined muscles. He was cocky and proud, but in a quiet and self-assured way. He obviously didn't come from a good background, but there was a dignity in him, a smoothness and harmony of features, and a quick intelligence.

He made an attempt at picking Ree up one afternoon as he was cleaning the pool. The pick-up attempt was more playful than serious, but Ree liked it and played along with him, and they went out for a drink after Juan got off work that evening.

They played games for the first few weeks, each pretending that they weren't serious at all about the other. Even when Juan made his first pass at Ree, and when they ended up in bed later that night, it was all like a game, as if they were testing the absurdity of the match-up. The Loehrs were one of the wealthiest families in South Florida. Juan was a nobody, a boy from inner city Philadelphia who had gone to Penn State for a year on scholarship and then had dropped out and come South to Miami.

The tease matches went on and on until they finally turned into something they probably never should have become. Ree was, despite all her problems, a very loving and sincere girl deep down, probably the most loving and sensitive of the four Loehr girls. Juan was a troubled young man. He had grown up Cuban and a refugee, but he was no foreigner. He'd been chosen as the most outstanding young man at a tough public high school in Philadelphia. He had been given awards and asked to give banal booster speeches at civic clubs. He had won a scholarship to Penn State, which had made his mother so proud she cried, but it was given in the spirit of tokenism by men he despised- wealthy, shallow men who would never have given him the time of day if it hadn't been convenient for them. And everything he had ever done to get where he was- all the set speeches and responses the all-American boy is expected to give- had always been fatuous to him. Of all the torment American society exacts from a disadvantaged young man, the worst may be that he cannot once speak the truth about the system that is lifting him up as an example.

Ree and Juan quickly developed one of those affairs that is carried on mostly in private. It was inconvenient for the couple to be seen together in public.

Neither one was particularly proud of the other. I would say they went together for two or three months, as seldom as once every couple of weeks, as often as once every couple of days, before the incident at the Loehr's house.

The Loehrs had a house on Green Turtle Cay in the Abacos, and they left the first week in September for a two-week vacation there, taking Mrs. Rodriguez along with them. Ree stayed alone in their Coral Gables house. She had Juan Jose over to cook steaks on the grill the first night they were gone. He ended up spending the night, and as the week went on, he came over every afternoon after work and spent the night with Ree in the bedroom she had lived in as a child.

It was the first time Juan had ever moved at ease in a house like that, although he wasn't entirely at ease. I should say it was the first time since he was four or five years old that he stayed in a house like that, but those memories were so old and so early that they were more like dreams than memories.

Thursday morning Juan had the day off from the swim and racket club. They got up fairly late, and Ree was in the kitchen cooking breakfast. Juan was sitting at the long counter that overlooked the sunken cooking area, watching her cook. They had the T.V. on, and Juan got tired of watching the "I Love Lucy" rerun that was playing. He had lated "I Love Lucy" since he was a little boy. So he got up and went to the Loehr's bedroom, where he and Ree had spent the night before, and got one of the porn tapes out of the VCR they had been watching. He brought it back into the kitchen and plugged it into the VCR there, and there was instant action on the tube.

Then he rolled a joint from the ounce of Colombian Ree had bought on Monday, and which they had half emptied. They lit the joint and were smoking as the bad rock music and moaning and cursing came from the television set. They were smoking dope and laughing at the video tape. Juan was wearing his swim trunks. Ree was wearing only an oversize T-shirt that rode up whenever she bent over the stove, and things didn't last too long like that.

Juan came around the counter and started fondling her. She waved him away with one hand while she tried to cook and smoke the joint with the other. Juan finally turned the stove off underneath the scrambled eggs, took the joint away from Ree, and blew her a shotgun. He took a toke himself and put the joint out in the ashtray beside the stove. Then he got her to climb up on the island in the middle of the cooking area, a cutting board surface some five or six feet square. He slipped the T-shirt off and skinned out of his swim trunks. Ree was giggling. She was mocking the woman on the videotape as Juan positioned her on her hands and knees facing the television. Then he climbed up on the island behind her.

The pot smoke was hanging thick in the air, and Ree and Juan were just beginning to stop kidding around and beginning to breath with a purpose, when they heard a sound behind them. Ree turned to look, and as she turned the door leading to the garage swung open, and in walked Mr. Loehr, pushing two heavy suitcases in front of him. Mrs. Loehr and Mrs. Rodriguez were right behind him.

This was an awfully hard thing to face, I'm sure. Ree jumped off the counter and hid on her hands and knees behind the counter. Poor Juan, there he was, out in the open as Mrs. Rodriguez and Mrs. Loehr backed out of sight into the garage. Mr. Loehr stood shocked for a moment, then he exploded. Juan had to run naked through the house, grab his pants out of the Loehrs' bedroom, and jump out of the bedroom window to get away. Mr. Loehr picked up the VCR and threw it across the breakfast room into the glass cabinet where the crystal was stored. Ree was crying and screaming at her father to stop, and he was screaming at her. It was a bad scene. I'm glad there were no guns handy, because I think someone might have been shot.

That was the final straw for Loehr. The rest of the day and that evening were really terrible with Ree. You know how you get in those fights with someone you love, and you feel it just has to get better soon because you love them, but it only gets worse every time either one of you opens your mouth. He hit her that evening in his paneled den, with the picture of him and Mrs. Loehr posing with the Vice President at the Waldorf. She left the next morning.

Ree had been kicked out of the house before, but this time was different. Loehr didn't give her any money, and the next week he went to his lawyer's offices and had her written out of his will. He told her, that morning after the incident, when she was still lying in the bed, and he walked into the doorway of her bedroom, and she rolled over looking out the window and praying that he would come take her in his arms and rock her, he told her, standing in the doorway of her room, that he didn't love her any more.

She listened to the footsteps of his wingtip shoes as he walked back down the hall and left for work.

Well, so there we are. Things were bad then, but they just kept getting worse. This is a hard tale, because you know how life sometimes can just get horrible, where you're convinced there's no way out of the mess. It gets worse than you ever really want to remember, the days, or the nights really, when you want to give up, when you think of killing yourself, or you want to kill someone you love. Life gets that bad, and I used to think it only got that bad for some people, but maybe it gets that bad for everybody- worse than any of us wants to be reminded of. The only thing is it all passes, and someday down the road you'll be somewhere, somewhere you never imagined you would be- with me the other day it was in a deer stand, in the top of a pine tree at the top of a low hill, where I could see three or four miles out over the pine forest and pasture land. It was a hot deer spot, too, a natural salt lick, just torn up with deer tracks, and my cousin had missed an eight-point buck out of that same stand that morning. We were bow-hunting, and the deer had come in behind him where he couldn't get turned around to draw without spooking him.

I'm way off track here, but anyway, life had been pretty bad for me for a few months. I didn't see any deer at all that afternoon. It was a beautiful cool day, with bright, low October sunshine. I was facing east, and trying to keep still, so I didn't see the sunset behind me. All I saw, and it happened just for a couple of minutes, was that there were these light whiffs of high clouds, that you could hardly see in the blue sky, but when the sun went down they lit up orange with a light, well, I can't describe it. It's like trying to describe what life is. Anyway, I'm way off the subject.

Loehr didn't speak to Ree. I suppose he didn't see her for months after that incident. She moved out of his house and moved into Juan's apartment in Little Havana. This tore Loehr up, I'm sure. Ree and Juan lived together for several months, and then they got married, more to spite Loehr I suspect than anything, although it's absurd to think that anyone would get married without secretly hoping in their hearts that this is going to be a love like none they have ever felt, that will last and last, and life will turn out like they only dream it will.

Ree didn't have a job. She took a job for a couple of months in a friend's boutique, but she quit that. Juan had to quit his job as a lifeguard and start driving a taxi and working nights as a bouncer at a nightclub. The marriage went bad quickly. Ree was doing a lot of cocaine and was smoking dope most of the day and watching soap operas. They had ferocious fights.

As for Mrs. Serna- or Mrs. Riera as she had lived the last fifteen or sixteen years- she was still living with Andres in Philadelphia. Mrs. Riera was a cleaning woman for a large insurance company downtown. It was a good job, and she had it almost since they came to Philadelphia. She worked for a year and a half or so in a machine factory, and then that closed down, and she went to work for the insurance company and stayed there. She made pretty good wages and had good benefits and was something of an institution on the three floors she cleaned every evening.

People knew her by name, and whenever one of the white-collar workers was working late and she would come around to clean, they would stop and have a conversation with her. Some of the men who had been around a long time even had learned enough about her in these conversations to ask how Juan Jose was doing, and she would lie to them. Well, not really lie, but she tried not to tell the story as she believed it to be. He had moved to Florida, she said, and she hoped that he would be going to the University of Miami in the fall. But she really hadn't heard from him in months when he called one evening to say that he had been married.

Mrs. Serna and Andres lived in an apartment in North Philadelphia, close enough to Chestnut Hill to pretend to respectability, but really in a bad neighborhood. They lived on the third floor of a duplex row house, red brick, with elaborate Victorian woodwork on the cornices and porch, most of which was rotting and beginning to fall down. Their house was the only original Victorian house still standing on their block, and there were a lot of ratty apartment buildings on the next block over.

It's not surprising she would have had some trouble with the boys, because that was a rough neighborhood to grow up in. She didn't have enough money to send them to private school, either, although she had sent Andres to parochial school his first three years. It's amazing they turned out as well as they did. Andres wasn't the student and the leader his brother had been, but he was nowhere near as fiery, either, and he had been Mrs. Riera's baby. Juan had always had some sub-surface hatred against the woman Andres considered to be their mother. But by this time she was having trouble with Andres, too.

When Juan called from Miami, Mrs. Riera was telling him this in Spanish, going on and on about how worried she was about Andres, and how much she missed Juan, and how she really did love him.

Andres was out of the apartment with his girlfriend, and he probably wouldn't come home until after midnight. It was a school night. She didn't know what to do with the boy. Juan finally cut her off and told her he had gotten married. He told her what a nice girl Ree was, and what a good family she came from, which sounded like a lie. Mrs. Riera said, well, good, she was proud of him. He should remember what he came from, and he came from very good people, the best, and it was fitting that he would marry someone like that. She told him good-bye and asked him please to write her and send her a photograph of his new wife.

When she hung up the phone she cried herself to sleep on her bed, and she didn't even wake up when Andres came home in the early morning.

I guess the Mariel boat lift was some four or five months later. Let's see what else had gone bad by that time. Ree was getting really hooked up with the drugs, and Mr. and Mrs. Loehr were going every week to a very expensive psychiatrist to see how to deal with it. The psychiatrist kept telling them to go to Al Anon, but they weren't the type of people to do that, and Loehr was very angry and resentful that he was spending so much money and time with this man. At the sessions, since they weren't making much progress talking about Ree, Mrs. Loehr spent a lot of time talking about why she was unhappy in her marriage. This caused a great deal of tension between the two of them, as if there weren't enough tension already.

Ree had lost a lot of weight. She had dark circles under her eyes, and the skin on her face was sagging. She smoked cigarettes constantly, and there even seemed to be gaps growing between her teeth. Juan stayed away from her as much as he could, but whenever he was home, they usually had a terrible fight. Usually late in the night after these fights they would end up having torrid sex, like they were trying to kill each other.

In Philadelphia, Andres had gotten his girlfriend pregnant. She was spunky little girl, half Irish and half Italian. Her father was a policeman, and he and her mother did not approve of Andres at all. They wanted her to have an abortion, and Andres had gone to Mrs. Riera to ask her to help him raise the money. Mrs. Riera went to church and said the rosary every evening for a week, and after a long and very honest searching of her conscience, she decided that abortion was nothing less than murder. It began to eat at her, then, just like it would eat at you if someone was seriously talking to you about killing their child. Well, not just like it, but almost.

She told Andres that she couldn't give him the money. She said he should marry his girlfriend. He threw a tantrum and told her all the reasons that would never work. And soon Mrs. Riera was so panicked by the thought of an abortion that she lost control of herself and said some very unkind things about Andres and his brother. Then she began crying and begged him to forgive her, to please try to understand, that a child was a gift from God, that all her life she had prayed for God to give her a child, and that it was unthinkable to kill the gift that God ...

She caught herself too late, and she tried to keep on with the conversation to cover up her mistake. Andres had no way of knowing that she wasn't his real mother. She had always acted like his real mother, and Juan Jose had never told him anything different. But we all have those secret suspicions of the truth somewhere inside us. When he heard what she said, it registered with him immediately. He asked what she meant, that she had always prayed that God would give her children. If God was mentioned in the question, Mrs. Riera couldn't very well lie. She tried to lie, but it wouldn't come out, so she ended up telling Andres the truth about his real family and the incidents surrounding their escape from Cuba. This was a terrible shock to Andres. He was very angry. He threw Mrs. Riera's china vase, the faded green one with gold scrolling on it, against the wall, and he said some things to her he never should have said. He left the apartment and didn't come home that night. And late that night was one of those bad times for Mrs. Riera. She had lost everything she ever loved, too. That bedroom in the back of a row house in a noisy, dirty section of Philadelphia, late in the early morning hours, waiting and praying for someone you love to come home- I don't want to think about this any more.

In this very bad time for all of these people, the only one who was not suffering much was Mrs. Rodriguez. Sure, she was very fond of the Loehr girls, since she had raised them all, but she was detached from them also. They weren't her children. She just had lost so much, her family and her home and her dignity and a large part of her sanity, that she didn't hold on as tightly as the rest of us do. To her, watching Ree slip away toward death was not as hard as it is to most people. Still, I suppose there were mornings when she was very angry at life, or at the way things are. I don't think you could watch all of those people fall apart and not be angry at the way things are.

That was before the television and radio stations began carrying reports of Castro's opening the port of Mariel. Mrs. Rodriguez was in the kitchen serving Mr. Loehr's breakfast of bran flakes and bacon. Mr. Loehr was watching the *Today* show on the television. Mrs. Rodriguez never paid any attention at all to the news, but there was something that caught her interest- the mention of Cuba, or the name Mariel, even though the American news readers pronounced it entirely differently from the way she had heard it all her life. Anyway, she stopped to watch the report briefly. Mr. Loehr was paying close attention, too, and he caught her watching and realized she was thinking the same thing.

He didn't discuss it with Mrs. Rodriguez that morning, but that evening he discussed it with his wife. When they went to dinner they heard the television on in the kitchen and Walter Cronkite talking about the refugees pouring out of Mariel and the flotilla of small boats that was going over to pick them up.

Mrs. Rodriguez never watched the news, as I said, so when she brought their dinner into the dining room, they asked her to sit down at the table with them. She was hesitant, but when she did sit down, it was with a hint of the pride and self confidence they hadn't seen in their old friend in over fifteen years. It was just a hint, though, held firmly in by that fear that keeps us all from hoping as much as our hearts were meant to hope.

Anyway, they had a tentative discussion that evening, and a rather heated discussion the next morning before breakfast, that ended with Mrs. Rodriguez running to her bedroom in tears, and Mrs. Loehr following to comfort her. Mr. Loehr, against Mrs.

Rodriguez's expressed wishes, located an unchartered fishing boat on Sanibel Island, drove to Sanibel Island on the Tamiami Trail late that afternoon, and left that night for the long run to Cuba.

The next day he arrived in Mariel, and after one miserable afternoon and night trying to fight his way through the crowd and the hostile soldiers and police and bureaucrats, he found his friend Rodriguez trying to get aboard a shrimp boat out of Murrel's Inlet, South Carolina.

He hardly recognized his old friend. Fifteen years change a person enough, but fifteen years of what Mr. Rodriguez had been through changed a man almost beyond recognition. He appeared there before Loehr, standing on the beach in a ragtag crowd of people trying to buy their way aboard a dinghy to carry them out to the shrimp boat. Mr. Rodriguez was fairly fit, not plump but not skinny. He had a thick beard salted with gray, and he was wearing a swordfisherman's long-billed cap. He was smoking the last of a thick cigar, puffing and puffing on it and chewing it as the sleazy people around him scrambled to get ahead of one another. He was deciding whether to throw out the last bit of who he was and join the scramble, too.

Mr. Loehr went up to him quietly, touched his elbow, and said his name. The two men embraced and wept.

The reunion with Mrs. Rodriguez, well, you want to think it was all dramatic, but it wasn't particularly so. It was like so much of life, in the fabulous moments of it, in that it was a little awkward, and the weather and the sun and the sea, the breeze blowing all that graying hair, it was just nothing particularly out of the ordinary.

Except that once he stepped onto the dock and hugged her, after a moment or two, they held on tight to each other and sobbed so hard you could see their chests heaving, and nobody else knew what to do.

You know, frankly, it's all a kind of a strange story, that I've never found particularly easy to tell. I mean one part doesn't flow particularly smoothly into another. Juan Jose saw all the reports of the Mariel boat lift, too, and they created a great deal of confusion in him. He didn't have any way to do anything about it right off the bat. He was still awfully scared of his past. It was the irretrievably lost past, as far as he knew, and it would be much easier to carry on with life. There was just no clear way to try to see if his father would come out of Cuba. He wasn't terribly sure he knew enough about his father to know how to look for him. It would have been one of those things that is far easier simply to let lie. But that was not like Juan Jose.

He went to the Immigration and Naturalization Service office in Miami. The place was a mob scene, full of Cubans and Haitians and Jamaicans, but mostly Cubans, and most of them were wild with fear and hope. Juan had to take a number and take a seat and wait for his name to be called. The first afternoon his name wasn't called. For some reason, and this wasn't at all like him, he called in sick for work and went the next morning and waited all day and still he wasn't called.

He went back the third day, and about 9:30 his name was called.

He told the harried case worker he was looking for his father. She got very apprehensive, as if he was trying to get someone into the country fraudulently, but eventually he explained to her that all he wanted her to do was check her computer files and see if someone with his father's name had come in from Cuba. The case worker, an ugly fat woman in her early twenties, with greasy, dark hair, was almost rude as she typed the name into her computer, but she suddenly smiled and said, "Yes, you're in luck. He's come."

She gave Juan an address where his father could be found. All fairly sloppy bureaucratic procedure, I imagine, but Juan was a very good-looking young man, and he could get women to do almost anything he wanted them to do. Plus, the poor girl had been working in a state of confusion for weeks.

Juan was so excited it didn't even occur to him what house he was going to. He knew it was on the Loehrs' street, but it was just one of those things that was so impossible he never even thought about it. When he pulled up in front of their house (he had not been back there since he had been married), he checked and rechecked the address. There was just no sense to it, but then he remembered that Ree had told him Mr. Loehr had once owned a hotel in Cuba. So there was some possibility there. As he was walking up the front walk, it became a possibility that he could accept as real, and then the rest of reality began to appear to him. It was so blinding he resisted thinking about it, until he rang the doorbell, and the thought became so clear to him that he couldn't help but fight it, and then his mother opened the door.

Some day, it might be far off, or maybe it has already come, things will happen to you that you will have no desire to talk about. At that time, words seem worthless, and what you have needed for so long is all there, even if it's there for only a moment.

I won't tell what happened when Juan Jose's mother opened the door for him. I have no desire to tell it. I would tell something about Andres and Mrs. Riera and Andres's little fiancee coming to Miami. The fiancee has always been a very striking part of the story for me. She was only sixteen, a small girl with long, auburn hair and blue eyes, and she was just beginning to show a little from her pregnancy. When she came into the Loehr's house on that unseasonably cool day for Miami, and when Mr. Loehr took the light blue angora sweater from her shoulders, her auburn hair cracked with electricity, and her cheeks flushed with modesty.

No, though, honestly, I don't want to tell that part of the story either. As many times as I have ever tried to tell it, I didn't really want to.

So I will tell you, to close it all, that the Loehrs had quite a wonderful week or two in their house, when their daughter Ree came home with her husband, and when all of the Rodriguez family and their maid Mrs. Serna were reunited. The Cubans sat up night after night and laughed and talked to each other in Spanish that was so fast and so full of life that the Loehrs stood by and listened and smiled, and only understood bits and pieces here and there.

The Seventh Tale
Jennifer Sills circles the globe.

Before I got married, when I was working on my father's farm, my brother and I were out cruising bars in Spartanburg one weekend, and we wound up with a few friends after closing time at one of the mill owner's houses. The mill owner's daughter was home visiting from New York and invited us over to cook breakfast. To be honest, I don't even remember clearly who all was there, or how my brother and I got invited. All these people I didn't know very well and didn't like particularly much were in the kitchen making an egg and sausage casserole and passing a bottle of schnaps around. And somehow, as the night blurred on, my brother and I ended up in one of the sitting rooms talking to Mary Rogers.

I never have particularly cared for Mary Rogers, if I had to come right out and tell the blunt truth. I've always thought she was a little boarding school snot, overweight and not particularly good-looking. She smoked cigarettes like a tar-sampling machine, with her wrist flapped back and the cigarette waving toward the floor between every puff. I probably judge her too harshly.

I'm thinking back, and this must have been sometime soon after I got back from Europe, I would say a year or so after I got out of college, because this is the first time I remember hearing the story of Jennifer Sills, and certainly I couldn't have been back in town too long, because the story really made the rounds of Spartanburg the year or two after she reappeared. Mary was good friends with Lacey Helms, Fred R.'s daughter, and Lacey was one of Jennifer Sill's oldest childhood friends, so Mary knew a lot of details to the story that I never heard anywhere else. And I'm kind of proud of myself that I never have repeated most of those details until now.

When I was in junior high school I was the class nerd, fat and bookish and not athletic.

No girls would have anything to do with me. That was when others my age were going steady or going to spin-the-bottle parties and coming to school on Monday and telling all about it. I was never invited to any of those parties. I had never kissed a girl. I had never been close to kissing one. But the adolescent stirrings were in me, and I needed to fall in love just as much as the other kids, so I fell in love in my daydreams, sitting in French class and staring across the room at Jennifer Sills.

My love for Jennifer Sills was a fantasy of the wildest sort, like Grace Kelly daydreaming at age thirteen about becoming a princess. Jennifer had fully developed breasts and long, blond hair and blue eyes. She was quiet and intelligent and a cheerleader, and she went steady with whatever athlete was the coolest guy in school at the time. Don't get me wrong, she wasn't a puffhead. In this case still waters ran deep.

You know life whirls all around us, and as irrational as our daydreams may be, they are rarely as irrational as the future turns out to be. By the time I was a senior in high school, Jennifer Sills was still the most beautiful girl in our class, although her breasts were no longer quite as large relative to the other girls'. She was still a cheerleader, and she was still quiet and intelligent and kind, and she still had long blond hair and blue eyes. She was getting a little shy as she got older. But by that time I was no longer quite the class nerd. Intellect had become an asset instead of a liability. I had grown out of some of my fat. I was fresh back from a summer in Europe. I smoked pot and wrote poetry and was always the rebel in the class discussion, and I guess it wasn't inconceivable that Jennifer would develop a crush on me.

This crush was a great embarrassment to me. Jennifer Sills was everything I had professed to despise in my transformation from class nerd to intellectual malcontent. She dated jocks. She was in the student government. She went to church youth group gatherings and led the singing. I caught a lot of ribbing from my friends about her. When she came outside with a friend to talk to me during lunch, my friends gave me hell about it for a week. I was terrified even to talk to such a good-looking and self-possessed girl. Jennifer made a fool of herself throwing herself at me and talking about me to anyone who would listen in our senior year of high school, but I never so much as asked her out on a date.

I felt like a fool when I ran into her a couple of years later at U. Va. I had driven up with some fraternity brothers from Chapel Hill for Midwinters, and I ran into her in the front yard of the St. A. house about two o'clock in the morning. I was stumbling drunk and carrying one handle of a cooler, with one of my cruder Eastern North Carolina frat brothers carrying the other handle. He kept making lewd advances to Jennifer, but she was sober and pretty and rosy cheeked from the cold, and she was escorted by a future President of the United States. She had completely recovered from her crush on me. She was nice, and mildly interested in what I had to say, but I felt like a slug.

And that was the last time I saw Jennifer before she disappeared, so everything from this point on is just what I have heard here and there. Jennifer was majoring in Economics at U. Va., writing her honors thesis on the development patterns of third world economies, and her parents decided to send her to Tanzania on an exchange for one semester of her senior year. This was exactly the kind of thing I would have expected from Jennifer's parents, by the way.

The August of her senior year, after a pretty going-away party at her parents' home in Spartanburg, Jennifer flew to London. There she boarded a chartered jet filled with American and British exchange students destined for Tanzania. The plane was a small, intracontinental jet chartered from an African airline. It was old. The seats were uncomfortably close together, and the ventilation system stank of too many bodies and too many years of cigarette smoke. The plane's range was insufficient to make the flight from London to Tanzania non-stop, so they had to stop in the Central African country of, well, let's call it Ubaway, to refuel.

Once the plane got on the ground in Ubaway, there was a miserable delay in refueling and resupplying the plane. The air conditioning system was shut down, and the students sat for the better part of an hour shut up in a sweltering plane, indignant and complaining, as only American rich kids can complain. The whole charter had been a planning snafu, and everyone, crew and passengers and Ubawayan airport officials, was hot and angry. Finally the students were allowed to deplane and proceed directly to a quarantine lounge in the airport where they could wait without clearing customs and immigration. They left their luggage on board the plane. The tour guide left all of their passports and health certificates on board, since they would need none of that stuff in the brief layover.

The refueling took a couple of hours at least, so the students, many of whom were still suffering the jet lag from flying to London, were dozing sitting upright on the few wooden benches available. When they were told they could reboard the plane, all of them filed groggily out of the door of the lounge and across the tarmac, except a group of seven young Americans, three young men and four young women, who had passed the time in one corner of the lounge joking and saying outrageous things to each other about the charter company and the exchange program and the government and people of Ubaway. Jennifer was with this group, and they hung back and stayed in the lounge as long as possible, determined not to go stand in line in the sun on the tarmac waiting to climb the movable stairs to the plane.

It was a slow line. The mid-day tropical sun was brutal. Jennifer and the other six stayed in the lounge until the last passenger began climbing the stairs, and the Ubawayan customs officer at the door of the lounge began shouting at them in French and gesticulating toward the plane. (Ubaway was a former French colony, and practically no one they encountered could speak more than a few words of English.) So the students started reluctantly out onto the tarmac, laughing and joking. And when they were about halfway across the ramp toward the plane, the jet exploded.

There was a sharp bang, and a puff of smoke from underneath the plane, and then as the Ubawayan ground crew began shouting and running away, there was another, deeper explosion like a roar, and the entire plane was lost in a fireball. The explosion was a mystery for some time, but I heard my father, who is an amateur pilot, say once (this must have been when I was home sometime during my senior year of college) that the investigators had determined there were two bombs, the first to rupture the fuel tanks and vaporize the fuel, and the second an incendiary device to ignite the cloud of vaporized fuel.

Anyway, that wasn't clear until after the investigation, many months later. Jennifer and the other six students were still far enough from the plane to escape injury, but everyone aboard was incinerated instantly. The bodies were burned beyond recognition, beyond counting, even, meaning I suppose that some of the bodies were blown into pieces.

I'm sure it was more awful than you and I could want to imagine. At any rate, this was the part of the story as I knew it when Mary Rogers started telling me about it late that night at ___________'s house in Spartanburg. I knew that there had been an explosion, that all aboard had been thought for months to have been killed, and that Jennifer Sills had reappeared almost three years later. At least that in general is what I knew. I'm sure I added a lot of details from Mary's version in the part I just told you.

My brother really disliked that prep-school set, and even though Jennifer Sills had gone to public school like we had, she still had hung with that bunch, and he kept pushing a lot harder than I did to hear everything that happened to her. Mary was lighting cigarettes and drinking Michelob Light beer from a bottle with a cocktail napkin wrapped around it, feeding us the story in a "this is really outrageous scoop" tone. My brother wouldn't have been listening to her if it wasn't really outrageous.

After the terrorist bombs exploded, the airport erupted into bedlam. Sirens screamed, police and army and fire trucks swooped all over the airfield, but the fire never was put out until it burned itself out. The army quickly moved in, sealed off the airport, and squads of soldiers began storming through the crowds of stranded passengers, arresting and beating people seemingly at random.

Jennifer and the other students huddled together just inside the lounge they had been waiting in earlier. The held each other and sobbed, some of them hysterically, over the terrible thing they had just seen. When the soldiers found them, they had no papers of any kind, as everything had been burned up on the plane. It was a bad scene. The soldiers were shouting at them in French and several different African languages and waving machine guns in their faces. One of the boys could speak a few words of French, but so badly he only aggravated matters. He was one of these Americans who can antagonize people anywhere in the world with a self-righteous, well-fed look and phrase-book language skills.

Things were going very badly indeed. The soldiers had the students lined up facing a cinder block wall with their hands clasped behind their heads, and an Ubawayan airport employee was imploring frantically with the soldiers in some wild-sounding African language with so many guttural stops he sounded like he was choking. The American girls were sobbing, and the soldiers were kicking the boys and preparing to search the girls, when an officer arrived on the scene.

He was a young man, very black, tall and lanky. He stopped the soldiers from what they were doing, questioned the airport employee, and then said to the students in poor English, "You passeports, pilease." The young man who had known some French shouted indignantly and gesticulated that they were on the plane, and the soldiers almost beat him up for it.

"You have peppers. Any peppers. Photo," the officer said, but the students made him understand they had no identification of any kind. One of the young men had a booklet of traveler's checks in his pocket. The officer studied these for a few minutes and handed the checks back to the boy.

The officer had a long discussion in French with the soldiers, then he issued some orders. Two soldiers saluted with palms forward and fingertips to their helmets, and they ran off into the chaos of the airport crowd.

"You will coming with me, pilease," the officer said to the students. The boy who had spoken some French began demanding in English to speak to the American embassy, but the officer acted as if he didn't even hear him. The soldiers grouped tight around them and kept their guns trained on them as they were led through the airport. In the main lobby of the airport some hundred or two hundred people were sitting on the floor as soldiers stood guard over them. Other soldiers were searching several young men who were leaning against the ticket counters. The officer led Jennifer and the other American students out to the taxi stand. The male students were taken to a blue panel van with police lights and sirens on it. The one American boy who had been so loud was still demanding to be taken to the American embassy when the soldiers shut the rear door of the van in his face.

This left the four girls standing on the sidewalk with their guards. Jennifer reached for the door handle of the van, but the officer shooed her away, waving his hands and saying, "No for woman, no for woman."

Instead, the girls were taken to a waiting, late-model Mercedes limousine, with air conditioning and leather seats and that pungent new Mercedes smell. The officer got in the front seat with the driver, and the car sped away from the airport following the police van. After a very fast couple of miles through the outskirts of the capital of Ubaway, the van veered off to the left, towards the city, and the Mercedes kept straight.

The Mercedes sped down a paved highway, past warehouses and shut-down factories, and past shanty-towns, and then into the more open countryside. The driver drove like a madman. Pedestrians crossed the road without any regard for the oncoming traffic. There were several near misses.

Once the driver had to slam on the brakes and skid sideways to miss a woman carrying a live chicken. One of the American girls screamed in the back seat, and then she broke down and started crying, and Jennifer tried to comfort her.

Some fifteen or twenty minutes out of the city, the car turned onto a winding road up into the hills and inched around a man driving a string of donkeys. It then sped around hairpin curves for five or six miles and turned into a long driveway bordered by palm trees. The driveway led to a magnificent colonial mansion set on a hill overlooking thousands of acres of rubber plantation. The Mercedes pulled up in front of the mansion, the officer stepped out, the driver opened the door for the four girls, and the officer said. "Here is the home of General Kanahwa. You are his guests."

The mansion was two stories tall. The columns on the front porch rose to support the roof over a grand second floor portico. The French-style windows were huge, and were all open, and a hot breeze blew the gauzey drapes out of them. In the heat of the late afternoon the girls could hear raucous bird calls in the hills below.

The officer led the girls inside, where a double circular stairway rose out of the entrance hall floored in rose-colored marble. The house was sumptuously decorated. There were oil paintings and water colors by European painters with famous names, although the girls had never seen any of these particular paintings reproduced anywhere. There was sculpture and fabulous Second Empire furniture. Some rooms were decorated in an African motif, with devilish masks and multicolored tapestries and wooden and ebony sculptures with tremendously oversize genitalia.

Oh, I forgot the part where the girls protested and demanded to be taken to the American embassy. They did this when they first got out of the car, but the officer either didn't understand them or didn't want to listen to them. He led them into the house, handed them over to the General's servants, saluted, went back to the Mercedes, and was driven away.

One of the students with Jennifer was a white girl from Chicago. She was an attractive girl, a little fat, with tremendous bosoms, and a very pleasant personality. The other two were black girls from Washington, D.C., svelte and trendily dressed, even though they were crumpled and sweaty from their ordeal that afternoon. They were snobbish. They had been to boarding school together in Connecticut, and now one of them went to Bennington and one to Skidmore. They hadn't had much to say to Jennifer or the Chicago girl up to this point.

The girls were taken upstairs, where each was shown an elegantly appointed bedroom where they assumed they would be staying. But no one at the house could speak any English, and none of the four students could speak any French. The girls were astonished at the accommodations, but they were still in shock from the accident and from being wheeled out here to this strange place, and their first thoughts were to try to call home and tell their parents they were o.k.

They tried through sign language to make the servants understand this, but the servants just shrugged. The Chicago girl was adamant about it, and finally in frustration she ran through the house looking for a telephone. When she found one she picked it up and started dialing. She dialed and dialed, and couldn't get any kind of answer. She kept getting a dead line or some kind of staticky taped message. Finally she got an operator, but the operator spoke first in an African language and then in French, and the Chicago girl shouted in English and then tried Hebrew, and one of the black girls tried Spanish, but they couldn't get anywhere, and the operator finally hung up. They tried and tried after that, for the rest of the afternoon, but the phone was dead for long periods of time, and when it did work, they couldn't get anyone on it who could help them. They found a phone book and were able to find a listing for the *Ambassade des Etats Unis* (Jennifer could remember "*Etats Unis*" from a year of grammar school French), but when they dialed the number nothing happened.

When they finally got someone to answer, it definitely wasn't the American Embassy, and the person just shouted into the phone in gibberish and hung up.

On the one hand the girls were terribly distraught and confused after the plane explosion and being whisked out here to this strange place, but on the other hand they were glad to be alive, and they were being treated very well. The servants brought them cool fruit drinks and served them sandwiches and cakes and cookies. They took them upstairs to a closet full of women's clothes and let them find something fresh to wear. Each of the girls had a hot bath drawn for them in their own bathroom.

By the time they bathed and changed and got their hair dried, it was early evening. The evening isn't very long in the tropics. The sun goes down quick and early, but it was still up when a motorcade of Mercedes limousines and Army jeeps came whining down the long driveway and circled to a stop in front of the mansion.

A soldier hopped out of the front door of the longest limousine and opened the door for the general. The general stepped out of his limousine in a blue dress uniform, the front of which was nearly covered in medals and campaign ribbons. Gold braid hung from both shoulders. He wore Ray-Ban sunglasses and a dress kipi with gold braid. His boots were spit-polish shiny, but with a light coating of dust from the day.

The general was a huge man, jet black and probably three hundred pounds. He was over six feet tall. His hands were plump, and the fingers were long. He walked into his house like a king, followed by a retinue of aides and greeted by doormen, a butler, and several young, black women in French maid uniforms. Jennifer and the other American girls were in the entry hall to meet him. He took each girl's hand, politely bowed from the waist and kissed it, smiled a very engaging smile, and welcomed them in beautiful French. The girls tried to speak to him in English about what was going to happen to them, and when they would be able to contact the American Embassy, but he didn't appear to understand anything they were saying. Jennifer turned to one of his aides and asked him if he could speak English, but the aide's eyes got big, and he stiffened up and said something quickly to her in French.

The girls got nowhere trying to communicate with the general. They were led to the sitting room, where they were served aperitifs while the general freshened up and changed. He came back downstairs in a white dress uniform, starched and immaculate, and covered with somewhat fewer medals than the uniform he had worn earlier. He sat with the girls for a while and was very polite while they tried to talk to him, but he didn't understand a word, as far as they could see. His servants came quietly in and out of the room, bringing hors d'oeuvres and drinks.

Jennifer Sills didn't drink alcohol. I don't know how anybody could go through three and a half years at U. Va. and not drink, but as far as I know, Jennifer had never had anything to drink at all. Anyway, it was a nice gathering, but there was no communication at all. The American girls were astonished at the difficulty they had making even the most basic signs understood. The general was quickly getting bored. He got up and paced to one of the enormous windows to look out over the rubber plantations.

"I don't know if y'all have caught on yet," one of the black girls from D.C. said. "But it's perfectly clear to me what this guy is up to. He's after some fresh young American pussy, is what he's after, and he's going to keep us locked up out here as long as he can get away with it."

Jennifer was shocked. "I can't believe you're saying that," she said. "You don't really think he could get away with something like that. I don't think you're being fair to him at all. He seems like a perfect gentleman."

The girl from. D.C. stood up from the sofa where she had been sitting. The general turned from the window and watched them talk, smiling politely. This made the girl from Washington nervous, but she said anyway, "Listen, the handwriting's on the wall, girls. Watch out."

"Well, there's nothing to worry about here, I can assure you," Jennifer said. But then she had that little embarrassed pause at the end that white people have when they think they might have said something racist.

The other girl from Washington scowled straight at the general and said, "He's not laying a hand on me."

"We'll make a pact," the first girl from Washington said. "It'll be like NATO, a mutual defense treaty. He doesn't lay a hand on any of us, and each of us will watch out for the others, to make sure he doesn't catch anybody off guard."

Jennifer thought this was unnecessary, but she agreed, as did the other girl from D.C. The girl from Chicago agreed to join the pact, too, but not enthusiastically. The general began humming a strange, African-sounding song, with lots of rhythm, but very little melody. He smiled at the girls and paced back and forth in front of the windows. He came back to the sofa where he'd been sitting, picked up his glass of Pernod and water from the side table, and drank the rest of the glass. He looked a little perplexed, a little irritated, the way someone looks when they are faced with an insurmountable language barrier. He bowed curtly to the girls and left the room.

A few minutes later the butler, a man who looked like he would be more at ease in a loincloth than the white tie and tails he was wearing, came in and summoned the girls to dinner. He led them into the dining room, and even the girls from Washington were mightily impressed.

The table was set magnificently, with two centerpieces of brilliantly colored and fragile and fragrant African flowers. The crystal and china was exquisite. The place settings had five spoons, three forks, and four knives. Wine coolers were set at all four corners of the enormous dining room table, but only five places were set. The chairs were by Chippendale, or they could have been, and there were fourteen of them in a matched set. The nine that weren't to be used were placed along the walls, away from the table.

The meal was an eight-course meal of the most delectable and interesting combination of French and Central African cuisine. The servants hovered inconspicuously behind the girls, whisking soup dishes out and plates in, but only when they were absolutely sure the girls were finished. The general was a gracious and congenial host. He managed to get the girls' hometowns out of them, and he pronounced the names of the towns with a thick French accent. At least they thought he was trying to get their hometowns. He understood Chicago and Washington very well. In fact he pointed to himself and talked on and on about Washington, as if he had spent some time there himself. He couldn't understand Spartanburg at all, though, and when Jennifer repeated over and over "South Carolina, South Carolina," he finally nodded and smiled politely, but he obviously didn't know what she was talking about.

There were five different wines served with the meal, not counting the champagne with dessert. Now, as I say, Jennifer didn't drink, and when the general tasted the first wine, and nodded that it was o.k. to serve it , she politely declined. The general seemed worried and shocked at that. The other girls just raved over the wine though, and one of the girls from Washington lowered her voice and said between the floral centerpieces that it was one of the best vintages ever and would go for better than a hundred fifty dollars a bottle.

The general sat with a polite but bemused smile through most of the dinner, and Jennifer noticed as the evening wore on that he was looking more and more at her. She on several occasions turned to catch him staring at her, and while he at first turned his glance away and politely paid attention to the other girls, by the third or fourth course,the general would keep looking at her when she caught him, and when she smiled, he would smile. There was nothing forward about it. He was very polite, but very masculine, and not at all apologetic in his manner.

And I can't say that I blame him at all. You know people change, at least in the way they look, pretty fast. I had seen Jennifer Sills a couple of years before this, when I was up at U. Va. for that Midwinters, and maybe she didn't look quite as good in Africa, but she looked fabulous that evening, as cold as it was, and as muddy as the front yard of the St. A. house was, and as drunk as I was. I'm not talking about glitzy, pin-up beauty. That doesn't move men. At least it doesn't move me that much. I mean it only works on celluloid or at a distance, with women who are made-up and in fancy clothes. I'm talking about something else. It's an inner beauty that shows out. The features don't make devastating women. It's something about the eyes, or the smile. There, that's enough, that's what Jennifer Sills had, and she has had it as long as I've known her. I can think about it right now, as long as it's been since I've seen her, and knowing she's probably starting to show wrinkles, and she might be fat or have her hair screwed up in some New York hairdo, but I can still fall madly in love with her in my dreams.

Now as for the wine, the other three girls, about halfway through the third course, just started ribbing Jennifer something awful, saying she really ought to at least taste some of this wine, that is was so expensive and so fine she might never get a chance to taste anything like it again. And the general and his servants seemed genuinely dismayed to see that she was refusing their hospitality. So she had a glass of white wine with the crayfish course, and since it was such a heady evening, she had the red wines with the other courses, and even got into the champagne with dessert.

You know the first time you drink it's probably going to affect you pretty strongly, but Jennifer didn't just drink a little bit.

It was disguised as delicious wines with a leisurely, eight course meal, and she just kept drinking and drinking without realizing what she was getting into. Plus you have to realize that all four of these girls had just been through the most traumatic day of their lives, and after all of that, here they found themselves in the most elegant of surroundings, delightfully entertained, with an elegant and urbane host who spoke nothing but French. I guess it was awfully easy just to give in and enjoy themselves a little.

When dessert was served- bananas and plantains and papayas and other tropical fruits they had never seen, all flambeed at the table- the general gave a signal to his servants. Folding paneled doors at one end of the dining room were opened to reveal an adjoining room with African musicians and women dancers and singers in native garb. They played and sang and danced some of the most beautiful music, low and rhythmic, with harmonies ranging far apart. Some of the dancers were full-bodied middle-aged women, some were absolutely beautiful young women, and some were topless girls in their early teens, with breasts like tangerines. All were deep throated in their singing, and not at all self-conscious.

Jennifer and the other American girls were struck dumb for the first couple of songs. Then they began applauding and chattering enthusiastically among themselves after each song was over. They smiled at the dancers and let them know how thrilled they were to be seeing this.

After a little champagne on top of the three different wines, and with that vibrant African music in the humid night air, with the French windows open and the drapes blowing gently in the breeze, well Jennifer got in the mood, and she got up and danced with the African women. I want to say Jennifer even took her cotton safari shirt off and danced topless in her skirt just like the other women.

I'm imagining that, surely. Mary Rogers didn't tell me about it, but it sure is fun to imagine. Anyway, Jennifer did some very sensual things in her dance, because she was drunk for the first time, and because she had just been through a terrible experience, and because she was in an exotic place that was far, far away from everything and everybody she knew.

The other American girls saw what was happening. They ganged together to keep Jennifer awake and clothed the rest of the evening, after the dancing was finished and when they retired with the general to the sitting room for a brief after-dinner drink.

They got Jennifer up to her bedroom safely and got into their own rooms safely and thought they had done a good job. It was a very hot night. Jennifer stripped out of her clothes and climbed into bed naked. She lay with a sheet over her, surrounded by the mosquito netting, but after a while she got too hot, so she kicked the sheet off and lay naked in the bed in the moonlight.

That's how the general found her when he came into her room. As for the actual seduction (and it was precisely that, a seduction, according to Mary Rogers), well, I don't know how that went.

That's a hell of a picture, the enormous general with slender Jennifer Sills, but according to Mary, it was not an unpleasant experience for Jennifer at all, especially after all the wine and, well, after everything.

You should have seen Mary Rogers telling this part, by the way, you know, late at night when the three of us were in that sitting room by ourselves. You know how people will talk about something as being repulsive, but the way they keep talking about it you know it turns them on. We heard a lot about the general.

The next morning, when Jennifer woke up next to the general, she might have felt differently, but it was still very early, just as the sun was coming up, and the general woke up, too, and reminded her of all the reasons the previous evening had not been unpleasant. Then he dressed politely and masculinely and left through a back passageway into an adjoining room.

By the time Jennifer got up and dressed and got down to breakfast, the other girls were already there, and the general had left for the day. The girls compared notes on the previous evening. They all ribbed Jennifer about getting drunk, but the girl from Washington said maybe she had been too quick to judge the general, he seemed like a gentleman after all, and maybe she was just too used to American men. The other girls agreed, and Jennifer didn't tell them anything at all about her experiences.

You know that line, "Will you respect me in the morning?" That is the woman's line because she knows in advance she's not going to respect herself in the morning, but she wants to do it tonight anyway. Jennifer starting feeling really bad about what she had done. Remember, this is a girl who grew up in Spartanburg, South Carolina. She didn't tell the other girls about it at all, but as the day wore on, she determined she sure as hell wasn't ever going to do it again, no matter how charming the general was.

Jennifer didn't really expect to have to face the general. She expected she would be taken to the American embassy that morning and be put on a plane home. All the girls expected that.

But nobody came to pick them up. The servants made no preparations for them to leave. The day went pretty much as the previous afternoon had gone. Nobody in the house acted as if they understood anything the girls said to them. The girls spent hours on the phone trying to contact someone who could help them, but the phone was dead most of the time, and when they could get it to operate they couldn't find anybody who could even speak English. The servants were very polite. They served them lunch by the pool and did everything in their power to make them comfortable.

By late afternoon the girls were starting to get angry. They talked about stealing a car and trying to drive into the city themselves, but Jennifer pointed out that they might very well end up in an Ubawayan jail for that, and that if they did break the law of the country they were in there was nothing the United States embassy could do to help. They weren't being mistreated, she said, and there might be some very good reason they were being held out here. The best thing might be to sit tight and wait.

Jennifer was ill at ease when she said that. She was determined not to have anything to drink that evening and to be quite firm with the general if he tried to make advances. She thought of telling the other girls just so they would know to have their guard up, but she couldn't bring herself to tell anyone at all.

One of the girls from Washington said she was convinced the general could understand English, at least some English, and she was determined to sit down and have a firm, clear talk with him when he got home.

But the general didn't come home that afternoon. The girls waited for him to arrive. They dressed for dinner and were served drinks on the sun porch, and then they had dinner in the dining room, not quite as luxurious as the night before, but almost. There was an empty chair for the general, but he never came.

Around ten o'clock in the evening, as they were finishing their dessert , they heard a car drive up out front. They thought it was the general. But it was the officer who had found them at the airport. He seemed very agitated. He told the girls, again in English that was difficult to understand, that the general extended his regrets, that he would not be able to make it home to entertain them that evening. The girls should go on to bed after dinner, the officer said, brusquely.

One of the girls from Washington stood up and confronted the officer, demanding to know what was happening and when they would be taken to the embassy. The officer was offended. He didn't even answer her. He summoned a servant and gave her brisk instructions in an African language, then he said good-night and left the room.

The girls sat at the table for a while discussing this. The girl from Washington was furious, but the others calmed her down and pointed out that the situation might indeed be more complicated than they were aware of, and they ought to be thankful they were here and comfortable and safe. The best thing to do, they decided, was to go to bed and see what happened.

It was eleven o'clock or so when the girls went to bed. The officer was still in the house, in the General's office down the hall from the sitting room. The light was on in the office. Through the closed door they could hear the officer speaking quietly on the phone in French.

When Jennifer get to her room, she took a nightgown out of the closet, but then she had second thoughts about that. She got in the bed fully clothed and pulled the sheets up to her chin. She couldn't sleep at all, worrying about what she was going to do when the General came. He was so big.

Through the open windows came the sounds of the landlocked tropics, a thousand insect cries and trills, monkeys screaming like human children in the distance, so sharp and sudden and eerie that Jennifer trembled. She heard thunderstorms in the distance and saw lightning reflected on the clouds. An hour or so later, Jennifer heard a car drive up in front of the mansion, and she tensed up.

It was quite some time before she heard the heavy footsteps outside her door. There was a light knock, but Jennifer didn't answer. Then the door opened slowly, and in the light from the hallway, Jennifer could see the enormous silhouette of the general. She could barely breathe. The general came into the room and closed the door quietly behind him.

"Jennifair," he said softly, but with self-assurance. Jennifer didn't answer him. She saw him begin to take his uniform jacket off. He unbuttoned it and was slipping it back off his shoulders, when the door suddenly burst open behind him.

What happened then was so quick and so violent Jennifer couldn't see it. There was movement and struggling. Men came dashing in through the door. Two of them jumped on her bed, tore the mosquito netting down, and smothered her with a pillow so she couldn't scream out. Jennifer fought and kicked and screamed into the pillow, but she couldn't see a thing. There was a loud struggle and kicking and grunting near the door, and then a sickening sputtering and gurgling sound, and the light came on. The men let Jennifer go and took the pillow from her face.

Jennifer saw the General standing with his eyes wide open and his hands to his throat. Blood was spurting out between his hands like out of a fountain, spraying over the room and the foot of the bed. He fell to the floor. Behind him was the officer who had brought them from the airport. The officer was holding a bloody knife curved like a sickle. His hands and the cuffs of his uniform were covered in blood. He was breathing heavily and looked scared.

Jennifer screamed and screamed and screamed, not fighting any more, but the men quickly smothered her cries with the pillow again. She heard the general kicking on the floor and saw the blood spray a few more seconds, and then he was still.

The officer issued orders breathlessly to the soldiers holding Jennifer. The soldiers tore the bedsheets into strips and used them to gag her tightly and bind her hands and feet. Then they picked her up and carried her out of the room. The general's body was motionless on the floor. The soldiers carried Jennifer downstairs and out the front door to a waiting Mercedes. The officer followed a couple of minutes later carrying two boxes of documents. He jumped in the front seat of the Mercedes next to the driver. Jennifer was in the back seat between the two soldiers.

The officer spoke to the driver. The Mercedes roared away from the mansion, down the long, moonlit driveway without headlights.

It was a horrible drive all that night at speeds that would have terrified anyone, on roads that were curvy and full of potholes. Once a woman in a grass skirt ran in front of the car just like a rabbit runs in front of a car in the U.S. at night, confused by the headlights and the speed. Jennifer saw her and screamed. The driver tried to swerve, but he couldn't miss her. She was knocked up in the air, over the roof of the car. The driver cursed, but he never slowed down.

They drove all that night and on past the dawn, out of the hills and onto the plain, so that in the early daylight they were barreling down a sand track. The driver drove as fast as he could on the hard, rocky sections of road, and when he hit the soft sand and dust he would race the engine and down shift, working through the gears until the car slowed to ten miles an hour or less, plowing through the sand. Jennifer was so exhausted she was nodding in and out of sleep.

An hour or two after sunup they came to a village, a shanty town really, in the middle of the plain. The driver leaned on the horn to clear camels out of the road in front of them. They stopped in front of a ramshackle store. The owner of the store, a fat Asian man, came out onto the porch with his wife. When the officer got out of the car the store owner looked scared. The officer shouted at him in some language that was unknown to Jennifer. The Asian man put his palms together and nodded and bowed. He fueled the Mercedes from a stack of fifty-gallon drums beside the front porch.

The officer stood in front of the Mercedes and stretched and scratched himself. The sun was an orange disc low over the plain.

The officer said something in French to the two soldiers in the back seat. They unbound Jennifer, took her out of the Mercedes, and led her through the store to the owners' bedroom.

Jennifer was dressed in a khaki skirt and a purple polo shirt. The store owner and his wife glanced briefly at her as she passed through the store. They lowered their eyes.

The soldiers sat Jennifer down in a wooden chair and stood guard over her. The officer came into the room and paced nervously back and forth in front of Jennifer. He shook his head.

"You are beautiful woman, " he said. "American woman. Young and strong woman."

He paced some more.

"Kanahwa is pig. Is dead pig. I kill him for many reason. I am hero. But is dangerous. Is dangerous for me, for you is better. Kanahwa is pig. He will sell you."

This was all so confusing to Jennifer that she broke down and started to cry. She held her face in her hands and slumped forward in the chair and cried. The officer shooed the soldiers from the room. He pulled up a chair and sat in front of Jennifer and stroked her blond hair, which I imagine hung not quite to her shoulders at this time in her life.

"You are beautiful woman. Life take you," he said.

Jennifer just sobbed and sobbed and couldn't say anything. She couldn't resist as he held her and hugged her and stroked her hair. He was very gentle. He didn't force her at all. But there was nothing she could have done to resist. The soldiers were right outside, and she was in the middle of God knows where in the middle of God knows what, and nobody in the United States even knew she was alive, much less where she was. She had no papers of any kind, and she had just been involved in the assassination of a powerful general. There was nothing Jennifer could have done, maybe.

The bed was a canvas-covered straw tick. The officer didn't finish undressing himself or Jennifer. Jennifer was just in shock.

When Jennifer walked out of the bedroom with the officer afterwards, the store owner and his wife were wide-eyed. The soldiers got in the front seat of the Mercedes this time with the driver, and the officer and Jennifer got in the back. They sped away from the village on a track that was in even worse shape than the one they had been traveling on since before sunup. Jennifer could see tall, hazy, jungle-covered mountains in the distance.

"Now friends of Kanahwa try kill me," the officer said, holding Jennifer's hand between his like a doting husband. The cuffs of his uniform shirt were still bloody.

"We go to mountain. With rebels. *Les Marxistes.*"

Who knows what Jennifer was thinking at this time, really.

Maybe she was thinking about the other girls back at the general's mansion, and how the murder would have been discovered by this time in the morning, and what might be happening to them. Maybe Jennifer wasn't thinking that clearly at all. More than likely she was just completely overwhelmed, on the edge of a nervous breakdown. Think where she had come from in the last forty-eight hours, and what she had been through.

Anyway, here Jennifer was in the Mercedes bouncing across the plain, which was getting rougher and rougher, broken by small hills and ravines. The driver kept the Mercedes engine racing, but they were making very poor time. Plus, they had cut the air conditioner off because the engine was overheating, so they were driving with the windows down, and the day was getting hotter. They were covered in dust.

They must have gone on at least another hour or so. They were far away from the village. The two soldiers in the front seat spoke to each other occasionally, but no one else in the car could hear them for the roar of the engine. Jennifer noticed this, even as agitated as she was, and she began to wonder about it, but the officer was too fascinated by Jennifer to pay attention. He kept his arm around her shoulders, and Jennifer could see that there was a bulge in his trousers.

They had just climbed out of a ravine and were driving through a narrow pass at the top when the soldier nearest the driver pulled out his pistol and put it to the head of the driver and shouted to him. The driver stopped the car. The officer leaned forward to say something, but he never got a word out. The other soldier spun in the seat, stuck his pistol up to the face of the officer, and fired three bullets into his head.

Jennifer was very lucky none of the bullets hit her. But she was sprayed with blood and whatever came out of the back of the officer's head. He fell back onto her dead already. Blood soaked her clothes.

Jennifer was screaming. She pushed the officer's body off her and opened the door and jumped out, in hysterics. She ran down the road into the ravine screaming and crying and waving her hands like she was trying to sling the blood off them.

The two soldiers got out and chased her and, when she tripped over a rock, caught her at the bottom of the ravine. Jennifer fought them like a madwoman, biting and kicking, but they were very strong. They picked her up and carried her back to the Mercedes, laughing. The driver was sitting forlornly on the ground behind the car with his legs folded. The soldiers kicked him out of the way and shouted at him. Then they stripped Jennifer's clothes off her and tied her by her wrists naked to the rear bumper of the Mercedes. This was not an easy process, because Jennifer fought them hard, and they hit her several times very hard themselves before she stopped fighting.

One of the soldiers unbuckled his trousers and dropped them, but the other grabbed him playfully by the arm and pulled him out of the way. This other soldier then unbuckled his trousers and stepped up to go first, but the first one shouted at him good-naturedly and pulled him away. The soldiers were walking with their pants around their ankles, with erections. It started out as a joking argument in a language that sounded as strange to Jennifer as any human language could sound, but the argument quickly turned nasty, and then they were shouting at each other viciously.

The first soldier railed at the second, waving his finger and nodding his head and shaking his head. Whatever he said- and it took him a long time to say it- cowed the other soldier. The victor then stepped up behind Jennifer with an angry look and prepared to go first. When he turned his back on the other soldier, though, the other soldier bent down and pulled his pistol from his holster near his ankles and shot his companion in the back.

The force of the bullet knocked the first soldier across Jennifer and onto the ground. The one who had shot him came over, spat at him, and kicked him out of the way. Jennifer was kicking and screaming and trying to free her wrists, but the soldier held his pistol up to the back of her neck to make her hold still.

As he was just about to rape her, the soldier who had been shot rolled over, barely alive, raised his pistol, and shot the man who had shot him. He hit the man twice, once in the shoulder, which spun the man around, and then once squarely in the middle of the chest.

Now both soldiers were down and dying, and Jennifer was hanging by her wrists on the bumper and crying. The driver jumped up and ran to each soldier and kicked their guns away from them.

Then he paced around the car nervously, talking to himself and nodding his head for several minutes waiting for both of them to die.

They groaned and writhed for a while, but in the end they died, and the driver untied Jennifer from the bumper. He gestured for her to get in the car. But Jennifer was naked, and her shirt and skirt were torn to pieces. Jennifer stripped one of the dead soldiers and put on his pants. The driver stopped her from putting the bloody shirt on. He pulled off his uniform shirt and gave it to her, leaving himself with just his undershirt.

Jennifer was going to pull the dead officer out of the back seat , but the driver shouted at her, waved her away, and pushed her into the front passenger seat. He closed the rear doors and got in and drove.

It took nearly the rest of the day to drive into the foothills of the mountains. The officer's body stank of blood and open brains, and there were flies crawling over it in the back seat.

The transition from desert plain to the forest of the foothills was very abrupt. As soon as the road began to gain some altitude, tall, dry grass began to appear, dotted with lone trees, then with clumps of trees, and after two or three miles, they were climbing steeply into the forest on a road that looked like it hadn't been traveled by a car or truck in weeks or months. They hadn't gone far at all into this thick forest when a group of men in khaki bermuda shorts and old-style undershirts stepped out in the road in front of them. The were carrying World War I rifles. A couple of them were carrying machine guns and wearing bandoliers over their shoulders. The driver stopped the car. The rebels immediately surrounded it.

I remember hearing this part of the story from Mary Rogers. I remember her getting so wrapped up in the story that she reached right up under her boobs and pulled the underwire of her bra down to make herself more comfortable. You'd have to know Mary Rogers to appreciate that. And my brother was just loving the story, the High School head cheerleader and the three-hundred pound African despot.

Well, anyway, oh, to catch you up on it all, and I knew this part before I heard Mary Rogers's story, nobody in the U.S. knew that Jennifer and the others had survived the plane crash for something like six months afterwards. I know it was a terrible strain on Jennifer's family, because everyone was assumed dead in the explosion, I mean there was no report of any of the students having been off the plane when it blew up, but there was such a diplomatic stink and such complications from the coup (the general's murder had been part of a coup d'etat), anyway, the U.S. and British authorities didn't get hold of any of the remains for months, and by that time they were badly deteriorated, and it took a long time for them to sift through all the evidence and finally determine that six students had not died on board the plane.

By this time, Jennifer was either with the Marxists or in South Yemen. And again, I wasn't that close to the story at that time in my life, and I don't remember the exact details, but I do know Mr. Sills flew to Ubaway and spent weeks or months following his daughter's trail, raising all kinds of hell through Senator Thurmond to get the State Department and the CIA to cooperate. Mary Rogers said he never did find out anything at all about Jennifer in Ubaway.

Anyway, she said Mr. Sills wasn't able to trace Jennifer's track at all until one of the girls from Washington showed up in Tanzania a year later, having escaped from white slavery. That's what had happened to the three girls who were left at the general's house after the murder. The other two girls were never found, as far as I know, and an investigation much later turned up that the two boys had died in the violence of the coup there in the Ubawayan capital. Grisly stuff.

Anyway, so here's Jennifer in this Mercedes in the foothills of the jungle covered mountains, surrounded by the Marxist insurgency, and with the stinking corpse of the officer in the back seat. The driver, you see, had brought the corpse of the officer along as a sort of entrance visa. The driver jumped out of the car and began babbling to the guerillas, smiling and bowing his head and doing a sort of curtsy where one knee touched the ground. He pointed to the dead officer in the back seat and spoke excitedly for a long time, pointing his forefinger like a pistol barrel and saying, "Pah! Pah!" like he had shot the officer himself. The rebels stuck their heads in the back windows of the car to look at the body, and they seemed quite pleased. The officer had started to bloat by this time.

Then the driver pointed at Jennifer and told a long, loud story,. The rebels looked disapprovingly at her. They made her get out of the car and sat her on a log while their leader questioned the driver at length. Some of the rebels, many of them boys who didn't look much over thirteen or fourteen, stood around Jennifer and stared at her. One old man came over and touched her blond hair in fascination.

The leader of the rebels shouted at him and gave the group around Jennifer a long harangue, pointing at Jennifer like a Baptist preacher pointing toward the seedy section of town during his sermon.

You know this story can get awfully long, just drag and drag on out. It got long while Mary Rogers was telling it that night at the ___________'s house. The group in the kitchen must have gotten their egg and sausage casserole cooked and eaten, and a lot of them must have drifted on away. Anyway, the story falls apart a little bit for me here. Let me see if I can reconstruct it.

The rebels held Jennifer as a prisoner, in a low mud hut with guards at the door. The only thing that comes to my mind is those mud huts like the Masai build in Kenya. My mother went to Kenya year before last and was showing Mary Ruth and me pictures of a Masai village she had visited. But this wasn't Kenya, and these weren't Masai tribesmen. It was a low mud hut in a guerilla camp in the jungle-clad mountains of the far reaches of Ubaway.

Let's try to imagine how she got out of the mud hut and into the guerilla leader's hut. Doesn't take a lot of imagination, but this guy was a dedicated revolutionary, and surely he would have had to formulate his self-justification in a different way from, say, General Kanahwa or the two soldiers in the Mercedes. Anyway, this was the next of Jennifer Sills' lovers in the three years she was gone.

Mary Rogers didn't say much about him, except that he couldn't speak English either, and he tried and tried to teach Jennifer French, but he didn't get very far. He had one of the native women in the camp try to teach Jennifer an Ubawayan language, and apparently Jennifer learned enough to be able to ask for something to eat or drink, but not enough to be able to tell anyone anything about herself. This lack of facility in learning foreign languages is not surprising in an American, even in someone as intelligent as Jennifer, but it was particularly frustrating for the Ubawayans, who had lived all their lives in a multilingual society. Most of them had been polyglots since they were children.

The commander of the guerilla forces, a handsome young man in his thirties who had attended the Sorbonne and the University of Moscow, was not a very patient man. He railed at Jennifer and lectured her for hours in their tent after she had moved in with him.

He even hit her on one occasion, and I think by and large it was a bad five months for Jennifer. She lost a lot of weight and got sick and was even unable to get out of her cot for a couple of weeks. When she was well enough, the sex with the rebel commander was torrid, as the sex in stormy and unfounded relationships often is. The commander, whose name was X.lada.l, was a very strong willed and egotistical man. The guerillas did practically no fighting while Jennifer was with there, but the commander spoke to his troops every day while they sat cross legged on the open ground in the middle of the camp compound. X.lada.l was a mesmerizing speaker.

He would inspire the guerillas for hours, and they would raise their fists and shake them in unison and shout slogans and cheer. This was the only time Jennifer ever saw X.lada.l look happy. He never seemed happy when he was with her.

Jennifer's hair was cut very short while she stayed with the guerillas. She was dressed in khaki fatigues, and she wore water buffalo sandals. She ate native foods, a kind of doughy, unleavened bread and unknown meats and spicy bean concoctions. She didn't eat much, as it usually made her sick. X.lada.l was particularly cruel when she was sick.

All in all it was a bad time. You know when you get in a situation like that, no matter how miserable it is, you're surviving, and when the minimum conditions necessary for survival are there, that seems to be enough to trap most of us in inaction. You see it every day all around you, someone in a miserable marriage, living with an alcoholic mother or husband or child, staying with a wife beater or cowering daily in front of a scold. We all do it to a certain extent. Jennifer stayed in that camp in the wilds of Ubaway and became and acted like something it's difficult for me to imagine Jennifer Sills being, a pathetic creature. Oh well, I'm making a judgment there. There's probably a hell of a lot I don't know and never will know. Maybe there was a lot to X.lada.l that actually made him attractive to Jennifer.

After five or six months with the Ubawayan rebels, one day Jennifer noticed a great stir moving through the camp. It was early in the morning, when the smoke from the cooking fires made the camp air foul, and Jennifer's first thoughts were that there was actually going to be some fighting for once, and perhaps the camp was under attack.

But it was only a small column of more rebels, carrying a shipment of AK 47 rifles and ammunition. And leading the column was a white man, the first white man Jennifer had seen since the airplane blew up.

This man was a Bulgarian agent who was working with the rebels. He spoke the Ubawayan language with grace and ease. He also spoke English, a sort of school English, that had never had the polishing that comes from living in contact with native speakers.

But here was the first person in half a year with whom Jennifer could communicate.

She poured out her heart to him, and he translated much of what she told him for the rebels. The rebels were shocked to hear the story of the plane blowing up and her being kidnapped. The driver of the Mercedes had told them only that she was General Kanahwa's mistress.

To hear Mary Rogers tell it, this Bulgarian secret agent (or he could have been Hungarian, or maybe Romanian- I'm not sure Mary really knew herself), this guy was a sort of East bloc James Bond, a fabulously handsome and daring and self-possessed man, in his late thirties or early forties, with a hard body and acres of chest hair peppered with gray. He spoke half a dozen languages and was debonair and dashing and not at all flashy and not at all fake.

Anyway, Jennifer fell in love with this guy. I mean he was not just another in the string of men who essentially owned her over the next two and a half years. She genuinely was in love with him. She begged him to take her with him when he left the rebels.

The Bulgarian didn't like the idea of an American girl being held against her will by the rebels. He didn't really like the idea of Jennifer being American period. At any rate, if you think about it just a little bit, she would have been an enormous political liability to him, and he was above all a dedicated and devout Marxist revolutionary. Despite all that, or maybe partially because of it, he took Jennifer with him on the arduous cross-country trek into Ethiopia.

I would imagine that was an adventure of the highest sort, wouldn't you? Crossing the Central African wastes with a man like that. And sitting around a campfire in the desert night with him and the other five or six heavily armed Africans, all squatting on their lean haunches. The sky was full of stars as you and I may never see it. And here this man was telling her of all he had seen and done in exotic locations all over the world. And he, by example really, simply by being himself and not debating or arguing or trying to sell, almost convinced Jennifer of the inevitability and moral rectitude of Marxist revolution.

Listen, I'm fudging a little bit here, really, as if you couldn't tell. I don't remember this part of the story very well. What I do remember is almost more like a dream, and I think I may have taken some of what I heard and combined it with some of what I know and some of what I imagine about African geography and geopolitics. I remember Mary Rogers telling about Jennifer living in a castle overlooking the sea with the Bulgarian (or the Hungarian or Romanian- really, now, you don't think Mary Rogers would know the difference between those places?) And this place is very clear to me. It could have been in Ethiopia, come to think of it, but I've always imagined it being in South Yemen. It would have been medieval and Spartan, in a poor Marxist country of course, but the sun would be blindingly bright, like something out of a Camus novel, and the deep, blue Red Sea would stretch out against the desert blue sky, down the steep hill from the castle wall.

This was another hard time for Jennifer, because no matter how difficult it would have been to contact her parents from this place, it would have been possible. And I'm sure she knew full well what agonies they were going through, and I'm sure she was homesick. Jennifer was the kind of girl to whom family means a lot. I always would have picked her as the kind of girl who would marry a doctor and live in a small Southern town and join the Junior League, although I suppose I was all wrong about that in the end. Anyway, the Bulgarian must have been laying some heavy stuff on her in a very subtle way. Surely it took a lot to keep her from getting away from him and trying to contact her parents.

Well, to me it's easy to see the whole thing, the candlelight dinners- the long conversations in the Bulgarian's constantly improving English. The strong, mysterious, gorgeous man who was the only person with whom she could communicate. Sunbathing nude on the castle walls. Swimming in the Red Sea at night by moonlight, and making love on the rocks as the small waves lapped underneath them. Jennifer could have told herself she would stay only a little bit longer, planning all the while to contact someone who could get her back to the States. That's the easiest way to stay somewhere forever, just one day longer.

Jennifer would have gained weight, and she would be suntanned. Her hair grew back and was bleached by the sun. She was happy, and she had that glow around her of a woman in love.

There was a young Russian, a KGB agent named Aleksandr, who was stationed at the embassy in the ancient city where Jennifer and the Bulgarian were staying. Mary Rogers wasn't clear about how they met. I imagine it could have been at some embassy gathering, a picnic or an outing to the beach, or maybe the KGB agent was in fairly close contact with the Bulgarian and saw Jennifer there at the castle with him. And I've got to admit this is the only part of the story that I find difficult to understand. Maybe I'm just too phlegmatic by breeding and nationality, and it would take someone as fiery as a Russian to do what Aleksandr did, but he did everything he could to steal Jennifer away from the Bulgarian.

Jennifer didn't like Aleksandr even. He didn't bathe regularly. His breath stank of onions and garlic. He had a thick-lipped, circles-under-the-eyes look about him, and although he was young and very fit, Jennifer didn't find him attractive at all. If she realized he was trying to make moves on her, she didn't let on that she did. I don't think the Bulgarian considered Aleksandr to be enough of a threat to worry about. He didn't like the young Russian. He treated him the way a man treats someone who is in same business as he but who is not as successful or as renowned.

The Bulgarian occasionally left South Yemen or wherever they were for quick trips to Libya or Iraq or Lebanon. He was never gone longer than a few days, and when he left, Jennifer would have the castle to herself with two local serving women. She got lonely, but the Bulgarian's hold was so strong on her that she never took advantage of these times to try to contact her parents. I think she even began to think it might be better to let them think she was dead, and to go on and live another life, doing things she could never do as Jennifer Sills.

After Jennifer had been with the Bulgarian for many months, he left one weekend for a trip to Greece. Jennifer went about her normal routine after he left. She slept late, read an old paperback copy of a William Styron novel, and went out onto the parapet about eleven o'clock to sunbathe nude. The parapet was higher than any surrounding building, and the parapet wall shrouded her from view below.

Around noon, Jennifer heard a tremendous ruckus going on in the open courtyard of the castle. One of the serving women was shouting at a man, and from the sound of it she was having a scuffle with him. Jennifer threw on her robe and went down the stone steps to the courtyard. She was met on the way by Aleksandr, who looked wild.

The Russian could speak no English at all, and Jennifer certainly couldn't speak any Russian, so the two of them had never had a direct conversation in the brief time they had known each other.

Aleksandr began babbling to Jennifer in a voice that was crazy and desperate but firm. He tried to take her by the hand and pull her down the stairs with him, but she backed away. He babbled on and on. In the end he was on his knees on the stone steps, with tears in his eyes, begging her in lovely sounding Russian with lots of "zh" and "sh".

Jennifer might have felt a little sorry for Alexandr, and she certainly didn't have any honor left to preserve. Who knows? She was free at the moment to do as she chose, so if Aleksandr had found a little dignity within himself, he might have gotten lucky that afternoon without going to all the trouble he went to. But he found no dignity at all- if he ever looked.

Jennifer had turned around and was headed back up the stairs in her robe, when the Russian grabbed her from behind and threw her over his shoulders. He ran down the stairs and out of the tower into the courtyard. Jennifer was cursing him and pounding her fists on his back. The two serving women came running and tried to trip up the Russian. They were screeching at him in Arabic and clawing at his face and kicking at his heels, but he was a strong and sure-footed young man, and he just laughed at them and kept running.

He carried Jennifer out of the very small passageway that led through the seaward side of the castle wall. Just outside the passageway two Arab men were waiting. They beat back the two serving women who were chasing Aleksandr. Aleksandr carried Jennifer kicking and screaming down the rocky path to the sea.

Offshore was a large white ketch, a luxury yacht in the seventy- to eighty-foot range, a very rare sight in this part of the world. A rubber Zodiac dingy was already zipping in toward the shore to pick them up.

Oh, come on! you say. Right, the Russian makes love to her on the yacht and they sail away to some tropical island. Well, I'm not making the story up. I'm telling it as I learned it myself.

That's what happened. That's the story as I got it. Even though Jennifer wasn't really happy with this Alexandr guy, she had been through enough of this stuff that she was kind of hardened to it by now, so she made the best of the situation.

Mary said what really kept Jennifer going through the next three men was sex. That's what she said. She said Jennifer couldn't talk to them, and they kept her from getting out and talking to other people. As a matter of fact, when she was with the Pakistani fellow, for several months she didn't even know where on Earth she was. She was just despondent, had more or less given up on life, and had, I suppose, become almost an entirely different person from the one I had known, or from the one she was eventually to become after all of this was over. The sex was at least some form of intimate contact with another human being.

O.k., let's see, Aleksandr was the fifth man, so yes, I think there were three more after him. The story all over Spartanburg was that she had passed through the hands of eight men in those three years. This was the part of the story that was only told in low voices late at night, when the dirtiest dirt comes out. So I am inclined to believe it.

To be perfectly frank, I don't remember the part between the abduction on the sailing yacht and Indonesia. There was something about Malay pirates, I think. Surely Mary Rogers didn't know enough geography to have told that part of the story right, anyway. I just remember my brother clapping and laughing as she told each succeeding episode. I would have thought his behavior would turn Mary Rogers off, but the more he delighted in the story, the juicier her telling of it became. If I hadn't made my brother get in the car with me and go home, I wouldn't have been surprised if he had gotten Mary Rogers in the rack that night. He owes me a lot for saving him from that sight first thing in the morning.

Anyway, before this thing gets too long, let's jump on to Indonesia, which I think is the best part of the story, anyway. I'm convinced Mary Rogers has no earthly idea where Indonesia is, and

I would say she could have been talking about the Philippines or India or Madagascar, for that matter. But let's call it Indonesia.

Jennifer had been bought from the pirates by this Pakistani merchant living in Indonesia, and he made her his wife. She was with him the better part of a year, in some small seacoast town a hundred miles or so from Jakarta. Anyway, one afternoon, as Jennifer was sitting at an upstairs window of their house in the marketplace, leaning out the window with her chin in her palm, brooding and thinking about home, she noticed an American-looking man walking through the crowd. She watched him, because she happened to be thinking about home at the time. As she was watching, he looked up, and their eyes met. Now, Jennifer was still a beautiful woman, and she still had her long blond hair, which of course was very unusual here and very striking, and the man kept looking back up at her, and she kept catching him at it, and he would glance away, and after a moment glance back again, until his expression changed to one of puzzled recognition, and he stared at her without embarrassment. Jennifer was about to leave the window, when suddenly it struck her. She did know this man.

He was Fred R. Helms.

I doubt Fred R. knew Jennifer's parents. I doubt he knew Jennifer well enough to speak to her at a cocktail party. But Jennifer was a friend of his daughter, and he would have seen her around at his house a time or two, and he certainly would have heard the story of her disappearance, which was unusual enough even to have caught Fred R. Helms's attention.

Fred R., by the way, was in Indonesia looking into buying a factory that made T-shirts, and only by a stroke of the most outlandish fate was he killing an afternoon wandering through the marketplace of this smallish town.

Jennifer came running downstairs dressed in her sarong. She ran up to Fred R. with a little bow, almost third-world in her movements. It threw Fred R. back. But before long she was the girl from Spartanburg, South Carolina, gushing out all that had happened to her, well, not near all, really, but enough to explain vaguely what she was doing here and how happy she was to see him. In fact, after a few minutes there in the middle of the crowded street, with people standing around them and staring like they were freaks, she broke down and started crying and hugged him like he was her own father.

Fred R. took her back to his hotel. He bought her lunch and a drink in the restaurant while she told him as much of her story as she could bring herself to tell. (It took many months I think for the story I have told you to come out and gel on the gossip circuit. The early versions weren't nearly as juicy.) Her Pakistani husband had convinced her that if she traveled alone in Indonesia without papers, she would be picked up immediately by the police and thrown in prison, and that even he couldn't get her out, because she was in the country illegally.

The Pakistani was a kind man, and he worshiped her. He told her every day that she could never go back to her family and the way of life she had known before, and she eventually heard that so much that she began half to believe it herself. She believed it enough to stay with him and not try to run to Jakarta to the American embassy, even though she would lie in bed at night and tell herself she would go the next week. She had been doing that for better than six months.

Jennifer broke down again and cried in the hotel restaurant, a Dutch colonial place, with wing-backed wicker chairs and ceiling fans and ferns and tropical plants all around. She said the Pakistani might very well be right, that she could never go back and live that life, that she had been kept like a slave for three years, and she didn't know that she could ever be what an American woman was supposed to be.

This part about the American woman didn't move Fred R. too much, but he was moved by Jennifer's condition. She was still beautiful. She was more than beautiful. There was still that something I've been trying to get a handle on for all these years. She really could get to you.

Fred R. took her shopping and bought her a week or two's worth of western clothes and got her out of the sarong. He told her not to be ridiculous, that the Pakistani was just trying to keep her for himself, that she had nothing to worry about from him. Fred R. said this in the way a man like him says those things.

I imagine that there are plenty of places and bureaucracies in the world where even Fred R. Helms would find he had very little influence. But in Indonesia, where he was negotiating to buy a T-shirt mill from one of the most well-connected businessmen in the country, he had as much influence as he needed. He was able to get

Jennifer's traveling papers straightened out quickly enough for her to leave the country with him later that week.

They flew first to Hong Kong, and then to Honolulu, where they had a thirty-six hour layover booked to recover from jet lag. Fred R., as much as he jetted around the world, still suffered terribly from the time changes, and he made it a point to allow a day of rest for each six hours of change. Jennifer could have flown on home without him. In fact she was very anxious to get home to her parents, but for some reason she didn't. Maybe there was some problem getting a seat on the connecting flight. I don't know. For whatever reason, she and Fred R. spent the night at the airport Sheraton in Honolulu.

The story goes, and I heard this from more people than Mary Rogers, that Fred. R. was hot on Jennifer's trail from the first night or two she stayed in the hotel in Indonesia. I can't tell what makes a man behave like that. Halfway around the world, in an adventurous setting with a girl who had seen more of the world and more adventure than he had ever seen. And a beautiful girl at that, even if she was a close friend of his daughter. Well, when it comes to this area of human relations, nothing anybody does should surprise us.

Anyway, apparently by the time they got to Honolulu, after Fred R. spent the night on the plane trying to sleep in the seat next to Jennifer, well, he just lost his better judgment, and he made a pass at her that night in a crowded restaurant, a kind of tacky, plastic-tropical place downstairs in the hotel. He got a glass of red wine in his face for whatever he said.

Poor old Fred R. I mean think about it. After all she had been through, and as many hands as she had passed through in the previous three years, you would think she could handle a come-on a little more gracefully than that. Plus she had to spend eight hours sitting next to the man on the plane the next day.

Somehow they did that and arrived back in South Carolina the next evening to be greeted by Jennifer's family and the local press, who made quite a story of the whole affair for the next few months. Jennifer's family was as happy as human beings can be.

As for Jennifer, she apparently had very few problems adjusting to life back in the States. I imagine the first few months were traumatic enough, but she very soon moved to New York and found a job selling textiles to the garment industry. She married some fellow she met up there, and the last I heard she had two kids. I haven't seen her since before she get married. But the last I saw her she was still very good-looking. A little older and a little hard. A little too business-like for my tastes, but she certainly didn't look like a girl who had gone through what she went through.

If you think about it, though, and I certainly have thought about it over the years, I don't understand how she could have gone through what she did in that part of the world in those years without, and I know you hate to hear it, without being infected with that dread disease. Plus, figure all the times she had sex unprotected, and never got pregnant, and then she comes back to the States, gets married, and has two perfectly healthy kids, bang, bang. Maybe you don't like to think about those details, but I just can't shake them out of my mind when I think about the story.

It's bothered me enough that I asked my old college roommate about it a couple of years ago. He was doing his residency in gynecology up in Baltimore, and he and his wife were down visiting his family one Christmas, and I took him to my duck blind on the river. Anyway, you know how you get to talking about things in a duck blind when there aren't any ducks flying. I told him the story of Jennifer Sills, and when I got through, he anticipated my questions. I was expecting some scientific explanation from him. You know how young doctors love to use their medical vocabularies. But he just took a long draw on his cigar, turned up the pint of rum we had been sharing, swallowed, and twisted the cap back on the bottle. Then he belched and said, "Well, it just goes to show. You can't ever tell."

The Eighth Tale
Ramon Alejandro becomes another man.

Ramon Alejandro was the trusted aide to a member of the ruling junta of a certain Latin American country during the nineteen-sixties. Ramon was a tall, light-skinned and light-haired young man, in his mid-thirties. He wore a rather thick mustache and horn rim glasses that were so weak they looked like he wore them for ornament. His shoulders were broad, and though his stomach bulged considerably more than would be considered acceptable these days, he was quite a fit man for that time. He was handsome, too, undeniably so. Ramon was a widower, his wife having died giving birth to their daughter, their second child. The older child was a boy, and at the time this story begins he was no more than six or seven years old.

Above all else, I would say Ramon Alejandro was a man of honor. That's a slippery thing- honor- if you look at people in the clear light. No man can be entirely honest, and no man can be entirely fair. No man can be entirely courageous. Those people we look on as examples of honor are usually either very old, so we don't know them very well, or they're dead. You hear occasionally (in fact very occasionally these days) someone say such and so was an honest man, "Now there goes an honest man." But he has certainly told his share of lies in his lifetime, and certainly the truth he tells does not always include that portion that is inconvenient for him.

To my mind, Ramon was a very honorable man, in the sense that is entirely out of fashion in our society today. He never knowingly told a lie. He never took the convenient way out of a situation for cowardice's sake.

I don't know if you've ever met a man like this. It's easy for me to idealize him. I shouldn't. All human beings are different, and what set him apart was that he was a man almost everyone silently admired, so even when he did or said something less than manly or less than admirable, everyone was immediately willing to forgive it, because they preferred to have him be what they admired him for being.

Enough of this. You might hardly expect to find a man like Ramon Alejandro involved in politics, but that had a lot to do with his courage.

It's funny that I look back on Ramon Alejandro like this. I never knew him in his honorable and courageous days. Or maybe I did.

Ramon was the envy of the other generals in the ruling junta. He was loyal to his general- unfailingly so. He was handsome and articulate and strong, strong enough to have envied his general's power, or at least to let his ego make him want to handle more and take credit for more than he did. He could have gotten away with that. His general knew Ramon was a formidable young man, and he would have let Ramon go as far as he could before he tried to quash him. An older man like that knows what it takes to come to power, and he can recognize the younger men who will someday take his power away, just as he took power from his mentor. But Ramon was very loyal. The general had chosen him as a young lieutenant, and had brought him along in his career, and had been a friend, almost a father, during that very difficult time after Ramon's wife died.

Several of the other generals had made advances to Ramon that would have allowed him to leave his general and increase his stature and power, but Ramon would have nothing to do with them. Ramon's general was savvy enough to know this.

During the early seventies, when the Maoist insurgency in the jungle provinces was beginning to threaten the rule of the junta, Ramon's general was chosen to lead the national forces in the field. He chose Ramon to sit in his place on the junta while he was gone. He also asked Ramon to move into his house while he was away, so he could watch after the general's wife and mother in his absence. Ramon was hesitant to do this at first, but the general insisted. He said he was worried the guerillas might send infiltrators to harm his family, and that there was no one else on earth he could trust like Ramon to protect them. So when the rainy season ended, and the general left to lead the first offensive, Ramon and his little son and daughter moved into the general's estate on the plain outside the capital city.

It was a large mansion with some two hundred hectares of cropland and formal gardens surrounding it. Ramon's children, who had lived all their lives in Ramon's modest city house, were quiet and abashed the day they arrived, but soon they were running and playing all over the house and hiding and chasing each other in the formal garden.

The general's wife was nearly twenty years younger than her husband. She was a former actress, and she was still quite attractive for a woman her age. She had dark hair cut to curve in at the nape of her neck. She had medium-sized, firm breasts, and the kind of bottom that is considered very sexy in Latin societies. Well, it was a nice looking bottom, although there was that little jiggle in it that age brings. She had a sharp but pretty nose, and big, dark eyes. She usually wore very red lipstick.

The general's wife just couldn't stand it when Ramon moved into her house with his beautiful, rambunctious, happy children. She didn't have any children of her own. She was kind of a sad woman, because while her marriage to the general had given her wealth and status and respectability, it had never given her much in the way of love.

These two children were running around the estate doing what children do- making noise and irritating the general's wife and being scolded by his crotchety mother. But they were also quick to laugh and tease, and to fall asleep on their father's shoulder.

Ramon was better with them than you might think a widower would be. He managed to make up for a mother's tenderness and spoiling, and still to be firm and authoritative as a father should be. He would rock his daughter to sleep some nights, singing the mountain lullaby his nurse had sung to him when he was a baby.

All of this just drove the general's wife (whom we'll call Maria Luz) crazy. Ramon was so handsome and so strong and so- perfect. We all want to make someone perfect. Maria Luz made Ramon her perfect man.

At first she was content to tell herself this silently as he spoke to his children or when they came running to him when his chauffeur drove him back to the estate in the evenings. He occasionally had ministers or subordinates call on him at the estate, and Maria Luz would greet them on the general's behalf and then admire Ramon as he led them firmly and graciously into a sitting room (never the general's study) to conduct their business.

Thoughts and hopes feed on themselves and grow. Maria Luz began by admiring Ramon Alejandro. Then she idealized him. And after a couple of months of living in the same house with him and his beautiful children, she fell in love with him.

One afternoon when Ramon's chauffeur drove him back to the mansion in his Cadillac limousine, Maria Luz left word with the butler that she would like to see Ramon in the general's study. Ramon's children had taken a walk down to the river with their nurse, and the general's mother had been driven into the capital for her biweekly visit to the chiropractor.

Ramon checked his uniform and medals in the hall mirror, drew himself up with a click-your-heels-together move, and went up the grand stairway and along the second-floor hallway to the general's study.

Maria Luz was seated on the end of a chaise longue in the corner of the study, next to one of the six-foot-tall windows. She was dressed in a chaste cotton dress that was tight enough to show off her slim figure and ample curves. She wore a modest string of pearls. Her lipstick was fresh, and her hair was ever so slightly mussed. She remained seated when Ramon walked into the room.

She told him she wanted to talk to him about a problem with a couple of the servants. The mechanic and one of the cook's assistants had been caught, and here she blushed and was very embarrassed to go on. They had been caught making love in the back seat of the General's Rolls Royce in the garage.

"Well, they must be dismissed immediately," Ramon said.

But Maria Luz said, "No, please, I tell you this only because I know you are a good and kind man, much more kind than my husband."

There was an awkward silence here.

"This isn't the first time this has happened," she said.

"What, with the same girl?"

"No," she said, "No, I'm talking about these servant people. It's all you can expect from that class of people, really. You have to expect it. I don't want to dismiss them. I just- maybe you-" She turned and walked to the window and never finished her sentence.

"In a way I envy them," she said.

She looked quickly at Ramon Alejandro.

"They are in a way," she continued, "so much freer than we are. The upper classes are supposed always to be in control of our emotions."

This was ridiculous coming from her, because she had never been upper class until the general married her.

"She is quite a pretty young girl," Maria Luz said. "And she has the feelings that any young girl has. I think, you know, sometimes what we expect from these young servant girls is unrealistic. And who are we to say what is wrong for them? We must always conduct ourselves as if we had no real feelings ourselves, as if we had no hearts, or as if we could control our hearts."

Ramon was still standing almost as if he were at attention. "I will investigate this matter immediately," he said. "The general's household must not in any case be dishonored."

"Do you know what I'm saying?" Maria Luz said.

"Yes," Ramon said. "And you are a very perceptive woman."

"No," she said. "I don't know if you understand. I was foolish perhaps to ask you here."

"I'm sorry?" Ramon said.

Maria Luz walked toward him, walked up too close really, and looked him straight in the eyes.

Ramon began to leave the room. "I will try to handle this affair leniently," he said.

"Do you know what I'm talking about?" Maria Luz said. Ramon stopped, and she went to him again.

"Ramon Alejandro," she said, "I am also a young woman. Not as young as you, perhaps, but I am still a woman. A general's wife is expected to be something- to be something no one can be. I am not to be human."

You might think Ramon would hurry on out of the room, but he didn't. Maria Luz came to stand right in front of him. She looked at him with her big, brown eyes and her pouting, lipsticked lips.

"You are a man," she said. "You are the most powerful man I have ever known."

Ramon just stood there.

The general's wife put her arms around his neck and kissed him on the lips.

Ramon pushed her gently away and gave an embarrassed bow.

"Please forgive me," he said, and he started to leave.

"Forgive you for what?"

"I'm sorry," he said, "I must leave."

"No," Maria Luz said, "No please, I am talking to you of the human heart. I cannot help myself."

She tried to kiss him again, but he turned his head away.

"Do you realize who I am?" she said. "Do you know what I can do for you?"

Ramon was very confused. He was still a young man, he still believed in honor, and he still believed that even though life throws many curves at you, the honorable way will pay in the long run.

So Ramon caught himself here and he said, "You are a very beautiful and alluring woman. Please forgive me, but I must leave."

Maria Luz grabbed him and kissed him again, forcing her tongue into his mouth. He pushed her away again and started to leave.

"No, wait," she said, and she went back to the window. "I must explain myself."

She stood staring out of the window with her back turned toward Ramon. She held her hands in front of her, fidgeting.

"We are only human," she said. "You too, as fine a young man as you are, are only a human being, and I pray you will realize what makes me do this."

With that she reached to her shoulders and slipped her unbuttoned cotton dress off. It fell around her ankles, and she turned to face him stark naked except for a black garter belt and her stockings. The open window was behind her, overlooking the general's estate. Her body was a forty-year-old body, with a sag here and there and breasts that were no longer pointed up, but she looked very good. Her breasts were large, with large brown nipples. She had a thick bush of black pubic hair.

Ramon had trouble catching his breath.

"Make love to me here," Maria Luz said, gesturing to the chaise longue. "If you have any balls, make love to me."

Ramon said, "I beg you to forgive me," bowed low, left the room, and quickly closed the door behind him. He went straight downstairs and had the butler call his car around. As he was waiting for the car, he kept glancing fearfully back up the staircase. The car came some minutes later. Ramon had himself driven to his office, where he worked until two o'clock in the morning.

When Ramon returned to the General's mansion in the early morning hours, there were two unmarked police cars parked in front, and Ramon's first thought was that Maria Luz may have tried to commit suicide. When he went into the foyer, there was the butler with three secret policemen. The policemen were stout, short men in shiny suits.

"Colonel Ramon Alejandro Balladeros?" one of the policemen said.

Ramon clicked his heels lightly together, nodded stiffly, and said, "Yes."

"Colonel," the secret policemen said. "I am sorry to inform you, you are under arrest. "

Ramon felt the blood rising in his face. "On what charge?" he said.

"You will please come with us," the policeman said.

"I will go nowhere until I hear the charges. "

"Please Colonel," the policeman said, and the butler looked like he wished he could melt into the floor.

"What are the charges against me?" Ramon said, almost losing his composure.

Everyone was ashamed to look at him.

"Where is Dona _____________?" Ramon asked.

"Colonel Alejandro," the policeman said. "You are under arrest for attempted rape. Do you wish to come with us immediately, or do you insist on dishonoring yourself further?"

I'm not going to go into the story of Ramon's detention and the way he bought his way out of his cell, returned to the general's mansion, got his children, then had himself and his children flown out of the country in a drug-smuggling DC3. I'm not going to go into it because I can't remember it all clearly now. It's been some years since Ramon Alejandro told me these things, and you have to remember that at first I didn't believe anything he told me. I thought he was crazy, really, so I didn't make the effort to make his stories stick together in my mind until much later, and then it was too late to reconstruct everything he told me. I regret this.

There is one portion of the story I remember well, and I think this shows why Ramon fled his country with his children rather than try to clear his name in a court of law. Ramon had personally witnessed the general executing a young man on the desert plain outside the capital city. The young man was a university student, active in leftist organizations, who had many run-ins with the secret police. The young man apparently had slept with the general's niece and had later bragged around the university that he had done so. He even claimed she had slept with two of his friends at the same time.

Ramon said he and two military policemen seized the boy from his apartment at the university. They drove him out of the city into the desert, where they met the general and his driver. The general had them remove the boy's handcuffs. The general cursed the boy, challenged the boy to hit him, and when the boy spat in the general's face, the general beat him with his fists until he was nearly unconscious. Then the general took one of the military policemen's pistols and shot the boy in the head.

Then he put the gun barrel to the boy's crotch and blew his genitals off.

You should know that the general's niece was a plump and very shy girl with a harelip. Her harelip had only partially been corrected by plastic surgery. The girl's father was a drunkard who had left his family when his daughter was only three years old, and she and her mother (the general's sister) had moved in with the general. The general had raised her as if he were her father, as he had no children of his own.

There, that's the part of the story that takes place in Ramon's home country. Now to jump ahead a long time. I'm not sure I can say this is jumping ahead- it might be more of a complete departure, because I can never be sure that the story I just told you is completely true, but to jump ahead a long way, let me tell you how I met Ramon Alejandro.

This was after I had been farming three or four years. The first couple of years I didn't have enough acres of peach orchards to justify keeping my own crew of migrant workers, so I would just pick up a crew for a couple of days or a couple of weeks from another farmer whenever I needed them.

But in the third year, we had enough acres and a wide enough spread of ripening dates to justify building a labor camp of our own.

I was very proud of the new camp and never hesitated to take visitors to see it. It had flushing toilets. They were in a cinder block bath house about fifty yards from the old barn I had furnished with used prison beds, used electric stoves, and used refrigerators.

Nearly all the migrant workers who saw it told me it was an extraordinarily nice camp, by the way.

Since my labor camp was so nice, and my farm was so efficiently run in my mind, I decided, rather than work with a migrant labor contractor as most people did, I would have Javier, my foreman, recruit and supervise the workers, and I would put each of them on my farm payroll, so that I could be sure they were all fairly paid.

When thinning time came that spring, Javier started recruiting workers, starting with a lot of his family and friends from Texas and Mexico. He hired a few people who had drifted up from Florida since it was peach season. I didn't meet most of them until Javier had already hired them and they showed up for work in the morning. But I remember when Ramon Alejandro showed up.

I was over at Javier's house trailer, talking with Javier about how many more people we were going to need to finish the thinning. I was telling him to be careful not to hire any Cubans, or anyone who spoke Spanish with an unfamiliar accent. That was shortly after the Mariel boat lift, when press reports had begun appearing that many of the refugees were violent criminals or insane.

As we were talking, a car drove up with four migrant workers in it, three young men and one older man who could have been forty or fifty or sixty. I never could really tell with these Mexicans. They were looking for work, and I can remember being a little apprehensive about them, since I was worried about the Cuban thing. At that time my Spanish wasn't good enough to follow the conversation. Javier told me the three young guys were Mexican, and the old guy wasn't. But he wasn't Cuban either.

This older man was Ramon Alejandro, and other than Javier's father-in-law, he was the oldest man in the camp that year. He didn't have a lot to do with the other migrant workers. He was a rather tall man for a Mexican, with a paunch belly and shoulders that were narrow and stooped from hard living. He had light brown hair with some streaks of gray, a handsome but weathered face, and a prominent nose. Honestly, he wasn't a particularly striking fellow when I first met him, and the only thing that would have made me remember him was the fear that he might be a *Marielito*.

The first time I remember hearing anything about him that made me take interest was one day when we were picking Sunbrights in the North Carolina orchard. Sunbrights ripen in early July. I worked really hard back then, and I usually didn't have time to stop to eat lunch, so the migrant workers would often offer me some of their lunch whenever they stopped to eat. I felt a little bad taking their food at first, but there was no reason to. The poorer a person is, the more generous he is likely to be. I certainly never would have invited any of them into my house for lunch, but they invited me to eat with them whenever they could.

Anyway, I was munching on a taco, when I picked up a little of the conversation. They were laughing and pointing at Ramon Alejandro and giving him a hard time, saying he was *loco*. Even some of the nice boys were giving him hell, and he was beginning to get hot about it.

I couldn't pick up what they were talking about. I thought I heard the word Fascist in Spanish, but it was all so fast I couldn't make it out. They ended up laughing at Ramon, and he took up his pick sack and walked angrily away through the orchard, ducking under the peach tree limbs hanging low with fruit, and started picking, filling his sack and dumping the peaches so hard into his bin box that I really should have said something to him to keep him from bruising them.

All the others were still laughing about him. I asked Javier what was going on. He shook his head, and had that Mexican kind of smile. "He is a crazy man," he said. "He is saying he was a colonel in the Air Force in (he gave the name of Andean country.) And he is saying about how he flew his, I don't know how you call it, his airplane for fighting."

Actually, I met a lot of crazy migrant workers, especially among the American crews. These were the people you see on the steam grates in the big cities in the winter. When the weather was nicer and it was fruit picking time, the crew leaders would drive in to the cities and pick them up at the missions, or sometimes right off the street. Some were drunks who had been intoxicated so long they couldn't tell reality from fantasy. Others were just mentally ill.

I suppose I kind of got to like these people. Suppose hell, it was the best part of farming to me, and the part I miss the most. For five years or so I spent the better part of my summer working with and talking to drunks and crazy people, and I had gotten used to hearing their stories.

There was a young man who claimed to have been part of the Rev. Jim Jones People's Temple in San Francisco before they moved to Guyana. One older man claimed to be a prince from Jamaica.

There were those drunks who told fantastic stories that I could be sure were concocted entirely in their minds, even if they themselves honestly believed them. I thought Ramon Alejandro might be one of these.

That's how I got to know Ramon Alejandro, then. During the day, when they were picking and I was moving through the orchard supervising, I would stop to talk to him just like I would talk to any of the other workers. My Spanish was really lousy then, more pidgin Spanish than anything. But I could curse fluently and joke about the crude things you need to joke about in a peach orchard. Ramon didn't laugh at these jokes in any more than a polite way.

He was a dignified man, although he was dirty and shabbily dressed and his teeth were rotten, and he didn't carry his shoulders well at all.

Over the course of a few weeks he spoke English to me, here and there, just practical stuff like, "The tractor driver will not come," when his bin was full. I began to speak some English to him, but he acted as if he couldn't understand well.

So one day, this was when we were picking Jersey Queens (that would be mid-August), I was speaking Spanish, making a joke to the guy who was picking into the same bin as Ramon, and the joke just fell flat because of a ridiculous mistake I made in my Spanish.

Ramon stopped picking, looked frustrated, and explained to me in very clear and grammatical English what I had said wrong.

As he repeated the correct Spanish phrase to me, I noticed a marked difference between his pronunciation and all the other worker's pronunciation.

"You speak English very well," I said. "Are you American? I mean are you from Texas?"

He laughed to himself and said no, not at all. But that was all he said, and he left me to puzzle over it.

The first time he told me he had gone to Harvard, I couldn't help it. I burst out laughing and kind of embarrassed myself. This was the ultimate crazy migrant worker story. Harvard undergrad, Stanford MBA, and picking peaches.

"You think I'm mentally ill," he said. "I'm simply telling you the truth, and the truth is always something much more complex than you could ever imagine yourself."

That took me aback, but I didn't believe him. It was one of those situations where a little part of you tells you you ought to believe, but the rest of you finds it very inconvenient to do so, so you put the troubling thought out of your mind. The rest of the story I've told you so far came out over the next three weeks or so.

Now just try to imagine an old, rotten-toothed migrant worker in worn-out clothes telling you this story about himself. Try to imagine how you would react. I didn't know what to do. It was a fascinating and entertaining story, told in several installments, with contradicting facts spread throughout. In that respect, and this is an incongruous afterthought, his story resembled the New Testament.

What made it even more inconvenient was that Ramon's vocabulary and grammar were just way too good, and he talked about politics and power and geography in such a way that I could tell he had to be educated. Most of the people who worked for me couldn't have pointed out Mexico on a map.

Ramon told me after the general's wife accused him of rape, he had realized the general was going to try to kill him, so he took his children and fled the country. He told me he knew the general was seriously capable of killing him because he had seen the general execute that university student who had violated the honor of the general's niece. So Ramon had gotten all the money together from his Swiss and Bahamian and Costa Rican bank accounts. He arranged to set himself and his children up in Mexico City, and to go to work with one of his old classmates from Harvard or Stanford.

When he told me all this, he laughed like it was absolutely absurd. He told me his life in that era was evil, and Satan had led him from one evil to another.

You see, he said, that was back when the marijuana trade to the United States was just taking off, and Ramon's general had strong ties to those in his country who grew and smuggled the marijuana.

In fact, Ramon had done a good bit of work with them himself. These people were nowhere near as organized and as ruthless back then as the traffickers of today, but they were nonetheless an international network of criminals, with a lot of money and a lot of killers at their disposal. Ramon's general had turned to these people and had put out a contract on Ramon. And the first time they had tried to assassinate him was in Mexico City.

This, he said, was a terrible thing, to have someone trying to kill you, and not to know who they were or where they might be coming from or how they might be trying to kill you next. Worse, after he successfully escaped their assassination attempt in Mexico City, he began to fear that they would do something to his children.

That's why he said he began living as a peasant. Ramon explained it to me in great detail one afternoon late in the summer, after he had already told me the better part of his story. He told me about several former Nazis who had fled to his country after the Second World War. He told me how some of them had been found and kidnapped by Israeli Nazi-hunters and returned to Europe or Israel for trial. He said that the key to disappearing from resourceful hunters- and the *narcotraficos* were more resourceful he said than the Jews- the key to disappearing was to depart totally from your former identity. Changing your name and moving to a foreign country weren't enough, he said, because the hunters would expect that, and they would trace you some other way.

By this time I was enthralled, even though I thought the man was mentally ill, and perhaps gravely so. He said a good man-hunter examined closely the prey's former life, looked at his hobbies, what languages he could speak, what kind of friends he had, what kind of places he liked to vacation in, and then used those clues to search him out. A name, a vocation, a nationality, all those were easy to change, but tastes and habits and passions would stay with the prey. Nazis who were art lovers had been found through art dealers and auction houses. A yachtsman could be found by searching yacht clubs. The only way to evade the man-hunters surely and permanently, Ramon told me, was to change your life, your tastes, your class, everything. And so he decided to live as a peasant in Mexico.

He burned his and his children's passports, he said. I found it very hard to believe a rational man would do that. And he simply disappeared onto the streets of the city, without telling any of his friends or business associates what he was doing. But he found life as a peasant in Mexico far too difficult, and he was worried that his children might starve or die of some illness, so he came to the United States as an illegal alien.

"And that is when I became another man," Ramon said. "That is when God changed my life.

"You work every day with these people," he told me. "But you are not like them, and you can not understand them. I have spent close to twenty years with these people. What separates you is sin. The Marxists will want to claim it is a class difference, but I don't think that is it. I think you realize the sinfulness of your class, of your wealth, of your way of life, and that distances you from these people."

This just pissed me off to no end, to have a crazy old man tell me this. "Not that these people are without sin themselves," he said, "but their lives are better than your life. You know the life you live distances you from God."

This is how the man talked, and it was hard not to listen. And I've got to admit that some of what he said and thought eventually came to be what I said and thought myself, although it took me many months or years to allow myself to think those things, and I suppose I only thought them when I became convinced that I had thought them up myself.

The other workers in the camp took notice of how I was treating Ramon and listening to him, spending a lot of time with him, I suppose, and that gave him a new measure of credibility.

Before long, some people in the camp really did believe Ramon had been a colonel, and they paid him a lot more respect by the end of the summer than I really thought he deserved.

I should get to his daughter. I didn't ask Ramon what had happened to his children when he told me the parts of his story over the summer, because I didn't really believe him, and I wasn't searching for holes in the logic of his tale. But towards the end of the summer, when other people started to take him seriously, well, Ramon began to carry himself differently. He worked picking peaches with a sort of dignity that was almost ridiculous in him.

One day Ramon was lecturing me about sin and how I knew the society I lived in was wicked, when I asked him well what about the man who is just trying to provide for his family, and is trying to do the best he can for his children? Is it sinful for him to try to earn a respectable living?

Ramon didn't answer me directly, but he did tell me what had happened to his children when they were very young and he had just come to the United States and started working as a migrant worker.

It was very hard, he said, almost as hard as Mexico, because he made very little money, and that was before there were food stamps and the government programs they have now. He was picking tomatoes on John's Island in South Carolina, near the end of the tomato season, and his little girl got sick, he said. She came down first with what seemed to be a bad cold, and he still took her and his son out into the field with him and let them play with the other children in the bus while he worked. After a week or two the cold turned into a fever like the flu, and he left her for a few days with a teenage girl in the camp who didn't like to work. One evening when he came back to the camp, he found the teenage girl watching television while his daughter was in the bed covered with sweat and barely breathing. He picked her up and ran a half mile down the sand road to the crew foreman's house. He got the man to drive him into the hospital in Charleston. His daughter had pneumonia, and she spent three weeks in the hospital and almost died.

Tomato season ran out while she was in the hospital, and Ramon had no money to pay her medical bills. The foreman kept trying to run Ramon and his son out of the camp, because all the other workers had already left. The foreman called in the State Employment Agency people to help get Ramon off his back.

That's when Ramon realized that he could no longer take care of his little girl.

He got real quiet when he told me this, and he wouldn't look me in the eye. You could tell it hurt. Ramon said his daughter was very sick, and he had no way to take care of her, plus, he said, back then he was still scared the *narcotraficos* would trace him to the United States and find him.

"I couldn't sleep at night," he said. "I would wake up screaming. I would dream that they were there, telling me they were going to kill me."

So he went to the wife of the farmer he was working for and asked if she could take care of his little girl. She wanted nothing to do with it, but a couple of days later she drove up to the labor camp and tooted the horn and asked for him. She said there was a childless couple in Charleston. They had been trying to adopt a child for some time. They would consider taking the girl, who was five years old, as a foster child maybe.

Ramon left his little girl with the couple in Charleston and went on up the coast that summer and fall, working in North Carolina and then Delaware and New Jersey. He said, and it was hard for him to say this, like he never had really told anyone about it , but he said that after a while he realized his daughter was better off where she was than with him. They were a nice couple, and well enough off, "not very well bred, or very well educated," he said, "but they were middle class. I think the husband was an engineer, and his wife worked as a secretary in an office. I knew she could never have the life I once had, but I thought, this is a good home, with good people, and if she grows up here maybe she will live a good life, and never become involved with the things I have become involved with. She can have a family and children and live in peace."

So Ramon never went back to Charleston and never called or wrote.

The little boy he kept with him for the better part of a year.

Then he began to think that if he really loved the child, he should maybe leave him, too. But he couldn't make himself do it, and besides, he thought, a boy is tougher than a girl and could take this life better.

Ramon was in New Jersey, in the truck farming country, staying in a labor camp that looked out over the Atlantic City Expressway. One Sunday afternoon a car pulled up to the camp. A lot of guys in the camp were drunk, but Ramon had taken his son down to a pond behind the camp to go fishing. Ramon was resourceful and unbroken enough to figure out how to get together a couple of fishing poles and some hooks and bait and find something worthwhile to do.

He had taken his boy, who should have been in school by this time, to go fishing, and this car stopped up at the labor camp. Three well-dressed Latin men got out and asked around at the camp. Ramon could see them up there, but he didn't pay much attention until they got back in the car and started driving down the dirt track toward the pond. There was no one else at the pond except Ramon and his little boy.

The men in the car weren't dressed like migrant workers, Ramon could see as they got closer. With nothing more to go on, he took his little boy by the hand, left the fishing poles propped up on the bank, and walked around the edge of the pond. He led his boy into the thick brush at the far end of the pond, and as soon as he was out of sight of the approaching car, he picked up his son and ran for his life. He ran down a hedgerow that separated two fields, ran for half a mile or so until he was completely out of breath, and he looked back once. He thought he caught a glimpse of someone coming out of the brush down beside the pond. Ramon ducked immediately to the other side of the hedgerow and kept running out of sight. He ran until he came to a blueberry field a good half a mile long. Ramon put his boy down and got him to crawl between the rows of bushes, which were about three feet high and so thick you couldn't see through them. Ramon got down and crawled right behind his son. He kept him going by making all this seem like a game, telling the boy he couldn't put his head up over the bushes at all or they would be caught.

They crawled down the row in this blueberry field until they got right out in the middle of it, and they couldn't be seen from any direction. Ramon rolled over on the ground in the shade underneath the bushes and held his little boy. He stayed there until dark, holding his son while the boy napped, and playing and talking with him, and building a sand castle and a sand fort with him when he got bored. After nightfall they made their way out of the field to the Turnpike and went to a rest area, where they caught a ride southbound with two Mexicans in a van, leaving their clothes and all they had behind.

"I was in that field," Ramon told me, "and I was thinking, What? Am I a crazy man now? Every man I see now, I think he is going to kill me." After this incident Ramon found a temporary foster home for his little boy in New Jersey. He left him there and never went back, just as he had with his little girl.

Maybe I should go back to the attack on Ramon's life in Mexico City. After he told me about hiding in the field in New Jersey,

Ramon laughed and he said, "I never told you how they tried to kill me in Mexico, did I? You think I'm some crazy old bastard who's inventing all this as he tells it to you.

"O.k., I'll tell you where they tried to kill me. I had a nice apartment in the Zona Rosa, four bedrooms, a luxury apartment with gold plumbing fixtures. You think I'm making this up, but they were the kind of fixtures your parents have in their house right now."

I was trying to remember when he had been in my parents' house. I had taken some of the guys over there to wash windows early in the summer. Had Ramon been with them?

"Oh, and I had a maid, of course, and a nurse to take care of the children. I was working with my friend. We were exporting minerals from the Sierra Madre. This was a difficult business, with a great deal of risk. My friend specialized in exporting, oh I've forgotten how you say it in English now." He scratched his head. "Talcum. Talcum rock. It was mined in the Sierra Madre, and we exported it to West Germany and Luxembourg to make toilet bowls and lavatories.

"Oh, you don't want to know all that, or maybe you do, but I told you, that is all in my evil life, and there is no reason to remember it now.

"They tried to kill me in Mexico, the *narcotraficos*. They are very powerful there, because they buy the police. They control the politicians, so there is no way you can hide from them, and no way you can escape them. They kidnapped me as I was walking from my apartment to my office one morning. They stopped a car beside me, right in the middle of Mexico City, and forced me with a gun to get in the car with them. They drove me out of the city for three hours, until we stopped at a peasant's shack in the outskirts of a seedy little village filled with dirty children and garbage.

"They bound me and took me inside. My general was there. My general, whom I had loved so much. He told me that he should kill me for trying to rape his wife, and I said, 'What? I don't know what you're talking about. It was she who tried to rape me, but he hit me across the face, and spat on me, and called me a coward, and said he couldn't believe that I, of all men, would come to this. Then he laughed and said, 'It's always the honorable, self-righteous bastards who turn bad in the end.'"

He was a delightful story teller, each episode getting more and more outrageous. I've got to say he lost me on this one. By the time he got through with the story of the kidnapping and the meeting with the general, I was convinced he was nothing more than a crazy old man. I imagine he told me this story on a Monday morning, because he had liquor breath and an apparent hangover.

He said the general was going to have Ramon's balls cut off by one of the *narcotraficos*, but Ramon kicked over the table and stole one of the kidnappers' machine gun and shot two of the *narcotraficos* and stole a motorcycle and escaped. I could hear Javier laughing and repeating the story in Spanish a couple of rows over from us.

"You've lived a dangerous life, Ramon," I said, the way you humor a crazy man. I had more pressing things to do, and I didn't really have time to listen to him wrap this tale up.

It was getting to be the end of the peach season. We were picking Rio Oso Gems, and I was trying to give the hint to everyone in the camp that I wanted them out of there as soon as the picking was over and they had been paid. I didn't want a bunch of unemployed migrant workers hanging around after peach season, tearing the place up and bringing the food stamp and social services and legal aid people up there. Besides, I had had a bad year and was just finding the time to sit down at the computer and figure up how much money I was going to lose. Mary Ruth and I had already started discussing getting out of farming. I didn't have much time to listen to Ramon Alejandro. For the rest of the season I avoided him whenever I could. I could only spend a few minutes in the orchard before I would have to run back to the packing house. We were having a lot of trouble collecting from a broker in New York and one in Cincinnati, and I was on the phone as much as I could be.

One evening after work Mary Ruth had invited a couple of friends over to eat a beef tenderloin she was grilling. We raised registered Angus cows. We steered one of the bull calves every season and fattened it so we could keep a freezer full of beef. I knocked off work early, came home and showered, and was dressed in time to sit down for cocktails with our guests when they arrived. We were sitting in the living room, since it was a terribly hot August day, too hot to sit out on the front porch. We were telling jokes when there was a knock on the front door.

I answered it. There was Ramon standing on my front porch. He had walked over from the camp, and I was taken aback a little, because I don't think I had ever had one of my workers come up and actually knock on my front door. They would either sit in their cars and blow the horn, or, if they were on foot, they would walk back and forth in front of the house until I noticed them.

I invited him in, even though I really didn't want to. I don't know why I insisted still on inviting these people into my house, when I had learned long before that any of them over the age of twenty would feel terribly uncomfortable if they came in. But Ramon wouldn't come in. He wanted to go out in the front yard and talk. He had been drinking. I could see it in his eyes and the way he stood. He was acting just like a drunk migrant worker, crazy and irresponsible and conniving, and I really didn't want to have to bother with him right then. I knew he would want something, a loan or something else I shouldn't give him. They always did when they came like this.

But what he wanted, well, it was a pain in the ass. He told me he wanted to thank me. He said that in all these years, almost twenty years, no one had taken the time to listen to him and let him talk about his past and tell about all the things he had learned from his extraordinary life. Nobody else, he said, had ever seen things the way he had seen them, and he had a lot to say, but no one to tell it to.

"You don't know," he said. There were tears in his eyes, and his breath smelled like liquor even though I had had a couple of scotch and waters. "You don't know what it is like, to live your life with people who don't understand, who can never understand. Ignorant, uneducated people who have never seen the things you have seen, and who think you are crazy when you talk about them. No one has listened to me in I don't know how long. I can never go back to what I was, but at least now I have remembered it."

It's a pain in the ass when someone is drunk and starts talking like that. I didn't like it. I was waiting for him to hit me up for some money or for a year-round job, but what he wanted wasn't that.

He wanted me to help him find his daughter.

It floored me when he said it. First of all, I didn't believe there was a daughter. It was as if the man had asked me to help him recover his million-dollar fortune. The things Ramon Alejandro told me had long since lost the feel of truth to me. I had convinced myself that he was a pathological liar. I told Ramon I had guests, and I would talk to him about it the next day, but maybe we could work something out. He went away just like any migrant worker, not believing me.

So I did talk to him the next day about it. I made a point of searching him out in the field that afternoon, and you should have seen his eyes light up when he heard me call his name and saw me coming. He eagerly pulled out a slip of paper on which he had written a name and "Charleston, S.C." as the address.

He said that was the name of the couple that had taken his daughter in. He wanted me to try to get their telephone number and call. I said he could do that as well as I. But he said, "No, *patron*, please, you do this for me," and he put the piece of paper in my hand and folded my hand shut with his.

He didn't want to talk to his daughter himself, he said. He only wanted to know how she was doing. When he said that, well, it was one of those things in between believable and not.

I didn't know what the hell to do. The worst thing is, I called long distance information that evening when I got home, and the couple was listed, living in North Charleston. So then, that easily, I had a telephone number and an address. Then I didn't want to call at all. I just didn't want to get dragged into this thing, and I told myself I would maybe write a letter, or just give the information to Ramon and not have anything more to do with it.

Then I made the mistake of telling Mary Ruth, and she said, "Earnest, you have to call them tonight. Think of what this might mean to that man."

God I didn't want to do it. Mary Ruth badgered me for a couple of hours, until I snapped at her.

Then I paced up and down the hall and took one of her cigarettes from her pack in the kitchen and lit it up. I went to the den phone and sat in my Lazy Boy, got the piece of paper out, and dialed the number, same area code as mine.

I remember the phone rang several times, and I was hoping there would be no answer, so at least I could put the conversation off to later. I do this every time I make an inconvenient phone call. Pray for the other party not to answer. I don't know why I'm that way. But just as I was about to hang up, this nice sounding middle-aged woman answered with a Charleston brogue. And then what the hell was I going to say? I was mad at Mary Ruth for getting me into this. It was really one of the most absurd situations I had ever found myself in.

So I introduced myself and told where I was calling from just like I was making a business call. I said I was trying to locate Lucinda Alejandro.

There was a silence on the other end of the line. The woman asked if I could say again who was calling, and I told her my name and where I was from and said that I was a peach farmer, and she said very slowly, "Are you calling on behalf of her father?"

I couldn't say anything.

"Is her father still alive?" the woman finally asked. "Yes," I said. " I mean ..." But I didn't know what to say.

"Lucy's been trying to find him for two years at least," the woman said.

And after a very confused couple of minutes, she put down the phone and called Lucy, and I got to speak to the young woman myself.

I never actually met the girl. Never really got involved in the story much beyond that phone call. I've got a photograph of her, though. At least I think it's her. The photograph is in the back of the top drawer of my desk. I got it from them the Christmas after I made that telephone call. They wrote from South America, although they didn't tell me whether they were living down there or had just gone back for a visit. There was Ramon, looking older, but incredibly healthy and happy, and a rather plain and rather plump young woman who must have been his daughter, and a young man with a beard and sunglasses who may have been his son.

They were standing in a square in front of a building that looked like a cathedral. The note on the back says, "To my dear friend Earnest. My best wishes to your family for a merry Christmas and happy New Year. "

That was the only thing I got from Ramon after he left my farm. No call from the daughter or from her foster mother or anything, which, well, it goes with the rest of the story, I suppose. It still befuddles me completely. I drove Ramon to the bus station myself that next afternoon, but he was so excited I didn't get much out of him. Hell, there wasn't that much more to get out of him.

He had told me almost all of his story already. I just had refused to believe it. I dropped him off at the Greyhound station in Spartanburg, shook his hand, and he walked toward the station door carrying a paper grocery bag full of clothes. He looked back and smiled with his rotten teeth and waved. He picked his shoulders up inside his shirt in the way a man who has been beaten down for decades moves, almost as if he is apologizing to the world for being there. I put my truck in gear and drove away, and I never saw him again.

I sure would have liked to hear at least something, some explanation of what happened after that. But I guess they didn't really owe me anything. There was a return address on the Christmas card, and I fully intended to write back and start a correspondence with them and see what had happened.

But you know how you don't write, and then you start to feel guilty for it, and then so much time goes by and you move and they move, and the addresses are no good any more, and you just lose people.

The Ninth Tale.
Earnest learns of a secret heart.

I finally had to get a paying job nearly a year after the baby was born. I managed to finagle a job in Charlotte with three of my old fraternity brothers who were importing furniture from the Far East. It was an unlikely match, me in with these business school graduates.

The three of them, once I got in the office with them, started using me as someone to have on their sides in the little power and ego struggles that go on all day long on any job. That was a tiresome thing, especially when I had my share, or more than my share, of male ego myself.

One of the guys was Dolf Bradshaw- short, stocky, with curly blond hair, originally from Bishopville, South Carolina. His torso and shoulders were perfectly proportioned. At age thirty he was still fit, and his legs were well proportioned and well muscled. He still ran every day and lifted weights, but the legs were just too short to go with the rest of his body, and I always thought he looked awfully strange because of it.

Dolf was sex crazy. I don't know if it came from growing up in a small town or what. It seems kids who grow up in those isolated small towns get exposed to a lot of sex at an early age. Most of what Dolf talked about in college, and even in spare moments on the job after we had grown up some, was sex. When we were in college, having raunchy conversations about sex, Dolf would tell stories that sounded like the letters in the front of Penthouse magazine, only his were true. In fact, there were often one or more eyewitnesses who could confirm the veracity of his stories.

We loved to crawl out on the second-floor roof at the frat house and watch through the windows as these things went on. I remember watching as Dolf and three other guys were pulling a train with this girl we called the Orient Express. There were about five of us out on the roof, watching through two windows. The lights were on in the room. I didn't get there until late in the action, when she was angry at them and trying to pick her clothes up off the floor and put them on. Every time she would bend over to pick up a piece of clothing, Dolf would try to enter her from behind, and she would wave him away from her.

I must not have been far enough back from the window, and maybe my face was visible to her in the light from inside. After she picked up all her clothes, she stood in front of the window and stared straight at me for a while. I didn't move a muscle. Maybe she couldn't see me in the darkness outside.

Another of the three partners was Ralph Wheatley. Ralph was the finance guy in our organization. Unlike my other two partners, he didn't chase women a lot. Ralph was about my height, with curly brown hair and a slight weight problem. Ralph was unmarried. Rather than chase women, he would have long-term steady girlfriends, probably four in the period since I had known him, the last two of which he had actually lived with. I didn't particularly like Ralph's taste in girls. They were usually overweight, wore too much makeup, and were bitchy. But I did like working with him, because of the three partners, he was the most laid back. He was the one I would go to with my ideas and problems, because he would listen to what I said, weigh it, and give me a straight answer. My other two partners- or bosses to be more precise- wouldn't do that.

The third partner, the guy who cracked my ass the most after I had gone to work with him, was Mike Kowalski. Mike was from a suburb of Cincinnati originally. His mother was from North Carolina, which is how he ended up going to school there. Mike was about six-feet three, with blond hair and broad shoulders and a prominent, strong chin and blue eyes. He had played J. V. basketball at Chapel Hill. He was an awfully good looking guy, a very intelligent fellow who had gone to business school at Wharton, and an enormously captivating person when you first met him. He would look people boldly in the eye and shake their hand firmly, and his voice was low and sincere. Everything he said in the presence of someone he didn't know well was cultured, upbeat, positive, and very often inspiring.

Mike was married to a girl who I thought earlier in my life was the perfect woman. Lucy Kowalski was president of the Pi-Phi house when we were at Chapel Hill. She was brown-haired and pretty, with that sort of patrician pug nose and prominent chin. She was intelligent and well-adjusted. She had a good sense of humor and impeccable manners and was kind and said the wise and correct thing in any conversation I ever heard. She had something of a reputation for having a temper, but I had never seen her display her temper at all. She always spoke to me as if I was an old friend she was very glad to see. We went to the beach with her and Mike a couple of times when we were younger, and she looked very good in a bathing suit. Not like the girls in Sports Illustrated, but very good for a real human being seen up close.

Lucy was a chaste and proper young woman. She would blush when we told dirty jokes in front of her. She never cursed, and she never had any reputation at all for screwing around. She had seemed to me, and to everybody else who knew her in college, to be an unlikely match for Mike Kowalski when they fell in love our senior year. Because Mike was a whore.

It had been funny when we were in college, but after he and Lucy got married, and after I got married, I didn't think it was as funny.

I had been married five or six years, and I guess Mike had been married seven or eight years, with two little boys, when I went to work for him. It was there at the office after hours, when all the women had gone home, that I first heard him joking with the other two guys about his infidelities.

I don't know that you would call them infidelities so much. He just liked to have sex with whores when he was traveling. He, like all of us except Ralph, traveled around the world a good bit. In fact, he traveled more than anybody else in the company, to Europe and the Far East and South Asia. I don't know if it was Dolf or one of his expatriate friends who got Mike started on the whores, but apparently he started in the Philippines, where you could get a beautiful young girl for a week for a couple of hundred dollars.

He and Dolf compared notes on where the best and the cheapest whores were in the world. Bangkok was their favorite spot. When I came back from my first trip to the Far East, I babbled about being taken to the Volvo Club in Hong Kong,where the whores clocked in on electronic time clocks at your table. I didn't, by the way, do anything more than carry on a polite conversation with my hooker- just to humor my host. Anyway, when I came back astonished by that experience, Dolf and Mike treated me like some kid who comes back from New York gawking about the tall buildings.

Mike told us about one of his German expatriate friends who owned an electronics factory in the Philippines. The guy's name was Gregor. Mike said Gregor's latest thing was to have the girl apply ice to his scrotum as he was reaching orgasm. Dolf shivered and whooped when he heard this.

"Oh my God, stop it," he said. "You're getting my dick hard." He grabbed his crotch and walked out of the office.

Anyway, I thought a lot less of Mike after I went to work for him. A lot of what I resented in him was this running around on Lucy.

Like I say, we did a good bit of traveling in our business, although it was rare that all four of us traveled together to the same destination. One of those rare occasions took us all to New York, where we met with a Taiwanese tycoon we were trying to get to invest in a Caribbean factory.

This Taiwanese guy was indisputably an asshole, by the way. They had sent me to call on the guy on my first trip to the Far East. He reminded me of Ferdinand Marcos. He took me around town in a chauffeur-driven Rolls Royce. He barked orders to his chauffeur.

He took me back to his office after lunch, where I had a long meeting with his subordinates who could speak English better than he. He was from mainland China originally, and his English was very poor. He wandered in and out of the meeting, and every time he walked out of the room, not even quite out of my earshot, he would start yelling at his employees like they were coolies.

Fortunately, we only had to entertain the Taiwanese guy two nights, and the last night we were in New York, we got to go out with two old frat brothers who had moved up there after college.

We met them at a Chinese restaurant on the upper west side and went from there to cruise the bars.

One of the old frat brothers we met was Russell Wilkes. Russell worked for one of the major banks in corporate lending or something. I've never been real sure about what he did, except I remember when we were discussing cigars one time, he said how he liked to have one after lunch in the executive dining room at the bank. Russell was single at the time. The other guy with us was Chip Sturm. He worked for an ad agency, I think, or was it marketing for some big corporation? I don't know, and it doesn't matter. Chip was engaged to a girl from Colombia whom I've never met. He's married to her now.

So, back to the Chinese restaurant. There we were, the four of us and Russell and Sturm drinking beer and eating Hunan food and telling wild stories about where we had gotten drunk and where the ones who were still chasing skirts had been chasing skirts. I kept pretty quiet in this conversation. Usually when I heard this kind of conversation, I feigned disbelief and dismay at skirt-chasing stories of the bachelors, as if I really missed that kind of thing. If I told the truth I would say I didn't miss it at all. But it was by and large fun to listen to the stories. I enjoyed how my partner/bosses would do this occasionally, getting together to go out drinking so they would remember why they were friends in the first place.

Near the end of the dinner, when we were all getting kind of tight, and after we had talked about a lot of other stuff, like business and politics and literature and philosophy (I'm serious, we talked about this stuff) well, after we had talked about that stuff we got back to the skirt-chasing stories. Dolf was telling one about a black girl when he was in high school back in Bishopville, and Sturm said, "Goddamn, that's like animals, man."

"Animals don't do that kind of thing," I said. "It's like human beings. "

"Goddamn, Spud," Mike said, "can't you ever say anything normal?"

And I don't know what it was, if it was the beers, or being in familiar company where I was more of a friend and equal than employee, or if it was the experience of watching Mike pal it up with the Taiwanese warlord pig, or what, but I just snapped, "Man, fuck you, Mike."

There was a silence at the table, and I could see Mike's eyes getting hot.

"You know I got a goddamn brain," I said, drunk and angry and being an idiot, "You don't think I've done some serious and reflective thinking about all this shit I'm saying?"

In the earlier conversation, Mike and I had been arguing about Ayn Rand. He thought she was great philosopher, and I've always thought she was a lousy writer and a fool. Mike implied that if I didn't believe in Ayn Rand like a priest believes in Jesus, there was no hope for me in the business world.

"What in the hell are you talking about, Spud?" Mike said. "Half the time I can't even understand you're saying to us."

"What I'm saying," I said, and my hands were shaking, "is it's about goddamn time we started treating people like human beings, instead of just somebody else you can fuck."

"Spud," Sturm said, "get under control."

"I just want to know what the hell I said that brought this on," Mike said, spreading his arms out and smiling that 'after all, I'm such a terrific guy' smile. "I mean, Spud, what have I done to you? I haven't even seen you three times in the last month."

Well, it would have probably just died there with me looking like a damn fool and maybe losing my job, but Dolf had had enough to drink that he jumped in, too. "Mike, goddamn it," he said, "you gotta beat up on Spud again today? Gotta prove you're the boss?"

And all of a sudden I was completely out of it, and this was a battle between Dolf and Mike, whom I had seen have some fabulous fights before. See, I was still pretty soft from sitting at home and taking care of the baby and writing. I couldn't stand the pressure of these confrontations without losing my cool, but Dolf and Mike could go at each other with precise, controlled, devastating shots. I suppose this one would have proceeded along those lines, except this was the first of these fights I had ever seen where both of them were drunk.

It went for about a five or ten minute battle, with solid hits on both sides, before they broke off, and the conversation between everybody else at the table continued. This warfare was much more refined than my outburst. Dolf pointed out that Mike had dropped the ball on the Caribbean deal and that he had lost a client in France because he gave the guy this same kind of berating and then the "who, me, wonderful me?" posture he had used with me.

Mike was hurt. He countered with something about Dolf's sexual activities being far worse than his. Then the fight calmed, and the fighters caught their wind and let their anger stoke while the rest of us carried on a conversation and tried to make light of the whole thing.

The waiter brought the check, after most of the other parties in the restaurant had already cleared out, and Mike paid the whole tab with his platinum American Express card. We left to go out cruising the bars, leaving our fortune cookies untouched on the table.

We took a couple of cabs over to a surfing-themed bar. We got a table in the back room, and all the guys except me and Sturm (who was engaged, you remember) and Ralph started trying to pick up girls. With Dolf and Mike, and to some extent Russell, this was a very serious business. When you hit a bar you didn't waste your time talking to the other guys, you scoped out the pussy and started talking shit to the girls (this is the precise terminology they used.) They were not alone in this pursuit, even in the age of AIDS, which amazes me. I was astonished at how many girls were there, drinking too much, doing coke obviously, flirting with the guys, and how many guys were there trying to get some free sex.

Maybe it was just because Mike and Dolf and Russell were getting considerably older and considerably balder, but within an hour everybody but Russell was sitting back at the table. Mike and Dolf were still scoping out girls, nodding toward the good-looking ones across the room and discussing whether their asses were right or not.

"Oh, I forgot, Spud," Mike said, with mock concern. "These are human beings."

He and Dolf had just talked about how a certain Hispanic-looking girl's derriere poked out a little more than it should (she was wearing a black silk outfit that almost looked like pajamas, and she was swinging back and forth to the music as she talked to her girlfriends) .

"Oh, lay off Spud," Dolf said.

"Man, what the fuck is this?" Mike said. It snapped out, and he was hot. " I can't open my goddamn mouth without hurting Spud's feelings? What the hell is it I've done?"

Well, that got Dolf rolling. He loved to fight with Mike, as I've already said, and I can't remember how one thing led to another in this conversation. I just remember the most striking part, the part I remember word for word, was when Dolf said, "I suppose you'd like Lucy up here whoring around the way you do."

Boy, that stopped the conversation cold. "Don't you ever talk about my wife like that," Mike said, and the other three of us were sitting there stone silent. I honestly thought he and Dolf were going to start swinging at each other. Mike's face was red, and his eyes, God, how can a man's eyes get so threatening?

Dolf was drunk. His curly blond hair seems to go wild when he's that drunk, and the stumpy body, when it's swaying like that, gives him a "screw you" look that gets him into a lot of trouble. "Hey, yeh," he said, ignoring Mike's warning, "what if little Lucy was up here trying to cop some dick? Hell, what if she's down in Charlotte right now trying to cop some, Mike? You don't think she could do that sort of thing? I mean it would be perfect payback, wouldn't it?"

"You shut the fuck up," Mike said.

"Hey, wait a fucking minute," Dolf said. "I mean we're talking about human beings here, aren't we? Are you saying she ain't a human being like all the others in here?"

"Dolf," Mike said, "you're talking about my wife."

"She's a human being, Mike. That's all I'm saying. She's a human being, like Spud says. Only I say, Spud's wrong about human beings. If you treat people like human beings, then what you do is fuck em. That's what real human beings want, is to get fucked."

"That's not what Lucy wants," Mike said .

"You don't know what you're saying," Dolf laughed. "Man, everybody wants to fuck. I mean that's the basic drive." He held his forearm erect in front of him and thrust his pelvis back and forth a couple of times. "Hey, why do you think all these people are here chasing pussy and dick when there's AIDS and all that shit around? People want to fuck more than they want anything else in this world. They'd rather fuck than live."

"Man you're sick," Mike said. "You're really sick, you know that. I've never known how sick you were."

"Wait a minute," Dolf said, and he had that funny looking body of his swaying as he talked. "I'm not the one running around all over the world sticking my dick in anything that moves and then dragging it back home to the mother of my children."

Mike jumped up and was going to hit him. Ralph grabbed Mike and held him back, and Mike shouted, "You piece of shit. Don't you ever talk about my wife like that."

Dolf was just drunk and laughing. He would have loved to get in a fist fight. It was the small-town redneck in him. "All I'm saying is Lucy Kowalski is just the same as any woman in this bar. You think she couldn't be running around doing exactly the same thing you do?"

You would think Mike would have gone on and hit him, but like I say, Mike had gotten to be a calculating bastard, and he surprised me by shrugging Ralph off and sitting back down. He didn't say anything much for a while.

The rest of us got another conversation going, trying to leave the outburst behind, but all of a sudden Mike just broke in.

"All right, I'll tell you Dolf," he said. "You fuck a lot of women, don't you? You know I know it. You fuck more women than anybody I know. You even love to fuck married women."

"Mike," Ralph said. "Drop it, man."

But this just egged Mike on. "No, I'm serious, you talk about me, you love more than anything in the world to fuck other men's wives, don't you?"

It was getting way out of hand, and I was ready to pick it up and leave this place.

"What are you getting at?" Dolf said.

"Hey, I want to make a proposition to you, is all," Mike said.

He was chopping his hand through the air like an executive in a Business Week advertisement. "All I want you to do is try to fuck my wife. There." He spread his hands out and laid the proposal on the table. "Man, if anybody can fuck a married woman, it's you."

None of us could speak. It even shocked Dolf for a second, as drunk as he was.

"I tell you what," Mike said. "No, I'll make it better. Let's make it better. We'll put money on it. What you say? Five, no, hell no, let's make it ten thousand dollars. You fuck my wife I'll pay you ten thousand dollars cash, no questions asked."

I've got to hand it to Ralph. I didn't think he had the guts to do this, but he told Mike to shut up.

"No. Hell no," Mike said. "I'm serious. If you're going to sit there and say the things you've said about my wife, I want to see you do it. I'm leaving tomorrow from here, I go to Singapore and Bangkok for two weeks, I want you to go back to Charlotte and do your absolute best, Dolf, to fuck my wife. Everything you can do. And if you do it, I'll pay you ten thousand dollars on the spot."

Dolf just started laughing. He leaned over the table and said, "All right, I'll do it. In fact, I'll make it even better. If I don't do it before you get back, I'll pay you ten thousand dollars."

I'm sure my jaw was hanging slack. The two of them both stood up, reached across the Formica-covered table, and slapped their hands together in an obscene handshake.

Mike whipped two hundreds out of his money clip, threw them on the table to cover the bill, and walked out of the bar. We didn't see him again in New York. He was supposed to be leaving in the morning from JFK to fly to Tokyo, but we didn't even see him back at the hotel. As for the rest of us, well, we didn't have much more fun that night. We didn't even discuss what we had just seen. Dolf left us and started trying to pick up girls. The last I saw of him, he was walking out of the bar with the Latin girl in the black pajamas.

Well, Ralph and I flew back to Charlotte the next morning thinking some pretty black thoughts, and keeping them to ourselves. I had only been working with these guys about five months when all this happened. I had been unhappy the whole time. That was for sure. I had been feeling something was rotten there, but I was in a hell of a tight place. I was damn lucky to have the job at all, given my resume, and Mary Ruth wasn't about to put up with me leaving the job, so I was stuck as far as I knew.

Ralph was another matter, though, and I didn't learn until a couple of months later what was on his mind. Ralph had made some good money in the few years he had been with Mike and Dolf. They had taken the lion's share for themselves, but Ralph had enough to walk and do whatever he wanted, and he wasn't married. He did end up walking, even before the whole thing came down, but like I say, that was a couple of months later.

Dolf wasn't on the plane with us that morning. He missed the flight and caught a later plane down about lunchtime. He got into the office late that afternoon, and he just walked straight into his office, closed the door, and spent the rest of the day on the phone.

Dolf was in a lousy mood the next two weeks. We didn't see much of him. He stayed out of the office calling on clients or getting his Porsche fixed or buying new clothes or getting his hair cut or something. He didn't work much, and I didn't say much to him at all when I did see him. It was just Ralph and me in the office with the girls. I always liked it like that, much more peaceful and harmonious. You could do the right thing by somebody and not be made to feel like a sucker for doing it .

Mike's faxes from the Far East were terse and to the point.

They were addressed to Ralph or to me, never to Dolf. And so the two weeks went by, and I thought the whole affair in the bar in New York must just have been a drunken outburst, that nothing would come of it. I felt pretty damn foolish for having believed anything would. I figured this was another case of my overreacting to the rough and tumble world of business life.

Mike usually came in from the West Coast or the Far East at some ungodly hour of the morning, completely jet-lagged. He would come straight from the airport to the office, his desk full of faxes and letters and phone calls to return, and would just be a miserable asshole to be around for several hours- wound-up and abusive and acting like the whole world would collapse if he didn't see to it that things were done right.

He came in that way this time, on the red eye from L.A. I got chewed out bad before nine o'clock, not having been in the office more than forty-five minutes. He was back in his office after that, raking some poor guy over the coals on the phone, when Dolf walked in. The girls were in the back room having a coffee break. Dolf stuck his head into the break room, told them good-morning, and closed the door. Then he walked past my desk (I didn't have an office, just a desk out with the girls' desks), and straight into Mike's office.

Mike was still on the phone. I heard something ring like a coin being dropped on his desk. Mike stopped talking.

"Listen, can I call you back?" he said. "Something just came up. I'll call you back, O.K.?" He didn't wait for an answer before he hung up. I couldn't see all this, but I could hear it plain as day. I could hear anything that went on in Mike's office if I wanted to.

"Where did you get this?" Mike said.

Dolf didn't answer him for a long time. There was just silence.

Then Dolf spoke. "She has a shaved pussy. Right where the pubic hair should be, she has a red heart tattooed. About two inches in diameter. It's a broken heart."

There was a long, long silence again. Even Ralph had stopped moving in his office. Then there was a violent rustle of clothing, and the coin or whatever bounced off the window glass. (It turned out to be a St. Christopher's medal. It belonged to Mike and stayed on his dresser at home). I heard a desk drawer open. A thump on the desk. Then no sound for thirty seconds. I didn't know what was happening. I didn't know if he was going to kill Dolf or what. I didn't know if I should run in there or what.

Then I heard the unmistakable rip of a check being torn from its place in the checkbook. A second or two later, Mike walked straight out of his office, without looking at me, and walked out the front door. I could see him through the glass door as he was getting into his BMW. I had never seen him look so terrifying.

Dolf walked into his office and slammed the door. When the girls came out of the break room chattering, I was sitting at my desk with head in my hands.

I got home that night, and I sure as hell couldn't tell Mary Ruth what had happened.

I never told anyone what had happened, until later at least. Jesus, you know I never even mentioned it to Ralph. Ever in my life. We sat there and listened to the whole thing happen, and both of us knew the other one was listening, and neither one of us ever said a thing to the other one.

Like I say, Ralph handed in his resignation a couple of months later. By that time things were getting really bad at the office between Dolf and Mike. There was the tension, sure, but the tension had always been there. But now things weren't getting done. Communication had broken down, promises weren't being kept. Phone calls and faxes weren't being answered. I was getting a lot of angry people calling up wondering what the hell was going on, and Mike and Dolf were doing most of their communicating with each other through me.

I started looking for a job seriously when Ralph announced he was leaving. I finally took one a couple of months later with the fellow I'm working with now.

Mike and Lucy broke up the summer after I left, and Dolf and Mike closed the business down about that same time. I don't know any details of what happened. I didn't have anything to do with either of them at all after I left them. Didn't have any desire to. I heard about Lucy and Mike splitting up just through friends, and then I didn't say anything about it, and didn't act like I would know anything about it, or like I even cared. I might have said, "Well, that's too bad. She's a nice girl." That was the most I might have said to anyone, and I usually didn't say that much.

I didn't care if I ever saw Mike again or not. I did as much as I could to avoid seeing him, if the truth be known. We ran into him at a couple of cocktail parties, but he traveled so much and was such an asshole anyway he didn't get invited to many parties. And when I did see him, I managed to stay on the other side of the room or in a different part of the house after we said hello and exchanged a few sentences.

As for Lucy, hell. Lucy Kowalski. I had always hated her married name. To me she was Lucy Williams, president of the Pi-Phi house, the finest, most sensible, good-looking, level-headed, mature girl in Chapel Hill. The kind of girl you would think would grow up to be like Barbara Bush. But Lucy Williams with a red heart tattooed over her shaved who-ha? Lucy Williams in bed with Dolf Bradshaw in her own house? The first I just couldn't imagine at all. Where in the hell did she get the thing? Sure, we all do crazy things when we're in college and drunk. But Lucy Williams at the tattoo parlor with her legs spread while some sleazy tattoo artist worked?

Dolf must not have had to try too hard, either. I mean two weeks, with her husband out of town and her having to take care of the two boys. And to get her to do it right there in their bedroom.

So anyway, things go on. The really absurd parts of our lives, the screaming fights with our wives or husbands, the times when we humiliate ourselves in front of someone, we somehow put them behind us enough to go on. I went on, and like I say, I never discussed Mike's and Dolf's bet with anybody at all, and they went on out of my life. After the business closed up, Dolf moved to Houston and went to work with a company we had never heard of called Enron. After Mike and Lucy split, Mike moved to Atlanta.

After almost a year of things being more or less sorted out by falling out, Lucy and Mary Ruth started becoming friends.

I don't know how it happens. Maybe it's a woman's thing. Maybe it's just Mary Ruth. She grabs onto these girls, and they're her best friend for life for six months or a year. They share all their deep, dark secrets, meaning mostly they talk terrible trash about their husbands, prefacing it with, "well, he is a truly wonderful person." Not that the husbands don't deserve to have trash talked about them, but the husbands don't run around sharing all their deep dark secrets with their friends. At least not that way.

Anyway, they met, as best as I can remember, at the Junior League. They were working together on some charity project. I shouldn't say they met. They had known each other before through me and Mike, but I remember when Mary Ruth came home from a meeting one night and said, "She's a really nice girl."

Anyway, Mary Ruth got to be pals with Lucy, and then it got to be awfully hard for me to hold in everything I knew. I think I was pretty cold to Lucy the few times I saw her during that period, to tell the truth. She was starting to show the signs of some bad strain, too. She didn't look good. She looked every inch of thirty years old, which she was, and then a lot more. I suppose this was understandable. It would be no fun whatsoever to live with Mike Kowalski, but it would be a hell of a lot worse to be going through a divorce with him.

You also have to take into account that there was a good bit of money at stake here. And child support and custody. It had all the makings of a very nasty divorce fight. And then add to that the charges of adultery, if he wanted to throw them in.

The strange thing was, as Mary Ruth started coming home to me and telling me the stories that Lucy told her about the divorce, there was no mention at all of the affair with Dolf Bradshaw. On second thought, that wasn't strange. You only get one side of the story from each party in a divorce, and I shouldn't have been surprised that Lucy was covering up. It did irritate me a little though to have to sit there and listen knowing what I knew.

To hear Mary Ruth tell it, Lucy was completely mystified why Mike had left her. He had just become a real jerk, detached, angry, stopped talking, and it got a lot worse after he and Dolf closed the business down. They weren't in financial trouble at all. Mike had plenty of money to start or buy another business or to coast until he found a job. But Lucy thought it was because of the business maybe. She just didn't know, and it was tearing her up.

Then Mary Ruth started bad-mouthing Mike to me. As if I hadn't been bad-mouthing him to her for the past year or so. But it's one thing when you are badmouthing a former friend, and it's another thing to have to listen to your wife badmouth the guy. It sort of pricks up my natural argumentativeness, I guess.

Well, Mary Ruth came home from the Junior League meeting one night. She had been out for a couple of beers with the girls after the meeting. I was finished writing, and the baby was in bed. I was up watching T.V., too tired to do anything else. Mary Ruth came in smelling like beer, and she sat on my lap in my La-Z-Boy, all smiles and kisses. The show I was watching on PBS was really interesting. I ignored her and tried to look around her to watch the T.V . She finally got up pouting and went to sit on the sofa. Then she wanted to talk.

I had to give up on the T.V. show, a fascinating documentary on the effects of the A-bomb on Hiroshima. Mary Ruth said Mike was trying to get custody of the boys and was being really nasty about it. Apparently he had been planning to leave Lucy for some time before he actually did. He had liquidated everything he could, even borrowed up to the limit on their home equity line, and had squirreled the money away God knows where, probably out of the country.

I really would rather have been watching the A-bomb show, and I guess I was a little short with Mary Ruth, and she just got mad.

"You haven't heard a word I've said," she said, getting up to storm into the kitchen. "You men are all alike. You don't appreciate us at all. You can just go to hell."

"Hey, wait a goddamn minute," I said. "Don't you talk to me like that." I hit the mute button on the T.V. remote. "You come in here bitching and badmouthing my friend, and you expect me to like it?"

"I don't believe this," she said. She laughed right at me. "You're telling me I'm badmouthing Mike Kowalski? After all the crap I've had to listen to about him for the past year?"

I was getting hot, now. "All I'm saying is there are two goddamn sides to every story, and you don't know the half of it."

Mary Ruth puffed her chest out and mocked me, shaking her finger at me, "Goddamn it, you don't know the goddamn half of the goddamn story." She giggled.

"Well, you don't." I was really hot now. I hate when she goes out drinking with the girls. "You think Lucy Kowalski's some kind of saint?"

"Yes, " Mary Ruth said. "Yes, as a matter of fact, I think she just about is. And she was married to one of the biggest male pigs on the face of the earth. Or is that redundant?"

She can really get me going sometimes, and I've said a lot of stupid things to her on those occasions, things I wish I never had said. "Well, for your goddamn information," I said, "did you know Lucy went to bed with Dolf Bradshaw about four months before Mike left her? Right there in Mike's and her own bedroom?"

That shut her up. If she were entirely sober she would probably have stormed out of the room and slammed the door. But she was just tipsy enough to realize the tremendous potential for heavy dirt here, and she walked back to the sofa, sat down, and stared at the television set.

Her brow was furrowed. She tried to look serious and concerned.

I switched the T.V. sound back on. The narrator's voice was running over film of a hydrogen bomb test on Bikini Atoll.

She let the time pass a little before she started digging for more dirt. That was a tactical error on her part, because by that time I had calmed down, and I told her it was a mistake that I said that, and that she was never to tell anyone else ever that I had said it, and then I clammed up. Which just about killed her.

Mary Ruth and Lucy got to be even better friends after that, though. Lucy would bring the boys over to play with the baby, and we would have her over for dinner.

It's that way with good friends. You can't remember how you got to be good friends. It happened that way with Lucy. We just saw more and more of her, and I guess she was lonely enough to use a couple of good pals. She was, really, just as wonderful a girl as she had ever been. She had lost a lot of the prettiness of ten years before, but she was still smart and level-headed, and non-judgmental, and attractive, and, well, fun to be around.

That spring we took Lucy to Mary Ruth's cousin's house at Edisto Beach for a rainy weekend. It was just the three of us. Lucy was supposed to have brought a date, but the date fell through at the last minute, and we told her to come on anyway. Which put me in an awkward situation. Lucy was pretty down and out about this guy not coming. The divorce hearing was in a month or so, and she was depressed already. She had lied to everybody about the date coming to the beach with her, because technically she was only separated.

Mary Ruth's cousins' house was a huge clapboard place built in the early fifties. The house was up on stilts above the retreating sand dunes. It was a rainy, cool weekend, with the sea gray and the surf heavy. A perfect weekend to be at the beach for me. But not the perfect weekend to be locked up in a big house with just two women for company. I suppose we made the best of it, and I certainly heard the steadiest stream of juicy gossip I had heard in a long time. I feigned disinterest, but it was all fascinating.

The ugly part came on Saturday night. We had driven up the highway to a seafood place and had a good bit to drink while we were there, and then when we got back out to the beach house I fixed everybody some white Russians in those big plastic football-game cups. We ended up getting pretty tight. The night wore on, and the sea breeze whipped the rain up against the screen porch and the window glass. We started talking about those things you only talk about late at night in very small groups, and after too much to drink. And the conversation got around to the divorce.

Lucy was talking about the problems they had had, the bad fights and all, and we were telling her that we had had all the same problems, except the problem of having too much money (which is a serious damn problem in a marriage, it seems to me). Lucy didn't really want to hear that we had had the same problems, when here we were still married.

Then Lucy started talking about Mike's running around. I hadn't known she knew about it. She didn't know about most of it, but she knew of one girl one time in New York. She had thought it was a real love affair, and that there was some reason Mike was dissatisfied with her, and that he had taken on this girlfriend because Lucy had been so wrapped up in motherhood and fixing their huge house up and driving the kids around town in the Volvo station wagon. I didn't like hearing that. How could you tell her that the girl was just another of a hundred pieces of strange to him?

The only thing unusual about her might have been that he didn't have to pay for it.

Well, I was sitting there listening to all this when I didn't really want to be listening to it, and I sure didn't intend at all to tell the things that I knew, but damn it, all of a sudden, here bursts in Mary Ruth wanting to tell the whole world about everything.

"Lucy," she said, and she cupped her white Russian in her hand. The wind whined on the eaves of the house. "I think I should tell you this, and please forgive me, Earnest." She took a sip. "Ernest told me all about you and Dolf. There. It's out in the open, now, and it was something all three of us knew about, so there's no sense in pretending we didn't."

Lucy looked puzzled. "What do you mean?" she said. But she wasn't just trying to cover up. She really didn't know what Mary Ruth was talking about.

Well, Mary Ruth just looked at me.

And then what the hell was I supposed to do? Was Lucy that good a liar? Frankly, I can usually spot a liar a mile off. There is some little thing that registers with me, although I often override that little thing and believe something I shouldn't. But this woman obviously had no idea what Mary Ruth was talking about.

"Earnest," Mary Ruth said.

And Lucy was looking at me like you would look at one of those tacky used car salesmen on T.V. if you met him in person. That has to get to those people, by the way, being looked at that way by every legitimate person they ever met. But hell, I was being legitimate, as far as I knew. Only there was no way I could tell her what I knew.

"Earnest," Lucy said. "What the hell are you talking about?"

I wanted a nuclear attack or a waterspout or Judgment Day to save me. I shook my head and took a cigarette from a pack on the coffee table and lit it.

This just heightened the anticipation from the two of them.

"Lucy," I said. "Ralph knows about it. Mike knows about it. And I know about it. All four of us knew. I'm sorry."

"Knew about what?" Lucy said.

"About you and Dolf," Mary Ruth said.

"What the hell about me and Dolf?" Lucy said. "I've never had anything to do with Dolf Bradshaw in my goddamn life."

"Earnest," Mary Ruth said, "you better tell me what you boys were talking about at the office."

Oh my Lord God. Jesus, why did my parents have to be so good and true to me when I was a little boy? I don't know how to tell lies. I just can't tell one unless I believe it myself or I'm pretty bad drunk. Well, maybe that's not entirely true, but I have a tendency to tell the whole truth, when I could probably get away with telling a lot less.

I told them there, that evening, with the wind whipping outside and opening and slamming the screen porch door every now and then, I told them the whole story of the evening in New York and the fight and the bet. Lucy and Mary Ruth looked like they were going to barbecue me as I told this part of the story, but when I got to the part about Dolf walking into Mike's office and telling about the heart tattoo, Lucy's mouth dropped opened, and she turned as scarlet red as I have ever seen any human being in my life. That saved me more or less with Mary Ruth, by the way, who was just as shocked as I had been to hear about the tattoo.

"I have never," stammered Lucy. "He has never ... There is absolutely no way ..."

Well, that's how the story got out. Like I say, that was not a fun weekend at the beach for me. The ride back to Charlotte the next day (and I was pretty damn lucky I wasn't walking back) was the longest period of time I have ever spent in an automobile, even though it's not but a two-hour drive.

Now, that's as far as I knew until the divorce hearing. I was thoroughly in the black as to what the truth was in this matter, but to tell the truth, the whole affair had caused me such misery I was just mad at the whole damn bunch of them-- Mike, Dolf, Lucy, even Mary Ruth, for having involved me at all. I could give a rip what the truth was, or if Dolf Bradshaw had been boinking Lucy Kowalski three times a day for the last fifteen years. I just wanted to be left out of it all.

Two things wouldn't let it out of my life though. One was Mary Ruth, who had just about had it with me by that time, I guess. And the other was the haunting image of Lucy's secret tattoo, whose existence had been undeniably confirmed.

Then there was a third thing that kept me involved in the story, and that was the subpoena that was served on me one evening as I was watching Tom Brokaw on the T.V. after work. The doorbell rang. I opened the front door. It was still daylight outside, and there was a nice-looking young guy in his twenties, in blue jeans, with longish blond hair. I opened the screen door, and he said, "Mr. Earnest _________?"

"Yes," I said.

He pulled the papers out from behind his back, slapped them up against my chest, and dropped them before I had time to react. He stepped down off the front stoop and hurried across the lawn to his car, jumped in, and sped off, without looking back.

I picked the papers up off the stoop and opened them. It was a subpoena to appear at the divorce hearing.

I went to a lawyer to see if I could get out of going. Even paid him one hour's fee to get him to call Lucy's lawyer and see if they would let me out of it. But no dice. I was summoned, and I had to go.

The hearing was on a very nice day in May or April. One of those balmy, breezy days, when the blossoms are all out and the oak leaves are no bigger than a possum's ear. My grandmother used to say that about the possum's ears. Anyway, I went downtown to the courthouse, had the usual hell of a time trying to find a parking place, and finally parked on the street and stuffed the parking meter.

Well, when I got in that little family court courtroom, there was a motley crowd in there. Mostly young, some middle age, and a couple that looked like they were in their seventies at least, all waiting for their chance to call it quits. And across the room, seated up near the front, were Lucy and her lawyer. About two rows behind them were Mike and his lawyer. I was standing in the doorway, wondering where I could sit to hide, when the swinging doors hit me from behind. I turned to apologize for blocking the way, and Dolf Bradshaw walked in dressed in one of his Hong Kong tailored suits, with a collar pin and bright red tie with large, silver paisleys. I hadn't seen Dolf since I stopped working with them.

Dolf just nodded, "Hey, Spud." He offered his hand without even looking at me anymore. Then he didn't stay to talk. He walked to the far back corner of the room and took one of the empty chairs

I had been thinking of taking. It was completely out of view of Lucy and Mike.

That left me to sit in the corner over near the door.

Divorce court is no fun. It's mostly one case after another being called, and the formalities being gone through in front of the judge. Almost every case had been worked out in advance, so the judge issued the decree and both parties, as hurt and as full of anger and as empty they were likely to get in their lives, just shuffled out the door dressed in their best clothes, trying to avoid looking at each other.

It had to be hard on the judge doing that every day.

There were a couple of cases where the money was going to be contested, and the judge put those off until later in the day. So I had to sit there for a couple of hours and watch all this. I've been to court on a few occasions. While there is almost never any high drama like you see on T.V. and in the movies, there are a lot of absurd stories and absurd characters. But this was too painful, and I was too nervous about what was coming up. I didn't like it at all.

Mike and Lucy's case was called, and their lawyers went up and spoke quietly to the judge at his bench. They were obviously the most highly paid and heavy-hitting lawyers there that day. The case was put off until right before lunch. Mike looked to be sweating. It wasn't hot in the courtroom.

About eleven o'clock, almost all the cases had been cleared. The couple in their seventies was still there with their lawyers, both the old people looking angry as hell. Their lawyers were wearing cheap suits and their ties were too short. There was one middle-aged black couple still left with their lawyers. The judge talked to all of these people's lawyers directly, by name. He told them that he was going to call their cases after lunch, and that Mike's and Lucy's case was going to be heard right now, and he was going to clear the courtroom. Everybody who had to leave looked pretty perturbed to have to be doing it, but they went without complaining.

That left me to be called as the first witness. I stepped into the witness stand, and a bailiff made me swear to tell the whole truth. Lucy's lawyer came up and asked in one of those sickeningly soft Southern drawls all the questions that made me tell the whole truth, as best I could remember it. It was in a way good to tell the story, sort of like going to confession. But in confession you don't have the people you are damning sitting right in front of you staring back at you.

You could tell Lucy's lawyer and the judge were hopping mad by the time I got through testifying. The judge didn't say anything. He just cleared his throat and was red in the face. He was a short, fat man with black hair that could have been a toupee, and jowls that spilled over his shirt collar. He had a shaving rash. He had been hard and cold all morning long to everybody who appeared before him.

The next witness they called was Dolf. The bailiff swore him in, too. I had seen Dolf look scared before. Not often, but once or twice I had seen him look scared. But Dolf wasn't scared in the least as he took that stand. He looked like he didn't give a rat's ass.

Lucy's lawyer stood up to question Dolf. He walked over and put his hand on the edge of the witness box.

"Mr . Bradshaw," he said. "Did you hear the testimony Mr. __________ just gave?"

"Yes," Dolf said.

"Was Mr. __________ 's testimony   accurate, as far as you know?"

Dolf pursed his lips up and thought. "Yes," he said.

"The story of the bet between you and Mr. Kowalski is true?" the lawyer said.

"Yes," Dolf said.

"And is it true that you confronted Mr. Kowalski in his office, told him of his wife's tattoo, presented him with his St. Christopher's medal, and that he paid you ten thousand dollars?"

Dolf was a little uneasy. But he said, "Yes, that is true."

"Was that the first wager for money that the two of you had made?"

"No. "

"It was common practice in fact for the two of you to make wagers?"

"More or less. "

"In fact, had Mr. Kowalski won a great deal of money from you in these wagers?"

"No. As a matter of fact," Dolf said, "I would say I had won ten, fifteen thousand dollars on the whole from him over the years. He made stupid bets. Always has been a stupid gambler. I even tried to keep away from betting with him. It made me feel bad. The guy threw his money away, and I knew he had a family to support."

"Mr. Bradshaw, have you ever had sexual relations with Lucy Kowalski?"

Dolf let that question hang just long enough for the dramatic effect. "No," he said.

"Have you ever told anyone you had sexual relations with Lucy Kowalski?"

"No."

Mike put his head down in his hands. I was thinking back. I was confused, but hell, that was the truth, come to think of it. "What did you tell Mr . Kowalski on the day you presented him with his St. Christopher's medal in his office?"

"Word for word?" Dolf said.

"Yes, please, exactly what did you tell him?"

"I told him Lucy had a red heart tattooed just above her private parts. Her shaved private parts. A broken heart."

"Did you tell him anything else?"

"No."

"Did he write you a check for ten thousand dollars?"

"Yes."

"Did you accept that check?"

"Yes."

"Did you cash that check?"

"Yes."

"What did you do with the proceeds?"

"I gave the money to Lucy Kowalski after she and Mike split up. I told her it was a business debt he had paid me, and I wanted her to have it."

"Why did you do that?"

Dolf just shrugged. Well, the lawyer let all of this sink in a little bit. I don't know what anybody else's reaction was, to tell the truth. I was too stunned myself. I think everybody there was as stunned as I was, except Lucy.

"Mr. Bradshaw," Lucy's lawyer said, "how did you know that Lucy Kowalski had the tattoo you described?"

Well, Dolf told his story then. When Mike left for the Far East after their bet, Dolf called Lucy at home every day, ostensibly over mundane office matters, until he found out that she was taking the boys over to her mother-in-law's house for dinner one evening. She didn't like her mother-in-law, and she was not looking forward to the evening.

Dolf worked late that day. When he knew Lucy would be gone, he left the office, drove over to Mike's house,and rang the doorbell. When he was convinced nobody was at home, he let himself in the garage door with the key Mike kept in the top drawer of his office desk. Dolf had parked his car in the church parking lot behind the house. It was after dark, and he crossed the back yard from the church parking lot.

When he got in, he went upstairs to Mike and Lucy's bedroom and took the St. Christopher's from Mike's chest of drawers. It was that quick, and he was ready to leave, but apparently one of the boys had gotten sick and thrown up over the mother-in-law's dining room table, so Lucy came home early. As Dolf was about to leave, he heard Lucy driving into the garage. She and the boys came in the garage door ,through the laundry room, and into the kitchen.

Dolf didn't have any way to get out. The master bedroom had two walk-in closets, both with louvered doors. One was Mike's with only Mike's clothes in it, and the larger of the two was Lucy's, with only Lucy's clothes in it.

Dolf ducked into Mike's closet, hoping he could sneak out as Lucy gave the boys a bath and put them to bed. He never got a chance, though. The boys' bathroom was opposite the head of the stairs, and there was no way for him to get past it without being seen.

Dolf had broken into the house, as far as I could tell from his story, for the express purpose of gathering evidence to substantiate his false claim to having slept with Lucy. He got a lot more evidence than he had ever hoped to get.

After Lucy put the boys to bed, she came into her bedroom and watched T.V. for an hour or so, as Dolf watched through the cracks of the louvered closet door. Then she got up and turned the T.V. off.

Dolf watched Lucy undress. He watched her plug an exercise tape into the VCR and do the exercises in the nude. He watched her go in to take a shower. He watched her put on a t-shirt after her shower. And he watched her kneel beside the bed, say her prayers, get into bed, and go to sleep. He stayed awake all night, leaning up against the door jam in Mike's closet, so he wouldn't snore or talk in his sleep. The next morning, when Lucy took the boys off to nursery school, he sneaked out of the house, walked back to his car, and drove home.

Dolf told this story, and it hurt to have to listen to it. It was one of those stories, to tell the truth, that show the side of us we don't want to see. Human beings are often far from poetic.

Lucy's lawyer tried to get Dolf to go into his motivations for doing what he had done. But Dolf just shrugged the questions off. I don't think he understood his own motivations. Then Mike's lawyer got up and tried to shoot holes in Dolf's story. But it became clear after a few minutes of questioning that Dolf was telling the truth. When a man is coming clean, you can't shoot holes in what he's saying. He's not being cautious enough about what he's saying to be inconsistent.

The judge really screwed Mike to the wall. I sat and listened through that part. Lucy got the house, a tremendous alimony settlement, the car, the boys, the dog and cat. Mike was going to be held in contempt of court if he didn't turn over a detailed accounting of where all his money was in overseas banks and corporations. Mike's lawyer tried to argue against this, but the judge wouldn't hear his arguments.

When it was over, I didn't stay around waiting for the dust to settle. As soon as they said I could go, I went. I didn't talk to anybody on the way out.

I might as well go on and skip ahead here. Because the oddest part of this story, I think, is how it all turned out, I mean with Lucy and Mike remarried. The divorce was granted and finalized, so when they got back together, they had to get remarried, even though they had been divorced for only a couple of months.

You know, there's a thing about marriage, and about life. You just can't ever really tell how anybody is doing at it- at life or at marriage that is. They're just living it, and surviving it, and you won't be able to say how well they did it until it's all over. You can't tell how the future is going to treat them.

So, here, from a snapshot right now, of the little I know about them, and the little I know about how well they are doing, I would have to say that Mike and Lucy are a happy couple. They certainly have two fine boys they ought to be proud of. Mike is a different man as far as I know. I haven't seen him but once since the divorce hearing. We were down at Hilton Head with some friends for the weekend. Mary Ruth was the one who suggested we go by to see Mike and Lucy. They had opened a small French restaurant set back out of sight in a shopping mall on the highway. The place was well kept, but tiny. I would say no more than ten tables. We made reservations with the girl who worked for them that afternoon, so they didn't know we were coming, and we caught them just as they were beginning to get busy.

Lucy and Mike were both friendly as they could be. A little distant, but Lucy gave Mary Ruth and me a hug, and Mike shook my hand. There was something there that kept them distant, but Mike, if I have to think back on it, was nothing like he was when he was a rich, young man.

They had had a baby, too, which I hadn't heard about. It was a girl. They pulled out pictures of her, and she was really the prettiest baby I have ever seen. I mean lots of babies are ugly, but she had a full head of pretty brown hair, and the biggest, deepest brown eyes and rosy cheeks. Looked just like her mother.

They had to get back to work, but the meeting went so well we invited them to our hotel for a drink the next afternoon, and they agreed to come.

The next afternoon Lucy called to say one of the boys had cut his lip falling off his bicycle and had to go get stitches, so they wouldn't be able to come. We didn't see them that weekend, and we haven't seen them since.

Which isn't to say we won't see them again, I guess.

The Tenth Tale
Wendy Potonovsky teaches her husband.

Ben Widerman was distinguished professor of Medieval Literature at an Ivy League University, a famous man in his field, which meant other professors around the country made their graduate students read his analyses of metaphor and irony in medieval frame tales. Some of those same students, eager to please their dissertation advisers, would skim through Ben's long deconstructions of the Arabic sources of those tales and cite them in their dissertation footnotes.

Not that Ben was such a bad writer. In fact, being from the old school (and as much as he tried to avoid acting like it, he was undeniably from the old school), his articles and both his books were quite readable. This lowered the graduate students' estimation of him.

Ben was also quite a popular teacher. I knew Ben. He was a humane and approachable guy for an Ivy League professor. I often wondered about him. He was pale, with large circles under his eyes and two battered pairs of horn-rimmed glasses that he constantly switched so he could see to read and then see to talk to his students. He always looked like he hadn't slept well, and his oily gray hair was always mussed. He dressed in inexpensive, button-down, oxford-cloth shirts, Ivy League ties, a blazer or tweed jacket, and scuffed cordovan wingtips.

I always assumed Ben was gay. He was in his late fifties when I knew him, and he had never married. Other graduate students asked me about him, and I would say I didn't know, but I was almost sure, in that way you become sure when you work with large numbers of homosexuals. That's what I thought about Ben Widerman, and I guess I was all wrong, or at least partly wrong. Because when Ben was sixty years old, he fell in love with and married one of his dissertation advisees, Wendy Potonovsky. Wendy was writing on the duality of meaning in morality plays. She was an awfully good-looking woman for an English graduate student.

In fact, Wendy was a woman who would have stood out as a looker in the general population, not just in the English department. And she didn't do much more than was required by her academic set to make herself look bad. She had long brown hair, probably hazel eyes, because her eyes still stick with me. Of course I remember her ass, which was somewhat protruding, but not enough to look bad. She had nice legs and boobs about the size of oranges. This is the kind of thing I was really thinking about in all those seminars I sat in on with her.

I often fantasized what Wendy would look like in one of those Sports Illustrated bathing suit issues.

Anyway, Wendy married Ben Widerman when he was sixty years old and she was, I'm guessing, twenty-seven or twenty-eight. Really, of all the professors I knew, the last one I could imagine hitting on his dissertation advisee, at least his female advisee, was Ben Widerman. I had dropped out of grad school by then, but I imagine it might have evolved as one of those entirely sexless things, the pure love of the mind, not Platonic, because that means something else to me, but just two people beginning to feel awfully comfortable with each other, and maybe feeling that way because they're not thinking all the time about the possibility of screwing each other.

They were married in a non-religious ceremony in the botanical gardens, repeating vows they had written themselves. The guests were a few of their colleagues, along with Wendy's family (her parents were divorced and attended with their boyfriend and girlfriend), and Ben's sister and her husband.

On their honeymoon they went to Cuba. Cuba was a beautiful place. Even though they weren't allowed to travel around much, Wendy had never been to a tropical island before, and she loved it, with the trade winds and the crystal clear water and the friendly people, and the interesting tourists from Europe and the Soviet Union. She had a fantastic time, the kind of time she had always dreamed about having on her honeymoon, except for one thing.

Ben was gentle and loving enough, but let's face it, Wendy was twenty-eight years old, and she was really turned on. The only times she had had sex before were when she gave in to the seduction attempts of drunk young men. She hadn't had a very high opinion of sex at all. But now with someone she loved and was married to, that was something else.

So Wendy was a tiger the whole honeymoon. Ben did everything he could to turn her attention elsewhere. Whenever she began to make advances, he engaged her in a discussion on some esoteric and surprising topic, and quickly caught a contradiction in her logic, which got her so worked up that she would debate with him for hours.

Ben tried once when they got home to explain to Wendy that he didn't feel he could keep up with her sexual stamina, but she just got sullen, and when he tried to comfort her, she burst into tears and said it must be her fault, that all the men she had ever been with had said that she was an iceberg. She ended up taking him to bed and trying to prove her seductiveness, which just turned Ben off. He couldn't do it at all, and this got Wendy all the more upset. They had the first night of tears and shouting and wondering whether they were going to make it through such agony, and believing theirs was the most screwed up marriage on earth.

But the next night, or maybe it was the next one after that- anyway, it was a cold winter night- Ben sat up by the fire and Wendy sat on the floor at his feet, and he read from *Beowulf* and *The Battle of Maldon* to her in Anglo-Saxon, with the rhythm and the stress where they should be, so that the poetry was as magnificent as words can be when you don't understand most of them. This was one of the things that had made Wendy fall in love with Ben. He really did love the poetry, in a magical way.

They made love the following week, or maybe it was two weeks after that. Wendy again did all she could to prove that she was a sex demon, and poor Ben had severe chest pains for several hours after that. Even though he tried to downplay it, Wendy and he were terrified that he had had a heart attack.

After that, Ben found every excuse not to go to bed with Wendy. He had some book to read, or a chapter of his new book on Old Norse Skaldic verse as anti-poetry that he absolutely had to have finished by the end of the term, or he had to prepare his report for a faculty committee meeting the next week. It just dragged out after that, something that both of them knew was not good, but that was a lot easier to live with and try to ignore than to try to fix.

Wendy was still happy with her fatherly crusader. She put her energies into working on her dissertation and teaching, and raising the consciousness of her own students, and showing them how their values were all in the wrong place.

One thing Wendy especially loved about Ben was his knack for drumming up funding for great trips. He was an expert at writing grants and tagging along on student tours, not just to those places where dead Germanic languages had once been spoken, but also to those political hot spots where he considered that right was pitted in the struggle against wrong.

Ben worked up another trip for them about a year after their honeymoon, this time a fact-finding trip to Nicaragua, where they would go out into the countryside and see how the Sandinistas were improving the lives of the peasants in the small villages. They went as soon as they could get away in exam time in May and met in Washington with the other members of the peace and human rights group who were sponsoring the junket.

After a prayer session that was designed not to offend the sensibilities of the irreligious among them, the group went to the Capitol and staged a small, fist-shaking protest. Then they went to the airport and boarded an Air Canada flight, all of them wearing name tags and feeling elated, chatting over the seat backs and standing bent over in the aisles to talk to each other.

They spent three days in Managua, where they joined in another fist-shaking protest led by a phalanx of school-children, and where all the members of the group were impressed by what the Sandinistas were doing to improve the lives of the people. And they were genuinely angered by what the U.S. government was doing to undermine their efforts.

It was a giddy time, almost like a religious retreat, and Ben became in many ways the priest or father of the group. The others looked to him for the pithy advice of a man who had patiently stood by the cause for almost half a century. All the group members admired him as he stayed up late every night- until the early morning hours- leading them in political discussions.

All except Wendy. Even though seeing Ben at his most fervent made her in one way proud, she also found herself resenting him as he preached with that self-assured smile on his face.

They had been married a year, you see, which might have been enough to cause the little pangs of resentment, but also, the late-night political discussions were just another good excuse for Ben to be too tired to do anything when he got in bed. He usually got there several hours after Wendy had already gone to sleep.

These late-night political discussions continued after the fact-finders made their way into the countryside, where they were shown all the things the Sandinistas were trying to do for the peasants. They met other American true believers who were there to make things work the way they wanted them to work, and they slept in little huts the government provided for them. Everything was just keen.

Until they came to the southern village of Labanana in the second week of their fact-finding mission. Labanana was a sleepy village with wide, dusty streets, set in the middle of a very wide and very flat valley filled with banana plantations. They toured a state-owned banana plantation where all the machinery was in shambles, they were told, because of the economic pressure the U.S. government was putting on the Sandinistas. The peasants were hard at work picking fruit, but to be perfectly honest, they looked just the same as peasants or fruit pickers anywhere, like they would a hell of a lot rather be doing something else, especially what you are doing, if all you are doing is standing there in your nice clothes and watching them work.

Anyway, that night after dinner Ben and Wendy had an indecorous fight, although they tried to keep their voices low so the other people in the tour wouldn't hear them. Wendy was tired and had a developing case of Montezuma's revenge, and she was really bitchy the last couple of days. Ben started to lecture her about one sharp remark she had made to the tour guide, and before long they were having a bad argument.

So Wendy went to bed early, and Ben stayed up late to discuss politics with the locals, long past the point where they all looked like they were ready to go to bed, too. It was one or two o'clock in the morning when the guerillas attacked. At first there was a rifle shot out near the edge of the village, and the government guides and soldiers looked very nervous, but when nothing else happened they began to calm back down. Then three or four minutes later, there was another shot, and after thirty very anxious seconds of silence, while the soldiers moved toward the doors and windows, automatic weapons fire broke out all around them in the distance. People started screaming, and the soldiers ran out into the street. Livestock squawked and bellowed and squealed. There was a crescendo of small arms fire, and then explosions.

Ben and the members of the tour who were still in the political meeting huddled low against the adobe walls of the building. Children were crying and screaming throughout the village. The gunfire was ferocious all around them. They could hear the soldiers shouting to each other. The night was lit up by explosions.

The firefight sounded terrible. A lot of the people in the tour, and a lot of the villagers in the house with them, were crying. The fighting started on the outskirts of the village and moved closer until it sounded like some of the gunfire was only a couple of houses away, and then, about two hours after the fighting started, the guerillas apparently began to retreat. The gunfire and shouting and explosions drew farther away and became more sporadic.

By sunup the firing had stopped, and Ben and the others left the safety of the house to see what had happened.

The soldiers were bringing one dead government soldier down the street, a short, very young man with Indian features whose chest had been blown open by shrapnel. Other soldiers behind them were pushing a captured guerilla in jungle camouflage. The fact-finders rushed over to see and photograph this, but not Ben. He went dashing down the street toward the bungalow where Wendy had been sleeping, to see if she was o.k.

When he got there he saw the door had been knocked off the hinges. He dashed inside and found the furniture had been thrown against the walls, the screens had been broken out of the windows, and the floor was covered with spent shell casings. There was no one in the house.

Ben was frantic. He ran through the streets, calling for Wendy and dashing into houses to look. He grabbed villagers and asked them in fragmentary Spanish if they had seen his wife, and he tried to describe her with his hands, but they just shrugged and shook their heads. The village was shot up, and livestock was running loose in the streets. The front of one building on the main street had been demolished by an explosion, but Ben saw no more wounded or,dead people. There was a dead ass lying up against a house on a back street. Flies were crawling all over it.

Ben ran and walked over all the village looking, until he was gasping for breath The early morning sun was just beginning to heat up. Ben got back to where the tour members were still gathered around the dead soldier, and he frantically told the tour guides that his wife was missing, so all the fact finders spread out over the village to look for her.

The prisoner was lying in the mud against a house, with his legs bound and his arms tied tight behind his back. As soon as the fact-finders dispersed, the government soldiers took turns kicking him and spitting on him, sticking their gun barrels up his nose and threatening to shoot his head off.

It was a long time before the fact-finders came to the conclusion that Wendy had been kidnapped. They had to search the whole village over and over, and then they had to search the fields surrounding the village for hours, and then they started searching in the banana plantations. They searched as far out as the edges of the jungle, but they could not find her. They were able to see the direction the rebels had come from and the direction they retreated. One *campesino* even found where they had bivouacked on a jungle ridge the day before, waiting until the middle of the night to attack. There was blood, and the tracks of a body being dragged away on the retreat trail, and this made Ben so scared he got nauseous. But the soldiers pointed out that the contras would never have dragged a wounded gringa back into the jungle with them.

Surely that was the worst day of Ben Widerman's life. Just stop a moment and try to get in his shoes yourself. You are in a very strange place in a very strange country, and after spending the night in the middle of a battle, wondering whether you were going to survive and whether your wife who was in a house a hundred meters away was going to survive as well, after all that, you spend the next day searching for your wife who is missing, presumed dead at first, but as the day wears on, presumed kidnapped.

If you were a bad actor starring in the movie version, you would run all over the set, covered in jungle dirt and sweat, shouting in a high-pitched voice at everybody who wasn't doing enough to help find her. But in reality what I would do, and I think what you would do, is to fight very hard to control your emotions and to keep cool on the outside, this fight being as much to keep you from going crazy as anything else. This is how Ben handled it, with cool determination, although the strain was easy to see on his face, and his hands shook, and a few times during the day he broke and shouted at people. The cool stayed with him until late in the afternoon, when one of the *campesinos* found the prints of Wendy's running shoes along the jungle trail where the rebels had retreated, and then about fifty meters later, he found several buttons off of Wendy's safari shirt, and, hanging in a bush five meters off the trail, her brassiere.

Ben just collapsed then. He collapsed and wept and cursed Nicaragua and cursed himself for bringing Wendy there. Several of his fellow fact-finders tried to pick him up and help him walk, but he was overcome. The soldiers were very cold about this.

Oh, it was a terrible time for Ben Widerman. Ben knew he couldn't go into the jungle after her. There was no way Ben Widerman could go into that jungle. A lot of the reasons were entirely rational, physical, logistical. But a lot of it also was because of who he was. Ben Widerman didn't go into jungles to look for his kidnapped wife. He couldn't even do it in his dreams. When he dreamed about it after he had returned to the States, he walked past the edge of the banana plantation, not two or three hundred yards into the jungle, and then he was in Los Angeles, looking for her in a Mexican barrio, trying to speak Spanish. A street gang was harassing him, and then there were five police cars full of Los Angeles Police Department patrolmen to protect him, but a gun fight broke out, and Ben ran away from it as fast as he could run in his dreams, which wasn't fast enough, like running in slow motion.

Ben's mother was in his dream. He ran to her, and she took him through a shopping mall in an affluent neighborhood. She helped him pick out some nice, Ivy League clothes, but all the time he knew he shouldn't be in the shopping mall with his mother- he should be in the jungle looking for Wendy.

Oh Ben. I suppose what he did for the next year and a half of his life really does testify to the capacity of men for courage. Ben fought a terrible fight with the State Department in Washington, enlisting the help of the media and several Congressional leaders. He searched for Wendy for over a year, spending nearly all his life's savings, and taking a sabbatical from teaching for one semester. He put his book on Old Norse versification on hold.

The official State Department story, after they admitted (and that was several months later) that Wendy might indeed be missing, their official story was that she had been kidnapped by a band of heavily armed *bandidos* who were not at all connected to the Contra guerillas. Ben put a lot of effort into ridiculing that in his lecture tours and all the press he could drum up, even after he became convinced himself that it was true.

The stink and hassle created by Ben, as well as other developments in Central America, led the Assistant Undersecretary of State to whom Wendy's case had been assigned to step down. The man who replaced him was a wooden bureaucrat, and he called Ben down to Washington and invited him into his office shortly after his appointment.

The new Assistant Undersecretary was not a man who shot straight. Ben could sense that when he walked into the room with him.

This Assistant Undersecretary of State invited Ben to have a seat at the conference table in his office. Ben was very hostile to the man. Immediately he began shouting questions and accusations that made the Assistant Undersecretary so angry his hands shook. But the Assistant Undersecretary had orders to carry out, so he asked Ben to sit down. The A. U. opened up a manila envelope stamped "Confidential," pulled some papers and photographs out, and told Ben, "You never saw any of this, Dr. Widerman."

There were several eight-by-ten, glossy, black-and-white photographs of a portly, bald white man. Pudgy might be a better word for him. The hair that still grew around the sides of his head was too long. In one picture he wore a salt and pepper stubble beard. The man looked to be in his mid- to late-forties.

In one picture the man was wearing a bikini bathing suit. He was sunning on a beach along a rocky coast. The photograph had been taken with a telephoto lens. The other photographs were of this man in sunglasses or with a hat covering his forehead as he stepped into or out of a car, or as he was walking through an airport.

This man, the assistant undersecretary told Ben, was an international drug and weapons dealer, one Wallace Schuler, a.k.a. Thomas Wallace, or Shuler Thoms. His real name was Chester Thoms, of the Thoms shipping fortune family, originally from Newport and Palm Beach.

"Probably one of the most dangerous men in the international weapons trade," the assistant undersecretary said, in a way that made it clear his only knowledge of this matter came from his assistant's briefing earlier that morning.

"This is the man who kidnapped your wife," the assistant undersecretary said. "We're still trying to figure out what he was doing in Nicaragua, but we know from sources that are much too sensitive to compromise that he has your wife with him. I'm sorry Dr. Widerman, I know this is a very emotional issue with you. But we have known for some time that your wife was with Thoms. We had to wait until it became common knowledge in a much larger circle of that underworld before we could declassify our information and make it known to you. I'm sorry, but we're dealing here with the fate of agents who risk their lives every day to defend your freedom."

The diplomat threw Ben so off guard with the whole presentation that Ben just nodded quiescently and then thanked the man as he was being shown the door. This really pissed Ben off when he had had thirty or forty minutes to think about it. He had been used.

That started the long process of verifying what the Assistant Undersecretary of State had told him, and then of actually searching for Wallace Schuler, or whatever his name now was. Ben exhausted his own personal savings, even had to sell his one-week-a-year time-share condominium in the Berkshires. He enlisted the aid of some political organizations and raised money on lecture tours where he outlined the case that the contras had kidnapped his wife and the U.S. government had done everything they could to cover it up.

He traced Schuler to Hong Kong in a stroke of luck after countless dead ends. If you spend enough time with your ear to the ground in any walk of life, you soon begin to pick up on the inside flow of information. It's really not so hard. Not nearly as hard as everyone imagines. Ben spent enough time reading about and getting to know people in the international weapons trade that he eventually started to know things he never would have imagined he would know.

Ben had heard of a major illicit shipment of Israeli Uzi machine guns to an African country early in the second summer of his search. Then he read on the fifth page of the New York Times an account of the guerilla insurgency there, and how the guerillas were being supplied by the Chinese government. The connection didn't hit him until he was in the shower a couple of days later. A disaffected DEA agent in Miami had told him several months earlier of one major arms dealer who operated out of Hong Kong and shipped for the Communist Chinese government, managing a number of shady, hard-currency transactions, some of which had wound up in a Cayman Islands account being watched by the DEA.

Anyway, Ben had heard, months and months before, that Schuler was working with those particular African guerillas, which was why he had read the article with interest. While he was in the shower, it hit him all at once. The man in Hong Kong was Schuler.

And so, one day Ben was in his shower in New England, dejected and depressed and convinced he was never going to get anywhere, and the next he week he was on a flight from Los Angeles headed for Hong Kong.

The first day or two in Hong Kong was maddening for Ben, as he encountered the trouble of trying to find people and places in an Oriental city. He screamed and cursed at a taxi driver one morning after he had stood in a queue for an hour to get a taxi, and the driver pretended not to understand the address in English, although every street sign in the city was written in English.

Ben had the desk clerk at his cheap hotel try to find a phone number and address for Wallace Schuler. Ben had to call the desk several times over a couple of days to get them to give him an answer. The answer finally was that there was no such listing.

After a long, frustrating afternoon of his second day in Hong Kong, Ben walked from his hotel far out on Nathan Road on the Kowloon side all the way down to the Star Ferry pier. The sidewalks were crowded with hundreds of thousands of Chinese shoppers, stopping to stare at the goods on display in the open shops. The ferry terminal was steamy hot until Ben walked onto the covered pier over the water. The crowd here was noisy and tightly packed. Old Chinese men coughed up phlegm and spat it at the bottom of the walls.

Ben rode the ferry over to Hong Kong. He walked up the hill from the ferry pier, aiming to take the Peak Tram to the top of Victoria Peak for a little sightseeing, but he got so hot and tired and depressed that he went into the Hilton, walked through the lobby to a bar, and ordered a drink that he couldn't possibly afford to order. Ben had run his Visa and Mastercard both perilously close to their limits.

A fat, short man with an open shirt and curly dark hair and a chest covered with gold chains was sitting at the bar when Ben came in. As soon as the man realized Ben was alone, he struck up a conversation with him. The man was a China trader, a loud and obnoxious man from Long Island, who loved to curse and badmouth the Chinese. This man would have offended Ben to no end a year and a half earlier, but Ben had changed in all his searching, and he accepted this man more or less as he had accepted all the strange and unsavory characters he had met.

Ben lied that he was in Hong Kong calling on toy manufacturers for a friend in New York who was in the import business. He kept the conversation going as he had learned to keep one going. He was unobtrusive and friendly, picking information out of the little fellow, letting him open up and warm up. Ben didn't have any particular designs for this man. As far as he knew, the man had nothing to offer him, but it was getting to be a habit for Ben to do this, whether he was looking for something or not. And after an hour or so, when they had ordered another round, Ben began to loosen up a bit himself.

He said he was having a little trouble doing business here in Hong Kong. He was terribly frustrated trying to find this fellow, one Wallace Schuler, whom his friend in New York had asked him to locate, and that he suspected the trouble was because this Schuler fellow was not exactly the kind of above-board businessman people went to look for themselves. They sent acquaintances to look for him .

"Well shit, he could be any of a million guys like that in Hong Kong," the China trader said. "You know what I'd do?" He spread his palms open and poked his belly out. "You go down to the World Trade Council building, show them your foreign business card, subscribe to their little magazine- you know they send you their magazine with all the shit you can buy from Hong Kong- tell them someone you were doing business with suggested you contact this guy, what do you call him, Schuler? Say, you know, say like you're telling the truth, say you tried to get them to trace him at the hotel, but they couldn't find him. Look like you're shooting the straight shit, they'll probably look him right up for you. If he does any business overseas, which it sounds like he does. It's worth a shot anyway."

So Ben paid for the guy's drink and did what he suggested.

He took a cab the half a mile or so down to the World Trade Council building, walked in, handed the girl at the counter one of the bogus business cards he had had printed up over the past year, and after some hemming and hawing she referred him to another girl in an office down the hall. That girl had a long conversation in Cantonese, spiced with worried looks and laughing, with another girl in the office. Then she gave him a phone number and address for Wallace Schuler.

It turned out to be a home address. Ben had the girl write it for him in English and Chinese, and he stood in a queue again for a taxi. He handed the address to the driver, who was really perturbed when he read it. It turned out to be the address of a house way up on Victoria Peak overlooking the harbor. The taxi ride took a good half an hour, and they got up there after dusk. When Ben saw the white stucco house, just outlined against the setting sun through the trees past the electric gate, something in him stirred. He was finally so close to the bastard, to this man he had been searching for for over a year.

It also hit Ben for the first time that Wendy was probably no longer alive.

Anyway, it was almost dark, and he just couldn't find it in himself to try anything else that night. He paid the return fare to have the taxi driver take him all the way back down to the Star Ferry Pier. Ben joined in the crush of people moving down the wide hallways out to where the ferry loaded. The Star Ferry is a delightful boat, something out of the nineteen-twenties, with wooden decks and wooden bench seats and a flat roof and straight smokestack. The ride across Hong Kong harbor in the early evening darkness is so exhilarating, with conversations in Chinese and English and French and Japanese all around you, and the water slopping up against the bow, and the harbor just mad with boat traffic, ferries and hydrofoils and tramp steamers and yachts and junks, all dodging in and out among each other. And the city on both sides of the harbor, climbing up the mountain sides and brightly lit and the skyscrapers hung with giant neon signs. It has to move you. It moved Ben like he was living a dream, like he couldn't really be in this place doing what he was doing.

Ben walked from the Kowloon side pier all the way back to his hotel, stopping along the way to stare into shop windows. He ate peanuts at the hotel bar for dinner that night, and he drank enough to help him go to sleep. When he went up his room, he took a beer from the refrigerator, turned on the T.V., and watched a bad Australian movie before he finally passed out.

The next morning was Sunday. Around nine o'clock, Ben left his hotel and retraced his route across Kowloon, across the harbor, and back up the Peak to the road in front of Wallace Schuler's estate. The house, what little of it he could see, looked bigger in the daylight. The ornamented steel gate was closed, and the high stucco wall was unscalable. Ben thought he could catch a glimpse of razor wire on the back side of the top of the wall, just out of sight.

Ben stood for a moment in front of the gate, his heart pumping and the blood throbbing in his neck. Then he walked up to the intercom beside the gate, rang, and announced himself. To his great surprise, after a very short wait, the electric motor switched on and the gate slid open.

Ben walked up the curved driveway, surrounded on both sides by thick, short trees and shrubs. Two Chinese men wearing bulky jackets and too-short ties came down the driveway to meet him.

They didn't smile. They led Ben around the side of the house and along a walkway to the back of the house, where they opened the gate. Ben walked onto the deck of a swimming pool with a stunning view of the harbor and the New Territories in the hazy distance beyond.

On a folding lounge chair, taking in the sun, lay Wallace Schuler, fat and tan and bald, in a bikini bathing suit like the one he had been wearing in the State Department photograph. When Ben walked through the gate, Schuler got up immediately and graciously offered Ben his hand.

"Hello, Dr. Widerman," Schuler said. "I understand you've been searching for me for some time." The accent was vintage Newport, Martha's Vineyard, Palm Beach. Ben had encountered it among his students in years past. He had always hated it.

Schuler was slightly short, decidedly pudgy and decidedly middle aged, with a pinkish sunburn. He was self-assured, but in a classy, humble way. He was gracious and seemed like a very straightforward guy. He asked Ben to take a seat and asked if he would like a drink, at least a cola, or a cup of coffee, perhaps.

Ben really was thirsty, so he ordered a cola, which one of the Chinese stiffs who had met him in the driveway brought to him on a serving tray.

"Listen, Professor Widerman," Schuler said, as they were walking along the edge of the swimming pool terrace, and he was pointing out the sights to Ben. "I know why you've been searching for me, and I know how long you've been searching for me. I'd like to help you. Obviously, I'm a very busy man, and I don't have time to help most of the people who want my help. I don't have time to speak to most people. But I admire a man who would stick with it the way you have.

"There," he said suddenly, pointing down into the harbor. "A U.S. Navy ship coming to call. Guided-missile frigate, Farragut class."

Ben couldn't have cared less.

"Anyway," Schuler said, taking a sip from his Bloody Mary, "I think you've been dealt a bum hand in this matter. It's outrageous what the State Department did about this. Those little spineless desk riders. Jesus you come to despise them in this business.

"Dr. Widerman, they've sent you on a wild goose chase. They knew how hard it would be to find me. They've made me this hard to find themselves, but they know I'm in no real danger, so they use me to send the occasional innocent on a wild goose chase. 'Schuler, the amoral bastard, has kidnapped some nubile leftist in the jungles of Central America this time.'" Shuler laughed and shook his head and belched a little belch.

"Listen, I really hate this degree of informality, you and I weren't brought up this way, but could I call you 'Ben?' Ben, it's absurd, you and I from the worlds we come from, here beside a swimming pool overlooking Hong Kong harbor, playing these games. I never stop marveling at life." Schuler looked then like a part of him was hurting, like he really missed something that was gone.

And Ben began to like this guy. Ben had been run around a lot in the past year, and he'd never had someone come clean to him like this.

"Listen, Ben," Schuler said, "I used to spend a lot of time in Central America. You might even have run across my trail there a couple of times, but I can assure you, as many bad things as I was doing there, I was never running around in the jungle kidnapping Americans. I mean come on, where do these bastards come up with this stuff? Their boys, their former National Guardsmen or gangsters or whoever they could drag into their band, they took her, and frankly, Ben, I'm sorry to say this, but I'm sure you've considered the possibility, I doubt she survived."

This hit Ben pretty hard.

"Not that, not that they did anything to her, probably. Frankly, Ben, my guess, and I've even heard this around on the grapevine, is that your wife was hit in the crossfire, that they either dragged her back in the jungle to help her, or just to remove the evidence of a gringa being killed in their fight. I mean come on, these are jungle peasants, they don't know anything about the world. They don't know about the kind of manipulating bastards who sent you looking for me."

The U.S. guided-missile frigate was coming to dock in front of the Prince of Wales building on the Hong Kong side. Ben had tears welling up in his eyes.

"Chester," a female voice said behind them. "Chester baby, are you going to want your rubdown?"

Ben was too worried about regaining his composure to look, but Wallace Schuler acted like he was going to choke, so Ben turned around to see what would get him upset.

It was a gorgeous young woman. She was practically naked, except for the bottom of a tiny string bikini. She had hips that were full enough to be inviting and alluring, not the emaciated look that's supposed to be in these days, but enough hips to make the string bikini look good. She was tan and shiny with oil, and her breasts were good-sized breasts, full and sagging just a little from their own weight, but still pert and pointed, just like Wendy's had ...

It couldn't be. Ben didn't even recognize her at first. The difference, even the sun bleached color of the hair, much longer now, and the laid-back expression, and here, half naked, no, mostly naked, and with more weight on her.

Ben couldn't even speak for a moment.

"Wallace," the girl said, "are you going to be working all morning again?"

"Wendy," Ben said.

The girl just looked at him.

"Wendy, my God, what have they done to you?"

"I'm sorry," the girl said, flipping her hair back over her shoulders. "What are you talking about?"

"Wendy."

"Sorry, wrong girl," the girl said. "Wallace, I'm sorry to interrupt. I didn't know you had company." She turned quickly and walked down the steps from the swimming pool towards the house, her tanned cheeks flexing with each barefoot step.

"Wendy, my God!" Ben shouted, but the girl kept on walking.

"Wendy! I'm your husband." Ben ran after her, and the two Chinese thugs came out from beside the house and caught him just as he grabbed her arm. She wouldn't look at his face.

"Wendy, please," Wallace said, but the Chinese thugs yanked him away from the girl and twisted his arm so far behind his back he shouted out in pain. Schuler said something forcefully in Cantonese, and they let Ben go.

"Chester, let me talk to him please," the girl said, and Schuler nodded and clapped his hands. The thugs stepped back and prepared to leave.

"Bring me a robe," the girl said. When she said that, Ben knew it was Wendy, and he knew she was not entirely the girl he had known. Well, I don't know about that. I don't think people change much. I think the hidden parts of them just come out more at different times in their lives.

Anyway, one of the thugs came trotting out with a terry cloth robe, which the girl put on. Schuler nodded curtly to Ben, and he followed the thugs into his house. As soon as Schuler was gone, Ben said, "Wendy, what has happened? I'm your husband."

The girl walked along the edge of the pool with her arms crossed. She laughed.

Ben just stood there with his arms open. "Wendy, what has this bastard done to you?" Come on, let's go." He grabbed her by the arm, but she yanked her arm away and laughed at him.

"You poor old ..." she shook her head.

"Wendy," Ben said, "I'm your husband. Come with me now. You can't stay here."

For the first time Wendy looked him in the eyes. Her sun-bleached hair was blowing in front of her face, and the morning haze was thickening over the harbor and New Territories behind her.

"You weren't my husband," she said. "You were my school teacher. You were a college professor. You were my daddy, but you weren't my husband."

"Wendy," Ben said. "Oh my God, if you only knew what I've been through." He was about to cry, and he tried to hug her, but she turned away.

"You know what a husband does?" she said. "You know what a husband and wife do? What Wallace and I do every night. Not just every night, but several times a day. What we do here in the pool, or down on the beach, or on his boat, or in his plane up in the air. That's what a husband does."

"Wendy, you can't be speaking like this. What have these people done to you?"

"You want me to tell you again? I just told you. I saw what the hell I had been missing. I mean look around you. Look at all this. Did you ever give me any of this? Did you ever give me anything but a goddamn lecture on how I was supposed to be? Or a goddamn guilt complex for not thinking and talking and acting the way I was supposed to? Look at all this. Don't tell me you wouldn't love to have it."

"Wendy, this is not you. Do you mean, what are we talking about? Wealth, power, or, or sex ..."

"Yes, goddamn it, that's exactly what we're talking about. We're talking about adventure, and exotic places, and yachts and airplanes and fast cars and clothes, and money. We're talking about going in the goddamn store and charging it. We're talking about having fun, goddamn it, and not having to feel like we're a bad little girl for having it. You know what kind of books Wallace reads, Ben? He reads whatever the hell he wants. And if he doesn't like it, he puts it down and tries something else. You know I've tried it myself, just reading for fun. I read spy novels. I read whatever I want to, and nobody makes me feel guilty for it. And we don't have to discuss the damn things either, or deconstruct them, or discuss politics, or be politically correct or socially conscious. It feels great, Ben."

"Wendy, I just refuse to believe that this is you talking," said Ben, and he was wagging his head.

But by the time Wendy finished, Ben was chopping his hand through the air. "This is not right," he said. "This is wrong. This is everything that is wrong in this world. This man is an exploiter, he's..." Ben got so flustered he couldn't speak.

"I don't give a shit, Ben. Frankly, I don't give a shit. If this is what it's like to be exploited, then I might just go in and get exploited a little this afternoon. On the billiards table maybe."

Well, it just got worse and worse, and how Ben survived that afternoon without having a stroke, I don't know. Ben left Wallace

Schuler's estate without Wendy. He never went back, and she never went back to him, and he never saw or heard from his wife again.

That was a bad year for Ben. He returned to school and was teaching again that fall. The people who had financed his travels the previous year were expecting a book or an article or at least a press release, but Ben kept putting them off or evading them. He was an old pro at that by now, so he was able to stretch things out until nothing came of it at all. He dropped out of politics anyway, and those people had less and less to do with him, so the matter resolved itself after a while, without too many hard feelings.

As for the rest of his life, well, it wasn't that much different from the life he had led for over thirty years. It didn't take him long to convince himself that Wendy was a bad egg and had always been, so he was in a way lucky to get rid of her.

Ben really burrowed back into his medieval texts and started taking special interest in the stories about the frailty and infidelity of women. He even wrote several scathing articles on the subject and dug up some particularly misogynistic texts that had been neglected in the past couple of decades. He sent one of those articles off to be published, in one of the journals that usually published anything he sent them, but the editor of that journal was now a woman, and the rejection letter she sent Ben brought him to his senses. He took the rest of his articles and stuck them back in his files and quietly spent the few years remaining till his retirement reading *Beowulf* and *The Battle of Maldon* and *The Canterbury Tales* to his students in the original, and letting them enjoy the sound and the rhythm of it, since most of them didn't study and couldn't understand what he was saying anyway.

Retraction

I hope all who read this young man's book, if they find anything in it that pleases them, will consider that it may be in here simply by the grace of God. And if they find anything that upsets them, I hope they realize it may have came from the author's own ignorance more than from any willful malice on his part.

Old men look back at the young men they were, and they shake their heads and judge. They don't particularly look forward to being judged by someone else. But that is inevitable, is it not?

That leaves the old men nothing to do but pray for forgiveness. Fortunately, they are old, and experience leads them to hope those prayers just might be worthwhile.

Acknowledgements

I owe an enormous debt of gratitude to those whose feedback, encouragement, and frank advice over the many years made this book possible. Come to think of it, it's been so many years, a good many of these people are no longer with us. I'd like to thank them anyway- especially Romulus Linney, Jill Birdsall, Shaye Areheart, Lisa Bankoff, Brian Wilson, Ann Evans, Paul Barnes, Dick Lang, Mike Grubbs, Matt Christopher, and Mary Boone. And thanks to Doug and Tom Hollingsworth for their love and support in those early years of writing.

Many thanks to Fayssoux Evans for the cover design and to Betsy Teter, Anne Waters, Kel Landis, and John Cribb for their publication advice.

And most of all, thanks to my wife, longtime partner, and closest friend, Ann Evans, for decades of love and the patience of Job.

www.ingramcontent.com/pod-product-compliance
Lightning Source LLC
Chambersburg PA
CBHW051131120726
47905CB00005B/1503